Anton Pavlovich Chekhov (1860–1904) was the son of a small shopkeeper and the grandson of a serf. After finishing school in his native town, Chekhov went to Moscow, where he entered the University to study medicine and started publishing tales, anecdotes, jokes, and articles. By the time he took his medical degree, writing had become his main interest and occupation. His literary reputation grew with the publication of the book *Motley Stories* (1886). In 1888, he was awarded the Pushkin Prize for the collection *In the Twilight*. This and the publication of the long story "The Steppe" marked the beginning of Chekhov's recognition as one of Russia's leading writers. The first production of his famous play *The Sea Gull* (1896) was a miserable failure. But in 1898, the play was revived at the Moscow Art Theater and proved a resounding success, as did the theater's productions of *The Three Sisters* and *The Cherry Orchard*. Chekhov married the actress Olga Knipper just three years before he died of tuberculosis.

George Pahomov, who emigrated to the United States from the Soviet Unon at an early age, holds a Ph.D. in Russian Language and Literature from New York University and is a professor in the Russian Department of Bryn Mawr College. The author of two books and numerous articles on Russian literature, he served as principal editor of the five-volume translation of *The Nikonian Chronicle*.

ANTON CHEKHOV

SELECTED STORIES

Translated by Ann Dunnigan

With an Introduction by
George Pahomov

SIGNET CLASSICS

SIGNET CLASSICS
Published by New American Library, a division of
Penguin Group (USA) Inc., 375 Hudson Street,
New York, New York 10014, USA
Penguin Group (Canada), 90 Eglinton Avenue East, Suite 700, Toronto,
Ontario M4P 2Y3, Canada (a division of Pearson Penguin Canada Inc.)
Penguin Books Ltd., 80 Strand, London WC2R 0RL, England
Penguin Ireland, 25 St. Stephen's Green, Dublin 2,
Ireland (a division of Penguin Books Ltd.)
Penguin Group (Australia), 250 Camberwell Road, Camberwell, Victoria 3124,
Australia (a division of Pearson Australia Group Pty. Ltd.)
Penguin Books India Pvt. Ltd., 11 Community Centre, Panchsheel Park,
New Delhi - 110 017, India
Penguin Group (NZ), 67 Apollo Drive, Rosedale, North Shore 0632,
New Zealand (a division of Pearson New Zealand Ltd.)
Penguin Books (South Africa) (Pty.) Ltd., 24 Sturdee Avenue,
Rosebank, Johannesburg 2196, South Africa

Penguin Books Ltd., Registered Offices:
80 Strand, London WC2R 0RL, England

Published by Signet Classics, an imprint of New American Library,
a division of Penguin Group (USA) Inc.

First Signet Classics Printing, November 1960
First Signet Classics Printing (Pahomov Introduction), April 2003
10   9   8

such characters, for we do not recognize ourselves in them. The comic low type is simple, his actions predictable and his motivation primitively linear. He is quantifiable. Any traits that might individualize him as a unique being are excluded. This is the matrix of Chekhov's early stories, such as "The Confession" (1883) and "The Milksop" (1885). But a turning point is sensed in "Agafya" (1886) when in the very last paragraph the central figure, suddenly graced with will and dignity, becomes a full person. And in "The Kiss" (1887), Chekhov shatters the external mode of description and enters the complexity of mind and consciousness of the protagonist.

The scientific mind, in dismissing the unique and singular in favor of the typical, acts in a profoundly antihumanist fashion when it examines humankind. When attempting to gain meaning from human experience, in trying to draw order from what otherwise were discrete, unrelated occurrences, the early Chekhov relied on his scientific rationalism. But scientific rationalism does not address the need to find meaning in life, the universal imperative of intellect.

In answer to this search for universal meaning, rationalism discovered laws of nature that legitimated the rule of tooth and claw, with the disadvantaged, the feeble and the naive becoming natural victims. Yet people aspire to a state of nature that is harmonious, equitable, just and beautiful. The possibility of such a state had once been a matter of faith. The rationalist replaced faith with knowledge and committed himself to a theory of progressive human development.

But no rational theory is comprehensive enough to make sense of the arbitrary and chaotic world in which we live. The uncommon, uniquely individual events remain a mystery. (The thinking character in Chekhov on occasion comes to this realization, e.g., Laptev in "Three Years" [1895]. Rationalism gives him no ultimate answers; faith he

does not possess; he is therefore left in total meaninglessness.) The absolute inevitability of natural processes suddenly becomes an absolute tyranny. The individual is not his
own master and cannot change himself. The law of nature,
rather than offering answers, is found to have total indifference for the seeker. This gives nineteenth-century "opti-
mistic" positivism its dark edge of pessimism for, in the
phrase of Russian philosopher Lev Shestov, "the certainty
that the existing order is immutable is for certain minds syn-
onymous with the certainty that life is nonsensical and absurd." Such were the intellectual parameters of Chekhov's
world.

Given the sense of a human being as a mere pawn in an
absurd world, Chekhov could only write of ruin and loss,
with time as thief and nature as ravager, and man as both
victim and instrument of this universal order. It is a grim vision. But the dark task of reporting it is lightened when the
victim of the absurd world is a mindless buffoon, the object
of the narrator's joke. Both the narrator and reader are untouched, protected by laughter.

Occasionally the laughter stills when the writer sees
that in the world of fools there are also children, the pure
and the innocent. With the shielding veil of laughter stripped
there remains only the recognition of absurdity and a result-
ant hopelessness, for no uplifting higher order presents itself. The last vestige of an individual's striving to transcend
the brutal reality of nature is his recognition of meaninglessness, the loss of hope in ever achieving transcendence.
The state of hopelessness thus becomes the sole reminder
that humans are still somehow noble.

With every cell of his body Chekhov must have felt
helpless before the invisible and unrelenting laws of nature.
He himself was being consumed by a faceless organism,
eaten alive by an unrelenting beast with the neutral scientific
name of *Mycobacterium tuberculosis*, the bacillus of consumption. As a doctor he knew there was no cure. Every

hour, every cough, must have reminded him that human beings will lose to the forces of nature.

Yet Chekhov, the stoic scientist, surely needed comfort.
He found it in those of his characters who, through suffering
or loss, rose to hopelessness. In their breakout achievement
they became his brothers and sisters. In his imagination he
presses them close to his chest, holds them dear, cherishes
them in a common bond. Hopelessness becomes a virtue
that separates them from the herd of humanity. Note the end-
ing of "The House with the Mansard" (1896) for the gentle
presentation of the artist's futile lament, and the tender treatment of Olga's descent into hopelessness in "Peasants"
(1897). Think of the endings of Chekhov's four major
plays—when his characters reach hopelessness Chekhov
embraces them with great sympathy.

And yet that is not all there is to Chekhov, for he is a
study in quiet contrast. Like the Russian Orthodox funeral
service, the *panikhida*, which at the nadir of grieving and
lamentation introduces a motif of hope and redemption,
softly progressing from minor to a subtle major, Chekhov
whispers of freedom, human potential and dignity. His art is
a continuing and heroic creative act in the face of malevo-
lent nature and nihilism. The creative act is an emanation of
freedom. Though creation needs *materiel* (a preexisting cul-
tural context), it itself is unprecedented; this is the freedom
that gives it unique life. Though freedom, human communion, conscience and love are rare in Chekhov's world, he
implicitly accentuates their value by showing their scarcity.

Time in Chekhov is an unrelenting destroyer, the distant
twin of Nemesis in classical tragedy. In making human
imagination and creation ruthlessly temporal, it effaces
hope. Yet Chekhov's creations live on, having easily outlived the seven years after his death, which he repeatedly
prophesied as the limit of the reading public's interest in
him.

Many Chekhov stories, early and late, are centered on

characters who deny the validity of the other. The central figures assume all human traits and aspects to themselves while denying them to others. Human relationships then become vertical, subject to object. Intersubjectivity—authentic communication among equals—is precluded. Agency, decision making, authority all belong to the subject who holds power. Nevertheless, this domination-submission model is at times overcome, almost always aided by the presence and recognition of beauty, the constant catalyst to which most people are blind. The relationship between Olga and her sister-in-law in "Peasants," for example, is transfigured by the contemplation of the church in the meadow across the river.

Many of the stories also expose the condition of *poshlost*, a Russian word describing a vulgar way of life, the surrender of the self to the fashionable and the popular, the cheap and the transient. It is the deadening of all authentic feeling and the striking of an affected pose. It means a life of unreflecting self-approval, a self-absorbed, triumphant mediocrity. In "Three Years" Yulia's father, the doctor, carries the symptoms of the condition and Panaurov, Nina's husband, is a particularly trenchant case.

As Chekhov's writing became increasingly subtle, the people in his stories moved from caricatures to characters, growing from flat to round, from cardboard to a vulnerable flesh that bled when injured. This makes their situation all the more poignant, for they are trapped in a reality that did not move with them. Chekhov saw the society of his time as thwarting human potential, individual development and personal freedom. Especially sharply drawn is the suppression and abuse of the defenseless—children and women. There appears a growing major theme of the spiritual imprisonment of women, especially educated women, who suffer from the lack of opportunity to manifest themselves and shape their lives. In "Three Years," Laptev cannot leave his environment because of his "habituation to captivity and his servile condition." The constraints that keep him a prisoner are internal. His wife's condition is even more frustrating, because her bonds are externally imposed and her intelligence makes her awareness of them achingly poignant.

Chekhov's deep understanding of the unequal treatment of women and his awareness that such repression deprives society of a source of energy, creativity and well-being are part of what mark him as a modernist. Nowhere in his works does he privilege one gender over the other. His affirmation that human frailty and human dignity are not gender specific but that the integrity of men is perhaps more fragile accentuates his prescience of modern sensibility.

Yet contemporary readers may readily undervalue Chekhov's innovativeness because his original style and techniques have been incorporated by generations of subsequent writers. The universal hallmark of the modern short story, which is the movement in consciousness from innocence to experience, was a structural innovation of Chekhov's. The movement away from external and objective description to a focus on the consciousness of the protagonist is another Chekhovian innovation. In "Three Years," Laptev's thoughts and meditations are revealed in inner speech, his voice coming close to that of the narrator. And there is also Chekhov's nonjudgmental narrator and the presentation of characters in whom experience creates the acute restructuring of moral nature without the establishment of moral certitude. All are major contributions to modern fiction. Because Chekhov died at the age of forty-four in 1904, we forget that he was of the generation of Freud (b. 1856) and Kandinsky (b. 1866), two figures who also shaped modernity.

His gift to modern sensibility is the intimation of indeterminacy. Before Chekhov, fiction was driven by passions, claims and counterclaims, action and counteraction, cause and effect—all the elements of the ageless plot. Chekhov eschewed them all, even dismissing causality. Plot then became meaningless. It is all chance happening in Chekhov, sheer accident. Could any stance be more modern? If there is no cause and effect, there can be no responsibility, no accounting for one's acts, only drift and the satisfaction of immediate urges. No wonder we embrace Chekhov; he is our father.

But if meaninglessness is the human condition, then acts of kindness take on a great significance, because there is no imperative for them. There is no value system that valorizes kindness; there is no reward for it. In fact, there is often only risk and cost. Kindness then becomes a purely existential act, a giving of the self at once heroic and tragic, as exemplified in the heroine of "The Darling" (1898).

What could be the source of such kindness? As expected, Chekhov gives no answer. But those who practice a giving of themselves—doctors, teachers, priests—are always the objects of sympathy and even reverence by Chekhov's narrators. Humans are imperfect, fallible and prone to error, he seems to say. And so the greatest human virtue is not moral certitude but charity, in its timeless sense of *caritas*, love of the heart, through which we see the deepest being of another and experience her or his inner life as if it were our own.

—George Pahomov

The Confession

IT WAS A COLD CLEAR DAY. I felt as elated as a cab driver who has been given a gold coin by mistake. I wanted to laugh, to cry, to pray. I was in seventh heaven: I had just been made a cashier! But I was rejoicing not because I now could get my hands on something—I was not a thief, and would have destroyed anyone who had told me that in time I should be one—I was rejoicing over the promotion and the slight increase in salary, nothing more.

And I was happy for another reason: on becoming a cashier I suddenly felt as if I were wearing rose-colored glasses. All at once people appeared to have changed. My word of honor! Everyone seemed to have improved! The ugly became beautiful, the wicked, good; the proud became humble, the miserly, generous. It was as if my eyes had been opened, and I beheld all man's wonderful, until now unsuspected qualities. "Strange," I said to myself, "either something has happened to them, or I have been stupid not to have perceived these qualities before. How charming everyone is!"

On the day of my appointment, even Z. N. Kazusov changed. He was a member of the board of directors, a haughty, arrogant man who always ignored the small fry. He approached me and—what had happened to him?—smiling affectionately, he clapped me on the back.

"You're too young to be so proud, my boy. It's unforgivable!" he said. "Why don't you ever drop in on us? It's shameful of you; the young people generally gather at our house, and it's always gay there. My daughters are forever asking me: 'Why don't you invite Gregory Kuzmich, Papa? He's so nice!'—But is it possible to get him to come? Well, in any case, I'll try, I told them. I'll ask him. Now, don't give yourself airs, my boy, do come."

Amazing! What had happened to him? Had he gone out of his mind? He had always been a regular ogre, and now look at him!

On returning home that same day I was astounded: Mama served not the usual two courses at dinner, but four! For tea in the evening there was jam and white bread. The following day, again four courses, again jam; and when guests dropped in we drank chocolate. The third day it was the same.

"Mama," I said, "what's the matter with you? Why this burst of generosity, darling? You know, my salary wasn't doubled. The increase was trifling."

Mama looked at me in surprise. "Humph! What do you expect to do with money—save it?"

God only knows what got into them. Papa ordered a fur coat, bought a new cap, took a mineral-water cure, and began to eat grapes—in winter!

Within a few days I received a letter from my brother. This brother could not endure me. We had parted over a difference of opinion: he considered me a selfish parasite, incapable of self-sacrifice, and for this he despised me. In his letter he now wrote: "Dear brother, I love you, and you cannot imagine what hellish torture our quarrel has caused me. Let us make it up. Let us each extend a hand to the other, and may peace triumph! I implore you! In expectation of your reply, I embrace you and remain your most loving and affectionate brother, Yevlampy." Oh, my dear brother! I answered him saying that I embraced him and rejoiced. Within a week I received a telegram: "Thanks. Happy. Send hundred rubles. Most urgent. Embrace you. Yevlampy." I sent the hundred rubles.

Even *she* changed. She did not love me. Once when I had made so bold as to hint that my heart was troubled, she accused me of being presumptuous and laughed in my face. On meeting me a week after my promotion, however, she dimpled, smiled, and looked flustered. "What's happened to you?" she asked, gazing at me. "You've grown so handsome. When did you manage to do that?" And then, "Let's dance. . . ."

Sweetheart! Within a month she had given me a mother-in-law. I had become that handsome! When money was needed for the wedding I took three hundred rubles out of the cash box. Why not take it, when you know you are going to put it back as soon as you receive your salary? At the same time I took out a hundred rubles for Kazusov. He had asked for a loan and it was impossible to refuse him; he was a big wheel in the office and could have anyone fired at a moment's notice.

A week before the arrest it was suggested that I give a party. What the devil, let them guzzle and gorge, if that's what they want! I did not count the guests that evening, but I recall that all eight of my rooms were swarming with people, young and old. There were those before whom even Kazusov had to bend the knee. His daughters—the oldest being my treasure—were in dazzling attire; the flowers alone with which they covered themselves cost me over a thousand rubles. It was very gay, with glittering chandeliers, deafening music, and plenty of champagne. There were long speeches and short toasts; one journalist presented me with an ode, another with a ballad. "We in Russia do not know how to appreciate such men as Gregory Kuzmich," cried Kazusov, after supper. "It's a shame! Russia is to be pitied!"

All those who were shouting, lauding and kissing me, were whispering behind my back, thumbing their noses at me. I saw their smiles and heard their sighs. "He stole it, the crook!" they whispered, grinning maliciously. But their sighing and smirking did not prevent them from eating, drinking, and enjoying themselves. Neither wolves nor diabetics ever ate as they did. My wife, flashing gold and diamonds, came up to me and whispered: "They are saying that you stole the money. If it's true, I warn you, I cannot go on living with a thief. I'll leave!" And she smoothed down her five-thousand-ruble gown. The devil take them all! That very evening Kazusov had five thousand from me. Yevlampy took an equal amount. "If what they are whispering about you is true," said my ethical brother, as he pocketed the money, "watch out! I will not be brother to a thief!"

After the ball I drove them all to the country in a troika. We finished up at six in the morning. Exhausted by wine and women, they lay back in the sleigh, and, as they started off for home, cried out in farewell: "Inspection tomorrow! *Merci!*"

My dear ladies and gentlemen, I got caught; or, to state it more fully: yesterday I was respected and honored on all sides; today I am a scoundrel and a thief. . . . Cry out, now, inveigh against me, spread the news, judge and wonder; banish me, write editorials and throw stones, only, please—not everyone, not everyone!

—1883

He Understood

IT WAS A STIFLING JUNE MORNING; the air was sultry, the leaves drooped, and the dry ground was cracked. One felt a longing for a storm, for rain that would relieve nature's distress. And a storm was brewing; in the west the clouds were growing dark. It would be welcome!

Along the outskirts of the forest a stooped, dwarflike little peasant moved stealthily. He wore mammoth gray-brown boots and blue trousers with white stripes; half the length of the boot tops had to be folded over. His completely threadbare, patched pants bagged over the knees and hung like coattails. A greasy rope belt had slid from his belly to his hips, and his shirt rode up to his shoulder blades.

He was carrying a gun that had a rusty barrel about two feet long with a sight resembling a good-sized bootnail. It was fitted with a white homemade butt, whittled out of pine and carved with stripes and flowers. Had it not been for the butt it would have borne no resemblance to a gun—and even so it looked more like something medieval than of our own time. The trigger was brown with rust and wound about with wire and thread. The most ludicrous part was the white, shiny ramrod that had been simply cut from a willow, and was fresh, damp, and much longer than the barrel.

The little peasant was pale, and his inflamed, crossed eyes darted in all directions. A wispy billy-goat beard quivered like a little rag under his lower lip. He took long strides, his torso bent forward; he was evidently in a hurry.

Behind him ran a large, shaggy mongrel, thin as a skeleton. Her long tongue hung out, gray with dust, and large patches of shed hair clung to her sides and tail. One hind leg was wrapped in a rag and had evidently been hurt. Every now and then the little peasant turned back to his companion. "Get out of here!" he kept saying, apprehensively. The mongrel would look around, and, having stood still for a moment, continue to follow her master.

The hunter wanted to slip into the forest, but it was impossible. Along the border there extended a dense, thorny wall of blackthorn bushes, and farther on a stretch of nettles. At last there was a path. The peasant again waved the dog off and darted along the path into the bushes. Here the ground had not yet dried; it made a sucking sound underfoot. The dampness made it easier to breathe. On both sides there was a mass of juniper and other shrubs, but the forest itself was about three hundred feet away.

Something made a sound like a wheel in need of greasing. The peasant started, then cocked an eye at a young alder tree in which he spied a moving black spot. He stepped nearer and made out a young starling sitting on a branch examining the under part of its lifted wing. The peasant stood still, dropped his cap, pressed the butt of the gun to his shoulder, and took aim; then he lifted the gun cock and held it to prevent its going off too soon. The spring was broken, the trigger did not work, and the gun cock failed to respond.

There was a whirring sound. The starling lowered his wing and looked with suspicion at the marksman. Another second and he would fly away. Again the hunter took aim and removed his finger from the cock, but to his disappointment it did not strike. He then cut a thread with his finger-nail, bent a piece of wire, and gave the cock a fillip. A click was heard, then a shot. The marksman's shoulder felt the strong kick of the gun; he had not been sparing with the powder. Dropping the gun, he ran to the alder tree and began fumbling about in the grass. Near a moldy, rotting branch he found a patch of blood and some down. Searching a little farther, he recognized his victim in the small, still warm body that lay near the tree trunk.

"Got him in the head!" he said delightedly to the mongrel. The dog sniffed at the starling and saw that his master had hit not only the head; on the breast was a gaping wound, one leg was broken, and a large drop of blood hung from the bill. The peasant quickly reached into his pocket, dropping rags, scraps of paper, and bits of thread, as he pulled out a new charge. He reloaded the gun, and, ready to continue the hunt, went on his way.

As if he had sprung from the ground, the Polish overseer, Krzewecki, appeared before him. The little peasant saw his arrogant, red-bearded face and grew cold with horror. His cap fell off as if by its own volition.

"What are you up to? Shooting?" asked the Pole in a mocking voice. "Very nice!"

The hunter timidly squinted to one side and saw a cart with brushwood and a group of peasants standing near it. He had been so carried away by the hunt that he had not even noticed anyone nearby.

"How dare you shoot?" Krzewecki asked, raising his voice. "So, this is your own forest? Or perhaps you think it's past St. Peter's Day? Who are you, anyway?"

"Pavel-the-Lame," the peasant feebly replied. "From Kashilovka."

"From Kashilovka! Damn it all, who gave you permission to shoot?" Krzewecki tried not to speak with the Polish inflection. "Hand over the gun!"

Pavel gave his gun to the Pole; he was thinking: "It

would be better to get one in the snout than to be spoken to so curtly."

"Hand over the cap, too."

He gave him the cap.

"I'll teach you to shoot! Damn it all! Come along." Krzewecki turned his back on the peasant and marched after the squeaking cart. Pavel, feeling the game in his pocket, followed behind.

An hour later they entered a spacious, low-ceilinged room with faded blue walls. This was the landlord's office. It was empty, but smelled strongly of life. In the middle of the room there was a large oak table on which were two or three ledgers, an inkstand, a sand glass, and a teapot with a broken spout. Everything was covered with a layer of gray dust. In one corner stood a large cupboard from which the paint had long since peeled; on it was a kerosene can and a bottle with some sort of mixture in it. In another corner there was a small ikon covered with cobwebs.

"A report of the case will have to be drawn up," said Krzewecki. "I shall inform the master at once and send for the constable. Take off your boots." Pavel sat down on the floor and silently, with trembling hands, pulled off his boots. "You won't get away from me," said the bailiff, yawning, "and if you do leave barefoot, it will be the worse for you. Sit here and wait till the constable comes." The Pole locked the boots and gun in the cupboard and left the room.

When he had gone, the peasant began slowly scratching the back of his head; he kept it up for a long time, as if trying to solve the problem of where he was, all the while sighing and looking around apprehensively. The cupboard, the table, the ikon, and the broken teapot all seemed to look at him reproachfully, sadly. A multitude of flies buzzed overhead so mournfully it became unbearably distressing.

"B-z-z-z-z," went the flies. "You got caught! You got caught!" A large wasp crawled across the windowpane. It wanted to fly out into the air, but the glass prevented it. It seemed to be tortured by its desire to get out. Pavel backed up to the door, took up his stand at the doorpost, dropped his arms to his sides and fell to musing.

An hour passed, then another, and still he stood at the doorpost, waiting and thinking. He squinted at the wasp and thought: "Why don't it fly through the door, the fool?" Two more hours passed. All was quiet, silent, dead. He began to think they had forgotten him, and that he, like the wasp, which now and then fell from the windowpane, would not escape for a long time. By nightfall the insect would go to sleep, but what would become of him? "Just like with people," he philosophized, looking at the wasp, "just like a person—there is a way it could get out, but it's ignorant, it don't know how."

At last a door slammed somewhere. Hasty footsteps were heard, and in a moment a short, plump man, wearing wide trousers with suspenders, entered the office. He was without a jacket or vest; between his shoulder blades and across his chest were bands of sweat. This was the master, Pyotr Yegorych Volchkov, a retired lieutenant colonel. His fat red face and perspiring bald spot suggested he would have given a great deal if, in place of this heat, the January frosts were suddenly to set in. He was suffering from the sultriness as well as the heat, and it was apparent from his swollen, sleepy eyes that he had only just got up from a soft and stuffy feather bed.

He paced the length of the room several times, as if he had not noticed Pavel; then he stopped in front of the prisoner and stared intently into his face for some time. He stared with a contempt that at first showed only in his eyes, then spread by degrees across his fat face. Pavel could not bear that look and lowered his eyes. He was ashamed.

"Now, show me what you've killed," whispered Volchkov. "Well, come on now, show it, you hero, you William Tell! Show it, you cretin!"

Pavel reached into his pocket and brought out the unfortunate starling; it had already lost its shape, was badly rumpled, and had begun to dry. Volchkov smiled scornfully and shrugged his shoulders. "Fool," he said. "You simpleton! You blockhead! Isn't that a sin? Aren't you ashamed?"

"I am ashamed, master," said the peasant, trying to control the swallowing movement that made it difficult for him to speak.

"Aside from the fact that—you robber, you Judas—you're hunting in my woods without permission, you dare to go against the law! Don't you know that the law forbids hunting out of season? The law says no one may hunt before St. Peter's Day. You didn't know this? Now, come here!" Volchkov went to the table and Pavel followed him. The landowner opened a book, leafed through it for some time, and then began to read in a high, drawling tenor, the statute prohibiting hunting before St. Peter's Day.

"So, you didn't know this?" he asked, when he had finished reading.

"Of course, we know it. We know it, Your Honor, but do we understand these things? Do we have such intelligence?"

"Ah? How does intelligence come into it if you senselessly destroy one of God's creatures? Here you've killed this little bird. Why did you kill it? Can you resurrect it? Can you, I ask you?"

"I cannot, master."

"But you did kill it. And what you have to gain from it I don't understand. A starling! It is neither meat nor feathers. So you killed it just like that, stupidly." Volchkov narrowed his eyes and began to straighten the starling's broken leg. The leg came off and fell onto the peasant's bare foot. "Damn you, you greedy beast!" Volchkov went on. "You did this out of greed. You saw the little bird and it annoyed you that she was flying free, glorifying the Lord. 'Here,' you said to yourself, 'let me kill it and devour it.' Human greed!—I can't look at you! And don't look at me with those eyes. You cross-eyed good-for-nothing! You killed her; and

she may have little ones. They may be peeping even now."
Volchkov made a tearful face and placed his hand close to
the ground to indicate how small the birds would be.

"I didn't do it from greed, Pyotr Yegorych. If I have a sin
on my soul, it is not greed or profit, Pyotr Yegorych. The
devil tempted me——"

"You, tempted by the devil? Why, you could tempt the
devil yourself! All you Kashilovka fellows are thieves."
Volchkov noisily blew out a stream of air, took a deep
breath, and continued in a low voice. "What am I to do with
you, eh? Considering how stupid you are, I should let you
go; but considering your action and your impudence, I
should give it to you. I should, without fail! I've coddled
you fellows enough. E-nough! I've sent for the constable;
we'll draw up a report; I've sent for him! The evidence is at
hand. You have only yourself to blame. It's not I who am
punishing you—your sins punish you. You know how to sin,
so you'll know how to bear the punishment. O-o-h, Lord,
forgive us sinners! Those Kashilovka fellows . . . Well, and
how are your spring crops?"

"All right, by the grace of God!"

"Why do you keep blinking?"

Pavel coughed into his fist with embarrassment and adjusted his belt.

"Why are you blinking?" repeated Volchkov. "You killed
the starling yourself, so why are you crying?"

"Your Honor," said Pavel, in a jarring falsetto, and
loudly, as if gathering his strength, "you, in your kindness,
are offended because I, let us say, killed the little bird. You
scold me, not because you are the master, but because your
feelings are hurt—because you're so kind. And do you think
my feelings aren't hurt? I'm a stupid man, without any understanding, but even I have feelings. May the Lord strike
me——"

"Why did you shoot it if you have feelings?"

"The devil tempted me. Let me tell you, Pyotr Yegorych,

sir. I'll tell you the whole truth, as before God! Let the constable come—it's my sin, and I'll answer for it before God and the judge. And to you I'll tell the whole truth, like at confession. Please—permit me, Your Honor!"

"What do you mean, 'permit you'? Whether I permit you or not, you won't say anything intelligent. What's it to me? It isn't I who am going to make out the report. Go ahead, talk! Why remain silent? Speak, William Tell!"

Pavel passed his sleeve over his trembling lips; his eyes grew even smaller and more crossed. "I don't get anything out of this starling," he said. "Even if there were a thousand of them, what good are they? You can't sell them, you can't eat them. They are nothing. You understand——"

"No, don't say that—here you are a hunter and you don't know—a starling, if roasted with a buckwheat gruel, is quite a morsel—or with a sauce—it's just like hazel hen. Almost the same taste." Then regretting the tone he had taken, he frowned and added, "You'll find out now what sort of taste it has—you'll see!"

"Taste means nothing to me, as long as there's bread, Pyotr Yegorych, you know that. But I killed the starling because I just couldn't help it. I *had* to."

"What do you mean?"

"God only knows! Please let me explain. It began to torment me right from the start of Holy Week, this feeling. *Let* me explain, sir. I went out that morning, after matins, after the Easter cakes were blessed. There I was on my way, with the women walking ahead and me behind them, I walked and walked, then I stopped by the dam. I stood there looking at God's world, seeing how everything happens in it, how every creature and every little blade of grass, you might say, knows its place. The day breaks, and the sun rises—I see all this—and there is joy in my heart. I look at the birds, Pyotr Yegorych, and all of a sudden my heart thumps!"

"Why was that?"

"Because I saw the birds. Right off the thought came into

my head. It would be good, I thought, to do some shooting, but, worse luck, the law doesn't allow it! And just then two ducks flew across the sky and a woodcock cried out somewhere beyond the river. I had a fierce craving to hunt! With this in mind I went home. I broke fast with the women, but the birds were there before my eyes! There I was eating, but the noise of the forest was in my ears, and the bird cries—'cheep! cheep!' Oh, Lord! I was dying to hunt, and that's all. And when I had some vodka with the Easter cakes, I was plumb crazy. I started hearing voices! I heard a kind of thin, as it were, angelic voice ringing in my ears and saying: 'Go on, Pashka, shoot!' It's as if I was under a spell! I can only suppose, Your Excellency, Pyotr Yegorych, that this was the devil's doing, and no one else's. And such a sweet, thin voice, like a baby's! From that morning on I was taken with this craving. I sat around outside, in a daze, my hands hanging, and I thought. I thought and I thought. And all the time your departed brother was in my mind, that is Sergei Yegorych, may he rest in peace. I remember how I used to go hunting with him. His Honor thought that as a hunter I was the best. He thought it was touching and amusing—me, cross-eyed, and a crack shot. He wanted to take me to a doctor in town to show him how skillful I was in spite of my trouble. It was wonderful and touching, Pyotr Yegorych. We used to go out at the crack of dawn, call the dogs, Kara and Ledka, and . . . a-a-h . . . twenty miles a day we'd cover! But what can I say? Pyotr Yegorych, I tell you honestly, that, excepting your brother, there is not, and there never was in this whole world, a real man! Cruel he was, harsh and quarrelsome, but as a hunter—nobody could stand up to him. His Excellency, Count Tierborg, tried and tried to outdo him with his hounds, but he went to his death envying him. How could he do it? He wasn't built for it. And he didn't have the gun your brother had, a double-barreled one, you know, from Marseilles, made by Lepelier and Company. At two hundred feet—a duck! No joke!" Pavel quickly wiped his lips, blinked, and went on: "I got this craving from him. When there's no shooting, I'm miserable, I can't breathe."

"Foolishness!"

"No, sir, Pyotr Yegorych! All Easter Week I went around like a madman—I couldn't eat, I couldn't drink! During St. Thomas's Week I cleaned my gun and mended it, then I felt a little better. But soon after that again I felt sick. I was drawn—pulled to it. I nearly burst! I tried vodka, but it didn't help, it made it worse. It isn't foolishness. After the blessing of the waters I got drunk. Next day it was worse than ever—as if I were being pulled out of the house. Pulled! A mighty thing! I took my gun and went to the vegetable garden. I started shooting blackbirds. I shot about ten, but I didn't feel any better. I was drawn to the forest, to the marsh. The old woman began scolding. 'How can you shoot a blackbird? That's not a noble bird. It's a sin before the Lord! The crops will fail if you kill a blackbird.'. . . Pyotr Yegorych, I took and smashed my gun. The hell with it! I felt better."

"Foolishness."

"No, sir! I tell you true, it isn't, Pyotr Yegorych! Let me explain it to you. Last night I woke up and I lay there thinking and thinking. My old woman was sleeping, and I had no one to say a word to. Could I fix my gun now or couldn't I? I thought. I got up and set to mending it."

"Well?"

"Well. . . . I mended it and ran out with it like a madman. And now I got caught. Serves me right. You ought to take this same bird and give me one across the snout—to teach me a lesson."

"The constable is coming right away. Go into the entry."

"I'm going, sir. . . . I even owned up to it at confession. Father Pyotr, too, said it was foolishness, but, according to my stupid way of thinking, as I understand this thing, it's not foolishness, it's a sickness—just like drinking. Same thing. You don't want to, but you can't help it. You would be happy not to—you make a vow before the ikon—but it forces you: 'Drink! Drink!'. . . I used to drink, I know."

Volchkov's red nose turned purple. "Drinking is another matter," he said.

"The same, sir. May God strike me! I tell you true!" A silence fell; they stood looking at each other. Volchkov's nose turned dark blue. "In a word, sir, drinking—as you are so kind, you understand what a weakness it is——"

The lieutenant colonel did understand—not from kindness, but from experience. "Off with you," he said to the peasant. Pavel was puzzled. "And don't get underfoot again."

"My boots, if you please, sir." The little peasant understood now, and was beaming.

"Where are they?"

"In the cupboard, sir."

He got his boots, cap, and gun, and went out of the office with a light heart. He cocked an eye at the dark clouds overhead. The wind played over the grass and the trees; the first spatter of rain was tapping on the hot roof; the heavy air grew lighter.

Volchkov pushed open the window; Pavel turned at the sound and saw the wasp fly out. Air! Pavel and the wasp celebrated their freedom.

—1883

At Sea

A Sailor's Story

ONLY THE DIMMING LIGHTS of the receding harbor were visible in an ink-black sky. We could feel the heavy storm clouds overhead about to burst into rain, and it was suffocating, in spite of the wind and cold.

Crowded together in the crew's quarters we, the sailors, were casting lots. Loud, drunken laughter filled the air. One of our comrades was playfully crowing like a cock. A slight shiver ran through me from the back of my neck to my heels, as if cold small shot were pouring down my naked body from a hole in the back of my head. I was shivering both from the cold and certain other causes, which I wish to describe.

In my opinion, man is, as a rule, foul; and the sailor can sometimes be the foulest of all the creatures of the earth—fouler than the lowest beast, which has, at least, the excuse of obeying his instincts. It is possible that I may be mistaken, since I do not know life, but it appears to me that a sailor has more occasion than anyone else to despise and curse himself. A man who at any moment may fall headlong from a mast to be forever hidden beneath a wave, a man who may drown, God alone knows when, has need of nothing, and no one on dry land feels pity for him. We sailors drink

16

a lot of vodka and are dissolute because we do not know what one needs virtue for at sea. However, I shall continue.

We were casting lots. There were twenty-two of us who, having stood watch, were now at liberty. Out of this number only two were to have the luck of enjoying a rare spectacle. On this particular night the honeymoon cabin was occupied, but the wall of the cabin had only two holes at our disposal. One of them I myself had made with a fine saw, after boring through with a corkscrew; the other had been cut out with a knife by one of my comrades. We had worked at it for more than a week.

"You got one hole!"

"Who?"

They pointed to me. "Who got the other?"

"Your father."

My father, a humpbacked old sailor with a face like a baked apple, came up to me and clapped me on the back. "Today, my boy, we're lucky!" he said. "Do you hear, boy? Luck came to us both at the same time. That means something." Impatiently he asked the time; it was only eleven o'clock.

I went up on deck, lit my pipe and gazed out to sea. It was dark, but it can be assumed that my eyes reflected what was taking place in my soul, as I made out images on the black background of the night, visualizing what was so lacking in my own still young but already ruined life....

At midnight I walked past the saloon and glanced in at the door. The bridegroom, a young pastor with a handsome blond head, sat at a table holding the Gospels in his hands. He was explaining something to a tall, gaunt Englishwoman. The bride, a very beautiful, shapely young woman, sat at her husband's side with her light blue eyes fixed on him. A tall, plump, elderly Englishman, a banker, with a repulsive red face, paced up and down the saloon. He was the husband of the middle-aged lady to whom the pastor was talking.

"Pastors have a habit of talking for hours," I thought. "He won't finish before morning." At one o'clock my father came to me, pulled me by the sleeve and said: "It's time. They've left the saloon."

In the twinkling of an eye I flew down the companion-way and approached the familiar wall. Between this wall and the side of the ship there was a space where soot, water, and rats collected. I soon heard the heavy tread of the old man, my father. He cursed as he stumbled over a mat-sack and some kerosene cans. I felt for the hole in the wall and pulled out the square piece of wood I had so painstakingly sawed. I was looking at a thin, transparent muslin through which penetrated a soft, rosy light. Together with the light, my burning face was caressed by a delightful, sultry fragrance; this, no doubt, was the smell of an aristocratic bedroom. In order to see the room it was necessary to draw aside the muslin with two fingers, which I hastened to do. I saw bronze, velvet, lace, all bathed in a pink glow. About ten feet from my face stood the bed.

"Let me have your place," said my father, impatiently pushing me aside. "I can see better here." I did not answer him. "Your eyes are better than mine, boy, and it makes no difference to you if you look from far or near."

"Be quiet," I said, "they might hear us."

The bride sat on the side of the bed, dangling her little feet in a foot muff. She was staring at the floor. Before her stood her husband, the young pastor. He was telling her something, what I do not know; the noise of the steamer made it impossible for me to hear. He spoke passionately, with gestures, his eyes flashing. She listened and shook her head in refusal.

"The devil!" my father muttered. "A rat bit me!"

I pressed my chest to the wall, as if fearing my heart would jump out. My head was burning.

The bride and groom talked at great length. At last he sank to his knees and held out his arms, imploring her. She shook her head in refusal. He leaped to his feet, crossed the cabin, and from the expression on his face and the movements of his arms I surmised that he was threatening her. The young wife rose and went slowly towards the wall where I was standing. She stopped near the opening and stood motionless in thought. I devoured her face with my eyes. It seemed to me that she was suffering, struggling with herself, not knowing what to do; but at the same time her features expressed anger. I did not understand it.

We continued to stand there face to face for about five minutes, then she moved slowly away and, pausing in the middle of the cabin, nodded to the pastor—a sign of consent, undoubtedly. He smiled happily, kissed her hand and went out.

Within three minutes the door opened and the pastor re-entered followed by the tall, plump Englishman whom I mentioned above. The Englishman went over to the bed and asked the beautiful woman a question. Pale, not looking at him, she nodded her head affirmatively. The banker then took out of his pocket a packet of some sort—evidently bank notes—and handed it to the pastor, who examined it, counted it, bowed and went out. The elderly Englishman locked the door after him.

I sprang away from the wall as if I had been stung. I was frightened. It seemed to me the wind was tearing our ship to pieces, that we were going down. My father, that drunken, debauched old man, took me by the arm and said: "Let's go away from here! You shouldn't see that. You're still a boy."

He was hardly able to stand. I carried him up the steep winding stairs. Above an autumn rain had begun to fall.

—1883

A Nincompoop

A FEW DAYS AGO I ASKED my children's governess, Julia Vassilyevna, to come into my study.

"Sit down, Julia Vassilyevna," I said. "Let's settle our accounts. Although you most likely need some money, you stand on ceremony and won't ask for it yourself. Now then, we agreed on thirty rubles a month. . . . "

"Forty."

"No, thirty. I made a note of it. I always pay the governess thirty. Now then, you've been here two months, so . . ."

"Two months and five days."

"Exactly two months. I made a specific note of it. That means you have sixty rubles coming to you. Subtract nine Sundays . . . you know you didn't work with Kolya on Sundays, you only took walks. And three holidays . . ."

Julia Vassilyevna flushed a deep red and picked at the flounce of her dress, but—not a word.

"Three holidays, therefore take off twelve rubles. Four days Kolya was sick and there were no lessons, as you were occupied only with Vanya. Three days you had a toothache and my wife gave you permission not to work after lunch.

20

Twelve and seven—nineteen. Subtract . . . that leaves . . . hmm . . . forty-one rubles. Correct?"

Julia Vassilyevna's left eye reddened and filled with moisture. Her chin trembled; she coughed nervously and blew her nose, but—not a word.

"Around New Year's you broke a teacup and saucer; take off two rubles. The cup cost more, it was an heirloom, but—let it go. When didn't I take a loss! Then due to your neglect, Kolya climbed a tree and tore his jacket: take away ten. Also due to your heedlessness the maid stole Vanya's shoes. You ought to watch everything. You get paid for it. So, that means five more rubles off. The tenth of January I gave you ten rubles. . . . "

"You didn't," whispered Julia Vassilyevna.

"But I made a note of it."

"Well . . . all right."

"Take twenty-seven from forty-one—that leaves fourteen."

Both eyes filled with tears. Perspiration appeared on the thin, pretty little nose. Poor girl!

"Only once was I given any money," she said in a trembling voice, "and that was by your wife. Three rubles, nothing more."

"Really? You see now, and I didn't make a note of it. Take three from fourteen . . . leaves eleven. Here's your money, my dear. Three, three, three, one and one. Here it is!"

I handed her eleven rubles. She took them and with trembling fingers stuffed them into her pocket.

"*Merci,*" she whispered.

I jumped and started pacing the room. I was overcome with anger.

"For what, this—'*merci*'?" I asked.

"For the money."

"But you know I've cheated you, for God's sake—

robbed you! I have actually stolen from you! *Why* this *'merci'?*"

"In my other places they didn't give me anything at all."

"They didn't give you anything? No wonder! I played a little joke on you, a cruel lesson just to teach you. . . . I'm going to give you the entire eighty rubles! Here they are in an envelope all ready for you. . . . Is it really possible to be so spineless? Why don't you protest? Why be silent? Is it possible in this world to be without teeth and claws—to be such a nincompoop?"

She smiled crookedly and I read her expression: "It is possible."

I asked her pardon for the cruel lesson and, to her great surprise, gave her the eighty rubles. She murmured her little *"merci"* several times and went out. I looked after her and thought: "How easy it is to crush the weak in this world!"

—1883

Surgery

A ZEMSTVO HOSPITAL. In the absence of the doctor, who has gone off to get married, the patients are received by his assistant, the feldscher Kuryatin, a stout man of about forty, whose face wears an expression of amiability and a sense of duty. He is dressed in a shabby pongee jacket, frayed woolen trousers, and between the index and middle fingers of his left hand carries a cigar that gives off a stench.

Into the waiting room comes the sexton, Vonmiglasov. He is a tall, heavy-set old man, wearing a brown cassock with a wide leather belt. He has a cataract on his right eye, which is half-closed, and on his nose there is a wart that from a distance resembles a large fly. He stands for a moment trying to locate an ikon; unable to discover one, he crosses himself before a bottle of carbolic acid, then takes a loaf of communion bread out of a red handkerchief and, with a bow, places it before the feldscher.

"A-a-a-h . . . greetings," yawns the feldscher. "What brings you here?"

"A blessed Lord's day to you, Sergei Kuzmich. I've come to your worship—verily and in truth is it said in the Psalter: 'Thou givest them tears to drink in great measure.' The other day I sat down to drink tea with my old woman and—dear Lord!—not a drop, nothing could I swallow. I was ready to lie down and die! One little sip and there was no bearing it. And it's not just the tooth itself, but this whole side—it aches and aches! It goes right into my ear, if you will excuse me, as if a tack or some such object was in there. Such shooting pains, such shooting pains! I sinned and I transgressed, shamefully have I besmirched my soul with sins, and in slothfulness have I passed the days of my life! It's for my sins, Sergei Kuzmich, for my sins! His Reverence rebuked me after the liturgy: 'You're stammering, Yefim, you talk through your nose. You sing and nobody can make out a word you say.'. . . And how do you think I can sing if I can't open my mouth? It's all swollen, if you will excuse me, and not having slept all night——"

"Hmmm . . . yes. Sit down. Open your mouth."

Vonmiglasov does as he is told. Kuryatin knits his brows and begins his examination. Among the teeth, all yellowed by time and tobacco, he discovers one that is ornamented with a gaping hole

"Father deacon told me to use an application of vodka and horseradish—that didn't help. Glikeria Anisimovna, God grant her health, gave me a little thread from Mount Athos to wear, and she told me to rinse the tooth with warm milk. Although I did put on the little thread, as for the milk, I did not take that—I'm a God-fearing man, I keep the fast."

"Superstition." The feldscher pauses. "It has to be pulled, Yefim Mikheich."

"You know best, Sergei Kuzmich. That's what you've been trained for, to understand this business; to know whether to pull it or use drops or something else. It's for this that you, our benefactors, have been put here, God give you health, in order that day and night, till they lay us in our coffins, we should pray for you, our fathers——"

"It's nothing," says the feldscher modestly. He goes to one of the cupboards and begins rummaging among the instruments. "Surgery is nothing; it's all a matter of a firm hand. Quick as you can spit! The other day the landowner Alexander Ivanich Yegipetsky came here to the hospital, like you, also with a tooth. He's an educated man, asks all kinds of questions, goes into everything, wants to know the how and the what of things. He shook my hand and called me by my full name. He lived in Petersburg for seven years and hobnobbed with all the professors. I spent a long time over him. 'In Christ's name, pull it out for me, Sergei Kuzmich!' Why not? It can be pulled. But—this business has to be understood; without understanding—impossible. There are teeth and teeth. One you pull with forceps, another with molar forceps, and a third with a key. To each according-ing.".

The feldscher takes up the molar forceps, dubiously gazes at the instrument for a moment, then puts it down and takes up the forceps.

"Now, sir, open your mouth wide," he says, approaching the sexton with the forceps. "We'll have that out quick as you can spit! I only have to cut the gum a little, get leverage on a vertical axis, and that's all." He cuts the gum. "And that's all."

"You are our benefactor! We are benighted fools, but the Lord has enlightened you——"

"Well, don't make a speech just because you have your mouth open. That will pull easily. There are some that give trouble; nothing but roots to them. This will—quick as you can spit!" He lays down the forceps. "Don't twitch! Sit still! . . . In the twinkling of an eye." Then, getting leverage: "The important thing is to get a deep enough hold," pulling, "so that you don't break the crown."

"Our Father!—Holy Mother!—O-o-o-h!"

"Don't do that—don't do that! What's the matter with you? Don't grab me! Let go my hands!" Beginning to pull again. "In a minute—now—*now!*. . . You know, this business is not so simple."

"Fathers! Saints!" screams Vonmiglasov. "Ministering angels! Oh! O-o-o-h! Pull—pull! Why do you have to take five years?"

"It's a question of—surgery. Impossible to do it all at once. Now—*now*———"

Vonmiglasov's knees come up to his elbows, his eyes bulge, his fingers twitch, and his breath comes in gasps; perspiration breaks out on his crimson face and tears stand in his eyes. Kuryatin breathes audibly, shifting his weight from one foot to the other, and pulls. An agonizing half minute passes . . . and the forceps slip off the tooth. The sexton jumps up, thrusts his fingers into his mouth, and feels the tooth intact.

"But you pulled it!" he cries in a wailing, and at the same time, derisive voice. "May they pull you like that in the next world! We humbly thank you. If you don't know how to pull a tooth, then don't do it! I'm seeing stars!"

"And why did you grab hold of me?" The feldscher is furious. "I'm pulling and you're shoving my hands away and saying stupid things. *Fool!*"

"You're a fool, yourself!"

"Do you think, you peasant, that it's easy to pull a tooth? Just try it! It's not like climbing up into a belfry and rattling off a few chimes! 'If you don't know how, if you don't know how!' " he mimics. "Look, an expert has turned up! How do you like that? When I pulled Mr. Yegipetsky's tooth— Alexander Ivanich, that is—he didn't say anything, not a word! He's a better man than you are, he didn't grab me. Sit down. *Sit down,* I tell you!"

"I'm still seeing stars—let me catch my breath! Oh!" Vonmiglasov sits down. "Don't drag it out so long, just pull it. Don't drag on it so, give it one quick yank!"

"Teach your grandmother to suck eggs! Oh, Lord, the ignorance of the people! Live with them and you go out of your mind. Open your mouth." He inserts the forceps. "Surgery is no joke, brother. It's not like reading the Scriptures from the pulpit!" Getting leverage: "Don't jerk! The tooth appears to have been neglected for a long time. The roots go deep." Pulling: "Don't move! There—there—don't move—now—*now*——" A crunching sound is heard. "I knew it!"

For a moment Vonmiglasov sits motionless, as if numb. He is stunned and stares blankly into space, his white face covered with sweat.

"Perhaps I ought to have used the molar forceps," mumbles the feldscher. "What a mess!"

Coming to himself, the sexton puts his fingers into his mouth. In place of the defective tooth he feels two sharp stumps.

"You mangy devil!" he cries. "They planted you on this earth, you fiend, for our destruction!"

"Go on, curse me some more," mutters the feldscher, putting the forceps into the cupboard. "Ignoramus! They didn't treat you to the rod sufficiently at your seminary. Mr. Yegipetsky—Alexander Ivanich, that is—lived seven years in Petersburg, he's a cultured man. One suit costs him a hundred rubles—and he didn't swear. What sort of peahen are you? Don't worry, you won't die!"

The sexton takes the communion bread from the table and, holding his hand to his cheek, goes on his way.

—1884

Ninochka

A Love Story

THE DOOR OPENED QUIETLY and my good friend Pavel
Sergeyevich Vikhlyenev entered. Although a young
man, he was sickly, old-looking, and, in general—with his
round shoulders, long nose, and gaunt features—unattrac-
tive. But, on the other hand, his face was so bland, soft, and
undefined that every time you looked at it you experienced
a strange desire to get hold of it with your five fingers and
to feel, as it were, the doughy soft-heartedness and warmth
of my friend. Like all bookish people, he was quiet, diffi-
dent, and shy; besides which, at this time he was paler than
usual, and for some reason violently agitated.

"What's the matter with you?" I asked, glancing at his
white face and faintly trembling lips. "Are you sick, or has
there been another misunderstanding with your wife? You
don't look yourself."

After hesitating for a moment Vikhlyenev coughed
slightly, then with a gesture of despair said, "Yes ... with
Ninochka again. I've been so miserable I couldn't sleep all
night, and, as you see, I'm barely alive. Damn it all! Other
people don't let things get them down; they take injury, loss,

or pain lightly. But it requires a mere trifle to depress and upset me."

"But what happened?"

"A trifle—a little domestic drama. But I'll tell you the whole story, if you like. Yesterday my Ninochka did not go out. She took it into her head to spend an evening with me and stayed at home. I was, of course, overjoyed. She usually goes out to a meeting somewhere at night, and since that's the only time I'm at home, you can imagine how I was . . . well . . . I was overjoyed. But then, you have never been married, so you don't know how cozy and warm it feels when you come home from work to find the woman you live for. . . . Ah!"

Vikhlyenev made an inventory of the charms of married life. Then he wiped the perspiration from his forehead, and continued. "Ninochka thought she'd like to spend an evening with me. Well, you know how I am—dull, heavy, and far from clever. It's not much fun to be with me; I'm forever at my drafting board or my soil filters; I never play, or dance, or joke. And you must admit that Ninochka is pleasure-loving. Youth has its rights, don't you think so? Well, I began by showing her various little things, photographs and one thing and another, told her some stories, and then I suddenly remembered that I had some old letters in my desk, among them some that were very funny. In my student days I had friends who wrote devilishly clever letters: you read them and you split your guts laughing! I pulled these letters out of the desk and commenced reading them to Ninochka. I read her one, then another, then a third, and suddenly—the whole thing broke down! In one letter she came across the phrase: 'Katya sends her regards.' To a jealous wife such a phrase is like a sharp knife, and my Ninochka—an Othello in petticoats! The questions rained down on my unfortunate head: Who is this Katya? And how? And why? I explained to her that she was in some way a kind of first love, something out of my young student life, my salad days, to which it was impossible to attach any significance whatsoever. Every youth, I told her, has his Katya; it would be impossible not to—but my Ninochka wouldn't listen. She imagined—God knows what!—and started to cry. After the tears, hysterics. 'You're vile, filthy,' she screamed. 'You hid your past from me! You probably have some kind of Katya even now, and you're hiding it from me!' I tried and I tried to reassure her, but to no avail. Masculine logic never convinced a woman. In the end I begged her forgiveness—on my knees. I crawled, and where did it get me? She went to bed in hysterics—she in the bedroom and I on the sofa in my study. This morning she was pouting, wouldn't look at me, and spoke to me as though I were a stranger. She threatens to move to her mother's, and she probably will—I know her!"

"Hm-m. Not a very pleasant story."

"Women are incomprehensible to me! Granting that Ninochka is young, pure, fastidious, and can't help being shocked by something so earthy—is that so hard to forgive? I may be guilty, but I begged her forgiveness—I crawled on my knees! I even, if you must know, wept!"

"Yes, women are a great riddle."

"My dear friend, you have a strong influence over Ninochka. She respects you; she sees in you an authority. Please, go and see her. Exert your influence, and make her understand how wrong she is. I am suffering, my friend. If this goes on one more day I won't be able to endure it. Go—be a friend!"

"But do you think that would be . . . proper?"

"Why not? You and she have been friends almost since childhood. She trusts you. As a friend, please go!"

Vikhlyenev's tearful pleading touched me. I dressed and went to see his wife. I found Ninochka engaged in her favorite occupation: she was sitting on the sofa, one leg crossed over the other, blinking her beautiful eyes and doing nothing. When I came in she jumped up and ran to me; then she glanced round, quietly closed the door, and, with the lightness of a feather, clung to my neck. (You must not think, dear reader, that this is a misprint. For a year now, I had been sharing with Vikhlyenev his conjugal obligations.)

"What deviltry have you thought up now?" I asked Ninochka, seating her beside me.

"What do you mean?"

"Again you have managed to torment your better half. He came to see me today and told me all about it."

"Oh—that! So he found someone to complain to!"

"What actually happened?"

"Oh, not much. I was bored last night . . . and got angry because I had no place to go, so, out of spite, I started nagging him about his Katya. I cried simply from boredom— and how can I explain that to him?"

"But you know, my darling, that's cruel and inhuman. He's so nervous, and yet you plague him with your scenes."

"Oh, that's nothing. He loves it when I act jealous. And there's no better blind than fictitious jealousy. But let's drop it. I don't like it when you start talking about my milksop; I'm fed up with him! Let's have tea."

"Well, in any case, stop tormenting him. You know, he's pathetic: he describes his happiness and his faith in your love so frankly and sincerely that it makes one uncomfortable. Do control yourself somehow; show him some affection; lie! One word from you and he's in seventh heaven."

Ninochka frowned and pouted, but a little later when Vikhlyenev came in and timidly looked into my face, she gaily and affectionately smiled at him.

"You're just in time for tea!" she said to him. "How clever of you, my pet, never to be late. Lemon or cream for you?"

Vikhlyenev, not expecting such a welcome, was moved; he kissed his wife's hand warmly, and embraced me. This embrace was so absurd and so untimely that both Ninochka and I blushed.

"Blessed are the peacemakers!" clucked the happy husband. "You've made her listen to reason; and why? Because you're a man of the world; you mingle in society, and you know all the fine points of a woman's heart! Ha! Ha! Ha! I'm a clumsy ox; when one word is needed, I say ten; when I should kiss her hand or something, I start to find fault! Ha! Ha!"

After tea Vikhlyenev led me into his study, buttonholed me, and mumbled, "I don't know how to thank you, my dear friend. Believe me, I suffered; I was tortured; and now I am so happy—I'm simply overwhelmed! And this isn't the first time that you've pulled me out of a terrible situation. My dear friend—now, don't refuse me—I have here a little something. . . . It's just a little model locomotive that I made myself; I got a medal for it at the exposition. Take it as a token of my gratitude . . . my friendship. Do me this favor!"

Naturally, I refused in every possible way, but Vikhlyenev was insistent and, like it or not, I had to accept his precious gift.

Days, weeks, months passed. Sooner or later the ugly truth was bound to be revealed to him in all its enormity. When, by accident, he did find out, he turned frightfully pale, sat down on the sofa, and stared dully at the ceiling without saying a word. A heartache has to express itself in some kind of movement, and he began to turn from side to side on the sofa in an agonizing way. Even these movements were circumscribed by his milksop nature.

A week later, somewhat recovered from the shock of this news, he came to see me. We were both embarrassed and avoided looking at each other. I began to spout some sort of nonsense about free love, marital selfishness, submission to fate.

"It wasn't about that—" he interrupted meekly, "all that I understand perfectly. In matters of the heart, no one is guilty. What concerns me is the other side of the business . . . the purely practical. You see, I don't know life at all, and where the actual arrangements . . . the social conventions are concerned, I'm a real greenhorn. So, help me, my friend! Tell me, what is Ninochka supposed to do now? Should she go on living with me, or do you think it would be better if she moved in with you?"

Having deliberated briefly, we left it at this: Ninochka would continue to live at Vikhlyenev's; I would go to see her whenever I liked, and he would take the corner room, which formerly had been the storeroom, for himself. This room was rather dark and damp, and the entrance to it was through the kitchen, but, on the other hand, he could perfectly well shut himself up in it and not be a nuisance to anyone.

—1885

A Cure for Drinking

THE WELL-KNOWN READER and comedian, Mr. Feniksov-Dikobrazov II, had been engaged to appear as a guest artist, and was arriving at the city of D—— in a first-class coach. Everyone who had come to the station to meet him knew that the celebrated actor had bought his first-class ticket only two stations back, for show, and that up to that point he had traveled third; they also observed that in spite of the chilly autumn weather he wore only a summer cape and a worn sealskin cap; nevertheless, when the sleepy, bluish face of Dikobrazov II appeared, everyone felt a quiver of excitement and an eagerness to meet him. The manager of the theater, Pochechuev, kissed him three times, in the Russian manner, and carried him off to his own apartment.

The celebrity was to have begun his engagement two days later, but fate decided otherwise; the day before the performance a pale, distraught manager rushed into the box office of the theater and announced that Dikobrazov II would be unable to play.

"He can't go on!" declared Pochechuev, tearing his hair. "How do you like that? For a month—one whole month—

it's been advertised in letters three feet high that we'd have Dikobrazov; we've built it up, we've gone all out, sold subscriptions, and now this low trick! Hanging's too good for him!"

"But what's the matter? What happened?"

"He's on a binge, damn him!"

"What of it? He'll sleep it off."

"He'll croak before he sleeps it off! I know him from Moscow; when he starts lapping up vodka, it's a couple of months before he comes out of it. This is a binge—a real binge! No, it's just my luck! And why am I so unfortunate? Whom do I take after to be cursed with such luck? All my life this dark cloud has been hanging over my head—why? Why?" (Pochechuev was a tragedian by nature as well as by profession; strong expressions, accompanied by beating his breast with his fists, were very becoming to him.) "What a vile, infamous, despicable slave am I to place my head beneath the blows of fate! Would it not be more worthy to give up this role of the eternal victim of a hostile fate, and simply put a bullet through my head? What am I waiting for? Oh, God, what am I waiting for?" Pochechuev covered his face with his hands and turned to the window.

Besides the cashier there were many actors and playgoers present in the box office, everyone offering advice, consolation, and encouragement, and the occasion bore a sententious and oracular quality; no one went beyond "vanity of vanities," "think nothing of it," and "maybe it'll turn out all right." Only the cashier, a fat dropsical man, said anything to the point.

"But, Prokl Lvovich," he said, "you should try curing him."

"Nobody in the world can cure a binge!"

"Don't say that. Our hairdresser cures them completely. He treats the whole town."

Pochechuev, by now ready to snatch at a straw, was overjoyed at this possibility, and within five minutes the theatrical hairdresser, Fyodor Grebeshkov, stood before him. If you will visualize a tall, bony, hollow-eyed man with a long sparse beard and brown hands, who bears a striking resemblance to a skeleton activated by means of screws and springs, and if you dress this figure in an incredibly threadbare black suit, you will have a portrait of Grebeshkov.

"Hello, Fedya!" said Pochechuev. "I hear, my friend, that you have the cure for a drinking bout. Do me a favor—not as an employee, but as a friend—cure Dikobrazov! You see, he's on a binge."

"God be with him!" Grebeshkov pronounced in a doleful bass voice. "Indeed, I do treat actors of the commoner sort, and merchants, and officials; but this is a celebrity, known throughout Russia!"

"Well, what of it?"

"In order to knock it out of him, it is necessary to produce a revolution in all the organs and members of the body. I will produce this revolution in him; he will get well; and then he will get on his high horse with me. 'You dog,' he will say, 'how dare you touch my person.' We know these celebrities!"

"No, no, don't shirk it, brother. One must take the thorns with the roses. Put on your hat and let's go."

When Grebeshkov entered Dikobrazov's room a quarter of an hour later, he found the famous man lying in bed, glaring malevolently at a hanging lamp. The lamp was motionless, but Dikobrazov did not take his eyes from it. "You'd better quit spinning," he muttered. "I'll show you how to spin, you devil! I smashed the decanter and I'll smash you, too. You'll see! A-a-a-h . . . now the ceiling's going round. I know—it's a conspiracy! But the lamp—the lamp! It's the smallest, but it turns the most. . . . Just wait. . . . "

The comedian got up, dragging the sheet after him and knocking glasses off the little table as he staggered toward the lamp; halfway there he stumbled against something tall and bony.

"What's that?" he roared, lifting his haggard eyes. "Who are you? Where'd you come from, hah?"

"I'll show you who I am—get into bed!" And not even waiting for Dikobrazov to follow his instructions, Grebeshkov swung his arm and brought his fist down on the back of the actor's head with such force that he fell head over heels onto the bed. In all probability he had never been struck before, because in spite of his drunkenness, he gazed up at Grebeshkov with wonder and even curiosity.

"You . . . you hit me? But, wait . . . you hit me?"

"I hit you. Do you want more?" This time the hairdresser struck him in the teeth. Either the strength of the blow or the novelty of the situation had an effect; the comedian's eyes ceased wandering and a glimmer of reason appeared in them. He jumped up, and with more curiosity than anger, began to examine Grebeshkov's pale face and filthy coat.

"You . . . you use your fists? You dare?" he mumbled.

"Shut up!" Again a blow in the face.

"Easy! Easy!" Pochechuev's voice was heard from the next room. "Easy, Fedyenka!"

"That's nothing, Prokl Lvovich. He himself will thank me for it in the end."

"Even so, take it easy!" exclaimed Pochechuev tearfully, as he glanced into the room. "It may be nothing to you, but it sends a chill down my spine. Think of it: in broad daylight, to beat an intelligent, celebrated man, who's in his right mind—and in his own apartment, too! Ach!"

"It's not him that I'm beating, Prokl Lvovich, but the devil that's inside him. Go away now, please, and don't upset yourself. . . . Lie down, devil!" Fedya fell upon the comedian. "Don't move! Wha-at?"

Dikobrazov was seized with horror. It seemed to him that all the whirling objects he had smashed had entered in a conspiracy, and now, with one accord, were flying at his head.

"Help!" he cried. "Save me! Help!"

"Cry! Cry out, you devil, you! The worst is yet to come!

Now listen: if you say one more word, or make the slightest movement, I'm going to kill you! I shall kill you without a regret. There is no one, brother, to intercede for you; even if you were to fire a cannon, nobody would come. But if you are quiet and submissive, I'll give you a little vodka. Here's your vodka!"

Grebeshkov took a pint of vodka out of his pocket and flashed it before the comedian's eyes. At the sight of the object of his passion, the drunken man forgot all about his beating and whinnied with delight. The hairdresser then took a dirty little piece of soap from his vest pocket and stuck it into the bottle. When the vodka became cloudy and soapy he set about adding all sorts of junk to it: saltpeter, ammonium chloride, alum, sodium sulphate, sulphur, resin, and various other "ingredients" that are sold in a chandlery. The comedian peered at Grebeshkov, avidly following the movements of the bottle. In conclusion the hairdresser burned a scrap of rag, poured the ashes into the vodka, shook it, and approached the bed.

"Drink!" he said, half filling a glass with the mixture. "At once!"

The comedian gulped it down with delight, gasped, and was immediately goggle-eyed. His face went white, and perspiration stood out on his forehead.

"Drink some more," suggested Grebeshkov.

"No, I don't want to! But, wait——"

"Drink, so you'll—— Drink! I'll kill you!"

Dikobrazov drank, then fell onto the pillow with a moan. A moment later he raised himself slightly, and Fyodor was able to satisfy himself that the mixture had worked.

"Drink some more! Let your guts turn inside out, it's good for you. Drink!"

And then the torture commenced: the actor's guts were literally turned inside out. He jumped up, then tossed on the bed, following with horror the slow movements of his merciless and indefatigable enemy. Grebeshkov did not leave his side for a moment, and sedulously pummeled him when he refused the mixture; a beating was followed by the mixture, the mixture by a beating. Never in all his life had the poor body of Feniksov-Dikobrazov II endured such outrage and humiliation; and never had the famous artist been so weak and helpless as he was now. At first he cried out and struggled, then he grew silent, and finally, convinced that the protests only led to further beatings, he began to weep. At length Pochechuev, who was standing behind the door listening, could bear it no longer, and ran into the room.

"Damn it all!" he cried, waving his arms. "It would be better to lose the subscription money, and let him have his vodka—only stop torturing him, please! He'll die on us, damn you! Look at him, you can see, he's absolutely dead! I should have known better than to get mixed up with you!"

"That's nothing. He'll be grateful for it, you'll see. Hey, you—what's going on there?" Grebeshkov turned to the comedian. "You'll get it in the neck!"

The hairdresser was busy with Dikobrazov till evening; he himself was tired, worn out. At last the comedian was too weak even to moan, and seemed to have petrified, with an expression of horror on his face. This state was followed by something resembling sleep.

The next day, to the great surprise of Pochechuev, the comedian awoke; it seems he was not dead! On awakening he examined the room with dull, wandering eyes, and then began to recall what had happened.

"Why do I ache all over?" he wondered. "I feel exactly as though a train had run over me. Shall I have a drink of vodka? Hey! Who's there? Vodka!"

Pochechuev and Grebeshkov were standing behind the door.

"He's asking for vodka!" Pochechuev was horrified. "That means you didn't cure him!"

"What are you talking about, Prokl Lvovich?" Grebeshkov was surprised. "Do you think you can cure anyone in a day?

I'd be thankful if he were cured in a week—and here you are talking of a day! You might even cure one of those weak fellows in five days, but this one has the constitution of a merchant. He's tough!"

"Why didn't you tell me this before, you devil?" roared Pochechuev. "Whom do I take after to have this luck? Cursed as I am, what more can I expect from fate? Wouldn't it be more sensible to end it all—to put a bullet through my head right now?"

Despite the gloomy view that Pochechuev took of his fate, Dikobrazov II was playing within a week, and the subscribers' money did not have to be returned.

Grebeshkov put on the comedian's make-up, handling his head with such deference that no one would have suspected his former treatment of the man.

"What vitality!" marveled Pochechuev. "I nearly died just watching that torture, but he, as if nothing had happened, not only thanks that devil Fedya, but wants to take him to Moscow with him! It's a miracle, that's what it is!"

—1885

The Jailer Jailed

HAVE YOU EVER NOTICED how donkeys are loaded? Generally the poor beasts are piled up with everything one can think of, regardless of bulk or quantity: kitchen paraphernalia, furniture, beds, barrels, sacks with infants in them; they are packed so that they look like huge formless masses, and even the tips of their hoofs are scarcely visible. Alexei Timofeyevich Balbinsky, public prosecutor of the Khlamov district court, looked somewhat like this when, after the third bell had rung, he rushed into the railway coach to secure a place. He was loaded from head to foot: bundles of provisions, pasteboard boxes, tin boxes, suitcases, a large bottle of something or other, a woman's cloak, and heaven only knows what more! Streams of perspiration ran down his red face, his legs were about to give way under him, and the light of suffering was in his eyes. His wife, Natasha Lvovna, followed him carrying her multicolored parasol. She was a small freckled blonde with a protuberant jaw and bulging eyes, and looked exactly like a young pickerel being drawn from the water on the end of a hook.

After wandering at length through several coaches, the prosecutor succeeded in finding places; he dropped his baggage onto the seats, wiped the perspiration from his fore-head, and headed for the exit.

"Where are you going?" his wife asked.

"I want to go into the station, sweetheart, to drink a glass of vodka——"

"You can put that idea out of your head. Sit down!"

Balbinsky sighed and sat down.

"Hold this basket—it has the dishes in it."

Balbinsky took the large basket and looked longingly out the window.

At the fourth stop his wife sent him into the station for hot water and there, near the buffet, he met his friend Fly-azhkin, assistant to the president of the district court of Plinsk, with whom he had planned to make this trip abroad.

"My dear fellow, what does this mean?" Flyazhkin swooped down upon him. "This is a dirty trick, to say the least. We agreed to travel together in the same coach; what the devil are you doing in a third-class coach? Why are you traveling third class? No money, or what?"

Balbinsky made a despairing gesture and began to blink his eyes.

"It's all the same to me now," he muttered, "I'd just as soon ride in the tender. It looks as if it's all over—everything we planned. I could throw myself under the train! You cannot imagine, my dear fellow, to what extent my wife has worn me out. I'm so exhausted it's a wonder I'm still alive! My God! The weather is magnificent . . . this air . . . the open country . . . nature . . . all the conditions for an undisturbed existence. Just the thought of going abroad ought to be enough to make me ecstatic. But no! Some evil destiny had to fasten that treasure round my neck! And observe the irony of fate: I invented this liver complaint for the sole purpose of getting away from my wife. I wanted to escape for a while—go abroad. All winter long I've dreamed of freedom; even in my waking dreams I saw myself alone. And now? I'm stuck with her for the trip! I tried one thing and then another—all for nothing! 'I'm going with you, no matter what!'. . . Well, she came. I suggested we go second class. Not for the world! 'Why,' she says, 'should we waste the money?' I gave her all the reasons—I told her we had the money, that we lose prestige if we travel third class, that it's stuffy, it stinks—but she wouldn't listen. A demon of frugality possesses her. Take this baggage, for instance. Now, why do we have to drag along such masses of stuff? Why all these bundles, boxes, suitcases, and other trash? Not only did we check ten poods of baggage, but we still require four seats in our car. The conductor keeps asking us to make room for others; the passengers get angry; she wrangles with them. It's a shame! Would you believe it? I'm on hot coals! But to get away from her? God help me! She won't allow me one step from her. I have to sit next to her and hold an enormous basket on my knees. Just now she sent me for hot water. Now, does it look proper for a court prosecutor to run around carrying a copper teapot? You know, there are probably some of my witnesses and defendants traveling on this train. My prestige is going to hell! But, from now on, my dear fellow, this is going to be a lesson to me! It's impossible to realize what personal freedom means! Sometimes you get carried away and, you know, for no reason at all, you stick someone in jail. Well, now I understand—it's penetrated. . . . I understand what it means to be in jail! Oh, how I understand!"

"I guess you'd be glad to get out on bail," Flyazhkin smirked.

"Overjoyed! Would you believe it—regardless of my circumstances I'd be willing to put up a bond of 10,000! But I've got to run. She's probably having a fit. I'll get roasted!"

In Verzhbolovo, when Flyazhkin was taking an early morning stroll on the platform, he caught sight of Balbinsky's sleepy face at the window of one of the third-class coaches.

"Wait a minute," the prosecutor beckoned to him, "she's

still sleeping—not awake yet—and when she's asleep, I'm relatively free. To get out would be impossible, but at least I can put this basket on the floor in the meantime. That's something to be thankful for! Oh, yes! I didn't tell you? I'm so happy!"

"Why?"

"Two boxes and one bag were stolen from us—now we're that much lighter. Yesterday we finished the goose and all the meat pies. I purposely overate so there would be less baggage. And the air in this coach! You could hang a hatchet on it. Whew! This isn't a journey—it's sheer torture!" The prosecutor turned and looked with bitterness at his sleeping spouse. "My Varvarka!" he whispered. "What a tyrant, what a Herod you are! With my luck, will I ever escape from you, Xantippe?... Would you believe it, Ivan Nikitich, sometimes I close my eyes and dream.... What do I dream? If ifs and ans were pots and pans, she would fall into my clutches as a defendant. I think I'd sentence her to hard labor. But—she's waking up—sh!"

In the twinkling of an eye he assumed an innocent expression, picked up the basket and set it on his lap.

At Eidkunen, when he came out to get hot water, he looked more cheerful.

"Two more boxes stolen!" he confided exultantly to Flyazhkin. "And we've eaten up all the rolls—we're that much lighter!"

When they reached Königsberg he ran into Flyazhkin's coach looking positively transfigured. He threw himself down on the divan and burst into laughter.

"My dear friend! Ivan Nikitich! Let me embrace you! I'm so happy, so perniciously happy! I am free! Do you understand? Free! My wife has run away!"

"What do you mean 'run away'?"

"She left the coach during the night, and she hasn't come back! She ran off, or fell under the train, or maybe she was left in a station somewhere. Anyway, she's gone! Oh, my angel!"

"But listen," Flyazhkin became alarmed, "in that case you ought to telegraph——"

"God forbid! I'm enjoying my freedom so much, I can't even describe it to you! Let's go out on the platform and walk up and down . . . breathe freely!"

The two friends went out and marched up and down the platform. With every breath the prosecutor exclaimed, "How good! I can breathe! Are there actually people that live like this all the time? Do you know what, brother?" He reached a sudden decision. "I'll move in with you. We'll spread out and live like bachelors." And he ran headlong to his own coach to get his things.

Within a few minutes he was back again, no longer beaming, but pale, stunned, and with the copper teapot in his hands. He staggered slightly, and clutched his heart.

"She's back!" He made a despairing gesture in answer to his friend's questioning gaze. "It seems that during the night she got confused about the cars, and went into the wrong one by mistake. And that's it, brother!"

The prosecutor stood before his friend with a dazed, despairing look on his face. Tears rose to his eyes. There was a moment of silence.

"Do you know what?" Flyazhkin said, taking him gently by the collar. "If I were in your place, I'd do the running away. . . . "

"What do you mean?"

"Run away, that's all; otherwise you're going to wither away. You should see yourself!"

"Run away . . . run away . . ." mused the prosecutor. "That's an idea! Well, I tell you what I'll do, brother: I'll get onto the wrong train at the next station, and—I'm off! Later I can tell her it was a mistake. Well, good-bye. . . . See you in Paris!"

—1885

The Dance Pianist

Two o'clock in the morning. I was sitting in my room filling an order for a *feuilleton* in verse, when suddenly the door opened and, quite unexpectedly, my roommate, Pyotr Rublyov, a former student at the M—— Conservatory, entered. Wearing a top hat and with his fur coat thrown open, he reminded me for the first time of Repetilov, but when I noticed his pale face, his singularly sharp, inflamed eyes, the resemblance disappeared.

"Why are you so early?" I asked. "It's only two o'clock. The wedding can't have ended so soon?"

He did not answer, but disappeared behind the screen, quickly undressed, and, with a sound of heavy breathing, lay down on his bed.

"Sleep, you beast!" I heard him whisper ten minutes later. "You went to bed, now sleep! . . . You're not sleepy—then you can go to the devil!"

"Can't you sleep, Petya?" I asked.

"I don't know what the hell's the matter with me. For some reason or other I can't sleep. And I can't help laughing—that keeps me from falling asleep. . . . Ha! Ha!"

"What's so amusing?"

46

"A funny thing happened. And the damned thing had to happen to me!" Rublyov came out from behind the screen and, laughing, sat down near me. "It's funny and . . . disgraceful," he said, rumpling his hair. "I have never in my entire life witnessed such a show. Ha! Ha! A first-class scandal, brother. A high-society scandal!" He brought his fist down on his knee, then jumped up and began to pace the cold floor in his bare feet. "They threw me out! That's why I came home early!"

"Stop it! I don't believe you."

"I swear it. They kicked me out—literally!"

I stared at him. His face was worn and sallow, but he looked so decent, honest, and refined, that I was unable to reconcile his crude "they kicked me out" with his sensitive expression.

"A first-rate scandal. I laughed all the way home. Oh, leave off writing that rubbish and I'll tell you. I'll pour out my soul . . . maybe it won't be so funny. Leave off, now, and listen; it's an interesting story. On the Arbat there lives a certain Prisvistov, a retired lieutenant colonel married to the illegitimate daughter of Count von Krach—consequently, an aristocrat. He is marrying his daughter to the merchant son of Eskimosov. This Eskimosov is a *parvenu* and *mauvais genre*—ill bred, a swine in a skull cap. But both papa and daughter would like to *manger* and *boire*, so there was no time to go into that. I set out for the Prisvistovs' around nine to play for the dancing. The streets were muddy, there was rain and fog, and I was feeling miserable at heart, as usual."

"Make it short," I said, "without the psychology."

"All right. I arrived at the Prisvistovs'. The ceremony was over, and the guests and young people were all gorging on fruit. I went to my post—the piano—and sat down to wait for the dancing to begin. The host caught sight of me. 'Ah, you have arrived! Look here, my friend, see that you play properly, and, above all, do not get drunk!' Brother, I'm so accustomed to that sort of welcome that I don't even take offense. Ha! Ha! One must take the thorns with the roses—right? And what am I, after all? A piano player, a domestic, a waiter that knows how to play the piano. In the homes of merchants I'm addressed as an inferior, given a tip, and—no offense intended.

"Well, having nothing to do till the dancing began, I was strumming a few chords, lightly, you know, just to loosen my fingers; and as I played I could hear that someone behind me had begun to sing along with the piano. I glanced over my shoulder—a young lady! She stood directly behind me, the sly one, sweetly gazing at the keyboard. 'Mademoiselle,' I said, 'I was not aware that anyone was listening to me.' She sighed, 'A lovely thing. . . . ' And I replied, 'Yes, it is. . . . Are you interested in music?' And then a conversation began. The young lady proved to be talkative; I didn't have to encourage her; she babbled on by herself. 'What a pity that the present-day youth does not study serious music!' And I, blockhead, fool that I am, so delighted to have someone paying attention to me—I still have my wretched vanity—assumed an attitude, and enlarged upon the indifference of youth, the lack of aesthetic standards in our society, and began to philosophize."

"But what's the scandal?" I asked Rublyov. "Did you fall in love?"

"Don't be silly. Love—that's a private catastrophe; but here, brother, we have something public, something in the realm of high society. Well, I continued chatting with the young lady, but before long I became aware that something was in the wind: I could hear whispering behind my back, and I caught the words 'piano player' followed by sniggering. They were talking about me. What could that mean? Something wrong with my necktie? I felt my tie, nothing out of place, so, naturally, I paid no attention and went on with the conversation. But the young lady was growing excited; she argued, and her face was flushed. She certainly was wound up! She let fly such a critique on composers, you had to hold onto your hat! . . . In *The Demon* the orchestration is good, but there is no melody; Rimski-Korsakov is a drummer; Varlamov is incapable of composing anything complete; and so forth. The boys and girls of today can hardly play their scales; they pay twenty-five kopecks a lesson and they're ready to write music reviews. . . . That gives you an idea of my young lady. I listened, but I didn't argue with her. I love it when some green young thing flares up and uses her brain.

"Well, the muttering and mumbling continued behind me. Why? All at once some fat peahen glided over to my young lady—one of those solid, red-faced mama-auntie types that you couldn't get your arms around if you stretched them—and, without so much as a glance at me, whispered something into her ear. And listen to this: the young lady blushed, clutched her cheeks with both hands, and recoiled from the piano as though she had been stung. What could it mean? It would take the wisdom of Oedipus to figure that out. I thought, either my coat had split down the back, or some disaster had occurred in the young lady's attire. How else could one explain such extraordinary behavior? In any case, before ten minutes had passed I went out into the lobby to inspect myself. I examined my necktie, my coat—tra-la-la—all in good order, nothing ripped. It was fortunate for me that a certain old hag with a bundle happened to be standing there; she cleared it all up for me. Were it not for her, I might have remained in blissful ignorance. 'Our young lady can't help showing what she is,' she was saying to one of the footmen. 'As soon as she saw a young man at the piano, she started her fooling, just as if he was a real—ach! what a joke! Just imagine, it turns out the fellow isn't even a guest, he's just a piano player—a musician! That's what she was talking to! It's a good thing Marya Stepanovna whispered something in her ear; otherwise she might have wandered off arm in arm with him. It's a shame!

Well, it's too late now; what's done is done.'. . . Well, what do you think of that?"

"The girl is stupid," I answered, "and the old woman's stupid. It's not worth paying attention to."

"I paid no attention; I was amused, that's all. I got used to that sort of performance a long time ago. In the beginning it was actually painful; but now I don't care a fig. The girl is young and stupid, and I'm sorry for her. . . . I returned to the piano and began playing—nothing serious, you understand—waltzes, crashing quadrilles, and a few thundering marches. If your musical soul is nauseated, you have only to take a drink, and you, too, can leap for joy with Boccaccio."

"But what was the scandal?"

"I was rattling away on the keys, not even thinking about the girl; I laughed, and that was all; but something was picking at my heart. And the gnawing in the pit of my stomach was like the gnawing of mice in municipal warehouses. Why I felt so miserable and sad I do not know. I reasoned with myself; I swore; I laughed; I even began to sing; but my soul was stung. A smarting pain tore at my chest; it pricked and gnawed. Suddenly something like a lump rose into my throat. I clenched my teeth and waited for it to pass; but it only stopped to begin again. What a thing to happen! And, as if to spite me, there came into my head the most abominable thoughts. I commenced thinking what rubbish I had turned out to be; that after traveling two thousand versts to reach Moscow, in the hope of becoming a concert pianist or a composer, I now find myself a dance pianist. . . . It's quite natural, in fact, it's even funny, but it turns my stomach. I thought of you, too. . . . There he sits, my roommate, scribbling. The poor devil is describing sleeping councilors, cockroaches in bakeries, foul autumn weather; describing, in other words, exactly what has been described time out of mind, chewed over and over again. . . . I thought about it, and for some reason

I felt so sorry for you—so sorry I could have wept. You're a good fellow, and you're sensitive; but you lack fire, spleen, force; you have no passion. Why you aren't a chemist or a cobbler instead of a writer, Christ only knows! ... I thought of all my unsuccessful friends, all the singers, painters, dilettantes. . . . There was a time when everything was stirring, seething, steaming to the heavens; but now—the devil only knows! ... Why such things came into my head, I have no idea. As quickly as I cast out thoughts of myself, my friends popped into mind; I got rid of them, and it was the girl. I merely laughed at her, she's of no importance. . . . But I couldn't get her out of my mind. What is it in the Russian character, I wondered, that makes it possible, as long as you are free, a student, or loafing around without a job, to drink with a man, slap him on the belly, flirt with his daughter; but as soon as you are in even a slightly subordinate relation to him, the shoemaker must stick to his last! Somehow, you know, I gagged on the thought; it stuck in my throat, gripping and strangling me, until at last I felt my eyes watering. My Boccaccio was cut short, and everything went to hell. The aristocratic reception room was filled with new sounds: I became hysterical."

"I don't believe you!"

"I swear it's true," answered Rublyov, flushing and attempting to laugh. "Quite the scandal, eh? After that I felt myself being dragged into the lobby . . . they put my coat on me . . . I heard the hostess say, 'Who got the piano player drunk? Who dared to give him vodka?' In conclusion, they threw me out. Quite a show—ha! ha! ... I didn't feel like laughing then, but now it seems terribly funny to me—terribly! A blundering idiot, tall as a fire tower, says 'how-do-you-do' and all at once has hysterics. . . . Ha! Ha!—Ha! Ha! Ha!"

"What's funny about that?" I asked, my eyes fixed on his

shaking head and shoulders. "Petya, for God's sake, why is that funny? Petya! My dear fellow!"

But Petya only continued to laugh, and in such a manner that I gradually realized he was hysterical. I quickly began ministering to him; and I cursed all Moscow lodging houses for not furnishing water at night.

—1885

The Milksop

IT WAS EVENING. Pantelei Diomidich Kokin, a secretary in the office of *The Goose Gazette,* a provincial newspaper, was on his way to the home of the manufacturer and Councilor of Commerce, Bludykhin, where there were to be amateur theatricals followed by a supper and dancing.

The secretary, happy, high-spirited, and pleased with himself, was imagining a dazzling future. . . . He pictured himself entering the ballroom, gallant, perfumed, and curled. He intended to affect an air of melancholy and indifference; to display self-respect in his bearing and the shrug of his shoulders; to speak negligently, reluctantly; and to try to bring to his glance an expression of weary mockery. In a word, he would conduct himself like a representative of the press. On passing him the ladies and gentlemen would exchange glances and whisper: "Member of the press. Not bad!"

As secretary of *The Goose Gazette* he was required to keep the addresses in order, take subscriptions, and see that the typographers did not steal the editor's sugar—and that was all. But who, of the general public, was to know the limits of his duties? Since he came from a newspaper, he was,

53

as a matter of course, a man of letters and custodian of editorial secrets. Ah, those editorial secrets, what an effect they had on a woman!

He would probably meet Klavdia Vasilyevna at the party. He intended to pass by her several times, as if he had failed to notice her; then, when she could bear it no longer, she would speak first. He would greet her indifferently, yawn, glance at his watch, and say: "What a bore! If only this nonsense would end soon. It's already midnight, and I have to get out an edition and look over certain articles." Klavdia would gaze up at him in awe, as one looks at a monument. Quite possibly she would ask him who, in the last issue, had written those scathing verses on the actress Kishkina Brandakhlytskaya. He would raise his eyes towards the ceiling and mumble mysteriously: "Mmmm . . . yes." Let her think he had written them! Then there would be dancing, supper, drinking . . . and the final state of bliss in which he would escort Klavdia home. Dreams . . . Dreams . . .

At the illuminated entrance to Bludykhin's house, the secretary saw two rows of carriages, the doors of which were being opened and closed by a corpulent doorman carrying a mace. The foyer was magnificent with carpets, mirrors, and flowers. Footmen in blue frockcoats over red waistcoats were taking the guests' overcoats, and Kokin casually dropped his into their hands. He approached the staircase where two footmen were tearing off the corners of tickets; he ran his hand over his hair, lifted his head with dignity and murmured: "From the press."

"Impossible! Impossible! Don't admit him!" came a sharp, metallic voice from above. *"Do not admit him!"* Kokin looked up. There, at the head of the stairs, looking straight at him, stood a fat man in a swallowtail coat. Being certain, however, that this sharp voice had nothing to do with him the secretary placed his foot on the first step of the staircase. To his horror, the footmen blocked his way.

"Do not admit him!" the fat man repeated.

"But—that is to say—why not?" Kokin was stunned. "I am from the press."

"That's exactly why, because you're from the press." The fat man bowed to a passing lady and repeated, "Impossible!"

Kokin stood as if struck over the head. He was horribly embarrassed. New gloves, curled hair, and the heavy scent of violet water are hardly compatible with the humiliating role of a man who has been denied admittance, whose way has been blocked by lackeys. All this in the presence of ladies—and servants! Apart from the shame, the bewilderment and surprise, the secretary felt empty and disillusioned, as if someone had taken a pair of scissors and cut out of him all dreams of future happiness. So must a man feel who has received, in place of some anticipated gratitude, a slap in the face.

"I don't understand—I'm from the press, let me in!" he stammered.

"We have been ordered not to," said a footman. "Step aside, you're blocking the way."

"Strange," faltered the secretary, forcing a dignified smile, "very strange . . ."

There was gay laughter and the rustle of fashionable gowns as one lady after another passed him. Each time the door slammed a draft flew across the vestibule, and another party of guests ascended the stairs.

"Why are they forbidden to admit me?" the secretary puzzled, still not himself after the unexpected rebuff. He could not believe his own eyes. "That fat man said it was because I was from the press that I could not be admitted. But why? . . . Curse them! I hope to God no one I know sees me standing here freezing. They would wonder what had happened. What a disgrace!"

Kokin made another attempt to go upstairs, but the footman barred his way. He shrugged, blew his nose, deliberated, and again approached the footmen. Again they stopped him. Upstairs the orchestra began to play. His heart fluttered

and he caught his breath in a quickening desire to be in the
great ballroom, his head held high, playing on Klavdia Vasilyevna's patience. At that moment the swelling of the music
awakened all the dreams with which he had beguiled himself on his way to the party.

"Listen," he cried out to the fat man, "why can't you let
me in?"

"What? . . . No one admitted from the press."

"But why? At least, explain."

"Mr. Bludykhin's orders. It's not my business. If he forbids it, I can't admit you. Please, let the lady pass. . . . Look
here, Andrei, no one from the press—the master's orders."

Kokin shrugged his shoulders; then feeling the stupidity
and pointlessness of the gesture, he moved away from the
staircase. What was to be done? The best thing he could
think of to do in such a case was to run to the editor's office
and let him know that that fool Bludykhin had issued such
an order. The editor, naturally, would be surprised, burst out
laughing, and say: "Now, isn't he an idiot? What a way to
take revenge for a review! He can't understand, the ass, that
if we go to his party, he's not doing us a favor, we're doing
him one. Ah, he is a fool, God forgive him! But wait: in tomorrow's issue I shall present you with a real carnation!"

Thus might the editor react to such an incident. And then
what? It would naturally follow that the secretary, like a respectable man, would be obliged to remain at home, to ig-
nore Bludykhin; both his pride and the dignity of the press
would require it. That is all very well in theory, but in fact,
when one has bought new gloves, paid a barber to curl one's
hair, and when, there, upstairs, both Klavdia Vasilyevna and
supper were awaiting him, it is far from well.

"I have been looking forward to this party for two
months," he thought. "I've dreamed of it, prepared for it.
For two whole months I ran all over town looking for a new
coat. I gave my word to Klavdia. And now—— No, it's impossible, there's been some sort of misunderstanding. It

must be a misunderstanding. There is no need to go to the editor; I have only to say a word to the manager."

"Listen," he addressed himself to the fat man, "just let me go upstairs—I won't go into the ballroom. I only want to speak to the manager or Mr. Bludykhin."

"Go ahead, but understand that on no account will you be admitted to the ballroom."

"Oh, Lord!" Kokin thought, as he started up the stairs, "those two ladies heard what he said. How humiliating! What a disgrace! I really ought to leave . . ."

Upstairs near the entrance to the ballroom stood the master of ceremonies, a short, redheaded man with a bow-knot in his lapel. An elaborately dressed lady sat at a little table handing out programs. The secretary appealed to them in a tearful voice.

"Tell me, please, why is no one from the press admitted? Why?"

"You gentlemen have only yourselves to blame," the redheaded man replied. "You are given complimentary tickets, you sit in the first row, and what do you write?—Libels!"

"Oh, good heavens, listen——"

At that moment loud applause was heard within, followed by the charming voice of Princess Rozhkin singing "Again I stand before you." The secretary's heart was palpitating; the tortures of Tantalus were not greater.

"What libels?" he appealed to the lady. "Granting, Madam, that there have been libelous statements in the paper, how am I guilty? The editor is guilty, the contributors, but I—how can I be guilty? I'm merely a secretary, a sort of bookkeeper, I'm not a writer at all. Really, I'm not! Listen, I'll even give you my word of honor I'm not a writer!"

"We can do nothing for you," sighed the lady. "The order was given by Bludykhin himself. However, you may buy a ticket."

"Damn! Why didn't I think of that before?" he thought. But he immediately recalled that he had only forty kopecks

in his pocket, which he had taken on the chance that Klavdia Vasilyevna might wish to be taken home in a cab. "In
any case, I'll have a word with Bludykhin," he said aloud.

"Wait for the intermission."

Kokin waited. From behind the door came a burst of applause, the sound of women singing, laughter; life was
seething in there. But the poor secretary stood outside a la
Henry at Canossa, in the attitude of a repentant sinner. Waiting for the intermission he stared at the door of the ballroom
like a horse who senses the nearness of oats but cannot see
them. He waited a long time. At last there was a clamor of
voices, the sound of chairs being moved, then the doors
were thrown open and the audience poured out.

" 'And happiness was so near, so possible!' " he thought,
watching the doors open. "No, it is most unlikely that they
will not admit me."

Soon Bludykhin himself appeared, rosy and beaming.
Kokin went up to him, but for some moments could not
bring himself to speak. Finally he said, "Excuse me, sir, if I
disturb you. You left orders, Anisim Ivanych, that no one
from the press was to be admitted. . . . "

"Yes. What about it?"

"I came here—but—I don't understand—you yourself
will agree— How can I be guilty? The editors, the contributors, they are guilty, keep them out, but I—word of honor,
I'm not a writer!"

"Ah-hah . . . but you are from the press?" Bludykhin inquired, throwing back his head and taking a stance with his
legs spread in the form of the letter A. "Naturally, you have
a grievance. Now listen to me. Let the public be my witness:
ladies and gentlemen, you will be the judges. Here is a gentleman, a correspondent, who has a gr-r-rievance against me
because I, so to say, I—ah—in some way pr-r-otested. My
views on the press are, I hope, well known. I have always
been for the press! But, ladies and gentlemen," here he made
a supplicating face, "ladies and gentlemen, there are limits!

Abuse the actors, the play, the set, if you will, but why write absurdities? Why? In the last issue of your paper there was a magnificent article—mag-ni-fi-cent! But, in describing the *tableau vivant* 'Judith and Holofernes,' in which my daughter happened to take part, he—*he* said—God knows why— 'The sword,' he said, 'which Judith held in her hands, was so long,' he said, 'that she could only have managed to kill him from a great distance, or by climbing up onto the roof.' Now, what has the roof to do with this? My daughter, when she read it, burst into tears! That, ladies and gentlemen, is not a review. No-o-o sir! Not at all! That is getting personal, to find fault with someone's sword! And simply to spite me!"

"I—I agree with you!" babbled Kokin, feeling that hundreds of eyes were focused on him. "I myself am against abusive criticism, but, actually, what has it to do with me? On my word of honor, I'm not a writer. I'm a secretary! And I'll tell you something else—but, just between ourselves, naturally—that article was written by the editor himself." (Why am I such a pig as to tell him this? he thought.) "But he's a good man, an honest man. If he wrote something like that, it was done accidentally, thoughtlessly——"

The secretary's sheeplike tone mollified Bludykhin. The Councilor of Commerce buttonholed Kokin and began once more to unfold his views on the press. A thousand feelings stirred simultaneously in the secretary's breast; it was very flattering to have someone as important as Bludykhin confide in him; he felt certain of immediate admission into the ballroom; the misunderstanding was at an end, his dreams were about to come true. At the same time he felt terribly ashamed and debased; thanks to his spinelessness he had betrayed himself and the editor of *The Goose Gazette* in public and before friends—like the worst kind of Judas. Instead he ought to have cursed them, spit on them, laughed at them; and he had, in fact, humiliated himself, begged, and nearly wept!

Bludykhin talked on and on; having assumed a role he was bent on playing it to the hilt. He took the secretary by the arm, they were about to enter Eden when a cry was heard: "Anisim Ivanovich! The general has arrived!" Bludykhin gave a start of surprise, left Kokin, and flew headlong down the stairs. The secretary stood still for a moment, adjusted his necktie and stepped forward; the moment had come when it was no longer necessary for him to wait and hope. The second act began and he approached the door. The master of ceremonies refused to admit him.

"Bludykhin said nothing to us. Impossible."

Ten minutes later the secretary was scraping along the icy streets in his big galoshes. He went home, but he would have been happier to have fallen through a hole in the ice. He felt ashamed and disgusted. Even the new gloves, the violet perfume, and his curled head sickened him. He could have hit himself over that head!

—1885

Marriage in Ten or Fifteen Years

EVERYTHING IN THIS WORLD IMPROVES: Swedish matches, operettas, locomotives, French wines, and human relations. And marriage improves. What it was and what it is you know; what it will be in ten or fifteen years, when our children have grown up, is not difficult to predict. So here is a sketch for the romance of the future.

A young lady of about twenty or twenty-five is sitting in her living room. She is dressed in the latest fashion and is seated on three chairs, only one of which she herself occupies; the other two accommodate her bustle. On her bosom is a brooch the size of a frying pan. Her coiffure, as becomes a well-bred young lady, is modest: twenty poods of hair brushed straight up, with a little ladder set in for the convenience of her maid. Her hat lies on the piano; it is trimmed with an artfully fabricated turkey, life-size, complete with eggs.

The doorbell rings. A young man enters. He is dressed in a red swallowtail, narrow trousers, and boots that resemble skis.

"I beg to introduce myself," says the young man, bowing before her, "Balalaikin, counselor-at-law."

"Pleased to meet you. What can I do for you?"

"I was directed to you by the Society for the Arrangement of Happy Marriages."

"Delighted. Please sit down."

Balalaikin sits down and says: "The Society brought to my attention several marriageable young ladies, but I found your conditions the most suitable for me. From this note of yours, which was given me by the secretary of the Society, it appears that you will bring to your husband a house in Plyshchikha, forty thousand rubles in cash, and about five thousand in personal property. Is that correct?"

"No. . . . Only twenty thousand comes with me," she replies coquettishly.

"In that case, Madam, forgive me for having troubled you. I shall take my leave."

"No, no! I was only joking," laughs the girl. "Everything in the note is correct, the money, the house, and the personal property. . . . The Society spoke to you, of course, about the redecorating of the house being charged to the husband's account—and—and . . . I'm frightfully embarrassed—and that the husband will not receive all the money at one time, but in installments over three years."

"No, Madam," sighs Balalaikin, "today *nobody* marries on the installment plan. However, if you insist on installments, as a special favor, I shall give you one year."

Balalaikin and the young lady begin to bargain. In the end she gives in, satisfied with installments of a year.

"And now, allow me to know your terms," she says. "How old are you, and where are you employed?"

"Frankly speaking, it is not I who am marrying; I am merely acting for my client. I am a broker."

"Oh! But I particularly asked the Society not to send me any brokers." The young lady is offended.

"Don't be angry, Madam; my client is somewhat advanced in years. He suffers from rheumatism . . . the dampness, you know, and he hasn't the strength to bustle about after a bride; so *volens-nolens,* he is obliged to act through a third party. But don't be concerned, I don't charge very much."

"Your client's conditions?"

"My client is a man of fifty-two, but despite his years, there are those who still are willing to lend him money. For instance, he has two tailors who dress him on credit. In the shops they put him on the books for as much as he likes. And no one knows better than he how to slip away from a cab driver at an entrance gate. And so forth. But let us not expatiate on his business abilities; let us just say, to round out the definition of his character, that he continues to get credit even from the chemist!"

"He lives only on credit?"

"Credit—that is his principal occupation. But inasmuch as he is a man of broad interests, he is not satisfied with this activity alone. Without exaggeration, one may say that no one knows how to dispose of a false stock coupon as cleverly as he does. Besides which, he is the guardian of his niece, which gives him about three thousand a year. And, he poses as a critic in the theater world, thus obtaining passes and free suppers from the actors. Twice he has been tried for embezzlement, and even now is on trial for forgery."

"Oh, is it possible that courts of law still exist?"

"Yes, as a remnant of the medieval morality we have not entirely outlived. But, we may hope, Madam, that this too will pass in a year or two, and cultivated men will relinquish these obsolete customs. Now, what answer do you wish me to give my client?"

"Tell him I'll think about it."

"What is there to think about, Madam? I do not presume to advise you, but, wishing you well, I cannot help expressing my amazement! An honorable man, in every respect brilliant, and you fail to agree immediately, knowing how disastrous this delay may be for you! Why, even while you are thinking, he may come to an agreement with another bride."

"That's true. In that case, I agree."

"You ought to have done so long since! May I please have your deposit?"

The young lady gives the agent ten or twenty rubles. He takes the money, bows obsequiously, and goes to the door.

"The receipt?" She stops him.

"*Mille pardons,* Madam. I completely forgot! Ha-ha!"

Balalaikin writes the receipt, bows again, and leaves. The young lady covers her face with her hands and falls onto the divan.

"How happy I am!" she exclaims, seized by an emotion she has never before experienced. "How happy I am! I love—and am loved!"

The end. Such is marriage in the near future. And, dear reader, was it so long ago that the bride wore crinolines and the groom flaunted striped trousers and a dazzling frock coat? Was it so long ago that a suitor, before falling in love with the girl, had to talk it over with her papa and mama?

Nightingales, roses, moonlight nights, perfumed notes, and love songs—all that is far, far away. To whisper together in a dark lane, to suffer, to long for the first kiss, and so on, is now as outmoded as dressing in armor or abducting the Sabines. Everything improves.

—1885

In Spring

THE SNOW HAS NOT YET melted from the earth, but the soul cries out for spring. If you have ever had the experience of recuperating from a serious illness, you know that beatific state in which your heart is filled with foreboding but you smile without reason. Nature appears to be going through just such an experience at the moment. The earth is cold, mud and snow squelch underfoot, and yet, how joyful, sweet, and gracious is the atmosphere! The air is so clear and transparent that if you were to climb up to a dovecote or a belfry you could see the entire universe, it seems, from one end to the other. The sun shines brightly, its smiling rays playing in pools of water with the sparrows. The rivulet awakes, swells, and grows murky; any day now it will begin to roar. The trees, though bare, give signs of living, breathing.

At such times it is good to take a broom or spade and drive the muddy water into gutters, to set boats to sail, or to dig your heels into the stubborn ice. It is also good to chase pigeons up into the sky, or to climb trees and catch starlings. In fact, everything is good at this happy time of year, especially if you are young and love nature, if you are not moody or hysterical, and if your work does not confine you within four walls from morning to night. But, it is not good if you are ill, if you are pining away in an office, or are in any way connected with the Muses. Yes, one should avoid having anything to do with the Muses in spring.

See how well, how splendidly, the simple people feel! Here is the gardener, Pantelei Petrovich, prematurely decked out in his wide-brimmed straw hat, and inseparable from the little cigar butt he picked up in the lane early this morning. Look, now; he stands arms akimbo before the kitchen window and tells the cook how he bought himself a pair of boots yesterday, his long, narrow frame, which won him the nickname "Stringbean," expressing self-satisfaction and dignity. His attitude toward nature is one of superiority over her. There is something proprietary, imperious, even disdainful, in his glance, as if, while sitting in his greenhouse or rummaging in the garden, he had made some particular discovery pertaining to the vegetable kingdom, something previously unknown to the world. It would be useless to explain to him that nature is sublime, formidable, and full of wonder-working miracles, before which a proud man should bow down. It seems to him that he knows everything—all mysteries, charms, and miracles; for him lovely spring is a slave no different from his narrow-chested, emaciated wife, who sits in the shed off the greenhouse, feeding her children Lenten soup.

And the hunter, Ivan Zakharov? Wearing a thick, worn jacket, and with galoshes on his otherwise bare feet, he sits on an upturned cask near the stables, making a wadding for his gun out of an old cork. He is preparing to go hunting. Closing his eyes, he visualizes the road that he will take, the paths with water beneath the snow, the brooks; he sees a long straight row of shapely trees under which he will stand, holding his gun, straining his sharp ear, and shivering from the chill of the evening air and his pleasurable emotion. He imagines that he hears the spitting sound the woodcock makes, the peal of bells that follows vespers in the neighboring monastery. . . . All is well with him; he is immeasurably, unreasonably happy.

But now, let us take a look at Makar Denisych, the young man who serves General Stremoykhov as a clerk or junior manager of his estate. He earns twice as much as the gardener, wears a white shirt front, smokes two-ruble tobacco, is always well-dressed and well-fed, and has the pleasure, when meeting him, of squeezing the general's plump white hand with the massive diamond ring on it. But, in spite of all this, how unhappy he is! He is forever at his books; his subscriptions to journals run to twenty-five rubles; and he writes and writes. . . . He writes every evening, he writes every day after dinner, he writes when others sleep, and he hides it all in his big trunk. On the bottom of the trunk are his neatly folded trousers and waistcoats; on top of these, a packet of tobacco with an unbroken seal, ten pillboxes, a crimson scarf, a piece of glycerine soap in a yellow wrapper, and all sorts of other things. Squeezed unobtrusively into one corner is a pile of papers covered with his handwriting, together with two or three copies of *Our Province,* the magazine in which his stories and correspondence have been published.

The entire district considers him a literary man, a poet. He is looked upon as someone out of the ordinary, but he is not liked. Everyone says there is something queer about the way he talks, the way he walks, and smokes.

One day, when summoned to be a witness in the district court, he irrelevantly gave his occupation as "writer," and then blushed as though he had been caught stealing a chicken.

Here he is, slowly walking in the lane, dressed in a blue overcoat, a plush hat, and carrying a walking stick. . . . He takes five steps, stops and stares into the sky or at an old rook sitting in a fir tree.

The gardener stands with his hands on his hips, the hunter has a crusty look, but Makar Denisych stoops, timidly coughs, and wears a bilious expression, as though spring weighed heavily upon him, suffocating him with her beauty. His soul is brimming with timidity; instead of exultation, joy, and hope, spring engenders in him vague and troublesome desires. And now he is walking up and down, unable to decide what it is he wants. As a matter of fact, what does he want?

"Ah, good day, Makar Denisych!" He suddenly hears General Stremoykhov's voice. "So, they haven't brought the mail yet?"

"Not yet, Your Excellency." Makar Denisych examines the carriage in which the jovial, robust general sits with his little daughter.

"Wonderful weather! A real spring day! Are you taking a stroll? Getting inspiration, I dare say!" But in his eyes Makar Denisych reads: "Untalented! Mediocrity!"

"Ah, my boy," the general says as he takes up the reins, "what a beautiful little piece I read over my coffee this morning! A trifle of only two pages, but how charming! It's a pity you don't know French, I'd give it to you to read. . . ." Hurriedly, in snatches, he recounts the little story, while Makar Denisych listens uncomfortably, feeling as though he were to blame for not being the Frenchman who wrote the piece.

"I don't understand what he sees in that!" he thinks as he watches the carriage disappear from sight. "It's commonplace, trite. My stories have much more content."

He is gnawed by envy. Author's egotism is a sickness of the soul; he who contracts it no longer hears the songs of birds, nor sees the sunshine and the spring; touch him but lightly on his weak spot and the whole organism contracts in pain. The infected Makar walks on and, passing through a garden gate, comes out onto the muddy road.

A high barouche rushes by with Mr. Bubentsov bobbing up and down in it.

"Hi, there, Author!" he shouts.

If Makar Denisych were merely a clerk or a junior manager, no one would dare to address him in that condescending, casual tone; but he is "a writer"; he is untalented, mediocre!

Those of Mr. Bubentsov's ilk understand nothing of art, and are even less interested in it; however, when they meet the untalented they are merciless, inexorable. They could forgive anyone except Makar, the unfortunate eccentric whose manuscripts lie in a trunk.

The gardener once broke an ancient rubber plant, and left some expensive plants to rot; the general has never done anything but live off others; Mr. Bubentsov, when he was justice of the peace, held court only once a month, and then he stuttered, talked all sorts of nonsense, and made a muddle of the law. All these things have been overlooked and forgiven, but they cannot overlook, cannot pass in silence, when they meet the untalented writer of indifferent verse and stories—they have to say something offensive.

That the general's sister-in-law slaps her maid and makes a row like a washerwoman when she plays cards; that the priest's wife never pays her losses; that the landowner Flyugin stole the landowner Sivobrakov's dog—no one made anything of these matters; but the fact that not long ago *Our Province* returned a poor story to Makar was known throughout the whole district, and brought forth gibes, endless talk, and indignation. Now they called him "Macaco."

If there is anything wrong about the way someone writes, they don't try to explain why it's "not right." They simply say: "Again that son-of-a-bitch has written something silly!"

Makar was prevented from enjoying the spring by the thought that he was not understood, that no one wanted to understand him or was even capable of it. Somehow, it seemed to him that if he were understood everything would be perfect. But how could he be understood—talented or not—when no one in the entire district ever read anything, or read only what was better left unread? How could he make General Stremoykhov understand that his little French piece was insignificant, flat, banal, trite—how, since he never read anything other than that sort of thing?

And the women—how they irritated him!

"Ah, Makar Denisych," they would say to him, "what a pity you weren't in the market place today! If you could have seen what an amusing quarrel took place between two men, you would certainly have written it up!"

All this was petty, of course, and a philosopher would have disregarded it, but Makar was constantly on hot coals. He felt solitary, orphaned, with a loneliness known only to bachelors and great sinners. Never once in his entire life had he stood arms akimbo like the gardener. Occasionally, perhaps once in five years, on the road, in the woods, or in a railway coach, he met another unfortunate eccentric like himself, and looking each other in the eye, they both brightened momentarily. Long conversations followed, arguments; in their delight with each other they were carried away and laughed so much that anyone catching sight of them might have thought they had lost their minds.

But, in general, even these rare moments did not pass untainted. At first, as a joke, Makar and his new acquaintance disclaimed each other's talent, unable to accept each other; envy, hatred, anger followed, and they parted enemies.

Thus his youth languished and wore away, without joy or love or friendship; without peace of mind; without everything, in fact, that he liked to write about during his moments of inspiration in the evenings.

And the spring passed with his youth.

—1886

Agafya

DURING MY STAY in the district of S—— I often used to go to the kitchen gardens of Dubovo to visit the gardener, Savva Stukach, or simply Savka. These kitchen gardens were my favorite spot for so-called "general" fishing—setting out with no thought of the day or hour of my return, supplied with every sort of fishing gear and a stock of provisions. As a matter of fact, it was not so much the fishing that appealed to me as the peaceful rambling, the meals at no set time, the conversations with Savka, and being for so long face to face with the serene summer nights.

Savka was a fellow of twenty-five, tall, handsome, sound as flint. He could read and write, rarely drank vodka, and had the reputation of being a sensible, reasonable fellow; but as a worker this brawny young man was not worth a penny. His powerful muscles, stout as ropes, were imbued with an invincible sloth. Like everyone in his village, he lived in his own hut and had his own plot of land, which he neither tilled nor sowed; nor did he work at any trade. His old mother picked up alms under windows, and he himself lived like a bird of the air: in the morning he did not know what he would eat at midday. It was not that he lacked energy, will, or com-

71

passion for his mother, but simply that he felt no inclination for work and did not see the value of it. . . . His entire being breathed serenity, and an innate, almost artistic passion for the purposeless, careless life. When Savka's healthy young body was physiologically impelled to muscular work, he briefly gave himself up to some sort of unrestricted but trifling occupation such as whittling superfluous pegs, or chasing a peasant woman until he caught her. His favorite posture was one of concentrated immobility. He was capable of standing in one place, his eyes fixed on one spot, for hours at a stretch without stirring. He never moved except on impulse, and then only when an occasion presented itself for swift, violent action: catching a running dog by the tail, pulling off a woman's kerchief, or jumping over a big hole. It need hardly be said that with such economy of movement Savka was as poor as Job and lived worse than any landless peasant. As time went on he must have accumulated tax arrears and, young and healthy as he was, the village commune sent him to be watchman and scarecrow in the community kitchen gardens—a job for an old man. No matter how much they laughed at him for his premature old age, he did not care a bit. This peaceful occupation, conducive to stationary contemplation, exactly suited his nature.

One fine May evening I happened to be at Savka's. I remember lying near the shack on a torn, threadbare sledge-rug, from which there rose a heavy, sultry fragrance of dry grass. With my hands clasped under my head I gazed before me. A wooden pitchfork lay at my feet; beyond it Savka's dog, Kutka, stood out like a black splotch, and not more than a dozen feet from him the ground abruptly ended in the steep bank of a little river. Lying thus I could not see the river, but only the tips of a dense growth of willow bushes on the hither side, and the sinuous, gnawed-looking edges of the opposite bank. Beyond the bank, on a dark knoll in the distance, the huts of Savka's village huddled together like frightened young partridges. Behind the hill the afterglow of the evening sunset was fading from the sky. A single strip of pale crimson remained, and even that was beginning to be covered with little clouds, like ashes on the embers.

On the right of the kitchen gardens a shadowy grove of alder trees quivered and softly whispered in the fitful breeze, and on the left there stretched a boundless field. There, where the eye no longer could distinguish field from sky, a bright light glimmered. Not far from me sat Savka, his legs tucked under him like a Turk, his head bent, as he gazed pensively at Kutka. Our hooks, with live bait on them, had long been in the river, and there was nothing left for us to do but abandon ourselves to the repose which Savka, never tired and always rested, loved so much. The afterglow had not yet faded from the sky, but already the summer night was enfolding nature in its tender, soothing embrace.

Everything was sinking into the first deep sleep with the exception of one night bird in the grove, a bird not known to me, who indolently uttered a protracted, articulate cry that sounded like: "Did you see Ni-ki-ta?" and then answered himself with: "I saw! I saw! I saw!"

"Why is it that the nightingales aren't singing tonight?" I asked Savka.

He slowly turned toward me. His features were coarse, but his face was as serene, gentle, and expressive as a woman's. Then he gazed with mild, dreamy eyes at the grove and the willows, slowly pulled a reed pipe from his pocket, put it to his mouth and piped the note of the female nightingale. And instantly, as if in answer to his piping, came the cry of the corn crake from the opposite bank.

"There's a nightingale for you!" laughed Savka. "Drag-drag! Drag-drag! Just like dragging at a hook, but I bet he thinks he's singing too."

"I like that bird," I said. "You know, when the birds migrate, the corn crake does not fly, but runs along the ground. It flies only over rivers and seas, otherwise it goes on foot."

"How do you like that, dog!" Savka murmured, with a respectful glance in the direction of the corn crake.

Knowing how much Savka enjoyed listening, I told him all I had learned about the corn crake from sportsmen's books. From the corn crake I imperceptibly passed to the migration of birds. Savka listened attentively, his unblinking eyes fixed on me, smiling all the while.

"In which country are the birds most at home," he asked, "ours or yonder?"

"Ours, of course. The bird is born here, and hatches its little ones here in its native country; they only fly over there to escape freezing."

"Interesting!" said Savka, stretching himself. "No matter what a person talks about, it's always interesting. Now, you take a bird, or a man . . . or take this little stone—there's something to think about in all of them. . . . Ah, if I'd known, sir, that you were coming, I wouldn't have told a woman to come here tonight. One of them asked to come today. . . ."

"Oh, please, don't let me interfere!" I said. "I can even lie down in the grove. . . ."

"Well, really, it's too bad! She wouldn't have died if she'd waited till tomorrow. . . . If she would just sit here and listen to the conversation—but all she wants to do is slobber. You can't talk sense with her here."

"Is it Darya you're expecting?" I asked after a pause.

"No. . . . A new one asked to come . . . Agafya Strelchikha. . . ."

Savka said this in his usual impassive, somewhat flat voice, as if he were talking of tobacco or gruel, and I started in amazement. I knew Agafya Strelchikha. . . . She was a young peasant woman of nineteen or twenty who, not more than a year before, had married a railway signalman, a fine young fellow. She lived in the village, and her husband came home to her from the line every night.

"All these goings on with women will end badly, my boy." I sighed.

"Well, maybe. . . . "

After a moment's thought Savka added, "I've said so to the women, but they pay no attention. . . . It's their foolishness—and they don't care!"

A silence followed. . . . Meanwhile the darkness was growing thicker, and objects began to lose their contours. The strip of sky behind the hill had completely disappeared and the stars grew brighter and more luminous. The mournful, monotonous chirping of the grasshoppers, the corncrake's cry, the calling of the quails, did not destroy the night's tranquillity but, on the contrary, only served to swell the great monotone. The soft sounds, enchanting to the ear, seemed not to come from birds and insects, but from the stars looking down upon us from the sky. . . .

Savka was the first to break the silence. Slowly he withdrew his gaze from black Kutka, looked at me and said, "I see it's getting dull for you, sir. Let's have supper."

Without waiting for an answer he crawled on his stomach into the shanty, rummaged about in it, causing the whole structure to tremble like a leaf, then crawled out again and set before me my vodka and an earthenware bowl containing baked eggs, rye cakes fried in fat, a piece of black bread, and other things. . . . We drank from a crooked little glass that would not stand, then set to work on the food. . . . Coarse gray salt, greasy, muddy-looking cakes, and eggs like rubber, but how savory!

"You live like a wretched fellow, but you have all sorts of good things," I said, pointing to the bowl. "Where do you get them?"

"The women bring them," Savka mumbled.

"Why is it that they bring them to you?"

"Oh . . . out of pity."

Not only Savka's menu, but his clothing, too, bore traces of feminine "pity." That evening I noticed he had on a new worsted belt, and round his dirty neck a bright crimson ribbon from which hung a copper cross. I knew that the fair sex had a weakness for Savka, and knew, too, that he did not like talking about it, so I did not pursue my inquiry. Besides, there was no time to talk. Kutka, who had been rubbing against us, patiently waiting for scraps, suddenly pricked up her ears and growled. In the distance we heard the intermittent splashing of water.

"Someone's coming by the ford," said Savka.

Two or three minutes later Kutka growled again, and made a coughing sound.

"Tsst!" her master hissed at her.

In the darkness there was the muffled sound of timid footsteps, and the silhouette of a woman appeared from the grove. Although it was dark, I recognized her—it was Agafya Strelchikha. She diffidently approached us, then stopped, breathing heavily. She was breathless, probably not so much from walking as from fear and the unpleasant feeling everyone experiences when fording a river at night. Seeing not one but two persons near the shanty, she uttered a faint cry and stepped back.

"Oh . . . it's you!" Savka said, stuffing a rye cake into his mouth.

"I . . . I—" she murmured, dropping a bundle of some sort onto the ground and darting a glance at me. "Yakov sends you his greetings, and he told me to give you . . . here's something for you. . . . "

"Now, why do you lie? Yakov!" Savka laughed. "There's no need to lie; the gentleman knows why you came. Sit down and have something."

Agafya looked askance at me and irresolutely sat down.

"I began to think you weren't coming this evening," said Savka after a prolonged silence. "Why do you just sit there? Eat! Or shall I give you a drop of vodka?"

"What an idea!" laughed Agafya. "Do you think you've got some sort of a drunkard here?"

"Oh, have a drink. . . . It warms the heart. . . . There!"

Savka handed her the crooked glass. She drank the vodka

slowly, without eating anything, then loudly blew out her breath.

"She brought something," Savka said in a jocular, condescending tone as he untied the bundle. "Women can never come without bringing something. Ah, a pie and potatoes! . . . They live well!" he sighed and turned to me. "They're the only ones in the whole village who've still got potatoes left from the winter!"

In the darkness I did not see Agafya's face, but from the movement of her head and shoulders it seemed to me that she could not take her eyes from Savka's face. To avoid being the third person at a tryst, I decided to go for a walk and got up. But at that moment two low, contralto notes of a nightingale were heard in the grove. Half a minute later there was a high, tiny trill, and thus having tried its voice, the bird began to sing. Savka jumped up and listened.

"It's the same one as yesterday!" he said. "Wait a minute! . . ." and noiselessly he ran into the grove.

"But what do you want with it?" I called after him. "Stop!"

With a wave of a hand, as if to say, "Don't shout!" he disappeared into the darkness. Savka was an excellent hunter and fisherman when he liked, but here too his talents were expended as fruitlessly as his strength. He was too lazy to do things in the conventional way and vented his passion for sport in idle tricks. For instance, he would catch nightingales with his bare hands, shoot pike with a fowling piece, and spend whole hours trying with all his might to catch a little fish with a big hook.

Left alone with me Agafya coughed, and repeatedly passed her hand over her forehead. She was beginning to feel a little drunk from the vodka.

"How are you getting on, Agasha?" I asked when the prolonged silence made it awkward not to speak.

"Very well, thank God. . . . You won't tell anyone, sir—" she suddenly added in a whisper.

"It's all right," I reassured her. "But aren't you being reckless, Agasha? What if Yakov finds out?"

"He won't find out. . . . "

"But if he suddenly——"

"No. . . . I'll be home before he is. He's on the line now, and won't return till the mail train brings him; I can hear it coming from here."

Agafya again passed her hand over her forehead and looked in the direction of the grove where Savka had vanished. The nightingale was singing. Some night bird flew down close to the ground, was startled by our presence, fluttered its wings, and flew to the other side of the river.

Soon the nightingale stopped singing, but Savka did not return. Agafya got up, restlessly took a few steps, and sat down again.

"What's the matter with him?" She could not contain herself. "The train won't wait till tomorrow! I ought to be going right now!"

"Savka!" I shouted. "Savka!"

I was not answered by so much as an echo. Agafya began to shift about anxiously, and again got up.

"It's time I was going!" she exclaimed in an agitated voice. "The train will soon be here. I know when the trains come in!"

The poor girl was not mistaken. In less than a quarter of an hour a sound was heard in the distance. Agafya kept her eyes fixed on the grove, moving her hands impatiently.

"Well, where is he?" she said with a nervous laugh. "Where can he have gone? I'm going! Really, sir, I must go!"

Meanwhile the sound was growing more distinct; the rattling of the wheels could be distinguished from the heavy gasps of the locomotive. A whistle was heard, then the hollow rumble of the train crossing the bridge . . . and in a moment all was still.

"I'll wait a minute longer . . ." sighed Agafya, resolutely sitting down again. "So be it. I'll wait."

At last Savka appeared in the darkness, softly humming. His bare feet made no sound on the friable earth of the kitchen gardens.

"Now, what do you say to that for luck?" he laughed merrily. "I just got to the bush and started to take aim with my hand when he stopped singing! Ah, you bald dog, you! I waited and waited for him to sing again, but—what do I care. . . . "

Savka awkwardly threw himself to the ground beside Agafya, catching her by the waist with both hands to keep his balance.

"And why are you scowling like a stepchild?" he asked her.

With all his soft-heartedness and good nature, Savka disdained women. He treated them in a negligent, lofty manner, and even went so far as to laugh contemptuously at their feelings for him. God knows, perhaps this scornful treatment was one of the causes of his powerful, irresistible fascination for the village Dulcineas. He was handsome and well built; his eyes always shone with a gentle friendliness, even when he was looking at a woman he held in contempt, but this fascination was not to be accounted for by external qualities alone. In addition to a favorable exterior and an original manner, one may assume that the touching role of acknowledged failure and unfortunate exile from his own hut to the kitchen gardens had an even greater influence upon the women.

"Now, tell the gentleman what you came here for!" Savka went on, still holding Agafya by the waist. "Come on, tell him, you wedded woman! Ho-ho! . . . Shall we have another drop of vodka, friend Agasha?"

I got up and, making my way between the vegetable beds, walked the length of the kitchen gardens. The dark beds looked like large, smoothed graves. They smelled of turned earth and the tender dampness of plants freshly covered with dew. . . . On the left the red light was still gleaming; it winked genially and seemed to smile.

I heard a happy laugh. It was Agafya. . . . "And the train?" I thought. "The train came in long ago."

I waited a little longer, then went back to the shanty. Savka was sitting motionless, Turkish style, and in a soft, scarcely audible voice was humming a song that consisted of words of one syllable, something like, "Fie on you, out on you . . . I and you. . . ." Agafya, intoxicated by the vodka, Savka's scornful caresses, and the sultry night, was lying on the ground beside him, spasmodically pressing her face to his knees. She was so carried away by her feelings that she did not even notice my arrival.

"Agasha, the train came in long ago!" I said.

"It's time—time you were gone," said Savka with a shake of his head as he caught my thought. "What are you sprawling here for? You're shameless!"

Agafya started, raised her head from his knees, glanced at me, and sank down beside him again.

"You ought to have gone long ago!" I said

Agafya turned round and got up on one knee. . . . She was suffering. For a moment her whole figure, as far as I could make out in the darkness, expressed conflict and vacillation. There was an instant when she seemed to recover her senses and drew herself up in order to rise to her feet, then some invincible and implacable force smote her whole body, and she threw herself down beside Savka.

"He can go to the devil!" she said with a wild throaty laugh, in which was heard her reckless determination, helplessness, and pain.

I quietly wandered off to the grove, and from there down to the river where our fishing lines were set. The river slept. A soft, double-petaled flower on a long stalk gently touched my cheek, like a child who wants to let you know he is not sleeping. To pass the time I felt for one of the lines and pulled it. It was slack and yielded to my touch—nothing had been caught. The opposite bank and the village were not visible. A light gleamed in one of the huts, but soon went out. I groped my way along the bank until I found a hollow I had seen in the daylight, and sat down in it as in an armchair. I sat there for a long time. . . . I watched the stars grow misty and lose their radiance, felt a cool breath pass over the earth, like a faint sigh stirring the leaves of the slumbering willows. . . .

"A-ga-fya!" came a hollow voice from the village. "A-ga-fya!"

The anxious husband had returned home, and in his alarm, was seeking his wife in the village. At that moment, from the kitchen gardens came the sound of unrestrained laughter: the wife had forgotten herself and, in her intoxication, sought to compensate for the torment that awaited her the next day, with these few hours of happiness.

I fell asleep. . . .

When I awoke Savka was sitting beside me lightly shaking my shoulder. The river, the grove, and both banks, green and washed, trees, fields—all were bathed in the bright morning light. Through the slender tree trunks the rays of the newly risen sun beat upon my back.

"So that's how you catch fish?" Savka laughed. "Come, get up!"

I got up, had a delightful stretch, and my waking lungs greedily began to drink in the moist, fragrant air.

"Has Agasha gone?" I asked.

"There she is," Savka replied, pointing in the direction of the ford.

I looked and saw Agafya. Disheveled, her kerchief slipping from her head, she was crossing the river, holding up her skirt. Her legs were scarcely moving. . . .

" 'The cat knows whose beard it licks!' " muttered Savka with a wink. "She goes back dragging her tail. . . . Sly as cats, these women, and skittish as hares. . . . She didn't go, the silly woman, in the evening when we told her to! Now she'll catch it; and they'll have me up in court. . . . Another flogging on account of women. . . . "

Agafya stepped onto the bank and went across the field

toward the village. At first she walked rather boldly, but soon agitation and fear got the upper hand: she turned round apprehensively, stopped, and took a deep breath.

"You sure are scared!" Savka laughed wryly as he gazed at the bright green trail left by Agafya in the dewy grass. "She don't want to go! That husband's been waiting for a good hour. . . . Did you see him?"

Savka spoke the last words with a smile, but they sent a chill through my heart. In the village, near the last hut, Yakov stood in the road staring straight at his returning wife. He did not stir, but was as motionless as a post. What was he thinking as he watched her? What words was he preparing for the meeting? Agafya stood still for a while, looked back again as if expecting help from us, then went on. I have never before seen anyone, drunk or sober, move as she did. It was as though she were shriveling under her husband's gaze. At one moment she walked in a zigzag, then raised and lowered her feet, bending her knees and swinging her arms, then moved backwards. After she had gone perhaps a hundred paces she looked round once more and sat down.

"You ought at least to hide behind a bush," I said to Savka. "If the husband catches sight of you . . ."

"He knows anyway who it is Agasha has been to. . . . The women don't go to the kitchen gardens at night for cabbages—everyone knows that."

I glanced at Savka's face. It was pale and contracted with a look of squeamish pity such as one sees on the faces of those watching tortured animals.

"What's fun for the cat is tears for the mouse. . . . " he sighed.

Agafya suddenly jumped up, shook her head, and with a bold step went toward her husband. Evidently she had mustered strength and was resolved.

—1886

The Kiss

O<small>N THE TWENTIETH OF MAY</small>, at eight o'clock in the evening, all six batteries of the N—— Reserve Artillery Brigade halted for the night on their way to camp in the village of Mestechki. In the thick of the commotion, while some of the officers were bustling about the guns, and others, gathered in the square near the church enclosure, were hearing the quartermasters' reports, a civilian riding a strange horse appeared from behind the church. The horse, a small bay with a fine neck and short tail, did not step straight forward but, as it were, sideways, with little dance movements, as though it were being whipped about the legs. Riding up to the officer the man on the horse raised his hat and said, "His Excellency Lieutenant General Von Rabbek, the local landowner, requests the pleasure of the officers' company presently for tea. . . . "

The horse bowed, began to dance, and retired sideways; the rider again raised his hat, and in a flash he and his strange horse disappeared behind the church.

"What the devil does that mean?" muttered several of the officers as they dispersed to the quarters. "You want to sleep, and along comes this Von Rabbek with his tea! We know what tea means!"

The officers of all six batteries vividly recalled an incident that had occurred the preceding year during maneuvers, when they, together with the officers of one of the Cossack regiments, had been invited to tea in the same way by a count, a retired army officer, who had an estate in the neighborhood; the hospitable and genial count gave them a hearty welcome, stuffed them with food and drink, and then refused to let them return to their quarters in the village, but made them stay the night. All this, of course, was very pleasant; they could have wished for nothing better. The trouble was the retired officer carried his enjoyment of his young guests to excess. He kept them up till dawn recounting anecdotes of his glorious past, led them from one room to another showing them valuable paintings, old engravings, rare arms, and reading them the original letters of celebrated men, and the weary, jaded officers who were longing for their beds, looked and listened, discreetly yawning into their sleeves. When at last their host released them, it was too late for sleep.

Might not this Von Rabbek be another such one? Whether he was or not, there was no help for it. The officers, brushed and in fresh uniforms, trooped off in search of the manor house. In the church square they were told that they could get to His Excellency's by the lower road—descending to the river behind the church and walking along the bank till they reached the garden, where they would find an avenue leading to the house; or they could go straight from the church by the upper road, which, half a verst from the village, would bring them to His Excellency's barns. The officers decided to take the upper road.

"But what Von Rabbek is this?" they wondered, as they walked along. "Surely not the one that commanded the N—— cavalry division at Plevna?"

"No, that was not Von Rabbek, but simply Rabbe—without the *von*."

"What glorious weather!"

At the first of the manorial barns the road divided; one fork went straight on and vanished into the evening dusk, the other, going off to the right, led to the manor house. The officers turned right and began to speak more quietly. On both sides of the road stood red-roofed barns built of stone, massive and austere, like barracks in a provincial town. Ahead of them gleamed the windows of the manor house.

"Gentlemen, a good omen!" said one of the officers. "Our setter has taken the lead; that means he scents game ahead!"

Lieutenant Lobytko, walking at their head, a tall, robust man with no mustache whatsoever (he was over twenty-five, but for some reason there was still not a sign of hair on his round, well-fed face), was famous throughout the brigade for his unerring instinct for divining the presence of women at a distance.

"Yes, there must be women here," he said, turning round. "I can feel it."

They were met at the portal by Von Rabbek himself, a handsome old man of sixty, in civilian dress. Shaking hands with his guests, he said he was happy and delighted to see them, but entreated them, for God's sake, to forgive him for not inviting them to spend the night: two sisters with their children, his brothers, and several neighbors, had all come to visit him, and there was not a single spare room left.

Though the general shook hands with everyone, made his apologies and smiled, one could see from his face that he was by no means so delighted as last year's count, and had invited the officers only because, in his opinion, good manners required it. And the officers, listening to him as they climbed the carpeted staircase, felt that they had been invited simply because it would have been awkward not to invite them, and at the sight of footmen hastening to light lamps in the entrance below and the anteroom above, they began to feel that by coming here they had introduced an atmosphere of confusion and annoyance. How could the presence of nineteen officers whom they had never seen before be welcome in a house where brothers, two sisters with their children, and neighbors had gathered, probably on the occasion of some family celebration or event?

Upstairs, near the entrance to the drawing room, the guests were met by a tall, graceful, elderly lady with a long face and black eyebrows, very like the Empress Eugénie. With a gracious and majestic smile, she said she was happy and delighted to see her guests, and only regretted that on this occasion she and her husband had been deprived of the opportunity of inviting the gentlemen to spend the night. From her beautiful, majestic smile, which instantly vanished from her face each time she turned away from a guest, it was apparent that in her day she had met countless officers, that she was in no mood for them now, and that if she invited them to her house and proffered her apologies, it was only because her breeding and position in society required it of her.

The officers went into a large dining room where, at one end of a long table, about a dozen men and women, both old and young, sat at tea. Behind them a group of men wrapped in a haze of cigar smoke was dimly visible; in their midst, speaking English in a loud voice and with a burr, stood a slender young man with red whiskers. Beyond this group, a brightly lighted room with pale blue furniture could be seen through a doorway.

"Gentlemen, there are so many of you that it is impossible to introduce you all!" The general spoke loudly, trying to sound very jovial. "Make one another's acquaintance, gentlemen, without formalities!"

The officers, some with very serious, even stern expressions, others with constrained smiles, and all of them feeling very awkward, bowed perfunctorily and sat down to tea.

The most ill at ease of them all was Second Captain Ryabovich, a short, stooped officer with spectacles and whiskers like a lynx. While some of his comrades assumed serious expressions and others forced smiles, his face, his lynxlike whiskers, and his spectacles all seemed to say: "I am the most shy, the most modest, and most colorless officer in the whole brigade!" On first entering the room, and later, when he sat down to tea, he was unable to fix his attention on any one face or object. The faces, dresses, cutglass decanters of cognac, the steaming glasses, the molded cornices—all merged into a single, overwhelming impression which inspired in him a feeling of alarm and a desire to hide his head. Like a lecturer appearing before the public for the first time, he saw everything that was before his eyes, but seemed to have only a vague conception of it (physiologists call such a condition, in which the subject sees but does not understand, "psychic blindness"). After a little while Ryabovich grew accustomed to his surroundings, recovered his sight, and began to observe. As a shy man, unused to society, what first struck him was that which he himself had always lacked—namely, the marked temerity of his new acquaintances. Von Rabbek, his wife, two elderly ladies, a young lady in a lilac dress, the young man with red whiskers, who, it appeared, was Von Rabbek's youngest son, very adroitly, as though they had rehearsed it beforehand, took seats among the officers, and immediately started a heated debate in which the guests could not avoid taking part. The lilac young lady fervently argued that the artillery had a much easier time of it than the cavalry and the infantry, while Von Rabbek and the elderly ladies maintained the opposite. A lively exchange followed. Ryabovich looked at the lilac young lady who argued so heatedly about something that was unfamiliar and utterly uninteresting to her, and he watched the insincere smile come and go on her face.

Von Rabbek and his family skillfully drew the officers into the discussion while keeping a vigilant eye on their glasses and their mouths to see whether all of them were drinking, or had sugar, or why someone was not eating biscuits, or drinking cognac. And the longer Ryabovich watched and listened, the more fascinated he was by this insincere but beautifully disciplined family.

After tea the officers went into the music room. Lieutenant Lobytko's instinct had not deceived him: there were many young matrons and girls in the room. The setter-lieutenant was soon standing beside a very young blonde in a black dress, and, bending over her with a dashing air, as though leaning on an unseen sword, he smiled and flirtatiously twitched his shoulders. He must have been talking some very interesting nonsense, for the blonde gazed condescendingly at his well-fed face and coolly remarked, "Indeed!" Had he been clever, the setter might have concluded from this unimpassioned "indeed" that he was on the wrong scent.

Someone began to play the piano; the melancholy strains of a waltz floated out through the wide-open windows, and suddenly, for some reason, everyone remembered that outside it was spring—a May evening. They all became aware of the fragrance of young poplar leaves, of roses, and lilacs. Under the influence of the music, Ryabovich began to feel the brandy he had drunk; he stole a glance at the window, then began to follow the movements of the women; and it seemed to him that the scent of roses, poplars, and lilacs, came not from the garden, but from the faces and the dresses of these women.

Young Von Rabbek invited an emaciated-looking girl to dance, and waltzed her twice around the room. Lobytko glided across the parquet floor to the lilac young lady and flew off with her. And the dancing commenced. . . . Ryabovich stood near the door among those who were not dancing and looked on. In all his life he had never once danced, never once put his arm around the waist of a respectable woman. He was enormously delighted to see a man, in plain sight of everyone, take by the waist a girl with whom he was not acquainted and offer her his shoulder for her hand, but he could in no way imagine himself in the position of such a man. There was a time when he had envied the valor and daring of his comrades, and was miserable at heart; the consciousness of being timid, uninteresting, round-shouldered, of having a long waist and lynxlike whiskers, deeply mortified him; but with the years he had grown used to this feeling, and now, watching the dancers or those who were talking loudly, he no longer envied them, but felt sadly moved.

When a quadrille was begun, young Von Rabbek approached those who were not dancing and proposed a game of billiards to two of the officers. They accepted and left the room with him. Having nothing to do, and wishing to take some part in the general activity, Ryabovich trailed after them. From the music room they passed through a drawing room, then along a narrow glassed-in corridor, and thence into a room where three sleepy footmen quickly jumped up from the divans. Finally, after traversing a long succession of rooms, Von Rabbek and the officers went into a small room where there was a billiard table. They started a game.

Ryabovich, never having played anything but cards, stood near the billiard table and indifferently watched the players as they walked about, coats unbuttoned, cues in hand, making puns and shouting words that were unintelligible to him. The players took no notice of him, and only now and then one of them, knocking against him with an elbow or accidentally catching him with a cue, would turn round and say, *"Pardon!"* Before even the first game was over he was bored, and it seemed to him that he was in the way. . . . He felt drawn back to the music room and went out.

On his way back he met with a little adventure. Before he had gone half way he realized that he was not going in the right direction. He distinctly recalled that he had met three sleepy footmen on his way to the billiard room, but he had already gone through five or six rooms, and they seemed to have vanished into the earth. When he became aware of his mistake he walked a little way back, turned to the right, and found himself in the semi-darkness of a small room he had not seen before. He stood there for a moment, then resolutely opened the first door that met his eye and walked into a completely dark room. Directly before him a strip of bright light made the chink of a doorway plainly visible; from beyond it came the muffled sound of a melancholy mazurka. Here, as in the music room the windows stood wide open, there was the fragrance of poplars, lilac, and roses. . . .

Ryabovich hesitated, in doubt. . . . At that moment he was surprised by the sound of hasty footsteps and the rustle of a dress; a breathless, feminine voice whispered, "At last!" and two soft, perfumed, unmistakably feminine arms were thrown around his neck, a warm cheek was pressed to his, and there was the sound of a kiss. Immediately the bestower of the kiss uttered a faint scream and sprang away, as it seemed to Ryabovich, in disgust. He very nearly screamed himself, and rushed headlong toward the strip of light in the door. . . .

When he returned to the music room his heart was throbbing and his hands were trembling so perceptibly that he quickly clasped them behind his back. At first he was tormented by shame and the fear that everyone in the room knew he had just been embraced and kissed by a woman. He shrank into himself and looked about uneasily, but after convincing himself that everyone in the room was dancing and chatting quite as calmly as before, he gave himself up to his new and never-before-experienced sensation. Something strange was happening to him. . . . His neck, round which the soft, perfumed arms had so lately been clasped, felt as though it had been anointed with oil; on his left cheek near his mustache, where the unknown lady had kissed him, there was a slight tingling, a delightful chill, as from peppermint drops, and the more he rubbed it the stronger the sensation became; from head to foot he was filled with a strange new feeling which continued to grow and grow. . . . He wanted to dance, to talk, to run into the garden, to laugh aloud. . . . He completely forgot that he was round-shouldered and colorless, that he had lynxlike whiskers and a "nondescript appearance" (as he had once been described by some ladies whose conversation he had accidentally overheard). When Von Rabbek's wife walked by he gave her such a broad and tender smile that she stopped and looked at him questioningly.

"I like your house—enormously!" he said, adjusting his spectacles.

The general's wife smiled and said that the house still belonged to her father; then she asked him whether his parents were living, whether he had been long in the service, why he was so thin, and so on. . . . When her questions had been answered she walked away, and after his conversation with her Ryabovich began to smile even more tenderly, and to think that he was surrounded by splendid people. . . .

At supper he automatically ate everything that was offered him, drank, and, deaf to what went on around him, tried to find an explanation for his recent adventure. This adventure was of a mysterious and romantic nature, but it was not difficult to explain. Probably one of the young ladies had arranged a tryst with someone in the dark room, had waited a long time, and in her nervous excitement had taken Ryabovich for her hero; this was the more probable as he had hesitated uncertainly upon entering the room, as though he, too, were expecting someone. . . . This was the explanation he gave himself of the kiss he had received.

"But who is she?" he wondered, looking around at the faces of the women. "She must be young, because an old woman doesn't make a rendezvous. And that she was cultivated one could sense by the rustle of her dress, her perfume, her voice. . . . "

His gaze rested on the girl in lilac, and he found her charming; she had beautiful arms and shoulders, a clever face and lovely voice. Looking at her, Ryabovich wished that she and no one else were his unknown. . . . But suddenly she gave an artificial laugh, wrinkling up her long nose, and she looked old to him. He then turned his gaze to the blonde in the black dress. She was younger, simpler, and more sincere; she had a lovely brow, and a charming way of drinking from her wineglass. Now he wished that it were she. But soon he found her face flat, and turned his eyes to her neighbor. . . .

"It's difficult to guess," he thought dreamily. "If you could take only the shoulders and arms of the lilac one, and the forehead of the blonde, and the eyes of the one on Lobytko's left, then . . ."

He effected the combination in his mind and formed an image of the girl who had kissed him—the image he desired, but which was nowhere to be seen at the table. . . .

After supper, replete and somewhat intoxicated, the guests expressed their thanks and said good-bye. Their host and hostess again apologized for not inviting them to spend the night.

"Delighted, delighted to have met you, gentlemen!" said the general, this time speaking sincerely (probably because people are always more sincere when speeding the parting guest than when greeting him). "Delighted! Come again on your way back! Don't stand on ceremony! Which way are you going? Up the hill? No, go through the garden below—it's shorter."

The officers went out into the garden. After the bright light and the noise it seemed very dark and still. They walked in silence all the way to the gate. Half drunk, they were feeling cheerful and content, but the darkness and the silence made them momentarily pensive. Probably the same thought had occurred to each of them as to Ryabovich: would the time ever come when they too would have a large house, a family, a garden; when they too would have the possibility—even if insincerely—of being gracious to people, feeding them, making them feel replete, intoxicated, and content?

Once they had gone through the gate they all began talking at once and loudly laughing for no reason. The path they followed led down to the river and ran along the water's edge, winding around bushes and gullies along the bank and the willows that overhung the water. The path and bank were barely visible, and the opposite shore was plunged in darkness. Here and there the stars were reflected in the dark water; they quivered and broke—and from this alone one could surmise that the river was flowing rapidly. It was quiet. On the other shore drowsy woodcocks plaintively cried, and nearby, heedless of the crowd of men, a nightingale trilled loudly in a bush. The officers stopped, lightly touched the bush, but the nightingale sang on.

"Look at that!" they exclaimed approvingly. "We stand right by him and he doesn't take the least notice! What a rascal!"

At the end the path ran uphill, and, near the church enclosure, led into the road. Here the officers, tired from their uphill walk, sat down and smoked. Across the river a dim red light appeared, and, having nothing better to do, they spent a long time trying to decide whether it was a campfire, a light in a window, or something else. . . . Ryabovich too peered at the light, and it seemed to him that it smiled and winked at him, as if it knew about the kiss.

On reaching his quarters, Ryabovich undressed as quickly as possible and went to bed. He shared a cabin with Lobytko and Lieutenant Merzlyakov, a mild, silent fellow, who in his own circle was considered a highly educated officer, and who always carried a copy of *The Messenger of Europe* with him, reading it whenever possible.

Lobytko undressed, paced the room for a long time with the air of a man who is dissatisfied, then sent an orderly for beer. Merzlyakov lay down, after placing a candle at the head of his bed, and plunged into *The Messenger of Europe*.

"Who could she have been?" Ryabovich wondered, as he gazed at the sooty ceiling.

His neck still seemed to him to have been anointed with oil, and near his mouth he felt the chilly sensation of peppermint drops. Into his imagination there flashed the shoulders and arms of the lilac young lady, the brow and candid eyes of the blonde in black, waists, dresses, brooches. . . . He tried to fix his attention on these images, but they danced, flickered, and dissolved. When they finally faded into the vast black background that every man sees when he closes his eyes, he began to hear hurried footsteps, the rustle of a dress, the sound of kiss, and—an intense, groundless joy took possession of him. . . . As he was surrendering himself to it he heard the orderly return and report that there was no beer. Lobytko was terribly indignant and began pacing the room again.

"Now, isn't he an idiot?" he said, stopping first before Ryabovich and then before Merzlyakov. "What a blockhead and a fool a man must be not to find any beer! Eh? *Canaille*—isn't he?"

"Of course you can't get any beer here!" said Merzlyakov without raising his eyes from *The Messenger of Europe*.

"No? Is that what you think?" Lobytko badgered him. "Good God in heaven, if you dropped me on the moon, I could find beer and women in no time! I'll go right now, and I'll find it—and you can call me a scoundrel if I don't!"

He spent a long time dressing and pulling on his long boots, finished smoking a cigarette in silence, and then went out.

"Rabbek, Grabbek, Labbek," he muttered, stopping in

the entry. "I don't feel like going alone, damn it all! Ryabovich, how about a promenade? Eh?"

Receiving no reply he came back, slowly undressed, and got into bed. Merzlyakov sighed, put *The Messenger of Europe* aside, and blew out the candle.

"Hm—yes-s," mumbled Lobytko, lighting a cigarette in the dark.

Ryabovich pulled the bedclothes over his head, curled up in a ball, and tried to assemble into a whole the images flashing through his mind. But nothing came of it. He soon fell asleep, and his last thought was that someone had caressed him and made him happy, that something extraordinary, ridiculous, but extremely lovely and delightful, had happened to him. And this thought remained with him even in sleep.

When he awoke, the sensation of oil on his neck and the peppermint chill near his lips had gone, but joy flooded his heart as it had the day before. He looked with rapture at the window frames gilded by the rising sun, and listened to the sounds of activity in the street. There was a loud conversation right under the window. Lebedetsky, the battery commander, had just overtaken the brigade, and, having lost the habit of speaking quietly, was talking to his sergeant at the top of his voice.

"What else?" he shouted.

"When they were shoeing the horses yesterday, Your Honor, Golubchik's hoof was pricked. The feldscher applied clay and vinegar. They are leading him to the side now. And also, Your Honor, Artemyev was drunk yesterday and the lieutenant ordered him put into the limber of the reserve gun carriage."

The sergeant also reported that Karpov had forgotten the tent pegs and the new cords for the trumpets, and that their honors, the officers, had spent the previous evening at General von Rabbek's. In the course of this talk Lebedetsky's red-bearded face appeared in the window. Squinting short-sightedly at the sleepy officers, he greeted them.

"Everything all right?" he inquired.

"The wheel horse has galled his withers with the new yoke," said Lobytko, yawning.

The commander sighed, thought a moment, and in a loud voice said, "I'm still thinking of going to see Alexandra Yevgrafovna. I ought to call on her. Well, good-bye. I'll catch up with you by evening."

A quarter of an hour later the brigade was on its way. As it moved along the road past the barns, Ryabovich turned and glanced at the manor house on the right. The blinds were down in all the windows. Evidently the household was still asleep. And she who had kissed him yesterday was sleeping too. He tried to picture her asleep. The open window of the bedroom, green branches peeping in, the freshness of the morning air fragrant with the scent of poplars, lilac, roses; the bed, a chair, and on it the dress he had heard rustling, little slippers, a tiny watch on the table—all this he clearly pictured, but the features of the face, the sweet, sleepy smile, just what was distinctive and important, slipped through his imagination like quicksilver through the fingers. When he had gone half a verst he looked back: the yellow church, the house, the river, and the garden, were all bathed in light; the river, with its bright green banks, its blue reflection of the sky, with here and there a glint of silver from the sun, was very beautiful. Ryabovich looked for the last time at Mestechki, and he felt as sad as if he were parting from something very near and dear to him.

On the road before him lay nothing but long familiar and uninteresting scenes. . . . To the right and left stretched fields of young rye and buckwheat in which rooks were hopping about; looking ahead there was nothing to be seen but dust and the backs of men's necks; looking back, dust and men's faces. . . . At the head of the column marched four men with sabers—this was the vanguard. Next came a crowd of choristers, and behind them the trumpeters on horseback. The vanguard and the singers, like torchbearers in a funeral procession, occasionally forgot to keep the regulation distance and marched far ahead. Ryabovich was with the first gun of the fifth battery. He could see all four batteries marching ahead of him.

To a civilian, the long, tedious procession of a brigade on the march appears to be a complicated, unintelligible muddle; he cannot understand why there are so many men around one gun, and why so many strangely harnessed horses are needed to draw it, as if it really were so terrible and heavy. To Ryabovich, however, it was all clear, and therefore extremely uninteresting. He had long known why at the head of each battery a stalwart sergeant major rode beside the officer, and why he was called the fore rider; directly behind this sergeant major were the riders of the next two pairs; he knew that the near horses on which they rode were called saddle horses and the off horses were called lead horses—all very uninteresting. Behind the riders came two wheel horses; on one of them rode a soldier still covered with yesterday's dust, and with a cumbersome, ridiculous-looking wooden guard on his right leg. But Ryabovich, knowing the purpose of the guard, did not find it ridiculous. The riders, every one of them, automatically flourished their whips and shouted from time to time. The gun itself was unsightly. On the limber lay sacks of oats covered with a tarpaulin, and the gun was hung with teapots, soldiers' knapsacks, bags, and looked like a harmless little animal which, for some unknown reason, was surrounded by men and horses. In its lee marched six gunners, swinging their arms. Behind the gun came more fore riders and wheelers, then another gun, as ugly and unimposing as the first. And after the second came a third, and a fourth, with an officer by it, and so on. In all, there were six batteries in the brigade, and four guns to each battery. The column covered half a verst. It terminated in a wagon train near which trotted the ass Magar, his long-eared head bent in thought—a most appealing creature that had been brought from Turkey by one of the battery commanders.

Ryabovich indifferently glanced ahead and behind, at the backs of necks, then at faces; another time he would have been dozing, but now he was completely absorbed in his pleasant new thoughts. In the beginning, when the brigade set out on the march, he tried to persuade himself that the incident of the kiss could be interesting only as a mysterious little adventure, that actually it was trivial, and to think seriously of it was, to say the least, foolish; but he soon dismissed logic and gave himself up to dreams. . . . At one moment he imagined himself in Von Rabbek's drawing room at the side of a girl who resembled the lilac young lady and the blonde in black; then he closed his eyes and saw himself with another, entirely unknown girl whose features were quite vague; in his imagination he talked to her, caressed her, leaned over her shoulders; he pictured a war, separation, and reunion, a supper with his wife and children. . . .

"Brakes!" rang out the command each time they descended a hill.

He too shouted "Brakes!" but he was afraid this cry might shatter his dream and call him back to reality.

As they passed a large estate Ryabovich looked over the fence into a garden and saw a long avenue, straight as a ruler, strewn with yellow sand and bordered with young birch trees. . . . With the avidity of a man who daydreams, he was beginning to see little feminine feet walking in the yellow sand, when, quite unexpectedly, he had a clear vision of the woman who had kissed him—the one he had succeeded in visualizing the evening before at supper. This image remained in his mind and did not leave him.

At midday there was a shout from the rear near the wagon train.

"Attention! Eyes left! Officers!"

The general of the brigade drove by in a carriage drawn

by a pair of white horses. He stopped near the second battery and shouted something that no one understood. Several
officers, Ryabovich among them, galloped up to him.

"Well, how goes it?" the general asked, blinking his red
eyes. "Are there any sick?"

Having received an answer, the general, a skinny little
man, chewed, pondered, then turned to one of the officers
and said, "The rider of your third gun wheeler took off his
leg-guard and hung it on the limber. *Canaille!* Punish him!"
He raised his eyes to Ryabovich and added, "It seems to me
your breeching is too long."

After a few more tedious remarks the general looked at
Lobytko and laughed. "You look very gloomy today, Lieu-
tenant Lobytko," he said. "Are you pining for Madame
Lopukhova?"

Madame Lopukhova was a very tall, stout lady, long past
forty. The general, who had a weakness for large women, regardless of age, suspected similar tastes in his subordinates.
The officers smiled respectfully. The general, delighted with
himself for having said something both caustic and funny,
laughed loudly, tapped his coachman on the back, and
saluted. The carriage rolled on.

"All that I am dreaming of, and which now seems to me
impossible and unearthly, is actually quite ordinary,"
thought Ryabovich, as he gazed at the clouds of dust that
followed the general's carriage. "It's all very ordinary and
everyone goes through it. That general, for instance, must
have been in love in his day, now he's married and has children. Captain Wachter is also married and loved, though the
back of his neck is very red and ugly and he has no waist.
Salmanov is coarse, and too much the Tartar, but he had a
love affair that ended in marriage. . . . I'm just like everyone
else, and sooner or later I'll go through it, too. . . . "

The thought of being an ordinary man with an ordinary
life delighted and heartened him. He pictured *her* and his

happiness, boldly, at will, and nothing inhibited his imagination now. . . .

In the evening, when the brigade reached its bivouac, while the officers were resting in their tents, Ryabovich, Merzlyakov, and Lobytko sat around a chest and ate supper. Merzlyakov ate deliberately, slowly munching as he read *The Messenger of Europe*, which he held on his knees. Lobytko talked incessantly and kept filling his glass with beer, but Ryabovich, whose head was in a fog from dreaming the whole day, remained silent and drank. After three glasses he felt relaxed, slightly drunk, and was moved by an irrepressible impulse to share his new sensations with his comrades.

"A strange thing happened to me at those Von Rabbeks'," he began, trying to speak in a casual, ironical tone. "You know, I went to the billiard room . . ."

He described the adventure of the kiss in exact detail; after a minute he fell silent. In that minute he had told everything, and he was shocked to find that the story required so little time. He had thought it would take him till morning to tell about the kiss. Lobytko, who was a great liar and consequently never believed anyone, looked at him skeptically and laughed. Merzlyakov raised his eyebrows and spoke without taking his eyes from *The Messenger of Europe*.

"Queer! She throws herself on your neck without addressing you by name. Probably a psychotic of some sort."

"Yes. . . . Probably. . . . " Ryabovich agreed.

"A similar thing once happened to me," said Lobytko with a look of awe. "Last year I was on my way to Kovno; I took a second-class ticket—the coach is packed, impossible to sleep. So I give the conductor a half ruble, he picks up my luggage, and leads me to a compartment. I lie down, cover myself with a blanket—it's dark, you understand—and suddenly I feel someone touching my shoulder, breathing on my face. I put out my hand and feel an elbow. I open my eyes and, can you imagine—a woman! Black eyes, lips the color of prime salmon, nostrils breathing passion, and the bosom—a buffer!"

"Excuse me," Merzlyakov placidly interrupted, "I understand about the bosom, but how could you see her lips if it was dark?"

Lobytko tried to extricate himself by making fun of Merzlyakov's obtuseness. All this jarred on Ryabovich. He left them and went to bed, vowing never again to take anyone into his confidence. . . .

Camp life set in. . . . The days flowed by, one very much like another. On all those days Ryabovich felt, thought, and acted like a man in love. Every morning when the orderly brought him water for washing, he drenched his head in the cold water, each time remembering that there was something warm and lovely in his life.

In the evenings when his comrades talked of love and women, he would listen intently, draw up closer, and his face took on the expression of an old soldier listening to the story of a battle in which he himself had taken part. And on those evenings when the officers, drunk, and with setter-Lobytko at their head, made Don-Juanesque raids on the "suburbs" of the town, though he took part, he was always sorry afterwards, felt deeply guilty, and mentally begged *her* forgiveness. . . . In idle hours or on sleepless nights, when he felt inclined to recall his childhood, his father, mother, and all that was dear and familiar, he always thought of Mestechki, the strange horse, Von Rabbek, his wife who resembled the Empress Eugénie, the dark room, the bright chink in the doorway. . . .

On the thirty-first of August he returned from camp, but this time with only two batteries instead of the whole brigade. He was dreamy and excited all the way, as if he were coming home. He had a fervent desire to see the strange horse, the church, the insincere Von Rabbek family, the dark room; that "inner voice" which so often deceives lovers whispered to him that he would surely see her. And he was tortured by questions: how would he meet her? what would he talk about? might she not have forgotten the kiss? If it came to the worst, he thought, even if he did not meet her, it would be a pleasure just to walk through the dark room and remember. . . .

Toward evening the familiar church and the white barns appeared on the horizon. His heart beat wildly. The officer riding beside him said something which he did not hear; he was oblivious to everything, and gazed eagerly at the river gleaming in the distance, the roof of the house, the dovecote, above which the pigeons were circling in the light of the setting sun.

When he reached the church, as he listened to the quartermaster's report, every minute he expected the messenger on horseback to appear from behind the church enclosure and invite the officers to tea; but . . . the report came to an end, the men dismounted and strolled off to the village, and the man on horseback did not appear.

"Von Rabbek will immediately learn from the peasants that we are back, and he will send for us," thought Ryabovich as he entered the hut; and he could not understand why one of his comrades was lighting a candle and why the orderlies were hurrying to start the samovars.

A painful anxiety took possession of him. He lay down, then got up and looked out the window to see if the messenger was coming. But there was no messenger to be seen. He lay down again, but half an hour later, unable to control his restlessness, he got up, went out into the street and walked toward the church. It was dark and deserted in the square near the church enclosure. Three soldiers were standing in silence at the top of the hill. Seeing Ryabovich they jumped to attention and saluted. He returned the salute and started down the well-remembered path.

On the other side of the river, in a sky washed with crimson, the moon was rising, and in a kitchen garden two peasant women were talking in loud voices as they pulled cabbage leaves; beyond the garden several huts loomed dark against the sky. But the river bank was the same as it had been in May: the path, the bushes, the willows overhanging the water; only the song of the stout-hearted nightingale was missing, and the scent of poplars and young grass.

When he reached the garden, Ryabovich looked in at the gate. In the garden it was dark and still. He could see only the white trunks of the nearest birch trees and a small patch of the avenue, all the rest merged into a black mass. He peered into the garden, listening intently; but after standing there a quarter of an hour without hearing a sound or seeing so much as a light, he slowly walked back.

As he drew near the river, the general's bathhouse, with white bath sheets hanging on the rails of the little bridge, rose before him. He ascended the bridge, stood there a moment, and without knowing why, touched one of the bath sheets. It felt rough and cold. He looked down at the water. The river was flowing rapidly, purling almost inaudibly around the piles of the bathhouse. The red moon was reflected in the water near the left bank; little ripples ran across the reflection, expanding it, then breaking it into bits, as though wishing to carry it off. . . .

"How foolish! How foolish!" he thought, gazing at the flowing water. "How stupid it all is!"

Now that he expected nothing, the incident of the kiss, his impatience, his vague hopes and disappointment, presented themselves to him in a clear light. It no longer seemed strange that he had waited in vain for the general's messenger, or that he would never see the one who had accidentally kissed him instead of someone else; on the contrary, it would have been strange if he had seen her. . . .

The river ran on, no one knew where or why, just as it had in May; from a small stream it flowed into a large river, from the river to the sea, then rose in vapor and returned in rain; and perhaps the very same water he had seen in May was again flowing before his eyes. . . . For what purpose? Why?

And the whole world, all of life, seemed to Ryabovich to be an incomprehensible, aimless jest. . . . Raising his eyes from the water and gazing at the sky, he again recalled how fate in the guise of an unknown woman had by chance caressed him; and remembering his summer dreams and fantasies, his life now seemed singularly meager, wretched, and drab.

When he returned to the hut he found not one of his comrades. The orderly informed him that they had all gone "to General Fontriabkin's, who sent a messenger on horseback to invite them." . . . . For an instant joy flamed in his breast, but he immediately stifled it and went to bed, and in his wrath with his fate, as though wishing to spite it, did not go to the general's.

—1887

The Father

"**T**O TELL YOU THE TRUTH, I've had a drop. . . . Excuse me, but on my way here I passed an alehouse, and because it's so hot I had a couple of small bottles. It's hot, my boy!"

Old Musatov pulled out of his pocket something that looked like a rag, and wiped his wasted, beardless face with it.

"I've come only for one little minute, Boris, my angel," he continued, not looking at his son, "but on a highly important matter. Excuse me, maybe I'm disturbing you. . . . Would you, my dear, have ten rubles—only till Tuesday? You see, yesterday I was supposed to pay the rent, but the money, you see—none! Not if they hanged me for it!"

Young Musatov went out without a word and could be heard whispering outside the door with the landlady and his colleagues who rented the *dacha* with him. He was back within three minutes and silently handed his father a ten-ruble note. Without even glancing at it the old man thrust it into his pocket and said, "*Merci*. . . . Well, and how are things going? It's been a long time since we've seen each other."

"Yes, a long time. Not since Easter, in fact."

105

"Half a dozen times I made up my mind to come and see you, but then, there was never time. First one thing and then another. It's simply killing! . . . But I'm lying. Everything I said is a lie. Don't believe me, Borenka. I said I'd pay you back the ten rubles on Tuesday—don't believe that either. Don't you believe one word I say. I haven't a thing to do; it's simply laziness, drunkenness. . . . And I'm ashamed to be seen in the street in these clothes. Excuse me, Borenka. Three times now, I've sent the girl to you for money, and I wrote pitiful letters. I lied. I'm ashamed of fleecing you, my angel. I know you can hardly make ends meet—you live on locusts—but I've got more gall than I know what to do with. Such gall you could exhibit for money! Excuse me, Borenka. I tell you this in all honesty because I can't look at your angel face and not be affected."

There was a moment of silence. Then the old man sighed deeply and said, "Would you treat me to a beer, maybe?"

The son said nothing but went out, and again there was the sound of whispering outside the door. A little later, when the beer was brought in, the old man became animated at the sight of the bottles, and his tone abruptly changed.

"I went to the races the other day, my boy," he said, with a furtive look in his eyes. "There were three of us; we each put up a ruble and bought a ticket on Frisky. And thanks to that Frisky, we got back thirty-two rubles apiece! I can't live without the races, son. The sport of noblemen. My old shrew always gives me a drubbing when I go. But I go anyhow. I love it, no matter what!"

Boris, a fair-haired young man with a melancholy, impassive face, slowly paced the room and listened to his father in silence. When the old man paused to clear his throat he turned to him and said, "The other day I bought myself a new pair of boots, but they seem to be too tight for me. Won't you take them? I'll let you have them cheap."

"If you like." The old man nodded and made a face. "But for the same price. No discount."

"All right. You can take them on credit."

The son crawled under the bed and got them out. The father took off his own clumsy boots, which were obviously secondhand, and tried on the new ones.

"Just right!" he said. "Very well, you let me keep them, and Tuesday, when I get my pension, I'll send you the money for them. . . . I'm lying again." Suddenly he fell into his former lachrymose tone. "That was a lie about the races, too—and the pension. . . . And you are deceiving me, Borenka. I am aware of your generous tactics. I can see through you! Your boots are too small because your heart is too big. Ah, Borya, Borya! I see it all . . . and I feel it!"

"Have you moved into a new apartment?" his son interrupted him, hoping to change the subject.

"Yes, my boy, I have moved. I move every month. With her temper my old shrew can't live long in one place."

"I went to your old place; I wanted to invite you to stay here at the *dacha* with me. It might do you good, considering your health, to spend a little time in the fresh air."

"No!" the father said, with a wave of his hand. "The old woman wouldn't let me. And I don't want to. You've tried to pull me out of the gutter a hundred times, and I've tried myself, but not a damned thing ever came of it. Give it up! I'll die in a ditch. Right now I sit here looking at your angel face, but at the same time something is dragging me back to my ditch. I guess that's fate. You can't lure a dung beetle to a rose. No. . . . But it's time I was going, my boy. It's getting dark."

"Wait a minute, I'll go with you. I have to go into town myself today."

The father and son put on their coats and went out. It was soon dark, and as they drove along in a cab, lights began to gleam in the windows.

"I've swindled you, Borenka!" muttered the old father. "My poor, poor children! It must be a great sorrow to have such a father! Borenka, my angel, when I look at your face

I cannot lie. Excuse me. . . . What my shamelessness has come to! My God! Here I have just come to you and swindled you, and embarrassed you by my drunken condition. I swindle your brothers, too, and disgrace them. . . . And you should have seen me yesterday! I won't conceal it from you, Borenka. Some neighbors dropped in on my old shrew—riffraff, the whole lot—I got drunk with them, too, and I was swearing like a heathen, cursing you children. I abused you, and complained as if you had deserted me. I wanted to make those drunken wenches feel sorry for me, so I played the unhappy father. That's what I always do. When I want to hide my own vices I heap all the blame on my innocent children. I can't lie to you, Borenka, or hide things from you. I came swaggering to you, but when I saw your gentleness, your compassion, I was tongue-tied, my whole conscience turned inside out."

"That's enough, now, Papa. Let's talk of something else."

"Mother of God, what children I have!" the old man continued, not heeding his son. "What splendor the Lord hath bestowed on me! Such children shouldn't belong to a good-for-nothing like me, but to a real man, with a soul and feelings! I'm not worthy!"

The old man took off his little cap with a button on top, and crossed himself several times.

"Praise be to Thee, Lord!" he sighed, glancing from side to side as though looking for an ikon. "Rare and remarkable children! Three sons I have, and every one alike. Sober, steady, businesslike—what brains! Cabby, what brains! Grigory alone has enough brains for ten men. He speaks French, he speaks German—and he can talk better than any of your lawyers. You could listen to him forever. . . . My children, my children, I can't believe you're mine! You, my Borenka, you're a martyr. I'm ruining you, and I'll go on ruining you. . . . You give to me endlessly, even though you know your money's thrown away. The other day I sent you a pitiful letter, describing my illness to you, but I was

lying—I wanted the money for rum. And you give it to me
because you're afraid of hurting me by refusing. I know all
that. I feel it. Grisha, too, is a martyr. On Thursday, my boy,
I went to his office, drunk, dirty, ragged—smelling like a
cellar from vodka. I went right up to him—a fine figure—
broke in on him with my filthy talk, and his colleagues, his
boss, and clients, all standing there. I disgraced him for life.
And he wasn't a bit embarrassed, he only turned a little pale;
but he smiled at me and came up to me as if nothing was
wrong. He even introduced me to his friends. Then he took
me all the way home—and not one word of reproach! I
swindle him worse than I do you. Now, you take your
brother Sasha, he's a martyr, too. He married a colonel's
daughter, you know, from an aristocratic circle—he got a
dowry with her. . . . You'd think he wouldn't be up to seeing
me. No, son, as soon as he got married, right after the wedding, he and his young spouse paid their first visit to me—
in my hole! As God's my witness!"

The old man sobbed, then suddenly began to laugh.

"At the time, as if it happened on purpose, we were eating grated radish with kvass, and frying fish, and there was
a stink in the place that would have turned the devil's own
stomach! I was lying down—I'd had a drop—and my old
shrew leaped out at the young people with her red mug . . .
disgraceful, in fact. But Sasha rose above it all."

"Yes, our Sasha's a good fellow," said Boris.

"Magnificent! You're all pure gold—you, and Grisha,
and Sasha, and Sonya. I plague you, torment you, disgrace
and rob you, and never in my life have I heard one word of
reproach, never have I seen a cross look. It would be all right
if I'd been a decent father to you, but as it is—tfoo! You've
had nothing but evil from me. I'm a bad, depraved man. . . .
Now, God be thanked, I've drawn in my horns, I've no more
spirit. But in former days, when you were all little, there was
strength in me—character. Whatever I said or did, I always
thought it was right. Sometimes I'd come home from the

club, drunk and mean, and yell at your poor departed mother
for the money she spent. I'd rail at her all night, but I
thought I was right. And in the morning when you got up to
go to school, I was still at it, showing character. Heavenly
kingdom, how I tortured her, poor martyr! And when you
came home from school, and I was sleeping, you didn't dare
have dinner till I got up. At dinner, again the music. You
probably remember. I wouldn't wish such a father on anyone. God sent me to you to test you. Exactly, for a trial. Hold
out, children, to the end! Honor thy father and thy days shall
be long. For your deeds may God send you long
life. . . . Cabby, stop!"

The old man hopped down from the droshky and ran into
a tavern. He returned half an hour later, drunkenly clearing
his throat, and climbed into the cab beside his son.

"And where's Sonya now?" he asked. "Still in boarding
school?"

"No, she finished in May; she's living with Sasha's
mother-in-law now."

"Well!" the old man exclaimed in surprise. "She's a fine
girl, she's following in her brothers' footsteps. Ah,
Borenka . . . and no mother, no one to comfort her. Listen,
Borenka, she . . . does she know how I live? Eh?"

Boris did not answer. Five minutes passed in deep silence. The old man gave a sob, wiped his face with the rag,
and said, "I love her, Borenka. You know, she's my only
daughter, and there's no comfort like a daughter in your old
age. I'd like to see her. Could I, Borenka?"

"Certainly, whenever you like."

"Really? And she wouldn't mind?"

"Of course not. As a matter of fact, she has been trying to
find you. She wanted to see you."

"By God! What children! Eh, cabby? . . . You arrange it,
Borenka, my darling. She's a young lady now, *delicatesse*,
consommé, everything very genteel; and I don't want to
show up before her in such a disgraceful condition. I tell you

what, Borenka, we'll organize it with strategy. For three days I'll stay off the spirits, to get my dirty drunken mug in shape, then I'll come to you, and you'll give me one of your nice suits for the occasion. I'll shave and get a haircut, then you'll go and bring her to your place. All right?"

"Very well."

"Cabby, stop!"

Once again the old man sprang out and ran into a tavern. Before they reached his apartment he jumped down twice more; each time his son silently and patiently waited for him. When they had dismissed the cab, and were making their way through a long, filthy yard to the "old shrew's" apartment, the father's face took on an utterly confused and guilty look; timidly he began clearing his throat and smacking his lips.

"Borenka," he said in an ingratiating tone, "if my old shrew starts saying anything to you, don't pay any attention, and . . . and try to be, you know, polite to her. She's ignorant and she's brazen, but . . . she's a good old woman. There's a warm, kind heart beating in her breast."

When they came to the end of the long yard, Boris found himself in a dark entry. The door creaked on its hinges, there was a smell of cooking and smoke from the samovar, and shrill voices were heard. Going from the entry through the kitchen Boris could see nothing but thick smoke, a line with washing hanging on it, and the chimney of a samovar through a crack of which gold sparks were falling.

"Here's my cell," the old man said, as he bent down to enter a low-ceilinged room, which, because of its proximity to the kitchen, was insufferably stifling.

Here three women sat at a table regaling themselves; on seeing a guest they exchanged glances and stopped eating.

"Well, did you get it?" asked one of the women, evidently "the old shrew," in a harsh voice.

"I got it, I got it," mumbled the old man. "Well, Boris,

welcome, sit down! We're plain people, young man. . . . We live simply."

He began to fuss about aimlessly. The presence of his son made him feel ashamed, but at the same time he wanted to strut before the women and act his accustomed role of the unfortunate, forsaken father.

"Yes, my friend . . . young man. . . . We live simply, nothing fancy," he muttered. "We're simple people, young man. . . . We're not like you, we don't care to put up a show. We're simple people, young man. . . . Yes, sir! . . . Shall we have a drink of vodka?"

One of the women—she was ashamed to drink before a stranger—sighed and said, "Well, I'll have one, on account of the mushrooms. . . . Mushrooms like that, they make you drink, even if you don't want to. Ivan Gerasimych, ask the young gentleman there, maybe he'll have a drink." She articulated the last word in a mincing drawl.

"Have a drink, young man!" said the father, without looking at his son. "We have no wines or liqueurs, my friend, we're simple people."

"He don't like our ways," sighed the "shrew."

"Never mind, never mind, he'll have a drink."

Not wishing to offend his father, Boris took a glass and drank it off in silence. When the samovar was brought, he drank two cups of revolting tea silently, with a sad expression, to please the old man, and listened without a word to the "shrew" making insinuations about there being cruel and heartless children in this world who abandon their parents.

"I know what you're thinking now!" cried the old man, who had reached his habitual state of drunken excitability. "You think I've debased myself, sunk into the mire, that I'm pitiful. But in my opinion, this simple life is a good deal more normal than your life, young man. I don't need anybody, and . . . and I don't intend to humble myself. I can't stand seeing some young puppy looking at me with pity!"

After tea he cleaned a herring and sprinkled onion on it;

this he did with so much emotion that his eyes filled with tears. He again began to talk of the races, his winnings, and of a Panama hat he had bought himself for sixteen rubles the day before. He lied with the same zest he displayed in drinking or eating a herring. His son sat in silence for an hour before taking his leave.

"I won't venture to keep you," said the old man haughtily. "You must excuse me, young man, for not living as you would like." He bristled, gave a dignified sniff, and winked at the women.

"Good-bye, young man!" he said, accompanying his son into the entry. *"Attendez!"*

There, where it was dark, he suddenly pressed his face against his son's sleeve and sobbed.

"I'd like to have a look at Sonyushka," he whispered. "You arrange it, Borenka, my angel. I'll shave, I'll wear your nice suit, and I'll put on a strict face. . . . I won't talk when she's there. Truly, I promise, I won't say a word."

He glanced timidly at the door through which the women's voices could be heard, and, repressing his sobs, in a loud voice said, "Good-bye, young man! *Attendez!*"

—1887

In Exile

OLD SEMYON, whose nickname was Preacher, and a young Tartar, whose name no one knew, were sitting by a campfire on the bank of the river; the other three ferrymen were inside the hut. Semyon, a gaunt, toothless old man of sixty, broad-shouldered and still healthy-looking, was drunk; he would have gone to bed long ago, but he had a bottle in his pocket and was afraid his comrades in the hut would ask him for a drink of vodka. The Tartar was worn out and ill, and, wrapping himself in his rags, he talked about how good it was in the province of Simbirsk, and what a beautiful and clever wife he had left at home. He was not more than twenty-five, and in the firelight his pale, sickly face and woebegone expression made him seem like a boy.

"Well, this is no paradise, of course," said Preacher. "You can see for yourself: water, bare banks, nothing but clay wherever you look. . . . It's long past Easter and there's still ice on the river . . . and this morning there was snow."

"Bad! Bad!" said the Tartar, surveying the landscape with dismay.

A few yards away the dark, cold river flowed, growling and sluicing against the pitted clay banks as it sped on to the

114

distant sea. At the edge of the bank loomed a capacious barge, which ferrymen call a *karbas*. Far away on the opposite bank crawling snakes of fire were dying down then reappearing—last year's grass being burned. Beyond the snakes there was darkness again. Little blocks of ice could be heard knocking against the barge. It was cold and damp. . . .

The Tartar glanced at the sky. There were as many stars as there were at home, the same blackness, but something was lacking. At home, in the province of Simbirsk, the stars and the sky seemed altogether different.

"Bad! Bad!" he repeated.

"You'll get used to it!" said Preacher with a laugh. "You're still young and foolish—the milk's hardly dry on your lips—and in your foolishness you think there's no one more unfortunate than you, but the time will come when you'll say to yourself: may God give everyone such a life. Just look at me. In a week's time the floods will be over and we'll launch the ferry; you'll all go gadding about Siberia, while I stay here, going back and forth, from one bank to the other. For twenty-two years now that's what I've been doing. Day and night. The pike and the salmon under the water and me on it. That's all I want. God give everyone such a life."

The Tartar threw some brushwood onto the fire, lay down closer to it, and said, "My father is sick man. When he dies, my mother, my wife, will come here. Have promised."

"And what do you want a mother and a wife for?" asked Preacher. "Just foolishness, brother. It's the devil stirring you up, blast his soul! Don't listen to him, the Evil One! Don't give in to him. When he goes on about women, spite him: I don't want them! When he talks to you about freedom, you stand up to him: I don't want it! I want nothing! No father, no mother, no wife, no freedom, no house nor home! I want nothing, damn their souls!"

Preacher took a swig at the bottle and went on, "I'm no

simple peasant, brother; I don't come from the servile class; I'm a deacon's son, and when I was free I lived in Kursk, and used to go around in a frock coat; but now I've brought myself to such a point that I can sleep naked on the ground and eat grass. And God give everyone such a life. I don't want anything, I'm not afraid of anyone, and the way I see it, there's no man richer or freer than I am. When they sent me here from Russia, from the very first day I jibbed: I want nothing! The devil was at me about my wife, about my kin, about freedom, but I told him: I want nothing! and I stuck to it; and here, you see, I live well, I don't complain. But if anyone humors the devil and listens to him even once, he's lost, no salvation for him. He'll be stuck fast in the bog, up to his ears, and he'll never get out.

"It's not only the likes of you, foolish peasants, that are lost, but even the well-born and educated. Fifteen years ago they sent a gentleman here from Russia. He forged a will or something—wouldn't share with his brothers. It was said he was a prince or a baron, but maybe he was only an official, who knows? Well, the gentleman came here, and the first thing, he bought himself a house and land in Mukhortin- skoe. 'I want to live by my own labor,' says he, 'in the sweat of my brow, because I'm no longer a gentleman, but an exile.'. . . 'Well,' says I, 'may God help you, that's the right thing.' He was a young man then, a hustler, always on the move; he used to do the mowing himself, catch fish, ride sixty versts on horseback. But here was the trouble: from the very first year he began riding to Gyrino to the post office. He used to stand on my ferry and sigh, 'Ah, Semyon, for a long time now they haven't sent me any money from home.'. . . 'You don't need money, Vasily Sergeich. What good is it? Throw off the past, forget it as if it had never hap- pened, as if it was only a dream, and start life afresh. Don't listen to the devil,' I tell him, 'he'll bring you to no good; he'll tighten the noose. Now you want money,' says I, 'and in a little while, before you know it, you'll want something else, and then more and more. But,' says I, 'if you want to be happy, the very first thing is not to want anything.' Yes. . . . 'And if fate has cruelly wronged you and me,' says I, 'it's no good going down on your knees to her and asking her favor; you have to spurn her and laugh at her, otherwise she'll laugh at you.' That's what I said to him. . . .

"Two years later I ferried him over to this side, and he was rubbing his hands together and laughing. 'I'm going to Gyrino,' says he, 'to meet my wife. She has taken pity on me and come here. She's so kind and good!' He was panting with joy. Next day he comes with his wife. A young, beautiful lady in a hat, carrying a baby girl in her arms. And plenty of baggage of all sorts. My Vasily Sergeich was spinning around her; couldn't take his eyes of her; couldn't praise her enough. 'Yes, brother Semyon, even in Siberia people can live!'. . . 'Well,' thinks I, 'just you wait; better not rejoice too soon.'. . . And from that time on, almost every week he went to Gyrino to find out if money had been sent from Russia. As for the money—it took plenty! 'It's for my sake that her youth and beauty are going to ruin here in Siberia,' he says, 'sharing with me my bitter fate, and for this,' he says, 'I ought to provide her with every diversion.' To make it more cheerful for his lady he took up with the officials and with all sorts of riffraff. And there had to be food and drink for this crowd, of course, and they must have a piano, and a fuzzy little lap dog on the sofa—may it croak! . . . Luxury, in short, indulgence. The lady did not stay with him long. How could she? Clay, water, cold, no vegetables for you, no fruit; uneducated and drunken people all around, no manners at all, and she a pampered lady from the capital. . . . Naturally, she grew tired of it. Besides, her husband, say what you like, was no longer a gentleman, but an exile—not exactly an honor.

"Three years later, I remember, on the eve of the Assumption, someone shouted from the other side. I went over in the ferry, and what do I see but the lady—all muffled up, and with her a young gentleman, an official. There was a troika. . . . And after I ferried them across, they got in it and vanished into thin air! That was the last that was seen of them. Toward morning Vasily Sergeich galloped up to the ferry. 'Didn't my wife pass this way, Semyon, with a gentleman in spectacles?'. . . 'She did,' says I. 'Seek the wind in the fields!' He galloped off in pursuit of them, and didn't stop for five days and five nights. Afterwards, when I took him over to the other side, he threw himself down on the ferry, beat his head against the planks, and howled. 'So that's how it is,' says I. . . . I laughed and recalled to him: 'Even in Siberia people can live!' And he beat his head all the more.

"After that he began to long for freedom. His wife had slipped away to Russia, so, naturally, he was drawn there, both to see her and to rescue her from her lover. And, my friend, he took to galloping off every day, either to the post office or the authorities; he kept sending in petitions, and presenting them personally, asking to be pardoned so he could go back home; and he used to tell how he had spent some two hundred rubles on telegrams alone. He sold his land, and mortgaged his house to the Jews. He grew gray, stooped, and yellow in the face, as if he was consumptive. He'd talk to you and go: khe-khe-khe . . . and there would be tears in his eyes. He struggled with those petitions for eight years, but now he has recovered his spirits and is more cheerful: he's thought up a new indulgence. His daughter, you see, has grown up. He keeps an eye on her, dotes on her. And, to tell the truth, she's all right, a pretty little thing, black-browed, and with a lively disposition. Every Sunday he goes to church with her in Gyrino. Side by side they stand on the ferry, she laughing and he not taking his eyes off her. 'Yes, Semyon,' says he, 'even in Siberia people can live. Even in Siberia there is happiness. Look,' says he, 'see what a daughter I've got! I suppose you wouldn't find another like her if you went a thousand versts.'. . . 'Your daughter,' says I, 'is a fine young lady, that's true, certainly. . . . ' But I think to myself: Wait a while. . . . The girl is young, her blood is dancing, she wants to live, and what life is there here? And, my friend, she did begin to fret. . . . She withered and withered, wasted away, fell ill; and now she's completely worn out. Consumption.

"That's your Siberian happiness for you, the pestilence take it! That's how people can live in Siberia! . . . He's taken to running after doctors and taking them home with him. As soon as he hears that there's a doctor or quack two or three hundred versts away, he goes to fetch him. A terrible lot of money has been spent on doctors; to my way of thinking, it would have been better to spend it on drink. . . . She'll die anyway. She's certain to die, and then he'll be completely lost. He'll hang himself from grief, or run away to Russia—that's sure. He'll run away, they'll catch him, there'll be a trial, and then hard labor; they'll give him a taste of the lash. . . . "

"Good, good," muttered the Tartar, shivering with cold.

"What's good?" asked Preacher.

"Wife and daughter. . . . Let hard labor, let suffer; he saw his wife and daughter. . . . You say: want nothing. But nothing is bad! Wife was with him three years—God gave him that. Nothing is bad; three years is good. How you not understand?"

Shivering and stuttering, straining to pick out the Russian words, of which he knew so few, the Tartar said God forbid one should fall sick and die in a strange land, and be buried in the cold, sodden earth; that if his wife came to him even for one day, even for one hour, he would be willing to accept any torture whatsoever, and thank God for it. Better one day of happiness than nothing.

After that he again described the beautiful and clever wife he had left at home; then, clutching his head with both hands, he began crying and assuring Semyon that he was innocent and had been falsely accused. His two brothers and his uncle stole some horses from a peasant, and beat the old man till he was half dead, and the commune had not judged fairly, but had contrived a sentence by which all three brothers were sent to Siberia, while the uncle, a rich man, remained at home.

"You'll get u-u-used to it!" said Semyon.

The Tartar relapsed into silence and fixed his tearful eyes on the fire; his face expressed bewilderment and fright, as though he still did not understand why he was here in the dark, in the damp, among strangers, instead of in the province of Simbirsk. Preacher lay down near the fire, chuckled at something, and began singing in an undertone.

"What joy has she with her father?" he said a little later. "He loves her, she's a consolation to him, it's true; but you have to mind your p's and q's with him, brother: he's a strict old man, a severe old man. And strictness is not what young girls want. . . . They want petting and ha-ha-ha and ho-ho-ho, scents and pomades! Yes. . . . Ekh, life, life!" sighed Semyon, getting up with difficulty. "The vodka's all gone, so it's time to sleep. Eh? I'm going, my boy."

Left alone, the Tartar put more brushwood onto the fire, lay down, and, looking into the blaze, began thinking of his native village, and of his wife: if she would come only for a month, even for a day, then, if she liked, she might go back again. Better a month or even a day than nothing. But if she kept her promise and came, how could he provide for her? Where could she live?

"If not something to eat, how you live?" the Tartar asked aloud.

He was paid only ten kopecks for working at the oars a day and a night; the passengers gave him tips, it was true, but the ferrymen shared everything among themselves, giving nothing to the Tartar, but only making fun of him. And he was hungry, cold, and frightened from want. . . . Now, when his whole body was shivering and aching, he ought to go into the hut and lie down to sleep, but he had nothing there to cover himself with, and it was colder there than on the river bank; here, too, he had nothing to put over him, but at least he could make a fire. . . .

In another week, when the floods had subsided and the ferry could sail, none of the ferrymen except Semyon would be needed, and the Tartar would begin going from village to village, looking for work and begging alms. His wife was only seventeen years old; beautiful, pampered, shy—could she possibly go from village to village, her face unveiled, begging? No, even to think of it was dreadful. . . .

It was already growing light; the barge, the bushes of rose-willow, and the ripples on the water were clearly distinguishable, and looking back there was the steep clay precipice, below it the little hut thatched with brown straw, and above clung the huts of the villagers. The cocks were already crowing in the village.

The red clay precipice, the barge, the river, the strange, unkind people, hunger, cold, illness—perhaps all this did not exist in reality. Probably it was all a dream, thought the Tartar. He felt that he was asleep, and hearing his own snoring. . . . Of course, he was at home in the province of Simbirsk, and he had only to call his wife by name for her to answer, and in the next room his mother. . . . However, what awful dreams there are! Why? The Tartar smiled and opened his eyes. What river was this? The Volga?

"Bo-o-at!" someone shouted from the other side. "Karba-a-s!"

The Tartar woke up and went to wake his comrades, to row over to the other side. Putting on their torn sheepskins as they came, the ferrymen appeared on the bank, swearing in hoarse, sleepy voices, and shivering from the cold. After their sleep, the river, from which there came a piercing gust of cold air, evidently struck them as revolting and sinister. They were not quick to jump into the barge. The Tartar and the three ferrymen took up the long, broad-bladed oars, which looked like crabs' claws in the darkness. Semyon leaned his belly against the long tiller. The shouting from the other side continued, and two shots were fired from a revolver; the man probably thought that the ferrymen were asleep or had gone off to the village tavern.

"All right, plenty of time!" said Preacher in the tone of a man who is convinced that there is no need to hurry in this world—that it makes no difference, really, and nothing will come of it.

The heavy, clumsy barge drew away from the bank and floated between the rose-willows; and only because the willows slowly receded was it possible to see that the barge was not standing still but moving. The ferrymen plied the oars evenly, in unison; Preacher hung over the tiller on his belly, and, describing an arc in the air, flew from one side of the boat to the other. In the darkness it looked as if the men were sitting on some antideluvian animal with long paws, and sailing to a cold, bleak land, the very one of which we sometimes dream in nightmares.

They passed beyond the willows and floated out into the open. The rhythmic thump and splash of the oars were now audible on the further shore, and someone shouted, "Hurry! Hurry!" Another ten minutes passed and the barge bumped heavily against the landing stage.

"And it keeps coming down, and coming down!" muttered Semyon, wiping the snow from his face. "Where it comes from, God only knows!"

On the other side stood a thin old man of medium height wearing a jacket lined with fox fur and a white lambskin cap. He was standing at a little distance from his horses and not moving; he had a concentrated, morose expression, as if, trying to remember something, he had grown angry with his unyielding memory. When Semyon went up to him with a smile and took off his cap, he said, "I'm hastening to Anastasyevka. My daughter is worse again, and they say there's a new doctor at Anastasyevka."

They dragged the tarantass onto the barge and rowed

back. The man, whom Semyon called Vasily Sergeich, stood motionless all the way back, his thick lips tightly compressed, his eyes fixed on one spot; when the coachman asked permission to smoke in his presence, he made no reply, as if he had not heard. And Semyon, hanging over the tiller on his belly, glanced mockingly at him and said, "Even in Siberia people can live. Li-i-ve!"

There was a triumphant expression on Preacher's face, as if he had proved something and was rejoicing that it had turned out exactly as he had surmised. The helpless, unhappy look of the man in the fox-lined jacket evidently afforded him great satisfaction.

"It's muddy driving now, Vasily Sergeich," he said when the horses were harnessed on the bank. "You'd better have waited a week or two till it gets drier. . . . Or else not have gone at all. . . . If there were any sense in going, but, as you yourself know, people have been driving about for ever and ever, by day and by night, and there's never any sense in it. That's the truth!"

Vasily Sergeich tipped him without a word, got into the tarantass, and drove off.

"See there, he's gone galloping off for a doctor!" said Semyon, shrinking with cold. "Yes, looking for a real doctor is like chasing the wind in the fields, or catching the devil by the tail, damn your soul! What freaks! Lord forgive me, a sinner!"

The Tartar went up to Preacher and, looking at him with hatred and abhorrence, trembling, mixing Tartar words with his broken Russian, said, "He is good—good. You bad! You bad! Gentleman is good soul, excellent, and you beast, you bad! Gentleman alive and you dead. . . . God created man to be live, be joyful, be sad and sorrow, but you want nothing. . . . You not live, you stone, clay! Stone want nothing and you want nothing. . . . You stone—and God not love you, love gentleman!"

Everyone laughed; the Tartar frowned scornfully and,

with a gesture of despair, wrapped himself in his rags and went to the fire. Semyon and the ferrymen trailed off to the hut.

"It's cold," said one of the ferrymen hoarsely as he stretched out on the straw that covered the damp floor.

"Well, it's not warm!" one of the others agreed. "It's a hard life!"

They all lay down. The door was blown open by the wind, and snow drifted into the hut. No one felt like getting up and closing the door; it was cold and they were lazy.

"I'm all right!" said Semyon, falling asleep. "God give everyone such a life."

"You're a hard case, we know that. Even the devils won't take you!"

From outside there came sounds like the howling of a dog.

"What's that? Who's there?"

"It's the Tartar crying."

"He'll get u-u-used to it!" said Semyon, and instantly fell asleep.

Soon the others fell asleep too. And the door remained unclosed.

—1892

Three Years

I

IT WAS STILL TWILIGHT, but here and there lights had already been lit in the houses, and from behind the barracks at the end of the street a pale moon was rising. Laptev sat on a bench by the gate waiting for the end of the vesper service at the Church of St. Peter and St. Paul. He was counting on Yulia Sergeyevna passing by on her way home from vespers, and he would speak to her, perhaps even spend the entire evening with her.

He had been sitting there for an hour and a half, and all that time he was picturing to himself his Moscow apartment, his Moscow friends, his footman Pyotr, and his writing table. He gazed in perplexity at the dark, motionless trees, and it seemed strange to him that he was living, not in his *dacha* at Sokolniki, but in this provincial town, in a house past which a large herd of cattle was driven every morning and evening, accompanied by dreadful clouds of dust and the blowing of a horn. He remembered recent conversations in Moscow in which he himself had taken part—long discussions in which it was affirmed that one could live without love, that passionate love is a psychosis, that there is no such love, but merely a physical attraction between the sexes—and all that sort of thing. Recalling these conversations he ruefully thought that if anyone were to ask him now what love was, he would be at a loss for an answer.

The vesper service was over and people were beginning to appear. With strained attention Laptev scrutinized the dark figures. The bishop had already been driven by in his carriage; the bells had ceased ringing, and one by one the red and green lights in the belfry—illuminations on the occasion of dedication day—had been extinguished; but people continued to come out, sauntering, talking together, and loitering beneath the windows. At last he heard the familiar voice, and his heart began to throb; then, when he saw that Yulia Sergeyevna was not alone, but with two ladies, he was seized with despair.

"This is awful, awful!" he whispered, suddenly jealous of her. "It is awful!"

At the corner, before turning into the lane, she stopped to say good-bye to her companions, and her glance fell on Laptev.

"I was just on my way to your house," he said. "I'm coming to have a little talk with your father. Is he at home?"

"Very likely," she replied. "It's still too early for him to go to the club."

There were gardens all along the lane, and by the fences lime trees grew, casting broad shadows in the moonlight, engulfing the fences and the gate on one side in complete darkness, out of which rose a whisper of women's voices, smothered laughter, and the sound of someone softly playing on a balalaika. The scent of lime trees and hay was in the air. This fragrance, and the whisper of unseen women, was tantalizing to Laptev. He had a sudden, passionate desire to embrace his companion, to cover her face, her hands, her shoulders, with kisses, to sob, to fall at her feet, to tell her how long he had been waiting for her. A faint, elusive odor of incense emanated from her, reminding him of a time when he too believed in God and attended vespers, a time when he used to dream of a pure, poetic love. And it seemed to him that because this girl did not love him, all possibility of the happiness he then had dreamed of was now lost to him forever.

She began to speak with concern about the health of his sister, Nina Fyodorovna. Two months ago she had undergone an operation for cancer, and now everyone was expecting a recurrence of the disease.

"I went to see her this morning," said Yulia Sergeyevna, "and it seemed to me that in the past week she has not so much grown thin as withered."

"Yes, yes," Laptev agreed. "There has been no relapse, but every day I notice she grows weaker and weaker; she's wasting away before my eyes. I don't understand what's the matter with her."

"Heavens, when I think how healthy, plump, and rosy-cheeked she was!" exclaimed Yulia Sergeyevna after a moment's silence. "Everyone here called her the Muscovite. And how she laughed! On holidays she used to dress up like a simple peasant girl, and it suited her so well."

Dr. Sergei Borisych was at home; he was a stout, florid man wearing a long frock coat that hung below his knees and made him look short-legged. He was pacing from one end of his study to the other, his hands thrust into his pockets, humming to himself, "Ru-ru-ru-ru. . . ." His gray whiskers were straggly, his hair uncombed, and he looked as though he had just got out of bed. And his study, with heaps of old papers piled in the corners, pillows strewn across the sofas, and a dirty, sick-looking poodle lying under the table, produced a similar unkempt, shaggy impression.

"Monsieur Laptev wants to see you," said his daughter, going into the study.

"Ru-ru-ru-ru." The humming grew louder as he wheeled into the drawing room, gave Laptev his hand, and asked, "What's the good news?"

It was dark in the drawing room. Laptev did not sit down,

but stood, hat in hand, apologizing for having disturbed him. He asked what could be done to enable his sister to sleep at night, and why she was growing so terribly thin; immediately he was disconcerted by the thought that he had asked the doctor these same questions earlier in the day, at the time of his morning visit.

"Tell me," he continued, "wouldn't it be well to send to Moscow for a specialist in internal diseases? What do you think?"

The doctor sighed, shrugged, and made a vague gesture with his hands. He was obviously offended. This was a suspicious man, quick to take offense and to whom it always seemed that he was mistrusted or insufficiently respected, taken advantage of by his patients, and a victim of his colleagues' animosity. He was forever ridiculing himself, saying that such fools as he were created for one purpose only—so that the public might walk all over them.

Yulia Sergeyevna lit the lamp. It was apparent from her pale, weary face and listless walk that she had exhausted herself in church and wanted to rest. She sat down on the sofa with her hands in her lap and sank into a deep reverie.

Laptev knew he was homely, but now he seemed to experience a physical sensation of his own ugliness. He was short and thin, with ruddy cheeks, and hair that had grown so sparse his head felt the cold. He lacked that refined simplicity of expression which makes even a coarse, plain face appealing. In the company of women he was awkward, garrulous, and affected. At the present moment he almost despised himself for it. He felt impelled to talk, for fear that Yulia Sergeyevna might be bored in his company. But what about? His sister's illness again?

He began talking about medicine, saying only what is generally said. He commended hygiene, and observed that he himself had long wished to found a workers' hostel in Moscow, and had even made an estimate of the cost. According to his plan, a workman, for five or six kopecks a night, could be given a bowl of hot cabbage soup with bread, a warm, dry bed, a blanket, and a place to dry his clothes and boots.

Yulia Sergeyevna usually remained silent in his presence, but by some mysterious means, perhaps a lover's intuition, he was able to divine her thoughts and intentions. And now he inferred from the fact that she had not gone to her room to change her clothes and drink tea after vespers, that she was going out to pay a visit.

"But I'm in no hurry with my hostel." Chagrined and irritated, he now addressed the doctor, who was staring at him dully, apparently puzzled, unable to comprehend what had impelled him to raise the question of hygiene and medicine. "It may be some time before I utilize our estimate. I am afraid the hostel might fall into the hands of our Moscow Pharisees and lady philanthropists, who always ruin any enterprise."

Yulia Sergeyevna got up and held out her hand to Laptev. "Excuse me," she said, "it is time for me to go. Please give my regards to your sister."

"Ru-ru-ru-ru. . . . " hummed the doctor. "Ru-ru-ru-ru. . . . "

Yulia Sergeyevna went out, and soon afterwards Laptev said good-bye to the doctor and went home. When a man is dissatisfied with himself and unhappy, what banality is conveyed to him by lime trees, shadows, clouds—all those complacent and impassive beauties of nature! The moon stood high in the heavens, beneath it sped the clouds. "But what an artless, provincial moon; what ragged, flimsy clouds!" thought Laptev. He was ashamed of what he had said about medicine and the night shelter; and he was appalled to think that again tomorrow he would be unable to resist trying to see and talk to her—only to be convinced that he was a stranger to her. And the day after, again the same. For what? When and how would it all end?

On reaching home he went in to see his sister. Nina Fyodorovna still looked strong and gave the appearance of being a well-built, vigorous woman, but her striking pallor made her look like a corpse, especially when, as now, she was lying on her back with closed eyes. Her elder daughter, Sasha, a girl of ten, sat by her side reading aloud from a school reader.

"Alyosha has come," the invalid said softly to herself.

Between Sasha and her uncle there had long been an unspoken agreement to take turns at the patient's bedside. Now Sasha closed her reader, and, without a word, quietly left the room. Laptev took an historical novel from the top of the chest of drawers, found his place in it, then sat down and began to read aloud.

Nina Fyodorovna was born in Moscow. She and her two brothers had spent their childhood and youth at home in Pyatnitsky Street, within the domestic circle of a merchant's family. It was a long and tedious childhood; her father treated her harshly—he had even flogged her on two or three occasions—and her mother, after a long illness, had died. The servants were dirty, coarse, and hypocritical, the house was frequented by priests and monks, and they, too, were coarse and hypocritical; they ate and drank their fill, crudely flattering her father, whom they disliked. The boys had the good fortune to be sent to school, but Nina was left uneducated; all her life she wrote a scrawling hand and read nothing but historical novels. Seventeen years ago, when she was twenty-two, she met her present husband, a landowner named Panaurov, at a *dacha* in Khimki. She fell in love with him, and secretly married him, against her father's will. Panaurov, a handsome, somewhat insolent man, who was given to whistling and lighting his cigarette from the ikon lamp, struck Nina's father as utterly worthless. Later, when the son-in-law began making demands for a dowry, the old man wrote his daughter that he was sending her furs, silver, various articles left by her mother, and thirty thousand rubles; but he withheld his parental blessings. Subsequently, he sent an additional twenty thousand. Panaurov ran through the dowry and the money, the estate was sold, and he moved with his family to town, where he entered a branch of the government service. There he acquired a second family, which became the cause of much talk, as this illicit family lived quite openly.

Nina Fyodorovna adored her husband. And now, listening to the historical novel, she was thinking of how much she had gone through, how much she had always suffered, and that if someone were to describe her life it would make a most pitiful story. As the tumor was in her breast, she was convinced that her illness had been caused by love and the life she led with her husband, and that she had been brought to bed by jealousy and tears.

Alexei Fyodorych closed the book and said, "The end, God be praised! Tomorrow we'll begin a new one."

Nina Fyodorovna laughed. She had always been given to laughter, but of late her brother had begun to notice that at times her mind seemed weakened by illness, and she would laugh at the least trifle, or even without cause.

"While you were out, before dinner, Yulia came," she remarked. "I gather she has very little faith in her papa. 'Let him go on treating you,' she said, 'but write in secret to the holy man and ask him to pray for you.' There is some sort of holy man living here. . . . Yulia forgot her parasol, you must take it to her tomorrow." Then, after a brief silence, she added, "No, when the end comes, neither doctors nor holy men can be of help."

"Nina, why don't you sleep at night?" Laptev asked, in an effort to change the subject.

"Because I don't, that's all. I lie in bed and think."

"What do you think about, dear?"

"About the children, you . . . about my life. You know, Alyosha, I've gone through a great deal. Once you begin remembering, you begin— Oh, my God!" she laughed again. "It's no joke to have borne five children and to have buried three of them. . . . Sometimes, just when I was about to be

confined, my Grigory Nikolaich would be at that very moment with another woman, and there would be no one to
send for the doctor or the midwife. And when I went into the
entrance hall or the kitchen looking for the maid, I found
Jews, tradesmen, moneylenders, all waiting for him to come
home. It made my head spin. . . . He didn't love me, though
he never said it in so many words. However, I have grown
more calm, and it's a relief; but when I was young, it hurt
me—hurt me, my dear . . . it hurt me terribly. Once—it was
when we were still living in the country—I found him in the
garden with a woman, and I walked away . . . I walked—I
don't know where. Later I found myself in the church por-
tico. I fell on my knees, 'Queen of heaven!' I prayed. . . .
And it was night. The moon was shining. . . . "

She had spent herself and was gasping for breath; after
resting a little she took her brother's hand and, in a weak,
stifled tone, said, "How kind you are, Alyosha! . . . How
clever! What a fine man you turned out to be!"

At midnight Laptev said good night to her; as he went out
he took with him Yulia Sergeyevna's forgotten parasol. In
spite of the late hour, both the men and women servants
were in the dining room drinking tea. Such disorder! The
children, too, were sitting there instead of sleeping in their
beds. They were talking in low voices, and no one appeared
to notice that the lamp was smoking and about to go out. All
of them, the children as well as the servants, were troubled
by a succession of inauspicious omens, and the atmosphere
was oppressive. The mirror in the entrance hall had been
broken; the samovar had been droning every day, and, as
though purposely, was doing so even now; it was said that a
mouse had jumped out of Nina Fyodorovna's shoe while she
was dressing. The awful significance of each of these signs
was well known to the children; the elder girl, Sasha, a thin
little brunette, sat at the table, inert with fear and misery,
while Lida, a plump, fair child of seven, stood at her side,
sullenly staring at the lamp.

Laptev went downstairs to his own apartment, where the low-ceilinged rooms were always close and smelled of geraniums. His brother-in-law, Panaurov, was in his sitting room reading a newspaper. Laptev nodded and sat down opposite him. Neither of them spoke. They sometimes spent entire evenings in silence, with no feeling of constraint.

The little girls came down to say good night. Without a word, Panaurov slowly made the sign of the cross over them several times, then gave them his hand to kiss. They curtsied and turned to their uncle, who also was obliged to make the sign of the cross and give them his hand to kiss. This ceremony of kissing and curtsying was repeated every evening.

When the children had gone Panaurov put aside his newspaper and said, "It's dull in this God-fearing town of ours! But, I must confess, my friend," he added with a sigh, "I'm very happy to see that you, at last, have found yourself a little diversion."

"What do you mean by that?"

"Recently I have seen you coming out of Dr. Byelavin's house. I presume you are not going there for the sake of the papa."

"Of course not," said Laptev.

"Well, of course not. And, by the way, you wouldn't find another such vulture as that papa if you searched high and low. You cannot imagine what a slovenly, incompetent, clumsy brute he is! You people there in the capital are interested in the provinces solely from a poetic viewpoint, that is to say, the picturesque, or *Hapless Anton* point of view; but I assure you, my friend, there is nothing in the least poetic here—there is barbarism, vulgarity, and meanness, nothing more. Take the local high priests of science, the so-called intelligentsia. Can you imagine, there are twenty-eight doctors in this town, every one of them has made a fortune and is living in his own home; meanwhile, the inhabitants remain in as hopeless a condition as ever. Here Nina had to have an operation—nothing of any consequence, actually—and we were obliged to send to Moscow for a surgeon! There was not a single man here that would undertake it. You cannot imagine! They know nothing, they understand nothing, they are interested in nothing. Just ask them, for example, what cancer is—what it is, what causes it."

And Panaurov began to explain what cancer was. He was an expert in every field of knowledge, and scientifically explained anything that happened to come up in conversation—but always in his own way. He had his own theory of chemistry, of astronomy, and of the circulation of the blood. He spoke deliberately, softly, convincingly, and he articulated the phrase "you cannot imagine" in an imploring tone, screwing up his eyes, languidly sighing and smiling, gracious as a king. It was obvious that he was very much pleased with himself, and that he never gave a thought to the fact that he was fifty years old.

"I feel like eating something," Laptev remarked. "I could eat something salty."

"Well, why not? That can be arranged immediately."

A few minutes later Laptev and his brother-in-law were sitting upstairs in the dining room having supper. Laptev had a glass of vodka and then began drinking wine. Panaurov drank nothing. He never drank and he never played cards, yet he managed to squander his own and his wife's property, and had acquired a great many debts. In order to spend so much in so short a time, one must have, not a passion, but special talent. Panaurov liked good food, elegant table service, music with his dinner, speeches, bowing footmen to whom he would casually toss a ten- or even twenty-five-ruble tip. He always took part in subscriptions and lotteries, never failed to send a bouquet on a friend's name day, bought cups, glass-holders, shirt buttons, neckties, walking sticks, scent, cigarette holders, pipes, puppies, parrots, Japanese knickknacks and antiques; his nightshirts were of silk, his bed was inlaid with mother-of-pearl, and his dressing gown genuine Bokhara. And for all this there was a daily expenditure of what he himself called "a pile of money."

During supper he continued to sigh and shake his head. "Yes, everything in this world comes to an end." He spoke softly, screwing up his dark eyes. "You fall in love and you suffer; you fall out of love, or you are deceived—and the woman doesn't exist who wouldn't deceive you—and you suffer; and you are brought to such a state of despair that you yourself will be unfaithful. But then, the time will come when all this will be merely a memory, and you will reason coolly, and consider the whole thing absolutely trivial."

Laptev was tired and slightly drunk; looking at the dark, handsome head, the clipped black beard, he thought he understood why women fell in love with this pampered, self-assured, and physically fascinating man.

After supper Panaurov did not stay at home, but went to his other family. Laptev accompanied him on his way. Panaurov was the only man in the entire town who wore a top hat, and every time he walked by the pitiful little three-windowed houses with their gray fences and nettle bushes, his elegant, foppish figure, his top hat and orange-colored gloves, created a strange and melancholy impression.

After parting from him Laptev unhurriedly returned home. The moon shone so brightly one could distinguish every straw on the ground. Laptev felt as though the moonlight were caressing his bare head, as though someone were passing a feather over his hair.

"I love . . . " he said aloud; and suddenly he had a desire to run, to overtake Panaurov, to embrace him, forgive him, bestow a large sum of money on him, and then to run off into a field, a grove, and go on running without looking back.

At home he saw Yulia Sergeyevna's parasol lying on a chair; he snatched it up and kissed it avidly. The parasol was silk, no longer new, and fastened with an old elastic band; the handle was a cheap one, made of ordinary white bone.

Laptev opened it and held it over his head, and it seemed to him that the fragrance of happiness was all about him.

He sat down, made himself comfortable without relinquishing the parasol, and began writing a letter to one of his friends in Moscow.

> *My very dear friend, Kostya,*
>
> *Here is news for you: I am in love again! I say again because six years ago I fell in love with a Moscow actress whom I never even managed to meet, and for the past year and a half I have lived with "a certain person" who is known to you—a woman neither young nor beautiful. Ah, my friend, how unlucky I have been in love! I never have had any success with women. And if I say again it is only because I find it somehow sad and shameful to admit, even to myself, that my youth has passed entirely without love, and that in a real sense I am in love for the first time only now, at the age of thirty-four. So let it be again!*
>
> *If you only knew the sort of girl she is! She could not be called beautiful—she is very thin, and her face is broad, but with such a wonderful expression of goodness when she smiles! And her voice—it sings and vibrates when she speaks. She never enters into conversation with me, so I do not know her; but when I am near her I sense in her a rare, exceptional being, a penetrating mind, and high aspirations. She is religious, and you cannot imagine how this touches me and elevates her in my eyes. On this point I am prepared to argue with you till doomsday. You are right, let it be as you say; all the same, I love it when she goes to church to pray. She is a provincial, but she studied in Moscow, loves our Moscow, and dresses in the Moscow style, and I love her for that, love her, love her. . . . I can see you scowling and rising to read me*

a long lecture on the subject of what love is, what sort of woman one can love, and what sort one cannot, and so forth. But, dear Kostya, before I fell in love, I, too, knew quite well what love was.

My sister thanks you for your greetings. She often recalls the time she took Kostya Kochevoi to the preparatory class, and to this day she continues to speak of you as "poor Kostya," still thinking of you as a little orphan boy. And so, poor orphan, I am in love. So long as it is a secret, do not say anything to a "certain person" there. Things will settle themselves, or, as one of Tolstoy's footmen says, "shape up."

When he had finished the letter, Laptev went to bed. He was so tired he could not keep his eyes open, but for some reason he was unable to sleep; the street noises seemed to prevent him. The cattle were driven by, the horn was blown, and soon afterwards the bells began to ring for early mass. At one moment he heard the creaking of a cart, at another the shrill voice of a peasant woman on her way to market. And the sparrows were chirping the whole time.

II

It was a gay, holiday morning. At ten o'clock Nina Fyodorovna, wearing a brown dress and with her hair neatly combed, was led into the drawing room, supported on either side; she walked a little, and briefly stood before an open window. Seeing her thus, with her broad, innocent smile, brought to mind the local artist, a drunkard, who said she had the face of a saint, and wanted her to sit for his painting of the Russian Shrovetide. Everyone—the children, the servants, her brother, and even she herself—all at once felt certain she would regain her health. The little girls were running about, chasing their uncle, and each time they succeeded in catching him the house resounded with their shrill laughter.

People came to inquire about her health; they brought communion bread and told her that in most of the churches prayers were being offered up for her that day. She was known throughout the town for her charity, and people loved her. She gave money with the greatest ease, like her brother, Alexei, who never stopped to consider whether it was necessary to give or not. She paid the school fees for poor students, distributed sugar, tea, and jam to old women, dressed impoverished brides for their weddings, and, if she happened to pick up a newspaper, she first looked to see if there was an appeal or notice of any sort concerning someone in distress.

At the present moment she held in her hand a bundle of notes authorizing certain of her poor petitioners to obtain goods at a grocer's shop; the previous evening they had been sent back to her by the shopkeeper, with a request for payment of eighty-two rubles.

"Now, see how much they've taken, the shameless creatures!" she exclaimed, scarcely able to decipher her own handwriting. "This is no joke! Eighty-two rubles! I shall simple refuse to pay it!"

"I'll pay it today."

"Why should you—why?" she asked, in agitation. "Isn't it enough that you and brother give me two hundred and fifty rubles a month? God bless you both," she added softly, in order that the servants might not hear.

"Well, I spend five hundred thousand in a couple of months," he replied. "I tell you again, dear, you have just as much right as Fyodor and I to spend the money. Understand this once and for all. We three are all father's children, and of every three kopecks, one belongs to you."

But Nina Fyodorovna did not understand it, and the expression on her face suggested that she was making a mental effort to solve a difficult problem. This lack of

comprehension where money was concerned never failed to
trouble and embarrass Laptev; moreover, he suspected that
she had personal debts she was ashamed to mention to him,
and which were causing her to suffer.

The sound of footsteps and heavy breathing was heard;
the doctor was coming up the stairs, disheveled and unkempt as usual.

"Ru-ru-ru-ru . . : " he hummed, "ru-ru-ru-ru. . . . "

Laptev went into the dining room to avoid meeting him,
then downstairs to his own rooms. It was clearly impossible
to be friendly with the doctor, or to drop in at his house in-
formally; even to encounter this "vulture," as Panaurov
called him, was disagreeable. That is why he so rarely saw
Yulia Sergeyevna. But if he were to take her parasol to her
now, he thought, while her father was not at home, he would
probably find her alone. His heart throbbed with joy.
Quickly, quickly! In a state of extreme excitement, he took
up the parasol, and flew on the wings of love.

It was hot in the street. At the doctor's house, in the enormous courtyard overgrown with nettles and tall grass, some
twenty boys were playing ball. They were the children of the
tenants, workmen living in the three unsightly old lodges,
which every year the doctor planned to renovate. The clear
young voices resounded through the yard. Far to one side,
near her own porch, Yulia Sergeyevna stood, her hands
clasped behind her, watching the game.

"Good morning!" Laptev called.

She looked around. Ordinarily when he saw her she appeared indifferent, cold, or, as yesterday, tired; now, however, her expression was animated and playful, like the boys
at their game of ball.

"See, in Moscow the children never play so merrily," she
said, coming to meet him. "Of course, there are not such big
yards there, they have no place to run. But Papa just went to
your house," she added, looking back at the children.

"I know, but I didn't come to see him, I came to see you,"

Laptev said, admiring her youthfulness, which he had never before observed, and which only now was revealed to him; he felt that he was seeing for the first time that delicate white neck encircled by a gold chain. "I came to see you," he repeated. "My sister sent you your parasol; you forgot it yesterday."

She put out her hand to take it, but he clasped it to his breast, and yielding to the same sweet rapture that had possessed him the night before when he sat under the parasol, he spoke passionately, without restraint.

"I entreat you, give it to me. I shall keep it as a souvenir of our acquaintance. Oh, how wonderful!"

"Take it," she said, blushing. "But there is nothing wonderful about it."

He continued to gaze at her in silent ecstasy, not knowing what to say.

"But why do I keep you standing here in this heat?" she said, after a brief silence. "Let us go indoors."

"I am not disturbing you?"

They went into the entrance hall and Yulia Sergeyevna ran up the stairs. Her white dress covered with little pale blue flowers made a rustling sound as she moved.

"It is impossible to disturb me," she replied, pausing on the staircase. "You see, I never do anything, Every day is a holiday for me, from morning to evening."

"What you are saying is inconceivable to me," he said, going up to her. "I grew up in an environment where people worked every day—everyone, without exception, men and women alike."

"But if there is nothing to do?" she asked.

"One must arrange one's life in such a way that work is necessary. There can be no pure and joyous life without work."

Again he pressed the parasol to his breast, and, to his own amazement, not even recognizing his own voice, he softly said, "If you would consent to be my wife, I would give everything. I would give everything—there is no price I would not pay—no sacrifice I would not make!"

She started, then stared at him in astonishment and dismay.

"What are you saying—what are you saying?" she exclaimed, growing pale. "It is impossible, I assure you! Excuse me." And with the same rustling of her dress, she ran to the top of the stairs and disappeared behind the doors.

Laptev understood what this meant, and his mood underwent an immediate and radical change; it was as though a light had suddenly been extinguished in his soul. Feeling the shame and humiliation of a man who has been scorned, who is disliked, offensive, or perhaps disgusting, and from whom people flee, he left the house.

"I would give everything!" he mocked himself, recalling the details of his proposal as he walked home in the heat. "I would give everything—exactly like a tradesman! Who needs your everything?"

Each word he had just spoken now seemed stupid to the point of being abhorrent. Why had he lied, saying he had grown up in an atmosphere where everyone without exception worked? Why had he spoken in that edifying tone about the pure and joyous life? It was neither interesting nor clever, but mere cant—typical Moscow cant!

Gradually he was overcome by that mood of indifference into which a criminal falls after receiving a severe sentence. He thanked God that it was all over, that the terrible uncertainty had come to an end, that he no longer had to spend whole days in expectation, exhausting himself, thinking only of one thing. Now everything was clear: he had to relinquish the prospect of personal happiness, live without desires, without hopes, never dreaming nor anticipating, and, in order to relieve the boredom he was so sick of nursing, he could occupy himself with the affairs of others, the happiness of others; thus, imperceptibly old age would come upon him, and life draw to an end—nothing more would be required. It was all the same to him now, he wanted nothing, and was able to reason coolly; but in his face, especially under the eyes, there was a certain heaviness; his forehead felt taut, stretched like an elastic band, and the tears were about to spurt from his eyes. Feeling a sensation of weakness in his whole body, he lay down on the bed, and within five minutes he was fast asleep.

III

Laptev's unexpected proposal had thrown Yulia Sergeyevna into a state of despondency. She had made his acquaintance by chance and knew very little about him; only that he was rich, a representative of the well-known Moscow firm of Fyodor Laptev and Sons, that he was always very serious, apparently clever, and anxious about his sister's illness. It had seemed to her that he never paid the least attention to her, and she was completely indifferent to him—and suddenly that declaration on the staircase, and his pitiful, enraptured face.

The proposal embarrassed her by its suddenness, by the fact that the word *wife* had been spoken, and by the necessity of refusing it. She could not even remember what she had said to Laptev, but she continued to feel traces of the violent, disagreeable emotion with which she had rejected him. She did not like him; outwardly he seemed like a salesman, and he was uninteresting. She could not have answered him otherwise; nevertheless, she felt uncomfortable, as though she had acted badly.

"My God, without even waiting to get into the room, but right there on the stairs!" she said miserably, addressing the little ikon that hung over her bed. "And never having courted me, it was somehow queer, extraordinary. . . . "

Her anxiety increased with every hour of solitude; it was

beyond her strength to cope with it alone. She needed someone to talk to, someone to tell her that what she had done
was right. But there was no one. She had lost her mother
long ago; she considered her father a strange person, and
was unable to talk to him seriously. She felt constrained by
his quirks, his excessive readiness to take offense, his in-
congruous gestures. One had only to begin a conversation
with him for him to start talking about himself.

She was not completely candid when she prayed, because
she did not know exactly what she should ask God for.

The samovar was brought into the dining room. Yulia
Sergeyevna, very pale, tired, and with a forlorn look, went in
to make the tea—it was one of her duties—and poured out a
glass for her father. Sergei Borisych, wearing the long frock
coat that hung below his knees, red-faced and uncombed, his
hands thrust into his pockets, was pacing the room in his customary manner, not from one end to the other, but back and
forth like a wild animal in a cage. He would stop at the table,
sip his tea with relish, and continue pacing, deep in thought.

"Laptev asked me to marry him today," Yulia Sergeyevna
said, and she blushed.

"Laptev? . . . Panaurova's brother?"

He was fond of his daughter; he knew that sooner or later
she would marry and leave him, but he tried not to think
about it. Solitude frightened him, and for some reason he believed that if he were left alone in that big house, he would
have an apoplectic stroke, but he did not like to speak of this
openly.

"Well, I'm very happy," he said, with a shrug of his
shoulders. "I congratulate you with all my heart. This presents you with an excellent opportunity to leave me—to your
great satisfaction. I fully understand you. To live with a father who is an old man, a sick man, half crazy, must be very
painful at your age. I understand you perfectly. And if I
should kick off a little sooner, and go to hell, then everyone
would be happy. I congratulate you with all my heart."

"I refused him."

The doctor was relieved at heart, but he was unable to stop himself and went on, "I am amazed—I have long been amazed—why is it that I have not yet been put into a madhouse? Why am I now in this coat, instead of a strait jacket? I still believe in truth, in goodness, I am a fool of an idealist—do you think that in our day this is not madness? And what do I get in return for my honesty, my fair play? They all but throw stones at me; they walk all over me. And I even get it in the neck from my nearest kin. The devil may as well take me, an old blockhead——"

"It's impossible to talk to you like a human being!" said Yulia.

Impetuously she got up from the table and went to her room. In her extreme anger she remembered how often her father had been unjust to her, but in a very short time she felt sorry for him, and when he left to go to his club she accompanied him downstairs and closed the door after him. Outside the weather was blustery; it was a disquieting night. The door shuddered from the force of the wind, in the passages there were drafts from every direction, and the candle was almost blown out. Upstairs Yulia Sergeyevna went from room to room making the sign of the cross over all the doors and windows. The wind howled, and it sounded as though someone were walking on the roof. Never before had it been so dismal, never had she felt so alone.

She asked herself if she had been right to refuse a man solely because his outward appearance was not to her liking. It was true, she did not love him, and to marry him would mean to relinquish forever her dreams, her notions of happiness and married life; but would she ever meet the man she dreamed of? And if she did, would he love her? She was already twenty-one. There were no marriageable men in the town. She thought of all the men she was acquainted with—government clerks, schoolteachers, officers; some of them were already married, and their domestic lives were thoroughly empty and dull. The others were uninteresting, insipid, silly, or immoral. Laptev was, after all, from Moscow, had a university degree, and spoke French. He lived in the capital where there were many clever, noble, distinguished people, where there was noise and bustle, beautiful theaters, musical evenings, superlative dressmakers, confectioners. . . . In the Scriptures it is written that the wife must love her husband, and in the novels love is given vast importance; but was there not a degree of exaggeration in all this? Was it really impossible to marry without love? After all, one often hears that love soon vanishes and only habit remains, that the whole purpose of marriage is not in love or happiness, but in duties, such as the rearing of children and domestic cares. . . . But perhaps what was meant in the Scriptures was that the wife ought to love her husband as her neighbor, respect him, and be merciful.

That night Yulia Sergeyevna diligently said her evening prayers, then knelt down, and, gazing at the ikon lamp, clasped her hands to her bosom and with deep feeling said, "Grant me understanding, Holy Mother, our Defender! Grant me understanding, oh Lord!"

She had often had occasion in the course of her life to meet elderly spinsters, poor, insignificant women, who were bitterly and openly remorseful because of once having rejected a suitor. Would the same thing happen to her? Ought she to go into a convent or become a Sister of Mercy?

After crossing herself and making the sign of the cross in the air around her, she undressed and went to bed. Suddenly the bell rang sharply and plaintively in the corridor.

"Oh, my God!" she exclaimed, feeling a painful irritation all through her body at the sound. She lay there thinking how meager, monotonous, and, at the same time, how vexing, was everything that happened in this provincial life! One was continually made to wince, to feel apprehensive, angry, guilty, and at last one became so nervous as to be afraid to peep out of the bedclothes.

Half an hour later there was the same sharp ring of the bell. Probably the maid was asleep and had not heard it. Yulia Sergeyevna lit the candle; shivering and annoyed with the servant, she began to dress. When she went out into the corridor the maid was closing the door downstairs.

"I thought it was the master, but it was someone from a patient," she said.

Yulia Sergeyevna returned to her room. She took a pack of cards out of the chest of drawers and resolved that if, after shuffling the cards well and cutting them, the bottom card was red, it would mean *yes*, she would accept Laptev's proposal; and if it was black, *no*. The card she turned up was the ten of spades.

This calmed her and she went to sleep, but in the morning, again she was wavering between *yes* and *no*. The thought that now she could, if she chose, change her life, weighed upon her, exhausting her to the point of making her feel ill; nevertheless, shortly after eleven o'clock, she dressed and went to call on Nina Fyodorovna. She wanted to see Laptev: perhaps now he would seem more attractive to her; perhaps she had been mistaken about him. . . .

She found it difficult to walk against the wind; holding her hat with both hands, and barely able to see anything for the dust, she made slow progress.

IV

When he entered his sister's room and unexpectedly saw Yulia Sergeyevna, Laptev again felt himself in the humiliating state of a man who is repulsive. He concluded that if she found it so easy to visit his sister and meet him after what had happened yesterday, it could only mean that he was beneath her notice, that she considered him utterly insignificant. But when he greeted her, and saw her pale face, the dust beneath her eyes, her sad and guilty expression when she looked at him, he understood that she, too, was suffering.

She did not feel well and stayed no more than ten minutes, then got up to go. As she was leaving she said to Laptev, "Will you see me home, Alexei Fyodorych?"

They walked along the street in silence, both holding onto their hats, he behind her, trying to shield her from the wind. In the lane it was less windy and they walked side by side.

"If I was unkind yesterday, please forgive me," she began, and her voice trembled as though she were about to burst into tears. "I have been in such torment—I didn't sleep all night!"

"And I slept soundly the whole night," he said, not looking at her, "but that doesn't mean that I'm well. My life is broken, I am deeply unhappy, and since your refusal yesterday, I walk around like someone who has been poisoned. Yesterday the most difficult part was said; today I no longer feel constrained and can speak freely. I love you more than my sister, more than my departed mother. . . . I can and have lived without my sister and my mother, but to live without you—for me this is meaningless, I cannot——"

And now, as always, he divined her intention. It was clear to him that she wanted to resume where they had left off yesterday, and for this reason had asked him to accompany her and was now taking him to her home. But what could she add to her refusal? What more could she have thought of? From everything, her smile, her glances, even the way she held her head and shoulders as she walked beside him, he could see that nothing had changed: she did not love him; he was a stranger to her. What, then, could she have to say to him?

Dr. Sergei Borisych was at home.

"Welcome, delighted to see you, Fyodor Alexeyich," he

said, interchanging his Christian name with his patronymic. "Delighted, delighted!"

Never before had the doctor been so affable, and Laptev concluded that he already knew of the proposal; this displeased him. He was sitting in the drawing room, a room that produced a strange impression with its poor, commonplace furnishings and bad pictures, and which, although it contained armchairs and an enormous lamp with a shade, nevertheless looked uninhabited, like a vast barn. Obviously, only a man such as the doctor could feel at home in this room. The next room, almost twice its size, was called the reception room, and contained nothing but chairs arranged as for a dancing class. As he sat in the drawing room talking to the doctor about his sister, Laptev began to be tormented by a certain suspicion: had not Yulia Sergeyevna come to his sister's and then brought him here to tell him that she had decided to accept his proposal? Oh, how awful! But the most awful part of all was that his soul was open to such suspicions. He visualized the father and daughter spending the preceding evening and the night in long deliberation, perhaps even in a protracted quarrel, before reaching the conclusion that Yulia Sergeyevna had acted rashly in refusing a rich man. He could hear the words used by parents on such occasions: "It may be true that you do not love him, but on the other hand, think how much good you will be able to do!"

The doctor was going out to visit patients. Laptev was about to leave with him, but Yulia Sergeyevna said, "Please, don't go."

She was worn out and depressed; she had convinced herself that to refuse a decent, good, and loving man, simply because he did not appeal to her—especially when this marriage offered the possibility of changing her dismal, monotonous, idle life, and when her youth was passing and the future looked no brighter—in such circumstances to refuse him would be madness, folly, caprice, for which God might even punish her.

The father went out. When the sound of his footsteps could no longer be heard, she stopped abruptly before Laptev, and all the color drained from her face as she resolutely said, "I thought for a long time yesterday, Alexei Fyodorych, I accept your offer."

He bent down and kissed her hand; awkwardly she kissed him on the head with cold lips.

He felt that in this betrothal scene the principal element—her love—was missing, and that there was a great deal in it that ought not to be. He had an urge to cry out, to run away, to leave for Moscow at once, but she was standing near him, and she seemed so beautiful that he was suddenly overcome with passion. He realized it was now too late to reason, and he clasped her to him in a passionate embrace, murmuring something, calling her *thou*, kissing first her neck, then her cheek, her hair. . . .

She turned from him and went to the window, frightened by his caresses; both of them already regretted their avowals; both were distractedly asking themselves: why has this happened?

"If you only knew how miserable I am!" she exclaimed, wringing her hands.

"What is it?" he asked, going to her. And he, too, began wringing his hands. "My darling, for God's sake, tell me—what is it? But only the truth, I implore you, nothing but the truth!"

"Pay no attention," she said, forcing herself to smile. "I promise you, I shall be a faithful and devoted wife. Come back again in the evening."

Later, as he sat with his sister, reading to her from the historical novel, he recalled everything that had happened, and he felt mortified to think that his glorious, pure, deep emotion had met with such a shallow response. He was not loved, and, very likely, his proposal had been accepted only because he was rich: what was valued in him was the very thing he thought the least of. One might assume that a pure girl like Yulia, who believed in God, had not once thought of money; but then, she did not love him, did she, therefore she obviously must have motives that were not disinterested—vague though they may have been, and not entirely calculated, they were there all the same. The doctor's house, with its commonplace furniture, was repulsive to him, and the doctor himself was like a miserable, fat moneygrub, a sort of operatic Gaspard out of *Les Cloches de Corneville*. Even the name Yulia had a vulgar sound. He thought of how he and his Yulia would go to the altar, virtual strangers to each other, without a modicum of feeling on her side, as if the marriage had been made by a professional matchmaker. And his only consolation—a consolation as banal as the marriage itself—was that he would be neither the first nor the last to enter into such a marriage; thousands of marriages were no different from his, and perhaps, in time, when Yulia came to know him better, she would grow to love him.

"Romeo and Juliet!" he said, as he closed the book. Then he laughed. "I, Nina, am Romeo. You may congratulate me. Today I proposed to Yulia Byelavina."

Nina Fyodorovna thought he was joking, but when she saw that he was serious, she began to weep. She was not pleased with this news.

"Well, then, I congratulate you," she said. "But why is it so sudden?"

"It isn't sudden. It has been going on since March, but you don't notice things. . . . I fell in love with her in March, when I met her here in your room."

"And I always thought you would marry one of our own friends in Moscow," she said after a pause. "A girl from our circle would be simpler. But what is most important, Alyosha, is that you should be happy, that's the important thing. My Grigory Nikolaich didn't love me, and—it's impossible to hide it—you can see how we live. Of course, any woman might love you for your goodness and your intellect, but, you see, Yulichka was educated at the Institute, she is of the gentry, and goodness and intellect are not enough for her. She is young, and you, Alyosha, are not so young, nor are you handsome." To soften her last words she stroked his cheek and added, "You are not handsome, but you are dear."

She became so excited that a slight flush appeared in her cheeks, and she talked with enthusiasm about whether or not it would be right for her to bless her brother with the ikon; after all, she was his elder sister, and took the place of his mother. She kept trying to persuade her dejected brother that the wedding must be properly celebrated, with all due solemnity and joy, so that no one could cast any reflection upon them.

As Yulia's betrothed, Laptev commenced going to the Byelavins' three or four times a day, and he no longer had the time to take Sasha's place and read aloud from the historical novel. Yulia received him in her own two rooms, which were at the end of the house, far from the drawing room, and he liked them very much. Here the walls were dark, the ikon case stood in one corner, and there was a fragrance of fine perfume and oil from the holy lamp. Her bed and dressing table were behind a screen. The small doors of the bookcase were covered on the inside with green curtains, and there were rugs on the floor, which made her footsteps inaudible; he concluded from this that she had a reticent nature and liked a quiet, calm, secluded life.

In her own house she was treated as though she were still a child: she had no money of her own, and occasionally, when they were out walking together, she was ashamed of not having so much as a kopeck with her. Her father gave her very little, not more than a hundred rubles a year for clothes and books. And, in spite of having a good practice, the doctor himself had scarcely any money. Every evening he played cards at the club, and always lost; besides which, he bought houses through a credit and loan society, and then rented them. The tenants were always remiss in their payments, nevertheless, he was convinced that these operations were most profitable. He had mortgaged the house he and his daughter were living in, and with the money had bought a barren plot of land on which he was building a large two-story house. This he also intended to mortgage.

Laptev now lived in a sort of fog, as though he were not himself but his double, and he did a great many things he could never have brought himself to do before. On several occasions he had supper with the doctor at his club, and, of his own accord, offered him money for his buildings. He even visited Panaurov's other family. It happened that his brother-in-law invited him to dinner, and without thinking, he accepted. He was met by a lady of about thirty-five, tall, extremely thin, with slightly graying hair and black eyebrows. She was evidently not Russian. Her face was blotched with white powder. She smiled cloyingly, and shook his hand so vigorously that the bracelets on her white arms jingled. Laptev felt that she smiled in this way to conceal from others and herself that she was not happy. He also saw two little girls, aged five and three, both of whom resembled Sasha. For dinner they were served a milky soup, soggy veal, and chocolate—it was sickly-sweet and unpalatable, but the table glittered with gold forks, bottles of soy sauce, cayenne pepper, a bizarre cruet stand, and a gold pepper pot.

Not until he had finished the soup did Laptev realize how inappropriate it was for him to be dining there. The lady was embarrassed, and continually smiled, displaying her teeth, while Panaurov didactically held forth on the subject of love, its nature and its cause.

"Here we have to do with one of the phenomena of electricity," he said in French, turning to the lady. "Under the skin of every human being lie microscopic glands that contain electric currents. If you meet an individual whose currents are parallel to your own, the result is love."

When Laptev returned home and his sister asked him where he had been, he felt uncomfortable and did not answer.

During all the time prior to the wedding, Laptev constantly felt himself to be in a false position. Daily his love grew stronger, and Yulia Sergeyevna seemed to him a poetic and exalted being, but the love was not mutual; in effect, she was selling herself, and he was the buyer. At times, as he thought about it, he was in utter despair, and he asked himself whether he ought to run away. He lay awake whole nights thinking of how, in Moscow, he would meet the woman he had referred to in his letter as "a certain person," and of what attitude his father and brother, difficult people, would take towards his marriage and Yulia. He feared that his father might say something rude to Yulia at their first meeting. And lately his brother had been behaving oddly; he wrote long letters on the importance of health, the influence of illness on the mental state, on what religion was, but not a word about Moscow or business. These letters irritated Laptev, and it seemed to him that his brother's character was changing for the worse.

The wedding took place in September. The ceremony was held after mass in the Church of St. Peter and St. Paul, and on the same day the bride and groom went to Moscow. When Laptev and his wife, who, in her black dress and long train, already gave the appearance of a matron rather than a girl, said good-bye to Nina Fyodorovna, the invalid's face was distorted with emotion, but she did not shed a tear.

"If I die, which God forbid, please take my little girls," she said.

"Oh, I promise!" Yulia Sergeyevna replied, her lips and eyelids twitching nervously.

"I shall come to see you in October," Laptev said, deeply moved. "Get well, my darling."

They traveled in a private compartment. Both of them felt sad and awkward. She sat in the corner, without taking off her hat, and pretended to doze; he lay on the divan opposite her, troubled by various thoughts about his father, "a certain person," and wondering whether Yulia would like her Moscow apartment. From time to time he glanced at his wife, who did not love him, and disconsolately thought: why has this happened?

V

The Laptevs had a wholesale notions business in Moscow; they dealt in fringe, braid, trimmings, crochet cotton, buttons, and so on. The gross receipts reached two million a year; what the net profits were, no one but the old man knew. His sons and the clerks estimated them to be approximately three hundred thousand, and said it would have been at least a hundred thousand more if the old man had not "spread it around," by which they meant, had he not extended credit indiscriminately. In the last ten years alone the accumulation of bad debts amounted to almost a million, and whenever the subject was mentioned the senior clerk would wink slyly and assert, "The psychological consequences of the age"—the meaning of which was not clear to everyone.

The chief commercial operations were conducted in the city market in a building that was known as the warehouse. The entrance to it was through a yard where it was always dusk, smelled of bast matting, and resounded with the clatter of dray horses' hooves on the asphalt. An unpretentious-looking iron-studded door led from the yard into a room with walls that had turned brown with damp and were all written over in charcoal; the light came from a narrow window with an iron grating over it. To the left was another room, somewhat larger and cleaner, with a cast-iron stove, two tables, and the same prisonlike window; this was the office, and from here a narrow stone staircase led to the second story, where the main room was located. It was a rather large room, but owing to the perpetual gloom, the low ceiling, the cramming together of boxes and bales, and people shoving their way through, it produced as disagreeable an impression on a newcomer as did the other two rooms. Upstairs, as well as in the office, goods lay on the shelves in piles, bundles, and cardboard boxes, displaying neither order nor artistry in the arrangement, and if one had not caught a glimpse here and there of a crimson thread, a tassel, or a tail of fringe, it would have been impossible to guess what sort of trade was carried on here. It was inconceivable, glancing at these crumpled paper bundles and boxes, that from such trifles millions were made, or that in this warehouse fifty men were employed daily, to say nothing of the buyers who came in

When Laptev went to the warehouse at noon on the day after his arrival in Moscow, the packers were hammering so loudly no one in the first room or the office heard him enter. A postman he knew was coming down the stairs with a bundle of letters in his hand, his face screwed up at the noise, and he, too, failed to notice Laptev. The first person to meet him upstairs was his brother, Fyodor Fyodorych, who looked so exactly like him that they were frequently thought to be twins. This resemblance had been a constant reminder to Laptev of his own appearance, and now, seeing before him a short, red-faced man with thinning hair, narrow, plebeian hips, completely uninteresting and unintellectual looking, he asked himself: Am I really like that?

"How happy I am to see you!" said Fyodor, kissing his brother and warmly shaking his hand. "I have been impatiently expecting you each day, my dear. When you wrote that you were to be married, I began to be tortured by curiosity, and then, I've missed you, brother. Think of it, six months since we've seen each other! Well? How are things? Nina's bad? Very?"

"Very bad."

"God's will," sighed Fyodor. "Well, and your wife? A beauty, I suppose? I love her already, she'll be my little sister. Between us we'll spoil her."

Laptev caught sight of the broad, stooped back—so long familiar to him—of his father, Fyodor Stepanych. The old man was sitting on a stool near the counter, talking to a customer.

"Papa, God has sent us joy!" Fyodor cried. "Brother has come!"

Fyodor Stepanych was tall and of such an extraordinarily powerful build that, in spite of his eighty years and wrinkles, he had the appearance of a vigorous, healthy man. He spoke in a deep, booming bass that came rolling out of his broad chest as from a barrel. He shaved his beard, but wore a clipped military mustache, and smoked cigars. As it always seemed hot to him, he wore an ample duck coat at all seasons of the year, in the warehouse and at home. Recently he had had a cataract removed; he did not see well, and was no longer active in the business, but sat drinking tea with jam and talking to the customers.

Laptev bent down and kissed his hand, then kissed him on the lips.

"It's been a long time since we've seen each other, my dear sir," said the old man. "A long time. So, am I to congratulate you on having taken the marriage vows? Well then, so be it, I congratulate you." And he put out his lips for a kiss. Laptev leaned over and kissed him.

"Well, and have you brought your young lady?" the old man asked, and without waiting for an answer, turned to one of the customers and said, "I herewith beg to inform you, Papa, that I am about to enter into marriage with such and such a maiden. . . . Yes. But as for asking Papa's blessing or advice, that's not in the rules. Nowadays they have their own ideas. When I married I was over forty, but I fell at my father's feet and asked his advice. Nothing like that today."

The old man was delighted to see his son, but considered it unseemly to be affectionate with him, or in any way to display his joy. His voice and his manner of saying "your young lady" plunged Laptev into the same ill-humor he always experienced on coming to the warehouse. Here every detail reminded him of the past, when he used to be whipped and put on Lenten fare; he knew that even now the boys were flogged and given bloody noses, and that when these boys grew up, they in turn would do the same. He had only to spend five minutes in the warehouse to feel that he was about to be scolded or punched in the nose.

Fyodor slapped one of the customers on the shoulder and said to his brother, "Here, Alyosha, let me introduce our benefactor from Tambov, Grigory Timofeich. He well might serve as an example to the young men of today—he's past fifty, and the father of infants!"

The clerks laughed, and the customer, a pale, scrawny, old man, joined them.

"Nature in excess of the norm," commented the senior clerk, who was standing near the counter. "Consider the source."

The senior clerk, a tall man of about fifty, with a dark beard, spectacles, and a pencil behind his ear, generally expressed his ideas abstrusely, with farfetched allusions, while a sly smile made it evident that he attached a particular and subtle significance to his own words. He liked to obscure his speech with bookish words, which he understood in his own way, and often gave to perfectly ordinary words a meaning they did not possess. For example, the word "notwithstanding"; when categorically expressing an opinion, in order to forestall any contradiction, he would extend his right arm and enunciate: "notwithstanding!" And the surprising thing was that the other clerks and the customers understood him perfectly. His name was Ivan Vasilich Pochatkin, and he came from Kashira. On congratulating Laptev, he expressed himself thus: "On your part it is the reward of valor, for the female heart is a Shamil."

Another important person in the warehouse was the clerk Makeichev, a plump, stolid man with a bald head and blond whiskers. He went up to Laptev and respectfully congratulated him in an undertone: "I have the honor, sir. . . . The Lord has heard your parents' prayers, sir. God be praised, sir."

The other clerks followed with their congratulations. They were all fashionably dressed and looked like thoroughly honest, well-bred men. Between every two or three words they put in a "sir," which made their rapidly spoken congratulations—"best wishes, sir, for happiness, sir"— sound like the hiss of a whip lash: "Whshsh-s-s-s!"

Laptev was soon bored with all this and longed to go home, but it was awkward to leave. For the sake of propriety he was obliged to spend at least two hours in the warehouse. He walked away from the counter and began asking Makeichev if everything had gone well during the summer, and whether there was anything new. The clerk, avoiding his eyes, answered him respectfully. A crop-eared boy in a gray smock handed Laptev a glass of tea without a saucer. A moment later another boy stumbled over a box in passing and almost fell, whereupon the decorous Makeichev was abruptly transformed; his face became fierce and malicious, the face of a monster.

"Keep on your feet!" he shouted.

The clerks were happy that the young master had married and at last returned; they cast inquisitive, friendly glances at him, each considering it his duty to make some deferential, agreeable remark in passing. But Laptev was convinced that it was all insincere, that they only flattered him because they feared him. He could never forget how fifteen years ago a clerk who was mentally ill had run out into the street barefoot, in nothing but his underwear, and, shaking his fists at the masters' windows, cried out that he was being worked to death, and how, when the poor man recovered, the clerks long afterwards continued to ridicule him, reminding him that he had shouted "Explorers!" instead of "Exploiters!"

Conditions in general were very bad for the employees at Laptevs', and it had long been a subject of talk for the whole market. The worst of it was that the old man, Fyodor Stepanych, adhered to a somewhat Asiatic policy in his treatment of them; thus, no one knew the wages of his favorites, Pochatkin and Makeichev; actually they received three thousand a year and bonuses, no more, but he made out that he paid them seven. Every year bonuses were given to all the clerks, but always covertly, so that those who received little were bound out of pride to say that they got more. Not one boy knew when he would be made a clerk; not one clerk knew whether or not his employer was satisfied with him. Nothing was directly forbidden, so they had no way of knowing exactly what was and what was not permitted. They were not forbidden to marry, but they did not marry for fear of displeasing the master and losing their jobs. They were allowed to have friends and pay visits, but at nine o'clock the gates were locked, and every morning the master suspiciously inspected each employee, trying to detect the smell of vodka: "Now then, breathe!"

Every holiday the employees were obliged to go to early mass and to stand in church where the old man could see them. The fasts were strictly observed. On festive occasions, such as the name day of the master or any member of his family, the clerks had to take up a collection and present an album or a cake from Fley's. They lived three or four in a room on the lower floor and in the lodge of the house in Pyatnitsky Street. At dinner, although a plate was set before each of them, they ate from a common bowl. If one of the masters came in while they were at the table, they all stood up.

Laptev was conscious of the fact that only those among them who had been corrupted by the old man's training could seriously consider him a benefactor; the others must have looked upon him as an enemy and an "explorer." Now, after an absence of six months, he saw no change for the better; there was even something new that boded no good. His brother Fyodor, who had always been quiet, thoughtful, and extremely refined, now ran about the warehouse with a pencil behind his ear, looking like an energetic businessman, slapping customers on the back and shouting "Friends!" to the clerks. He appeared to be playing some sort of role, and Alexei did not recognize him in the part.

The old man's voice boomed on uninterruptedly. Having nothing to do, he was giving advice to one of the customers, telling him how he ought to live his life and conduct his business, always holding himself up as an example. This boastfulness, this coercive, authoritarian tone, Laptev had heard ten, fifteen, and twenty years ago. The old man idolized himself; from what he said it always appeared that he had brought joy to his wife and all her relations, had been magnanimous to his children, a benefactor to his clerks and employees, and that the entire street and all his acquaintances felt impelled to pray eternally for him; whatever he did was right, and if things went wrong for other people, it was only because they had not consulted him—without his advice nothing could succeed. In church he always stood in the foremost place, and even made observations to the priests when, in his opinion, they were not conducting the service properly, and he believed that this was pleasing to God, because God loved him.

By two o'clock everyone in the warehouse was hard at work except the old man, whose voice went booming on. To avoid the appearance of idleness, Laptev took some trimmings from one of the workgirls and let her go; then he turned to one of the customers, a merchant from Vologda, listened to what he had to say, and told a clerk to attend to him.

"A.V.T.!" was heard on all sides (prices were denoted by letters in the warehouse, and goods by numbers). "R.I.T.!"

As he went out Laptev said good-bye to no one but Fyodor.

"Tomorrow I shall bring my wife to Pyatnitsky Street," he said, "but I warn you, if Father says one rude word to her, I shall not remain there an instant."

"You're still the same," sighed Fyodor. "Marriage hasn't changed you. You must make allowances for the old man. Till tomorrow, then. Eleven o'clock. We shall be waiting impatiently. Come directly after mass."

"I don't go to mass."

"Well, it's all the same. The important thing is not to be later than eleven, so you'll be in time to pray to God and have lunch with us. Greet my little sister, and kiss her hand for me. I have a presentiment I shall love her," he added with complete sincerity. "I envy you, brother!" he called after Alexei, as he descended the stairs.

"Why is it he keeps shrinking into himself in that shy way, as though he felt naked?" Laptev wondered, as he walked along Nikolsky Street, trying to understand the change that had taken place in Fyodor. "And he speaks a new language, too; 'Brother, dear brother; God has sent us joy; pray to God'—exactly like Shchedrin's Iudushka."

VI

The following day, which was Sunday, at eleven o'clock in the morning, Laptev and his wife were driving along Pyatnitsky Street in a light, one-horse carriage. He dreaded some possible vagary on the part of Fyodor Stepanych, and even now felt ill at ease.

After spending two nights in her husband's house, Yulia Sergeyevna considered her marriage a mistake, a catastrophe, the horror of which would have been unendurable had she been forced to live with him in any other city. But Moscow diverted her; she liked the streets, the houses, the churches, and if it had been possible to drive about in one of those splendid sleighs drawn by costly horses, to drive all day, flying along from morning to night, breathing the cold autumn air, perhaps she would not have felt quite so unhappy.

Near a white, newly stuccoed, two-story house, the coachman pulled up the horse and turned to the right. It was apparent that they were expected; two policemen stood at the gate with the porter, who was wearing a new caftan, high boots, and galoshes. The entire area, from the middle of the street to the gate and across the yard to the porch, was strewn with fresh sand. The porter took off his hat, and the policemen saluted. Fyodor, looking exceedingly grave, met them near the porch.

"Very happy to make your acquaintance, little sister," he said, kissing Yulia's hand. "You are very welcome."

He took her arm and led her upstairs, then along a corridor through a crowd of men and women. The anteroom was also crowded, and smelled of incense.

"I shall introduce you to our father presently," Fyodor whispered in the midst of a sepulchral silence. "A venerable old man, paterfamilias."

In the large reception hall Fyodor Stepanych, in obvious expectation, was standing by a table prepared for the service; with him stood a deacon and the priest in a calotte. The old man gave Yulia his hand without saying a word. Everyone was silent. Yulia was embarrassed.

The priest and the deacon put on their vestments. A censer was brought in, scattering sparks and giving off a smell of incense and charcoal. Candles were lit. The clerks entered the hall on tiptoe and stood in two rows along the wall. There was absolute silence, not even a cough was heard.

"The blessing of the Lord," began the deacon.

The service was read with great solemnity, nothing was omitted, and two canticles were sung: "To Sweetest Jesus," and "Holy Mother of God," the singers holding sheets of music up before them. Laptev saw how disconcerted his wife was. All during the singing of the canticles, and while the singers were intoning "Lord, have mercy on us" in different keys, he was under a mental strain, constantly expecting the old man to look round and make a remark such as: "You don't know how to cross yourself." Moreover, he was vexed: why this crowd? Why all the ceremony with priests and a choir? It was too bourgeois. But when Yulia, with his father, placed her head under the Gospels, and went down on her knees several times, he realized that she liked all this, and he felt relieved.

At the end of the service, during the Prayer for the Prolongation of Days, the priest gave the old man and Alexei the cross to kiss, but when Yulia Sergeyevna approached, he put his hand over the cross and indicated that he wanted to speak. Signs were made to the singers to stop.

"The prophet Samuel," began the priest, "was sent by the Lord to Bethlehem, 'and the elders of the town trembled at his coming, and said, Comest thou peaceably? And he said, Peaceably: I am come to sacrifice unto the Lord: sanctify yourselves and come with me to the sacrifice.' Even so, Yulia, servant of God, shall we ask thee of thy advent to this house: 'Comest thou peaceably?' "

Yulia flushed with emotion. When he had finished, the priest gave her the cross to kiss, then in a quite different tone he said, "Now Fyodor Fyodorych must marry. It's time."

The singing was resumed, people commenced to move about, and the room grew noisy. The old man, deeply moved, his eyes brimming with tears, kissed Yulia three times, made the sign of the cross over her face, and said, "This is your home. I am an old man and need nothing."

The clerks congratulated her and spoke a few words, but

the singing was so loud it was impossible to catch what they said. Lunch was served, and champagne. Yulia sat next to the old man, and he talked to her about families living together in one house, telling her it was not good to live apart, that separation and discord lead to disruption.

"I've made the money, and all the children do is spend it," he said. "Now, you come and live in this house with me, and hold onto it. It's time for an old man to rest."

Yulia was continually catching glimpses of Fyodor, so like her husband, except that he was shier and more restless; he kept fussing about her, frequently kissing her hand.

"We are simple people, little sister," he said, and spots of red came out on his face as he spoke. "We live simply, like Russians and like Christians, little sister."

Laptev was very pleased that everything had gone well, and that, contrary to his expectations, nothing untoward had occurred. On the way home he said to his wife, "You're surprised that such a powerful, broad-shouldered father should have such undersized, narrow-chested sons as Fyodor and me. But it's quite understandable. My father married my mother when he was forty-five and she was only seventeen. She used to turn pale and tremble in his presence. Nina was born first—born of a comparatively healthy mother, therefore she turned out better, stronger than we were. By the time we were conceived and born, Mother had been worn out by constant fear. I can remember Father training me, or, to put it bluntly, beating me, before I was five years old. He used to whip me with a birch rod, pull my ears, and hit me on the head; every morning when I woke up my first thought was: will I be beaten today? To play or romp about was forbidden us; we had to go to morning service and to early mass, kiss the hands of priests and monks, and sing hymns at home. You are religious, and you love all that, but I am afraid of religion; when I pass a church I think of my childhood and am horrified. As soon as I was eight years old I was placed in the warehouse; I worked like any common boy, and it was very bad for my health, because there I was beaten almost daily. Later, when I went to high school, I had classes till dinnertime, then I had to sit in that warehouse till evening; and this went on until I was twenty-two and met Yartsev at the university. That Yartsev did me a lot of good. I tell you what"—Laptev laughed delightedly—"let's go and visit Yartsev right now! He's a very fine person! How touched he will be!"

VII

One Saturday in November, Anton Rubinstein was conducting a symphony concert. It was very crowded and hot. Laptev stood behind the columns, while his wife and Kostya Kochevoi sat down in front in the third or fourth row. At the very beginning of the intermission "a certain person," Polina Nikolaevna Rassudina, quite unexpectedly walked by him. Since the day of his wedding the thought of a possible meeting with her repeatedly crossed his mind, causing him some anxiety. Now, her frank, straightforward gaze reminded him that in all this time he had not brought himself to make any explanation, had failed even to write two or three friendly lines, had behaved, in fact, as though he were hiding from her; he blushed with shame. Impetuously and warmly she pressed his hand.

"Have you seen Yartsev?" And without waiting for an answer, she rushed on, with broad strides, as though someone were pushing her from behind.

She was an extremely thin, homely woman, with a long nose, and a face that always looked tired and worn; it seemed to cost her a great effort to keep her eyes open and remain on her feet. She had beautiful, dark eyes, and an intelligent, kind, sincere expression, but her movements were angular and abrupt. It was not easy to talk to her, because she could neither listen nor talk calmly, and loving her was very difficult. Sometimes when she stayed with Laptev she would laugh a great deal, hide her face in her hands, declare that for her love was not the most important thing in life, and would be as coy as a girl of seventeen, and he would have to put out all the candles before kissing her. She was thirty years old, and married to a schoolteacher, but she had not lived with her husband for a long time. She supported herself by giving music lessons and playing in quartets.

During the *Ninth Symphony* she again appeared, as if by chance, but the crowd of men standing like a thick wall behind the columns prevented her from going on, and she was forced to remain there. Laptev saw that she was wearing the same velvet blouse she had worn to concerts last year and the year before. Her gloves were new, and she carried a new but cheap fan. She loved clothes, but she did not know how to dress, and grudged the money for it; as a result she dressed badly and negligently, and striding rapidly down the street on her way to a lesson she might easily have been taken for a young novice.

The audience applauded and shouted *bis*.

"You shall spend this evening with me," she said, going up to Laptev and looking sternly at him. "From here we'll go and have tea together. Do you hear? I demand this of you. You are greatly indebted to me, and you haven't the moral right to refuse me this trifle."

"Very well, let us go," Laptev acquiesced.

There were endless curtain calls after the symphony, and the audience was slow to leave. Laptev could not go without speaking to his wife; he waited for her at the door.

"I am desperate for tea!" Polina Nikolaevna complained. "My soul is parched."

"You can get tea here," said Laptev. "Let's go into the buffet."

"I have no money to throw away on bartenders. I'm not a merchant's wife."

He offered her his arm, but she refused in a long, tedious statement he had heard many times before, to the effect that she did not count herself a member of the weak, fair sex, and therefore did not require the assistance of gentlemen.

While talking to him she kept glancing at the audience and greeting her acquaintances, pupils, and fellow students in her courses at the conservatory. She grasped their hands convulsively, and gave them a quick, sharp tug. All at once her shoulders began to twitch and she trembled as though in a fever; then, with a look of dismay, she quietly said, "Whom have you married? Where were your eyes—were you out of your mind? What did you see in that silly, worthless girl? I loved you for your mind, your soul, while that china doll wants nothing but your money!"

"Let us drop that, Polina," he entreated. "Everything you can say to me about my marriage I have already said to myself—many times. Do not add to my suffering."

Yulia Sergeyevna appeared wearing a black dress and a large diamond brooch that her father-in-law had sent her after the service. She was followed by her retinue: Kochevoi, two doctors of their acquaintance, an officer, and a plump young man in a student's uniform, called Kish.

"You go on with Kostya," Laptev said to his wife. "I'll come later."

Yulia nodded and went on. Polina Nikolaevna gazed after her. A shudder ran through her body, she twitched nervously, and in her eyes there was a look of repugnance, hatred, and pain.

Laptev was afraid to go home with her, foreseeing a disagreeable discussion, bitterness, and tears; he suggested they have tea in a restaurant.

"No, no. We'll go to my place. Don't dare to mention restaurants to me!"

She did not like being in restaurants because she thought the air was polluted by tobacco smoke and the breath of men. She had a peculiar prejudice against any man she was not personally acquainted with, considering them all depraved and capable of attacking her at any minute. Furthermore, restaurant music irritated her to the point of making her head ache.

When they came out of the Hall of the Nobility, they took a cab in Ostozhenka and drove to Savelovsky Lane, where Rassudina lived. All the way there Laptev was thinking about her. It was true that he owed her a great deal. He had met her at Yartsev's, when she was instructing his friend in music theory. She fell deeply in love with Laptev, and her love was completely disinterested. Her relations with him did not alter her way of life; she continued to give lessons, and, as before, to exhaust herself with work. Thanks to her, he began to understand and love music, which he had cared very little for until then.

"Half my kingdom for a glass of tea!" she said in a stifled voice, having covered her mouth with her muff to avoid catching cold. "I gave five lessons today—curse them! My pupils are such blockheads, such rubber stamps! I was so infuriated, I nearly died! And I don't know when this slavery will ever end. I'm worn out. As soon as I can scrape together three hundred rubles I'm going to drop the whole business and go to the Crimea. I'll lie on the beach and soak up the ozone. How I love the sea—oh, how I love the sea!"

"You won't go anywhere," Laptev said. "First, you'll never save the money, and second, you'd begrudge spending it if you did. Forgive me, but again, I repeat: is it really less humiliating to accumulate this money kopeck by kopeck, from idlers who take your lessons merely because they have nothing else to do, than to borrow it from your friends?"

"I have no friends!" she replied irritably. "And I shall ask you to stop saying such stupid things. The working class, to which I belong, has one privilege: the consciousness of its incorruptibility, and the right to reject the patronage of tradesmen—and to disdain them. Oh, no—you don't buy me! I'm no Yulichka!"

Laptev made no attempt to pay the driver, knowing it would only provoke a deluge of words, all of which he had heard many times before. She herself paid.

Rassudina lived in a small furnished room in the flat of a solitary lady who provided her with meals. Her large Becker piano was for the present at Yartsev's in Great Nikolsky Street, where she went daily to practice. In her room there were armchairs in slipcovers, a bed with a white summer quilt, flowers that belonged to her landlady, and oleographs on the walls; there was absolutely nothing to suggest that the room was occupied by a woman—and a woman of education. There was no dressing table, no books, not even a writing table. She obviously went to bed as soon as she got home and went out as soon as she got up in the morning.

The cook brought in the samovar. Polina Nikolaevna made the tea and, still shivering—it was cold in the room—began to abuse the singers who had sung the *Ninth Symphony*. Her eyes closed with emotion. She drank one glass of tea, then another, and a third.

"And so you are married," she said. "Don't worry, I'm not going to pine away; I shall be able to tear you out of my heart. Only it's annoying and bitter for me to find out that you are just as rotten as all the others—that what you want in a woman is not a mind, an intellect, but a body, beauty, youth. Youth!" she snorted, as if mimicking someone. Then she burst into laughter. "Youth! You want purity, *Reinheit! Reinheit!*" When she had stopped laughing her eyes filled with tears.

"Are you happy, at least?" she asked.

"No."

"Does she love you?"

"No."

Laptev, agitated and unhappy, got up and began to pace the room.

"No," he repeated. "If you want to know, Polina, I am miserable. What can I do? I've made a stupid mistake, and now it cannot be rectified. One must take it philosophically. She married without love, foolishly, perhaps even for money, but without reasoning; now she evidently realizes her mistake and is suffering. I see it. At night we sleep together, but in the daytime she's afraid to be alone with me for five minutes, and seeks distraction, society. With me she feels ashamed and frightened."

"But she does take money from you?"

"That's stupid, Polina!" he cried. "She takes money from me because it makes absolutely no difference to her whether she has it or not. She's a pure and honest girl. She married me simply because she wanted to get away from her father, and that is all."

"And you are convinced that she would have married you even if you had not been rich?" Rassudina asked.

"I am convinced of nothing," he replied wearily, "of nothing. I don't understand anything. For God's sake, Polina, let's not talk about it!"

"Do you love her?"

"Desperately."

They fell silent. She drank her fourth glass of tea, and he paced the room, thinking that by now his wife was probably having supper at the doctors' club.

"But is it really possible to love without knowing why?" Rassudina asked with a shrug of her shoulders. "No, it's the prompting of animal passion! You're intoxicated! You're poisoned by that beautiful body, that *Reinheit!* Get away from me! You're filthy! Go back to her!" She made a despairing gesture, then picked up his hat and flung it at him.

He put on his fur coat and left without a word, but she ran into the passage after him, and, convulsively seizing his arm above the elbow, broke into sobs.

"Stop, Polina, that's enough!" he said, but he was unable to unclasp her fingers. "Calm yourself, please!"

She closed her eyes, turned pale, and her long nose became an unpleasant waxy color, like that of a corpse; and

still he could not unclasp her fingers. She fainted. He carefully lifted her up, laid her on the bed, then sat beside her for
ten minutes or more, until she regained consciousness. Her
hands were cold and her pulse was weak and uneven.

"Go home," she said, opening her eyes. "Go away, otherwise I shall begin howling again. I have to get control of
myself."

When he left her, instead of going to the doctors' club
where his friends were expecting him, he went home. On the
way he reproachfully asked himself why he had not
arranged his life with this woman who loved him, and who
was, in essence, his wife and friend. She was the only
human being who was attached to him; and besides, would
it not have been a more worthy and more gratifying task to
give happiness, peace, and refuge to that clever, proud
woman who was so oppressed by work? Was it for him, he
asked himself, to lay claim to youth and beauty, to that happiness which could not be, and which, like a penalty or
mockery, for three months now had kept him in a state of
melancholy and depression? The honeymoon was long over,
and yet, absurd as it seemed, he still did not know what sort
of person his wife was. To her school friends and her father
she wrote long, five-page letters, and could always find
something to say, but to him she talked only of the weather,
or informed him that it was time for dinner. When she said
her long prayers before going to bed, kissing her many
crosses and ikons, he watched her with animosity, and
thought: "There she is praying, but what about? What is she
praying for?" And in his thoughts he outraged both himself
and her, telling himself that when he took her in his arms he
was only taking what he had paid for; but it was appalling.
Had she been a lusty, bold, sinful woman, instead of a young
girl, meek, devout, with the pure eyes of innocence. . . . Before they were married her piety had touched him, but now
her conventional, established views were like a barrier behind which the real truth could not be seen. By now every

element in his life with her caused him to suffer. When she sat beside him in the theater and sighed or laughed, it pained him that she enjoyed herself alone and was unwilling to share her delight with him. She was on good terms with all his friends, and it was singular that they already knew what she was like, while he knew absolutely nothing about her, and could only brood in silent jealousy.

When he got home he put on his dressing gown and slippers and sat down in his study to read a novel. His wife was not at home. But within half an hour the bell rang, and Pyotr's muffled footsteps could be heard as he ran to open the door. It was Yulia. She went into the study, still wearing her fur coat, her cheeks crimson from the frosty air.

"There's a tremendous fire in Presnya," she announced breathlessly. "The sky is glowing! I'm going to see it with Konstantin Ivanych."

"Enjoy yourself."

Laptev felt reassured by the sight of her fresh, healthy face, with its look of childish fear. He read for half an hour, then went to bed.

The following day Polina Nikolaevna sent to the warehouse two books she had borrowed from him, and all his letter and photographs; with them came a note consisting of one word: *"Basta!"*

VIII

By the end of October, Nina Fyodorovna had undergone an unmistakable relapse. She was rapidly growing thinner, and there was a change in her face. She continued to believe that she was recovering, despite the severe pain, and each day she got up and dressed as though she were well, then lay on the bed the whole day. Toward the end she became very talkative. She would lie on her back and speak in a low voice, breathing with great difficulty. She died suddenly in the following circumstances.

It was a clear, moonlight night, and the sounds of people tobogganing on the fresh snow could be heard in her room. She lay on her back, and Sasha, who had no one to relieve her now, sat dozing at her mother's side.

"I can't remember his father's name," Nina Fyodorovna was saying in a low voice, "but he was called Ivan Kochevoi. . . . a poor clerk. He was a terrible drunkard, God rest his soul! He used to come to us every month, and we gave him a pound of sugar and two ounces of tea. And sometimes money, too, of course. Yes. . . . And then this is what happened: he began drinking so heavily, our Kochevoi, that he died—consumed by vodka. He left a son, a little boy of seven . . . a poor little orphan. . . . We took him in and hid him in the steward's quarters. He lived there a whole year, and Papa never knew. And when he did find out he only shrugged and said nothing. When Kostya, the little orphan, was eleven, I took him from one school to another, but not one would take him. And he cried. . . . 'What's the matter, little silly, why are you crying?' I asked him. Then I took him to the Razgulyai School, and there, God bless them, they took him. The little boy began going to school every day, from Pyatnitsky Street to Razgulyai and back again on foot. . . . Alyosha paid for him. By the grace of God, the boy studied hard, he grasped everything, and turned out well. Now he's a lawyer in Moscow, and Alyosha's friend . . . and he's highly educated. . . . We did not disdain a fellow creature, but took him into our home, and now, I suppose, he prays for us. . . . Yes. . . ."

She spoke more and more slowly, and with long pauses; after a brief silence she suddenly drew herself up to a sitting position.

"I feel . . . something is not. . . . Something seems to be wrong," she said. "God have mercy on me! Oh, I can't breathe!"

Sasha knew her mother was going to die soon; now, seeing her face suddenly grow pinched, she guessed it was the end and was frightened.

"Mama, dear, you mustn't!" she sobbed. "You mustn't!"

"Run to the kitchen.... Have them go for your father.... I am very ill...."

Sasha ran through all the rooms, calling, but none of the servants was in the house; she found only Lida, asleep on a chest in the dining room, with no pillow and all her clothes on. Sasha ran into the yard just as she was, without her galoshes, and then into the street. Her nurse was sitting on a bench at the gate, watching the tobogganing. From the toboggan slope by the river came the sounds of a military band.

"Nurse, Mama's dying!" Sasha sobbed. "You must go for Papa!"

The nurse went upstairs to the bedroom, and after looking at the sick woman, thrust a lighted candle into her hands. Sasha rushed about in terror, pleading with she knew not whom, to go for her papa. At last she put on her coat and a kerchief and ran into the street. She had learned from the servants that her father had another wife and two children with whom he lived in Bazarny Street. She ran out of the gate and turned left, crying and frightened of the strangers. Soon she began sinking into the snow and was shivering with cold.

She met an empty sleigh but did not take it, fearing perhaps that the man would drive her out of town, rob her, and throw her into the cemetery—at tea the servants had talked of such a case. She walked on and on, sobbing and panting with exhaustion. When she came to Bazarny Street she asked where Mr. Panaurov lived. A woman she did not know spent a long time explaining the way to her, then, seeing that she did not understand, took her by the hand and led her to a one-story house set back from the street. The door was unlocked and Sasha ran through the entry, down a corridor, and at last found herself in a bright, warm room, where her father was sitting by the samovar with a lady and two little girls. But by now she was unable to utter a word and only sobbed.

"I suppose Mama is bad? . . . Tell me, daughter, is Mama bad?"

He became alarmed and sent for a cab.

When they reached home they found Nina Fyodorovna propped up on pillows with a candle in her hand. Her face looked dark and her eyes were closed. Crowded together in the doorway stood the nurse, the cook, a housemaid, the peasant Prokofy, and several other simple people who were complete strangers. The nurse was giving them orders in a whisper, but they appeared not to understand. Lida, pale and sleepy, stood at the far end of the room by the window, staring at her mother with a grave expression.

Panaurov took the candle out of Nina Fyodorovna's hand and flung it onto the chest of drawers, scowling with disgust.

"This is dreadful!" he exclaimed with a shudder. "Nina, you must lie down," he said tenderly. "Lie down, dear."

She looked up, but did not recognize him. They laid her down on her back.

When the priest and the doctor, Sergei Borisych, arrived, the servants all devoutly crossed themselves and began to pray.

"It's a bad business," the doctor said thoughtfully, as he went into the drawing room. "And she was still young, not yet forty."

The little girls could be heard sobbing loudly. Panaurov, pale, with tears in his eyes, went up to the doctor and said in a weak, languid tone, "Will you be so good, my dear friend, as to send a telegram to Moscow? I'm definitely not up to it."

The doctor got out the ink and wrote the following telegram to his daughter:

PANAUROVA DIED EIGHT O'CLOCK THIS EVENING. TELL
YOUR HUSBAND: MORTGAGED HOUSE FOR SALE
DVORYANSKY STREET. NINE THOUSAND CASH. AUCTION
ON TWELFTH. ADVISE NOT TO MISS.

IX

Laptev lived in one of the lanes off Maly Dmitrovka, not
far from Stary Pimen. In addition to a large house facing the
street, he rented a two-story lodge in the yard for his friend
Kochevoi, a counselor at law, whom all the Laptevs called
Kostya, because he had grown up in their care. Opposite this
lodge was another, also of two stories, in which there lived
a French family consisting of a husband and wife and their
five daughters.

A 20-degree frost had whitened all the windows. When
he woke up in the morning, Kostya, with a preoccupied expression, first took fifteen drops of a certain medicine, then
got two dumbbells from the bookcase and set about his
gymnastics. He was tall and very thin, with a large reddish
mustache; but the most conspicuous feature of his appearance was a pair of extraordinarily long legs.

Pyotr, a middle-aged peasant wearing a jacket and cotton
breeches tucked into high boots, brought in the samovar and
made tea.

"'It's fine weather today, Konstantin Ivanych!" he said.

"Yes, it is. But it's a pity, brother, that we can't get on
without such exclamations."

Pyotr sighed out of politeness.

"What are the little girls doing?"

"The priest has not come, and Alexei Fyodorych himself
is giving them their lessons."

Kostya found a spot on the window that was not covered

with frost and trained his binoculars on the windows of the house opposite, where the French family lived.

"Can't see," he said.

Meanwhile, Alexei Fyodorych was giving Sasha and Lida religious instruction downstairs. They had been living in Moscow for the past six weeks, and, with a governess, were installed on the lower floor of the lodge. Three times a week a teacher from a city school, and a priest, came to give them lessons. Sasha was going through the New Testament, and Lida had recently begun the Old Testament. At the last lesson she had been set the task of learning everything up to Abraham.

"So, Adam and Eve had two sons," said Laptev. "Excellent. And what were their names? Now, try to remember!"

Lida, with her customary solemn expression, moved her lips without making a sound and stared at the table. Sasha, the elder girl, looked at her in misery.

"You know very well, don't be uneasy," said Laptev. "Now, what were Adam's sons called?"

"Abel and Cabel," whispered Lida.

"Cain and Abel," Laptev corrected her.

A big tear rolled down Lida's cheek and dropped onto the book. Sasha flushed and looked down; she, too, was about to burst into tears. Laptev felt so sorry for them he could not speak; there was a lump in his throat and he got up from the table to light a cigarette. At that moment Kochevoi came downstairs with a newspaper in his hand. The little girls stood up and curtsied without looking at him.

"For God's sake, Kostya, you give them their lesson," Laptev pleaded. "I'm afraid I shall cry, too, and I have to go to the warehouse before dinner."

"Very well."

Alexei Fyodorych went out. Kostya, looking very serious, sat down and drew the Scriptures toward him.

"Well, where have you got to?" he asked.

"She knows about the Flood," said Sasha.

"The Flood? Good! Let's finish off the Flood. Fire away!"

Kostya skimmed through the story of the Flood in the book and said, "I must point out to you that, actually, there never was a Flood such as they describe here. Nor was there any such man as Noah. Several thousands of years before the birth of Christ, there was a rather unusual inundation of the earth, which is mentioned, not only in the Hebrew Bible, but also in the books of other ancient peoples: the Greeks, the Chaldeans, and the Hindus. But, whatever it may have been, this inundation could not have submerged the entire earth. The plains, perhaps. But the mountains very likely came through. It's all right to read this book, of course, but I wouldn't take it too seriously."

Again the tears began to flow; Lida turned away and all at once began sobbing so loudly that Kostya jumped up from the table in consternation.

"I want to go home to my papa and nurse!" she wailed.

Sasha, too, began to cry. Kostya went upstairs and called Yulia Sergeyevna on the telephone.

"Darling, the girls are crying again. Can't do a thing with them."

Yulia Sergeyevna ran across from the big house with only a knitted shawl over her dress, and got chilled through: she immediately began to comfort the children.

"Believe me, do believe me," she pleaded, "your papa is coming today. He has sent a telegram. You're grieving for Mama, and I am, too, but there is nothing we can do. We must accept the will of God."

When they had stopped crying she wrapped them up and took them out for a drive. First they drove along Maly Dmitrovka and past the Strastnoi Monastery on Tvorskaya Street. They stopped near the Iverskaya Chapel, where they lit candles and knelt down and prayed. On the way back they went to Filipov's and had Lenten cakes sprinkled with poppy seeds.

The Laptevs dined between two and three. They were served by Pyotr, who, besides waiting on them, ran to the post office, to the warehouse, and to the district court for Kostya; he spent the evenings making cigarettes, the nights running to open the door, and at five o'clock in the morning he was lighting the fires in the stoves. Nobody knew when he slept. He delighted in opening Seltzer bottles, which he did deftly, noiselessly, and without spilling a drop.

"Good luck!" said Kostya, tossing off a glass of vodka before the soup.

At first Yulia Sergeyevna did not like Kostya; his bass voice, and his expressions, such as: "kicked him out," "land him one on the beak," "filth," "produce the samovar"; his habit of clinking glasses and becoming maudlin over a drink, all seemed trivial to her. But when she knew him better, she began to feel very much at ease with him. He was open with her, and liked to sit quietly talking to her in the evening; he even let her read the novels he had written, which up to that time he had kept secret even from such friends as Laptev and Yartsev. Because she did not want to hurt his feelings, she praised them, and this delighted him, as he intended sooner or later to become a famous writer.

In his novels he wrote only of the country and life on the estates of large landowners, although he had very rarely even seen the country—and then only when visiting acquaintances at a *dacha*—and had been at a country estate only once in his life, when on legal business in Volokolamsk. He avoided any element of love in his writing as though he were ashamed of it, but he put in frequent descriptions of nature, in which he liked using phrases such as "the wayward line of the mountains," "the wondrous forms of clouds," "the consonance of mysterious rhythms." The fact that his novels had never been published he attributed solely to censorship.

During dinner Laptev said: "It's an amazing business; again I am simply baffled by my brother. He said to me that we must find out the date of the firm's centenary so that we can petition to be elevated to the nobility! And he said this in all seriousness. What has happened to him? Frankly, I'm beginning to be worried."

They talked of Fyodor, and of how it now seemed to be the fashion to affect some sort of pose. Fyodor, for instance, was trying to appear like a simple merchant, though he no longer was one, and when the teacher from the school of which old Laptev was the patron came for his salary, Fyodor even changed his voice and his walk, behaving as though he were someone in a position of authority.

After dinner there was nothing to do so they sat in the study. They talked about the decadents, and *The Maid of Orleans,* then Kostya recited a monologue; he thought he gave a very successful imitation of Ermolova. Later they played vint. The little girls had not gone back to the lodge, but sat together in one armchair looking pale and sad; they were listening to the street noises, wondering if their father was coming. In the evening when it was dark and the candles had been lit they felt homesick. Everything upset them—the talk at the card table, Pyotr's footsteps, the crackling in the fireplace, and they could not bear to look at the fire. At such times they tried not to cry, but their hearts were heavy. They could not understand how anyone could talk and laugh when their mother was dead.

"What did you see through the binoculars today?" Yulia Sergeyevna asked Kostya.

"Today nothing. But yesterday the old Frenchman himself took a bath."

At seven o'clock Yulia and Kostya went to the Maly Theater, and Laptev was left with the children.

"Your papa should be here by now," he said, looking at his watch. "The train must be late."

The little girls sat in the armchair, huddled together like animals in the cold, while Laptev paced the room, impatiently glancing at his watch. It was quiet in the house.

Shortly before ten o'clock the bell rang and Pyotr went to open the door.

Hearing the familiar voice, the children screamed, sobbed, and ran into the hall. Panaurov was wearing a luxurious fur coat, and his beard and mustache were white with hoarfrost.

"Just a minute, just a minute," he murmured, while Sasha and Lida, laughing and crying, kissed his cold hands, his cap, his coat. With the nonchalance of a handsome man who has been spoiled by love, he caressed the children languidly, and went into the study.

"I shall not be with you long, my friends," he said, rubbing his hands. "Tomorrow I go to St. Petersburg. They have promised to transfer me to another city."

He was staying at the Dresden Hotel.

X

Ivan Gavrilych Yartsev was a frequent visitor at the Laptevs'. He was a healthy, vigorous man with black hair and an intelligent, pleasant face. He was considered handsome, but lately he had begun to grow stout, which marred both his face and figure; his appearance was also impaired by having his hair cut so close that the scalp showed through. When he was at the university his fellow students used to call him "Slugger" because of his tall and powerful build.

He had taken his degree in philology, together with the Laptev brothers, then he had gone into natural science, and now had a master's degree in chemistry. He had never held a chair in the department, nor even been a laboratory assistant, but taught physics and natural history in a modern school and two girls' high schools. He was enthusiastic about his students, especially the girls, and contended that the rising generation was a remarkable one. In addition to chemistry he studied sociology and Russian history at home, and occasional brief notes which he signed with the initial "Y" appeared in newspapers and journals. He discussed botany and zoology like an historian and approached the solution of any historical problem like a scientist.

Another friend who was like one of the family at the Laptevs' was Kish, known as "the eternal student." He had studied medicine for three years, then had transferred to mathematics, spending two years in every course he took. His father, a provincial pharmacist, sent him forty rubles a month, to which his mother added another ten without her husband's knowledge, and this sufficed not alone for his living expenses, but for such luxuries as an overcoat lined with Polish beaver, gloves, scent, and photographs (he often had photographs of himself taken and distributed them to his friends). He was immaculately clean, timid, and slightly bald, with golden side whiskers close to his ears. He had the air of a man always ready to oblige, and, in fact, was forever fussing over other people's affairs, rushing about with a subscription list, freezing in the early morning at a theater box office to buy tickets for ladies of his acquaintance, or, at the request of a friend, placing an order for a wreath or a bouquet.

It was always said of him: "Kish will go; Kish will do it; Kish will buy it." For the most part the results of these efforts were unfortunate; he was continually being showered with reproaches, or people would forget to pay him for the purchases he made, but he took it all in silence, with merely a sigh for the more awkward occasions. He was never particularly glad or sorry, his stories were long and boring, and his jokes provoked laughter simply because they were pointless. One day, for instance, intending to be funny, he said to Pyotr, "Pyotr, you're not a shoat!" Everyone laughed, he longest of all, so delighted was he with the success of his witticism. Whenever one of the professors was buried, he walked in front with the torchbearers.

Yarsev and Kish usually came to tea in the evening. If

their hosts were not going to the theater or a concert, tea was prolonged till supper. One evening in February, the following conversation took place:

"A work of art is significant and effective only when it contains an idea about some serious social problem," said Kostya, with an angry look at Yartsev. "If the work contains a protest against serfdom, or the author takes up arms against high society and its fatuousness, then it can be effective and significant. Those novels and tales where it's: Oh, she fell in love with him, and Ah, he fell out of love with her—such works, I say, are trivial, and the hell with them!"

"I agree with you, Konstantin Ivanych," said Yulia Sergeyevna. "One of them describes a love scene, another a betrayal, and a third a reconciliation. Are there no other themes? There are so many people who are sick, unhappy, and worn out by poverty; to them such books must be revolting."

Laptev was distressed to hear his wife, a young woman not yet twenty-two, reasoning about love with such sober detachment. He suspected the reason for it.

"If poetry does not have the answers to questions that seem important to you," said Yartsev, "you ought to consult books on technical subjects, criminal and financial law; read scientific pamphlets. What would be gained, if, say, in *Romeo and Juliet*, they had a discussion about freedom of speech or the disinfection of prisons, when you can find everything on the subject in special articles and manuals?"

"That's going to extremes, Uncle," Kostya interrupted. "We're not talking about the giants, like Shakespeare and Goethe, we are talking about the hundreds of talented lesser writers, who would be of far greater benefit to us if they would drop love and occupy themselves with propagating knowledge and humane ideas among the masses."

Kish, in a thick, nasal voice, began to recount a story he had recently read. He spoke deliberately, and without omitting the least detail; three minutes passed, five, ten, and still he went on. No one understood what he was talking about, and his face grew more and more apathetic and his eyes more dull.

"Kish, do get on with it!" Yulia Sergeyevna could endure it no longer. "It's really agonizing!"

"Shut up, Kish!" Kostya shouted.

They all laughed, including Kish.

Fyodor arrived. There were red spots on his face as he hurriedly greeted everyone, and immediately led his brother away to the study. Lately he seemed to avoid any gathering of people, preferring to be with one person alone.

"Leave the young people to their laughter, in here you and I can speak from the heart," he said, sitting in a deep armchair at a distance from the lamp. "We haven't seen each other for a long time, dear brother. How long is it since you were last in the warehouse? It must be a week."

"Yes. There's nothing for me to do there. And the old man, I must confess, is very tiresome."

"Of course, they could get on without you and me at the warehouse, but one must have some sort of occupation. 'In the sweat of thy brow shalt thou eat bread,' as they say. God loves work."

Pyotr brought a glass of tea on a tray. Fyodor drank it without sugar and asked for another. He drank a great deal of tea, and could drink as many as ten glasses in an evening.

"Do you know what, brother," he said, getting up and going to Alexei, "leaving sophistry aside, you must get elected to the town council, and then, gradually, by easy stages, we shall get you installed as a member of the board, then as assistant to the mayor. And, as time goes on—you're a clever man, with a good education—you'll be noticed, and they'll send for you in Petersburg. Active members of district and town councils are in vogue there, brother. And look, before you're fifty you'll be a privy councilor with a ribbon across your shoulder."

Laptev did not answer; he understood that all this—being

a privy councilor, wearing a decoration—was what Fyodor himself wanted, and he did not know what to say.

The brothers sat in silence. Fyodor opened his watch and stared at it with strained attention for a very long time, as though he were trying to observe the movement of the hands. The expression on his face struck Laptev as odd.

They were summoned to supper. Laptev went to the dining room, but Fyodor remained in the study. The argument was over and Yartsev was speaking in the tone of a professor delivering a lecture.

"Owing to the diversities in climate, energy, tastes, and growth, equality among men is physically impossible. But civilized man can render this inequality innocuous, as he already has done in the case of swamps and bears. One scientist succeeded in training a cat, a mouse, a falcon, and a sparrow to eat from the same plate, and it is to be hoped that education may yet accomplish as much with human beings. Life is continually advancing, civilization is making enormous progress, and it is plain to see that there will come a time when, for example, the position of the present-day factory worker will appear to us as absurd as the conditions under serfdom, when wenches were bartered for dogs."

"That won't be very soon, not so very soon," said Kostya, smiling ironically, "at least not before Rothschild finds his cellars full of gold absurd. And until that time comes, the worker will be held in a yoke, and grow bloated from hunger. No-o-o sir! That's not the answer, Uncle. We must not wait, we must struggle. If the cat eats from the same plate as the mouse, do you think it's because she's imbued with a consciousness of duty? Of course not! She is compelled to by main force."

"Fyodor and I are rich; our father is a capitalist, a millionaire, you will have to struggle with us!" Laptev said, rubbing his forehead with the palm of his hand. "The idea of anyone struggling with me is something I am unable to grasp. I am rich, but, so far, what has money brought me—

what has this power given me? In what way am I more fortunate than you? My childhood was unbearable; money did
not save me from the rod. When Nina was ill and died, my
money did not help her. If I am not loved, I cannot command
love, though I spend a hundred million."

"But you can do a great deal of good," said Kish.

"Good! What sort of good? Yesterday you spoke to me of
a certain mathematician who was looking for a job. Believe
me, I can do as little for him as you can. I can give him
money, but that's not what he wants. I once asked a well-
known musician to find a place for a destitute violinist, and
the answer I got was: 'You come to me simply because
you're not a musician.' And I say to you: You come to me,
confident of help, because you've never been in the position
of a rich man."

"Why this comparison with the well-known musician, I
do not understand!" Yulia Sergeyevna burst out, and then
blushed. "What has the well-known musician to do with it?"

Her face began to quiver with hatred, and she lowered
her eyes to conceal it. Not only her husband, but everyone
sitting at the table understood what that look meant.

"What has the well-known musician to do with it?" she
quietly repeated. "There is nothing simpler than helping
someone who is poor."

No one spoke. Pyotr served the woodcock, but they all
refused it and ate nothing but salad. Laptev could not remember what he had said, but it was clear to him that it was
not his words that were odious to her, but the mere fact of
his meddling in the conversation.

After supper he went back to his study; tense, his heart
pounding in anticipation of some further humiliation, he
tried to listen to what was going on in the hall. Another argument had begun. Then Yartsev sat down at the piano and
sang a sentimental song. He was a man of many talents: he
could sing, play the piano, and perform sleight-of-hand
tricks.

"You may do as you please, gentlemen, but I do not intend to sit at home," said Yulia. "We must go somewhere."

They decided to drive out of town, and Kish was sent to the merchants' club for a troika. They did not ask Laptev to go with them because his brother was with him, and, besides, it was not customary for him to join them on these drives; but he took it to mean that he bored them, that he was not wanted in the company of these gay young people. His disappointment and bitterness were so intense he almost wept, and he was positively glad that they were treating him so unkindly, so scornfully; he was glad that he was a stupid, dull husband, a moneybags; and it seemed to him that he would be more than glad if, this very night, his wife were to deceive him with his best friend, and afterwards, with a look of hatred, confess it to him. . . . He was jealous of their student friends, of actors, singers, of Yartsev, even of mere acquaintances; and now he passionately wished that she would actually be unfaithful to him; he wanted to find her in the arms of another man, to be outraged, once and for all to be set free from this nightmare. Fyodor drank tea in loud gulps. Now he too prepared to go.

"Our old man must have amaurosis," he said, putting on his fur coat. "His sight is becoming very bad."

Laptev also put on his coat and went out. He accompanied his brother as far as Strastnoi Street, then took a sleigh to Yar's.

"And this is what is known as 'family happiness'!" he said mockingly. "This is love!"

His teeth were chattering, whether from jealousy or some other cause, he did not know. At Yar's he walked about near the tables, listening to a singer of topical songs. He had no ready phrase prepared, in the event he met his own party, and was convinced that if he were to see his wife he would only smile foolishly and pathetically, and everyone would know what had impelled him to come there. He was disconcerted by the loud music, the electric lights, the scent of powder, and the fact that the women he passed stared at him. He stood at the doors trying to see or overhear what was going on in the private rooms, and it seemed to him that he was playing some low, contemptible role, on a level with those women and the singer. He went on to Strelna, but his friends were not there either, and only on his way back, as he was again driving up to Yar's, was he noisily overtaken by another troika. The driver was drunk and shouting, and he heard Yartsev's laugh.

It was after three o'clock when Laptev returned home. Yulia Sergeyevna was already in bed. When he saw that she was not sleeping, he went up to her and said sharply, "I understand your hatred, your aversion—but you might spare me in the presence of others! You might at least conceal your feelings!"

She sat on the side of the bed with her legs dangling, and in the lamplight her eyes looked black and very large.

"I am sorry," she said.

His whole body was shaking; he was so agitated he could not utter a word, but stood before her, silent. She, too, was trembling, and sat looking like a criminal, waiting to hear what he would say.

"How I suffer!" he said at last, clutching his head. "This is hell—I am going out of my mind!"

"And do you think it is easy for me?" she asked in a trembling voice. "Only God knows what it is like for me!"

"You have been my wife for six months now, but you haven't a spark of love in your heart for me—nor is there any hope—not a glimmer! Why did you marry me?" he went on in desperation. "Why? What demon thrust you into my arms? What were you hoping for? What did you want?"

She looked at him in horror, as though terrified that he would kill her.

"Did I fascinate you? Were you in love with me?" he continued, panting for breath. "No! Then, what? Tell me—

what?" he shouted. "Oh, the damned money! The damned money!"

"I swear to God—no!" she cried, crossing herself. She shrank under the insult, and for the first time he heard her cry. "I swear to God, no!" she repeated. "I didn't think of the money. I didn't want it. I simply thought I should do wrong if I refused you. I was afraid of ruining your life and my own. And now I am suffering for my mistake—suffering unbearably!"

She sobbed bitterly; he realized that she was suffering, and, not knowing what to say, he sank to the floor at her feet.

"That's enough, that's enough," he murmured. "I humiliated you because I love you madly." He suddenly kissed her foot, clasping it passionately. "If only a spark of love! Lie to me—tell me a lie! Don't say it's a mistake!" . . .

But she only continued to weep, and he felt that she endured his caresses as an inevitable consequence of her mistake. And she drew the foot he had kissed under her like a bird. He felt sorry for her.

She lay down and covered her head, and he undressed and went to bed. In the morning they both were embarrassed and did not know what to talk about, and it seemed to him that she limped slightly on the foot he had kissed.

Before dinner Panaurov came to say good-bye. Yulia was seized with an irresistible desire to go to her own home; it would be good, she thought, to go away, to have a rest from married life, from this turmoil, and the persistent awareness of having done wrong. At dinner it was decided that she would leave with Panaurov and visit her father for two or three weeks, until she grew tired of it.

XI

Yulia Sergeyevna and Panaurov traveled in a private compartment. He wore an astrakhan cap of an odd shape.

"No, I was not at all satisfied with Petersburg." He spoke deliberately, and sighed. "They promise a great deal . . . but nothing definite. . . . Yes, my dear, I have been a justice of the peace, a permanent member of the court, chairman of the district magistrates, and, finally, councilor of the provincial administration. It would seem that I have given sufficient service to the fatherland to have the right to some consideration, but, there you are! I can never manage to get transferred to another town. . . . " He closed his eyes and shook his head. "Naturally, I'm not an administrative genius, but, on the other hand, I'm a respectable, honest man, and even that is rare today. I'll admit that occasionally I've been somewhat deceptive with women, but in my relations with the Russian government, I have always been a gentleman. But, enough of that," he said, opening his eyes. "Let's talk about you. Why did you suddenly take it into your head to visit Papa?"

"Oh . . . I wasn't getting on so well with my husband," Yulia replied, gazing at his cap.

"Yes, he's a queer one, all right. All the Laptevs are queer. Your husband's not so bad, but his brother Fyodor is an absolute idiot." Panaurov sighed and then very seriously inquired, "But you've taken a lover, of course?"

Yulia looked at him in amazement and laughed.

"Heavens! What are you talking about?"

It was after ten o'clock when they got out to have supper in one of the large stations. When the train started again Panaurov took off his overcoat and cap and sat down beside Yulia.

"I must tell you, you're a very attractive girl," he began. "I hope you will forgive the gastronomical comparison, but you remind me of a freshly pickled cucumber; it still smells

of the hotbed, so to say, but already has a smack of the salt
and a whiff of fennel. In time you'll develop into a magnificent woman . . . a wonderful, elegant woman. If this little
journey of ours had occurred five years ago," he sighed, "I
should have considered it my delightful duty to join the
ranks of your adorers. But, now, alas, I'm on the retired list."
His smile was melancholy but gracious as he put his arm
around her waist.

"You must be mad!" she cried. She was flushed, and so
frightened that her hands and feet turned cold. "Stop it,
Grigory Nikolaich!"

"What are you afraid of, darling?" he asked softly.
"What's so awful about it? It's simply that you're not used
to it."

If a woman protested he interpreted it as a sign that he
had made an impression on her, that he attracted her. Holding Yulia by the waist, he kissed her firmly on the cheek then
on the lips, fully convinced he was affording her the greatest pleasure. When she had recovered from her fright and
confusion, Yulia began to laugh. He kissed her once more,
then put on his absurd cap and said, "And that is all the old
veteran is able to give you now. . . . A Turkish pasha, a kind-
hearted old fellow, once received a gift—or perhaps he just
inherited it—of a whole harem. When his beautiful young
wives lined up before him, he walked around them, kissed
every one, and said, 'That is all that I am now in condition
to offer you.' And I say the same to you."

All this seemed silly and fantastic to Yulia, but it amused
her. She began to feel mischievous. Standing on the seat and
humming, she took down a box of candy from the shelf,
threw him a piece of chocolate, and cried, "Catch!"

He caught it. She laughed loudly and threw him another,
then a third, and he continued to catch them and put them
into his mouth, while gazing at her with pleading eyes. She
found a great deal that was both feminine and childish in his
features and expression. When she breathlessly sat down be-

side him, and continued to look at him and laugh, he lightly ran two fingers along her cheek and ruefully said, "Naughty girl!"

"Take it," she said, giving him the box. "I don't like sweet things."

He ate it all, down to the last piece, then locked the empty box in his suitcase; he liked boxes with pictures on them.

"However, that's enough mischief," he said. "Time for the veteran to go night-night."

He opened his carryall, took out his Bokhara dressing gown and a pillow, then lay down and covered himself with the dressing gown.

"Good night, darling!" he said softly, and sighed as though his whole body ached. He was soon snoring. Without the least feeling of constraint, she too lay down and fell asleep.

The next morning, driving home from the station, the streets of her native town seemed empty and deserted; the snow looked gray, and the houses diminutive, as though someone had flattened them. She came upon a funeral procession in which the deceased was carried in an open coffin with banners.

"They say it's lucky to meet a funeral procession," she thought.

The windows of the house in which Nina Fyodorovna had lived were pasted over with white handbills.

With a sinking heart she drove into her own courtyard and rang the bell. The door was opened by a maid she had not seen before, a plump, sleepy girl in a thick quilted jacket. As she went upstairs, Yulia recalled that it was here Laptev had proposed to her; but now the staircase was unwashed and covered with traces of footprints. Upstairs in the chilly passage patients sat waiting in their coats. For some reason her heart beat violently, and she was so excited she was scarcely able to walk.

The doctor, stouter than ever, brick-red and disheveled,

was drinking tea. He was delighted to see his daughter, and even shed a few tears; it occurred to her that she was the only joy in this old man's life. She was touched, and warmly embraced him, telling him she would stay a long time—until Easter. After going to her own room and changing her clothes, she returned to the dining room to drink tea with him. He was pacing up and down the room with his hands in his pockets, humming "Ru-ru-ru-ru," which meant he was dissatisfied with something.

"You have a gay time of it there in Moscow," he said. "I'm glad for you. . . . I'm an old man, I don't need anything. It won't be long now before I'll kick off, and you'll all be rid of me. It's really a wonder that I have such a thick hide—that I'm still alive! Amazing!"

He went on to say that he was a tough old donkey everyone rode on; that they had burdened him with the care of Nina Fyodorovna, all the cares of her children, and her funeral; that that fop, Panaurov, who did not care to bother about anything, had even borrowed a hundred rubles from him, which he had never repaid.

"Take me to Moscow and put me in a madhouse!" he shouted. "I'm crazy—I'm a naïve child, I still believe in truth and justice!"

He then upbraided her husband for his shortsightedness in failing to buy houses that could have been bought so advantageously. And now Yulia began to see that perhaps she was not the only joy in this old man's life. While he was receiving patients, and later, when he went out to pay his calls, she walked through all the rooms, not knowing what to do or what to think. She no longer felt at home in the house in which she had been born, nor in her native town; she had no desire to go out into the streets, nor to see her friends, and even the recollection of these friends and of her girlhood awakened no feeling of melancholy, no regret for the past.

In the evening she dressed somewhat more stylishly and went to the vesper service. But there were only simple peo-

194 ANTON CHEKHOV

ple in the church, and her magnificent fur coat and hat made
no impression. It seemed to her that some change had taken
place in the church, as well as in herself. Formerly she had
loved the reading of the canon at the evening service, and
the choir singing a hymn such as "I Will Open My Lips";
and she had liked moving slowly in the crowd toward the
priest, who stood in the middle of the church, then feeling
the holy oil upon her forehead; now she was simply waiting
for the service to end. And leaving the church she had no
feeling other than a dread that beggars might approach her;
it would be so tiresome to have to stop and search her pockets—besides, there were no coppers in them now, only
rubles.

She went to bed early, but it was a long time before she
finally fell asleep. She kept dreaming of certain portraits,
and of the funeral procession she had seen in the morning:
the open coffin with the corpse was carried into the yard and
came to a stop before the door; there the coffin was swung
back and forth in a sheet, then violently flung against the
door. Yulia woke and jumped up in horror. Actually there
was the sound of knocking at the door downstairs, and the
bell wire whirred against the wall, but no ring was heard.

She heard the doctor cough. The maid went down and
came up again.

"Madam," she said, knocking at Yulia's door. "Madam!"

"What is it?" Yulia asked.

"A telegram for you!"

Yulia went out to her with a candle. Behind the maid
stood the doctor wearing an overcoat over his underwear.
He, too, carried a candle.

"The bell is broken," he said, yawning sleepily. "It ought
to have been repaired long ago."

Yulia opened the telegram and read:

WE DRINK TO YOUR HEALTH.
YARTSEV, KOCHEVOI.

"Oh, what idiots!" she said, and burst out laughing; and all at once her heart felt light and gay.

Going back to her room, she quietly washed and dressed, and spent the hours till dawn packing her things. At noon she left for Moscow.

XII

During Holy Week the Laptevs went to an exhibition at the school of painting. The entire household went, in the Moscow fashion, including the two little girls with their governess, and Kostya.

Laptev knew the names of all the well-known painters and never missed an exhibition. When he was at his *dacha*, he himself sometimes painted landscapes in oil; he thought he had a good deal of taste, and that if he had studied he might have become a good painter. When he was abroad he used to visit curio shops, examine the antiques with the air of a connoisseur, give his opinion, then buy at whatever price the dealer chose to ask. These purchases then lay for a long time piled up in crates in the coach house, ultimately disappearing, no one knew where. Or, stopping in at a print shop, he would slowly and meticulously examine engravings, or perhaps a bronze, make various observations on them, and end by buying a cheap frame or a box of worthless prints. In his home the pictures were all large, but never good; and even the best of them were badly hung. More than once he had paid large sums for things that had turned out to be crude counterfeits. It was remarkable that, timid as he was in most matters, when it came to an exhibition of paintings, he was exceedingly bold and self-confident. Why?

Yulia Sergeyevna looked at paintings, as did her husband, either through binoculars, or through the opening in a cupped hand held up to one eye. She was astonished that the people looked like live people, and the trees like real trees; but she understood nothing of art, thought many of the pictures were alike, and was convinced that the whole purpose of art was in figures and objects standing out as though real when peered at through a cupped hand.

"That forest is Shishkin's," her husband explained to her. "He always paints the same thing. But notice the snow: there is no such thing as lavender snow like that. . . . And the boy's left arm is shorter than his right."

When they were all tired and ready to go home, Laptev went to find Kostya. Yulia was left to gaze apathetically at a small landscape. In the foreground of the painting there was a small stream with a log bridge across it, and on the opposite shore a path disappearing into dark grass, then a field; on the right, part of a forest, and near it a campfire—probably that of night watchers—and in the distance a fading sunset.

Yulia imagined herself crossing the little bridge, following the path farther and farther, the stillness all round her, drowsy corn crakes calling, and the fire flickering in the distance. And for some reason she began to feel that long ago and many times before she had seen these same clouds extending across a glowing sky, a forest and a field. She had a feeling of loneliness, and she longed to follow the path on and on and on; the evening sunset held a reflection of something unearthly and eternal.

"How beautifully that is painted!" she exclaimed, surprised at her sudden understanding of the picture. "Look, Alyosha! Do you see how tranquil it is?"

She attempted to explain why the landscape appealed to her so strongly, but neither her husband nor Kostya understood her. She kept looking at the painting with a melancholy smile, and the fact that they found nothing exceptional in it disturbed her. She began walking through the rooms, examining the pictures again; she wanted to understand them, and no longer found them all alike. When she returned

home, for the first time she really looked at the large painting that hung above the piano in the drawing room. It
aroused a feeling of antagonism within her, and she said,
"Why would anyone want to have such pictures?"

From that day on the gilt cornices, the Venetian mirrors
with flowers, and paintings like the one that hung over the
piano—to say nothing of discussions of art by her husband
and Kostya—aroused in her a feeling of boredom and vexa-
tion, at times, even of hatred.

Life drifted on its accustomed course, day after day, holding no particular promise. The theatrical season came to an
end, the days began to grow warm, and there followed a period of magnificent weather. One morning the Laptevs decided to attend the district court to hear Kostya plead a case;
he had been assigned by the court to defend the accused.
They were late in starting and arrived after the examination
of the witness had begun. A soldier in the reserve was accused of housebreaking and burglary. There were a great
many witnesses, all washerwomen; they testified to the fact
that the accused frequented the house of their employer, the
proprietress of the laundry. On Holy Cross Day he had come
there late in the evening, begging money for a pick-me-up,
but no one had given him anything. He went away, but returned an hour later with beer and gingerbread for the girls.
They drank and sang till dawn. When they looked about
them in the morning, they discovered that the lock on the
door leading to the garret had been broken, and three men's
shirts, a petticoat, and two sheets were missing. Kostya, in
an ironic tone, asked each witness whether she had drunk
the beer the accused had brought on Holy Cross Day. He
was obviously implying that the laundresses themselves had
stolen the linen. He delivered his speech without the least
nervousness, all the while glaring angrily at the jury.

He gave an explanation of housebreaking with burglary,
and followed it with an explanation of simple burglary. He
spoke persuasively and in great detail, evincing an extraor-

dinary capacity for redundancy and solemnity of tone in matters that had long been common knowledge.

It was not easy to understand exactly what he wanted. From his long speech the foreman of the jury could have drawn only one conclusion: that it was a case of housebreaking but not theft, as the washerwomen themselves had sold the linen for drink; or, if it was theft, that it was theft without housebreaking. But evidently he said exactly what was required, as his speech moved both the jury and the public, and was very much admired. When the verdict of acquittal was announced, Yulia nodded to Kostya, and later warmly pressed his hand.

In May the Laptevs moved to their *dacha* at Sokolniki. By that time Yulia was expecting a child.

XIII

More than a year had passed. At Sokolniki, not far from the Yaroslav railway embankment, Yulia and Yartsev were sitting on the grass; near them Kochevoi was lying, his hands under his head, gazing up at the sky. All three had been for a walk and now were waiting for the six o'clock train to pass before going home to tea.

"Mothers always see something remarkable in their own children—that's part of nature's plan," said Yulia. "A mother will stand by the crib for hours admiring her baby's ears, his eyes, his nose—enraptured! If anyone kisses her child, she, poor thing, imagines that it gives him the greatest pleasure. And a mother talks of nothing but her child. I am aware of this weakness in mothers, and I keep watch over myself. But, truly, my Olya is exceptional. The way she looks at me when I'm nursing her! And how she laughs! She is only eight months old, but I have never seen such intelligent eyes in a child of three!"

"By the way, tell me," Yartsev asked, "whom do you love more, your husband or your child?"

"I don't know," she replied, "I never loved my husband very much, and Olya is actually my first love. You know, of course, that I didn't marry Alexei for love. I was stupid in those days, and used to suffer, imagining I had ruined his life and my own; now I see that love is not at all necessary, it's all nonsense."

"But if it is not love, what is the feeling that binds you to your husband? What makes you go on living with him?"

"I don't know . . . habit, I suppose. I respect him, I miss him when he's away for long—but that's not love. He's an intelligent, honest man, and that suffices for my happiness. He's very kind, and sincere. . . . "

"Alyosha's intelligent, Alyosha's kind," Kostya repeated, lazily lifting his head. "But, my darling, in order to find out that he's intelligent and kind, and interesting, you have to eat three poods of salt with him. . . . And of what use is his kindness or his intellect? He'll shell out all the money you like, that he can do, but when it comes to packing off some insolent, arrogant fellow, he shrinks and cowers. People like your obliging Alexei are absolutely useless in a struggle. In fact, they're useless in general."

At last the train appeared, spreading clouds of steam of an absolutely pink color above the grove; two windows of the end car flashed so brightly in the sunlight that it hurt their eyes to look at them.

"Time for tea!" said Yulia Sergeyevna, getting up.

Lately she had grown a little stout, and her walk was becoming matronly and rather indolent.

"Nevertheless it's not good to live without love," Yartsev said, following her. "We are forever talking of love, and reading about it, but we ourselves love very little, and this is decidedly wrong."

"It's all nonsense, Ivan Gavrilych," said Yulia. "That's not where happiness lies."

They had tea in the little garden where the mignonette, stock, and tobacco plants were in bloom, and the early gladioli were beginning to come out. Yartsev and Kochevoi could see by her face that Yulia was going through a happy period of inner peace and serenity, that she wanted nothing but what she already had, and they themselves yielded to a feeling of well-being and tranquillity. Whatever any of them said seemed apposite and wise; the pine trees were lovelier, the resin more wonderfully fragrant than ever before, the cream tasted delicious, and Sasha was a good and clever little girl. . . .

After tea Yartsev sang songs, accompanying himself on the piano, while Yulia and Kochevoi sat listening in silence. From time to time Yulia quietly rose and went to look at the baby and Lida, who for two days had been in bed, feverish and unable to eat.

" 'My friend, fond friend,' " Yartsev sang. . . . "No, ladies and gentlemen," he announced, shaking his head, "I'm hanged if I can understand why you're opposed to love! If I weren't occupied for fifteen out of every twenty-four hours, I should most certainly fall in love!"

Supper was served on the veranda; although the air was warm and still, Yulia wrapped herself in a shawl and complained of the damp. When it grew dark, she seemed not quite herself and she kept shivering and begging her friends to stay a little longer. She regaled them with wine, and after supper ordered brandy to keep them from going. She did not want to be left alone with the children and the servants.

"The summer residents are getting up a performance for the children," she said. "We've already got everything—actors, and a theater—now all we need is a play. We've been sent some twenty plays of various kinds, but not one of them is suitable. You like the theater, and you know history," she said, turning to Yartsev, "why don't you write an historical play for us?"

"Well, I might."

The guests finished the brandy and prepared to go. It was past ten, which was late for the summer residents.

"How dark it is! One can't see a thing," said Yulia, accompanying them to the gate. "I don't know how you will find your way. And it's so cold!"

She wrapped the shawl more tightly around herself and walked back to the veranda.

"My Alexei is probably playing cards somewhere," she called after them. "Good night!"

Coming from the lighted rooms Yartsev and Kochevoi were unable to see, and, like blind men, groped their way to the railway embankment and across it.

"Can't see a damned thing," said Kostya in his bass voice, stopping and peering up at the sky. "But the stars—those stars are exactly like brand-new fifteen-kopeck pieces! Gavrilych!"

"Ah?" Yartsev called out from somewhere in the darkness.

"I say: I can't see a thing. Where are you?"

Yartsev whistled as he came up to him and took his arm.

"Hey, you summer people!" Kostya suddenly shouted at the top of his voice. "We've caught a socialist!"

When he had been drinking he always became loud and troublesome, quarreling with policemen and cab drivers, and intemperately laughing and singing.

"The hell with nature!" he shouted.

"Come now," Yartsev tried to quiet him. "Don't do that. Please!"

They soon grew accustomed to the dark and were able to distinguish the silhouettes of tall pine trees and telephone poles. The sounds of whistles from the Moscow stations reached them from time to time, and the wires hummed plaintively. There was not a sound from the grove itself, and in this silence there was something majestic, powerful, and mysterious. By night it seemed that the tops of the pine trees almost touched the sky. The friends found a track and walked along it. It was quite dark there, and only from the long strip of star-strewn sky, and from the fact that under foot the earth was firmly trampled down, did they know that they were on a path. They walked side by side in silence, and both of them imagined that people were moving toward them. Their intoxicated mood forsook them. It came into Yartsev's mind that this grove was perhaps inhabited by the spirits of the Muscovite tsars, boyars, and patriarchs, and he was on the verge of telling this to Kostya, but he restrained himself.

When they reached the city gate day was just breaking. They continued to walk in silence along the wooden pavement, past the cheap summer cottages, the taverns, the stacks of timber; beneath the span of intertwining branches overhead, the damp air was chilly and pleasantly fragrant of lime trees; then a long, broad street opened before them, with not a soul, not a light on it. . . . When they reached the Red Pond it was daylight.

"Moscow—a city that will have to suffer a great deal more," said Yartsev, looking at the Alexeyevsky Monastery.

"What made you think of that?"

"I just did. I love Moscow."

Both Yartsev and Kostya had been born in Moscow; they adored their native city, and for some reason were hostile to all others. They were convinced that Moscow was a remarkable city, and Russia a remarkable country. When they went to the Crimea, the Caucasus, or abroad, they felt uncomfortable, bored, and ill at ease, but the gray climate of Moscow they found appealing and wholesome. On days when a cold rain beat against the windows and dusk descended early, when the walls of the houses and churches took on a somber brown color, and when one did not know what to put on when going out—such days were to them delightfully stimulating.

At last, near the station, they took a cab.

"As a matter of fact, it might be a good idea to write an

historical play—but, of course, without the Lyapunovs or the Godunovs—something from the days of Yaroslav or Monomachus. . . . I hate all Russian historical plays, with the exception of Pimen's monologue. When you are dealing with any kind of historical source material, or even when you read a textbook on Russian history, it appears that in Russia everyone is extraordinarily talented, gifted, and interesting; but when I go to the theater and see an historical play, Russian life begins to seem dull, morbid, and lacking in any originality."

Near Dmitrovka the friends parted, and Yartsev went on to his apartment in Great Nikitsky Street. Still thinking about the play, he became drowsy with the swaying of the cab. He began to imagine a fearful tumult, with clanking and shouting in some unknown tongue like Kalmuk; a village enveloped in flames, a neighboring forest covered with hoarfrost, faintly pink from the reflection of the fire, and for a great distance everything so clearly visible that each single fir tree was distinguishable, and flying through the village, savage people on horseback and on foot, all as crimson as the glowing sky. "The Polovtsy," thought Yartsev. One of them, a terrifying old man with a bloody face and covered with burns from the fire, was tying a young girl to his saddle. The girl had the face of a Byelorussian, and she was looking sadly and wisely at the old man as he shouted at her in a towering rage. Yartsev shook his head and woke up.

" 'My friend, fond friend,' " he hummed.

Even after he had paid the cabman and had gone upstairs to his own rooms, he was unable to shake off his dream; he continued to see flames enveloping a village, a crackling, smoking forest, a huge wild boar, panic-stricken, rampaging through the village. . . . And the girl bound to the saddle still gazing. . . .

It was already daylight when he arrived home. On the piano near some open sheets of music two candles had burned low. Lying on the sofa in a black dress with a sash was Rassudina, sound asleep with a newspaper in her hand. She had probably been playing the piano until late, waiting for Yartsev to return, and had finally fallen asleep.

"Look here! She's worn out!" he thought.

Carefully taking the newspaper from her hand, he covered her with a plaid, extinguished the candles, and went into the bedroom. As he lay down he was thinking of the historical play, and the melody of "My friend, fond friend" was still running through his head. . . .

Two days later Laptev dropped in to tell him that Lida had diphtheria and Yulia Sergeyevna and the baby had both caught it from her; and five days after that he received the news that Lida and Yulia were recovering, but the baby was dead, and that the Laptevs had left their Sokolniki *dacha* in haste and returned to Moscow.

XIV

Laptev now found it unpleasant to spend much time at home. His wife frequently went to the lodge, saying that she had to look after the little girls; but he knew she went there, not to give them their lessons, but to weep in Kostya's room. The ninth day came, then the twentieth, and the fortieth, and still he had to go to the cemetery, had to listen to the requiem, and afterwards, the whole day and night, to exhaust himself thinking of nothing but that unfortunate baby, and repeating all sorts of banal things to his wife in an effort to comfort her. He seldom went to the warehouse now, but occupied himself solely with charitable work. He devised various tasks and duties for himself, and was glad when the occasion made it necessary for him to spend an entire day driving here and there on some trifling matter. Lately he had thought of going abroad to make a study of hostels, and the idea appealed to him now.

It was an autumn day. Yulia had just gone to the lodge to weep, and Laptev lay on the sofa in his study, wondering where he should go. At that moment Pyotr announced Polina Rassudina. Laptev was delighted; he jumped up and went to meet this unexpected visitor, his former friend, whom he had almost begun to forget. She had not changed in the least since that evening when he had seen her for the last time; she was just the same as she had always been.

"Polina!" he exclaimed, extending both hands to her. "I have not seen you for ages! If you knew how glad I am to see you! Come in!"

Rassudina greeted him, jerked him by the hand, and, without removing her coat and hat, went into the study and sat down.

"I've come for one minute," she said. "And I haven't the time to talk of trivialities. Please sit down and listen. It's all one to me whether you're glad to see me or not; the gracious attentions of you lordly gentlemen are not worth a pin to me. I'm here only because I've tried five other places today and have met with refusals in every one—and this is a matter that cannot be put off. Listen," she went on, looking into his eyes, "five students of my acquaintance—limited, confused people, but unquestionably poor—have not paid their fees and have been expelled. Your wealth makes it your duty to go straight to the university and pay for them."

"With pleasure, Polina."

"Here are their names," she said, giving Laptev a list. "Go this instant; you'll have plenty of time to enjoy your domestic bliss later."

At that moment a noise was heard behind the door leading into the drawing room; it must have been the dog scratching himself. Rassudina turned red and jumped up.

"Your Dulcinea is eavesdropping," she said. "That is vile!"

Laptev was offended for Yulia.

"She is not here; she's in the lodge," he said. "And don't

speak of her in that way. Our baby died and she is terribly grief-stricken."

"You can console her," Rassudina said bitterly, and sat down again. "She'll have a dozen more. It doesn't require much wit to bring children into the world!"

Laptev remembered hearing this, or something like it, many times in days gone by, and it brought back the poetry of the past, the freedom of his solitary, bachelor life, when he felt young and as though he could do anything he wished, when there had been neither the love for a wife nor the memory of a child.

"Let us go together," he said, stretching himself.

When they reached the university Polina waited at the gate while Laptev went into the office; before long he came back and handed her five receipts.

"Where are you going now?"

"To Yartsev's."

"I'll go with you."

"But you'll interfere with his work."

"No, I assure you!" he said with an imploring look.

She was wearing a black, crepe-trimmed hat, as though she were in mourning, and a very short, threadbare coat, with bulging pockets. Her nose seemed longer than ever, and, in spite of the cold, her face was deathly pale. Laptev found it pleasant to be following her, obeying her, and listening to her grumbling. He was thinking as they walked along: what inner strength this woman must have, if, being so ugly, awkward, and so nervous, not knowing how to dress properly, or even comb her hair, and always somehow lacking in grace, she was, nevertheless, fascinating.

They entered Yartsev's apartment by the back door, through the kitchen, where they were met by the cook, a clean little old woman with gray curls; she was terribly embarrassed, and with a sweet smile that made her little face look like a pie, she said, "Please, come in."

Yartsev was not at home. Rassudina sat down at the piano

and, ordering Laptev not to bother her, set to work upon a tedious, difficult exercise. He sat on one side and without distracting her with conversation, turned the pages of *The Messenger of Europe*. Having practiced for two hours, her daily task, she ate something in the kitchen and went out to give her lessons. Laptev read the continuation of a story, then sat for a long time without reading and without feeling bored, quite content to think that it was now too late to go home for dinner.

"Ha-ha-ha-ha!" Yartsev's laugh was heard, then he himself appeared, red-cheeked, robust, and elated, in a new coat with bright buttons. "Ha-ha-ha-ha!"

The two friends dined together, then Laptev lay on the sofa while Yartsev sat near him smoking a cigar. Dusk was falling.

"I must be getting old," said Laptev. "Ever since my sister Nina died, for some reason, I often think of death."

They talked of death, the immortality of the soul, of how good it would be to be resurrected and fly off somewhere, to Mars, to be eternally idle and happy, and, above all, to think in some special way, unlike the way one does on earth.

"But, one does not want to die." Yartsev spoke quietly. "There is no philosophy that can reconcile me to death; I regard it as nothing but extinction. I want to live."

"You love life, Gavrilych?"

"Yes, I do."

"And here I am, in no way able to understand myself in this respect. I am either in a state of depression or indifference. I'm timid, lack confidence in myself, have an abject conscience, and am quite incapable of adapting myself to life or mastering it. Another man may talk nonsense or cheat people, and enjoy doing it, while it is my lot consciously to do good and yet feel nothing but anxiety or the most complete indifference. This I ascribe to my being a slave, the grandson of a serf. Before we rabble can find the right road, many of us will fall by the wayside in the struggle."

"All that is good, my dear," said Yartsev with a sigh. "It only proves once again how rich and varied Russian life is. Ah, how rich! Do you know, I am more convinced each day that we are now living on the eve of the greatest triumph, and I should like to live long enough to have a part in it. You can believe it or not, but, in my opinion, a remarkable generation is now growing up. When I teach these children, especially the girls, I revel in it! They are marvelous children!"

Yartsev walked over to the piano and struck a chord.

"I am a chemist, I think in terms of chemistry, and I shall die a chemist," he went on, "but I have a craving, and I'm afraid I shall die before I can satisfy it. Chemistry is not enough for me; therefore I take up Russian history, the history of art, pedagogy, music. . . . Last summer your wife suggested I write an historical play, and now I am longing to write; I could sit for three days and nights without getting up, just writing. I am overcome by these images, my head is crammed with them; I feel as though a pulse were throbbing in my brain. It's not that I have the least desire to become anything special, or to create something momentous; I simply want to live, to dream, to hope, not to miss anything. . . . Life, my dear fellow, is short, and one must spend it well."

After this comradely talk, which ended only at midnight, Laptev began visiting Yartsev almost every day. He felt drawn to him. Generally he arrived before evening, lay down and patiently waited for Yartsev to come home, never feeling the slightest boredom. Yartsev would return, have dinner, and sit down to work. When Laptev asked him a question, however, a discussion would spring up and work would be forgotten; at midnight the friends would part, well pleased with each other.

But this did not last long. One day when he arrived at Yartsev's he found Rassudina alone there; she was at the piano practicing her exercises. She looked at him coldly, almost with enmity, and without even shaking hands said, "Will you kindly tell me when this is going to end?"

"This—what?" Laptev asked, not understanding.

"You come here every day and prevent Yartsev from working. Yartsev is not a merchant, he's a scholar, and every minute of his life is precious. You ought to understand this and have at least a little tact."

"If you consider that I hinder him," Laptev replied meekly in embarrassment, "I shall put an end to my visits."

"And a good thing! You'd better go now; he may come in at any moment and find you here."

The tone in which this was said, and the look of indifference in her eyes, decidedly disconcerted him. It was apparent that she had absolutely no feeling for him other than a desire to see him go as soon as possible. What a contrast this was to her former love! He left without shaking hands with her, thinking she would call him back; but he heard only the piano scales, and he slowly descended the stairs, realizing that he was now no more than a stranger to her.

Three days later Yartsev came to spend the evening with him.

"I have news," he said with a laugh. "Polina Nikolaevna has moved into my place for good." He was somewhat embarrassed as he went on in a low voice, "Why not? Of course, we're not in love with each other, but I think that . . . that doesn't make any difference. I'm glad I can give her a refuge and peace, and make it possible for her not to work if she should fall ill. She believes that by living with me she will bring more order into my life, and that under her influence I shall become a great scientist. That's what she fancies. Well, let her think so. In the south they have a saying: 'A fool grows rich on fancies.' Ha-ha-ha!"

Laptev said nothing. Yartsev walked up and down the study, looking at the pictures he had seen many times before; then, with a sigh, he said, "Yes, my friend, I'm three years older than you, and it's too late for me to think of real

love. Actually, a woman like Polina Nikolaevna is a godsend
to me, and I shall spend my life quite happily with her till
I'm an old man. But the devil knows why it is one always
has to feel some sort of regret, some sort of longing; I go on
feeling as if I am lying in the Vale of Dagestan, dreaming of
a ball. In other words, a man is never satisfied with what he
has."

He went into the drawing room and, as though nothing
had happened, began singing sentimental songs, while
Laptev sat in his study with closed eyes, trying to understand why Rassudina had gone to live with Yartsev. It made
it sad to think that there were no lasting, constant attachments; he felt annoyed that Polina Nikolaevna had gone to
live with Yartsev, and annoyed with himself that his feeling
for his wife was no longer what it had been.

XV

Laptev was reading as he swayed back and forth in a
rocking chair; Yulia was also in the study reading. They
seemed to have nothing to talk about, and both had been
silent since morning. Now and then he looked at her from
over his book, thinking: whether one marries from passionate love, or without any love, doesn't it come to the same
thing? The days of his jealousy, worry, and suffering now
seemed remote. He had succeeded in going abroad, and now
was resting after the journey. He looked forward to the
spring, when he again planned to visit England, which had
greatly appealed to him.

Yulia Sergeyevna had grown accustomed to her sorrow,
and no longer went to the lodge to weep. That winter she had
given up shopping expeditions, the theater and concerts, and
stayed at home. She did not like large rooms and always sat
in her husband's study or in her own room, where she kept

the ikon cases that were part of her dowry, and where the landscape painting she had liked so much at the exhibition was hung. She spent almost no money on herself, and lived on as little as she had in her father's house.

The winter passed without gaiety. Wherever one went in Moscow there was card playing, and if anyone introduced a different kind of amusement, such as singing, reading, or drawing, it turned out to be even more boring. Since there were few talented people in Moscow, and the same singers and readers performed at all the evening parties, the delights of art itself gradually palled, and for many were reduced to a tiresome, monotonous social obligation.

Furthermore, never a day passed at the Laptevs' without its misfortune. Old Fyodor Stepanych was losing his sight, and the oculists said he would soon be blind. For some reason Fyodor also had given up going to the warehouse, and spent all his time at home writing. Panaurov had been transferred to another city with a promotion to Actual Civil Councilor, and was now staying at the Dresden; he came to Laptev almost every day to ask for money. Kish had at last left the university, and while waiting for the Laptevs to find him some sort of work, spent whole days at their house, telling his long, boring stories. All this was irritating and wearing, and made life continually unpleasant.

Pyotr came into the study and announced an unknown lady. On the card he brought in was the name Josephina Iosifovna Milan.

Yulia Sergeyevna lazily rose and left the room, limping slightly, as her foot had gone to sleep. In the doorway appeared a thin, extremely pale woman with dark eyebrows, dressed entirely in black. She clasped her hands to her breast and in a supplicating voice exclaimed, "Monsieur Laptev, save my children!"

Her powder-splotched face and the sound of jingling bracelets seemed familiar to Laptev; suddenly he recognized her as the lady at whose house he had so inappropriately dined one day before his marriage. It was Panaurov's second wife.

"Save my children!" she repeated, and her face quivered, suddenly looking old and pitiful. "You alone can save us. I have spent my last kopeck coming to Moscow to see you. My children will die of starvation!"

She made a movement as though she were about to fall on her knees. Laptev was alarmed, and seized her arm.

"Sit down, sit down . . ." he mumbled, putting her into a chair. "I beg you to be seated!"

"We have no money—not even for bread," she said. "Grigory Nikolaich is going to his new post, but he doesn't want to take the children and me with him, and the money you so generously have been sending us he spends only on himself. What are we to do? What? My poor, unfortunate children!"

"I beg you to calm yourself. I shall instruct the office to send the money in your name."

She began to sob, then grew calm, and he noticed that the tears had made little paths down her powdered cheeks, and that she had a mustache.

"You are infinitely generous, Monsieur Laptev. But, be our guardian angel, our good fairy, and persuade Grigory Nikolaich not to abandon me, but to take me with him. I love him, you see, love him madly, he is my solace!"

Laptev gave her a hundred rubles and promised to speak to Panaurov; he then accompanied her to the entrance hall, afraid that at any moment she might break into sobs or fall on her knees.

When she had gone Kish arrived. Then Kostya came with his photographic apparatus. Lately he had been captivated by photography, and several times a day took pictures of everyone in the house. This new pursuit caused him many disappointments, and he had grown even thinner.

Before evening tea Fyodor came in. Having seated himself in one corner of the study, he opened a book and stared unceasingly at one page, obviously not reading. He spent a long time drinking tea, and his face grew very red. In his presence Laptev felt heavy-hearted; even his brother's silence disturbed him.

"You may congratulate Russia on the appearance of a new pamphleteer," said Fyodor. "Joking aside, brother, I've turned out a little article—testing my pen, so to say. I've brought it to show you. Read it, my dear, and give me your opinion. But sincerely!"

He took a copybook out of his pocket and handed it to his brother. The article was called "The Russian Soul"; it was laboriously written in the colorless style generally employed by untalented writers with a secret vanity. Its principal idea was that the intellectual man has a right not to believe in the supernatural, but has a duty to conceal his disbelief so that he may not tempt believers to doubt; without faith there is no idealism, and idealism is destined to save Europe and guide humanity into the true path.

"But you do not say what Europe has to be saved from," said Laptev.

"That's understood."

"Nothing is understood," said Laptev, nervously pacing the room. "I don't even understand why you wrote it! But that's your business."

"I want to publish it in a special pamphlet."

"That's your affair."

"I shall forever deeply regret that you and I think differently. Ah, Alyosha, my dear brother! You and I are Russian, we are orthodox believers, men of breadth; what have we to do with all these German and Jewish vagaries? We're not upstarts or anything like that, you know, but representatives of an eminent merchant family."

"What do you mean—an eminent family?" Laptev exclaimed, trying to restrain his irritation. "Eminent! Our grandfather was flogged by landowners, and punched in the face by every insignificant little government clerk! Grandfather beat our father; our father beat us. What has this eminent family bequeathed to us? What sort of blood and nerves have we received as our heritage? For nearly three years now you've been discoursing like a sexton, talking all sorts of rot; and now you've written—this obsequious gibberish! And I—and I? Look at me. . . . No resourcefulness, no courage, no strength of will; I'm scared of every step I take, as though I were going to be beaten for it; I'm timid in the presence of nonentities, idiots, and brutes who are immeasurably beneath me mentally and morally; I'm afraid of porters, doormen, policemen, the political police; I'm afraid of everyone, because I was born of a mother who was persecuted, and because I was beaten and frightened in my childhood! You and I will do well to have no children. God grant that this eminent merchant family may die with us!"

Yulia Sergeyevna came into the study and sat down at the table.

"Were you having an argument?" she asked. "Am I interrupting you?"

"No, little sister," Fyodor replied. "We were having a discussion of principles. . . . Now you talk this way and that about the family," he said, addressing his brother, "but this family has created a business in the millions. That's worth something!"

"That's enormously important—a business in the millions! A man of no particular intelligence or ability quite by accident becomes a huckster, then, having grown rich, he goes on trading day after day, with no system of any sort, with no aim, not even the greed for money; he trades mechanically, and the money comes to him of itself, he doesn't even go after it. There he sits all his life, loving his work simply because he can tyrannize over his clerks and make fools of his customers. He's the patron of a school because he enjoys the feeling that the teacher is his subordinate and he can lord it over him, and he's an elder in the church because there he can domineer over the choristers and keep them under his thumb. What the merchant loves is not trade, but power, and your warehouse is not so much a commercial establishment as a torture chamber! And for a business like yours you need clerks who have been deprived of everything, who have lost their individuality—and you yourself prepare them for this by forcing them in childhood to go down on their knees to you for a piece of bread, from childhood inculcating in them the idea that you are their benefactor! It's not likely you'd ever take a university man into your warehouse!"

"University men are not suited to our business."

"That's not true!" Laptev shouted. "It's a lie!"

"Excuse me, but it seems to me you are spitting into the well from which you drink," said Fyodor, getting up. "You despise our business, yet you are able to enjoy the income from it."

"Ah-hah! At last you have said what you think!" Laptev laughed and then glared angrily at his brother. "Yes, if I did not belong to your eminent family, if I had even a scrap of will or courage, I should long since have flung away that income and worked for my living. But from my very childhood you and your warehouse deprived me of any sense of responsibility! I belong to you!"

Fyodor glanced at the clock and hurriedly made his farewells. He kissed Yulia's hand and went out, but instead of going into the hall, he went into the drawing room, then into the bedroom.

"I've forgotten the arrangement of the rooms," he said, in extreme confusion. "It's a strange house. Isn't it a strange house?"

Putting on his fur coat he acted as though he were stunned, and there was a look of pain on his face. Laptev was no longer angry; he became frightened, but at the same time he felt sorry for Fyodor, and his warm, sincere love for his brother, which seemed to have been extinguished during those three years, now awoke in his heart, and he felt an intense desire to express it.

"Fedya, come and have dinner with us tomorrow," he said, stroking his shoulder. "Will you come?"

"Yes, yes. . . . But give me some water."

Laptev ran into the dining room and picked up the first thing on the sideboard that came to hand; it was a tall beer mug, and he poured some water into it and took it to his brother. Fyodor eagerly began to drink, but suddenly bit a piece out of the mug; a crunching sound was heard, followed by sobbing. The water spilled all over his fur coat and frock coat. Laptev, who had never before seen a man cry, stood frightened and confused, not knowing what to do. While Yulia and the maid removed Fyodor's coat and led him back into the living room, he looked on helplessly, then followed after them with a feeling of guilt.

Yulia helped Fyodor to lie down then knelt beside him. "It's all right," she said comfortingly. "It's only nerves. . . . "

"My dear, I am so miserable!" he said. "I am so unhappy, so unhappy. . . . But all the time I've kept it hidden . . . hidden!" He put his arm round her neck and whispered in her ear, "Every night I see my sister Nina. She comes and sits in the armchair next to my bed."

When he went into the hall an hour later and again put on his coat, he was smiling, but embarrassed before the maid. Laptev accompanied him to Pyatnitsky Street.

"Come and have dinner with us tomorrow," he said, holding his brother's arm as they walked. "And at Easter we'll go abroad together. You must have a change, otherwise you'll grow rusty."

"Yes, yes . . . I shall, I shall go. . . . And we'll take little sister with us."

On his return home Laptev found his wife extremely agitated and nervous. The incident with Fyodor had upset her, and she was in no way able to calm herself. She did not weep, but she was very pale and kept tossing about in bed, plucking with cold fingers at the quilt, the pillows, and her husband's hands. Her eyes were large and frightened.

"Don't go away; don't go away from me," she said to her husband. "Tell me, Alyosha, why have I given up saying my prayers? What has become of my faith? Oh, why did you discuss religion before me? You've confused me, you and your friends. I can no longer pray."

He put compresses on her head, chafed her hands, and gave her tea to drink, and she pressed close to him in fear. . . .

Toward morning she fell asleep, exhausted; but because he sat beside her holding her hand, Laptev was unable to sleep. All the next day he felt jaded and dull; he wandered listlessly from one room to another, unable to think of anything.

XVI

The doctors said that Fyodor was mentally ill. Laptev did not know what to do with himself in the house in Pyatnitsky Street, and the dark warehouse, where neither Fyodor nor the old man ever appeared now, gave him the feeling of a tomb. When his wife told him that he ought to go to the warehouse and to Pyatnitsky Street every day without fail, he remained silent or began talking irritably of his childhood, saying that it was not within his power to forgive his father for the past, that the Pyatnitsky Street house and the warehouse were abhorrent to him, and so on.

One Sunday morning Yulia herself went to Pyatnitsky Street. She found old Fyodor Stepanych in the large reception hall where the service had been held the day of her first visit. Without a necktie, wearing his duck coat and slippers, he sat motionless in an armchair, blinking his sightless eyes.

"It is I, your daughter-in-law," she said, as she approached him. "I've come to see how you are."

He began breathing heavily with excitement. Touched by his misfortune and his loneliness, she kissed his hand, and he passed his hand over her face and head, as though to convince himself that it was she, and then made the sign of the cross over her.

"Thank you, thank you," he said. "I've lost my eyes, you know, and can see nothing. . . . I can just barely see the window and the fire, but I'm unable to make out people and objects. Yes, I'm going blind, and Fyodor has fallen ill; things go badly without the master's eye. If something goes wrong there's no one to look into it; people get spoiled. And why is Fyodor ill? Did he catch cold? Never in my life was I ailing, never took medicines, knew nothing of doctors."

And, as was his habit, the old man began boasting. Meanwhile the servants hurriedly laid a table in the reception room, setting out appetizers and bottles of wine. There were about a dozen bottles on the table, one of which looked like the Eiffel Tower, and a full platter of hot pies smelling of jam, rice, and fish.

"I invite my dear guest to have a bite," said the old man.

She took his arm and led him to the table, and then poured a glass of vodka for him.

"I'll come again tomorrow," she said, "and I'll bring your grandchildren, Sasha and Lida. They will feel sorry for you, and they'll be sweet to you."

"No need; don't bring them. They're illegitimate."

"Why illegitimate? Their father and mother were married."

"Without my consent. I did not give them my blessing, and I don't want to know them. Let them go."

"That's a strange way to talk, Fyodor Stepanych," said Yulia with a sigh.

"In the Gospels it is written that children must respect and fear their parents."

"Nothing of the sort. In the Gospels it says we must forgive even our enemies."

"In our business, that's impossible. If you were to forgive everyone you'd be done for in three years."

"But to forgive, to say a kind, friendly word to someone, even a guilty person, is far above business or wealth!"

Yulia longed to soften the old man, to inspire a feeling of compassion in him, to arouse his repentance, but he listened to her as an adult listens to a child, merely to humor her.

"Fyodor Stepanych," said Yulia resolutely, "you are now an old man; soon God will call you to Himself. He is not going to ask you what sort of trader you were, or if your business was successful, but whether or not you were kind to people, or were harsh to those weaker than yourself, such as your servants and your clerks."

"I have always been a benefactor to those that served me, and they ought to say eternal prayers for me," the old man said with conviction; then, touched by Yulia's tone of sincerity, and wishing to please her, he said, "Very well, bring the grandchildren tomorrow. I'll order some little gifts to be bought for them."

The old man was careless in his dress, and there were cigar ashes on the front of his coat and on his knees; evidently no one cleaned his clothes or shoes. The rice in the pies was undercooked, the tablecloth smelled of soap, the servants tramped about noisily. . . . Yulia was aware of the neglected look of the whole household, as well as of the old man, and she felt ashamed of herself and her husband.

"I shall come tomorrow without fail," she said.

She went through the house and gave orders for the old man's bedroom to be cleaned, and for the ikon lamp to be lighted. Fyodor was sitting in his own room gazing at an open book without reading. Yulia talked to him and ordered his room also to be put in order. Then she went downstairs to the clerks' quarters. In the middle of the room in which they dined there was an unpainted wooden column that had been placed there to support the ceiling and prevent it from collapsing. Here the ceilings were low, the walls covered with cheap wallpaper, and a smell of charcoal fumes and cooking was in the air. It happened to be a holiday and all the clerks were at home, sitting on their beds waiting for dinner. When Yulia entered the room they jumped to their feet and meekly answered her questions, sullenly staring at her like convicts.

"Heavens, what a wretched place you have here!" she said, clasping her hands. "Aren't you crowded?"

"Crowded, but not at odds!" said Makeichev. "We are deeply gratified by you, and shall offer up our prayers to our merciful Lord."

"The congruity of life with the aspirations of the individual," said Pochatkin.

Seeing that Yulia did not understand Pochatkin, Makeichev hastened to explain, "We are humble folk, and must live according to our rank."

She inspected the boys' quarters and the kitchen, made the acquaintance of the housekeeper, and was thoroughly dissatisfied.

At home she said to her husband, "We must move to your father's house as soon as possible, and stay there. And every day you will go to the warehouse."

They sat side by side in the study without speaking.

His heart was heavy; he had no desire to move to Pyatnitsky Street nor to go into the warehouse, but he guessed what his wife was thinking and was powerless to oppose her. He stroked her cheek and said, "I feel as though our life had already come to an end, and that a gray half-life is about to begin for us. When I learned that brother Fyodor was hopelessly ill, I wept. We spent our childhood and youth together; there was a time when I loved him with all my heart—and now, this catastrophe. It seems to me that in losing him I have been cut off from my past, irrevocably. And now, when you say that we must move to Pyatnitsky Street, to that prison, I begin to feel that there is no future for me either."

He got up and walked to the window.

"Be that as it may, one must relinquish all thoughts of happiness," he said, gazing out into the street. "There is none. I have never known it, and, probably, it doesn't exist. Once in my life, however, I was happy—the night I spent sitting under your parasol. Do you remember the time you left your parasol at Nina's?" he asked, turning to his wife. "I was in love with you then, and I remember sitting the whole night under that parasol in a state of perfect bliss."

Near the bookcase in the study stood a mahogany and bronze chest of drawers in which Laptev kept various useless things, and among them the parasol. He took it out and handed it to his wife.

"Here it is."

Yulia looked at it for a minute, recognized it, and smiled sadly.

"I remember," she said. "You were holding it in your hand when you proposed to me."

When she saw him preparing to go out she said, "Please come back early if you can. I miss you."

Then she went to her own room and sat looking at the parasol for a long time.

XVII

In spite of the complexity of the business and the huge turnover in the warehouse, there was no bookkeeper, and it was impossible to make out anything in the books kept by the office clerk. Agents came to the warehouse every day, German and English, with whom the clerks discussed politics and religion. There was an alcoholic nobleman, a sick, pitiful man, who came to translate the foreign correspondence in the office; the clerks called him "Bagatelle" and put salt in his tea. In general, this entire enterprise struck Laptev as being a monstrous eccentricity of some sort.

He now went to the warehouse every day and tried to establish new procedures; he forbade the clerks to whip the boys or mock the buyers, and he was beside himself when they gleefully consigned shopworn and worthless goods to the provinces under the guise of the latest and most fashionable stock. He was now the head of the warehouse, but he still did not know how great his fortune was, whether the business was doing well, how much the chief clerks were paid, and so on. Pochatkin and Makeichev considered him young and inexperienced, concealed a great deal from him, and continued to hold mysterious, whispered conversations with his blind old father every evening.

It happened that in the beginning of June Laptev and Pochatkin went to the Bubnovsky restaurant to discuss business over lunch. Pochatkin had worked for the Laptevs a long time; he had come to them at the age of eight, and was almost like one of them. They trusted him completely, and when he gathered up the daily receipts and stuffed them into his pockets on leaving the warehouse, it aroused no suspicion. He was the chief clerk in the warehouse, at home, and even in church, where he performed the duties of the elder in place of his master. Because of his cruel treatment of the boys and the subordinate clerks, he was nicknamed Malyuta Skuratov.

When they entered the restaurant he nodded to a waiter and said, "Bring us half a miracle, my boy, and twenty-four unsavories."

In a few minutes the waiter brought a tray on which there was a half bottle of vodka and several plates of various kinds of appetizers.

"Now as follows, my dear fellow," Pochatkin said to him, "give us a portion of the prime mover of all gossip and slander, with mashed potatoes."

The waiter did not understand and became confused; he was about to say something but Pochatkin gave him a severe look and said, "Notwithstanding!" After a moment of intent thought the waiter went into consultation with his colleagues and finally was able to surmise what was wanted: he brought a platter of tongue.

After they both had drunk a couple of glasses of vodka and had eaten, Laptev said, "Tell me, Ivan Vasilych, is it true that in recent years the business has begun to fall off?"

"Not at all."

"Speak out and tell me frankly what the profits have been, what they now are, and what our financial condition is. It's impossible, you know, to go on like this in the dark. Not long ago we had an accounting at the warehouse, but, if you will forgive me, I don't trust it; you apparently find it necessary to conceal something from me, and tell the truth to no one but my father. From early years you have been accustomed to playing politics, and now you can't do anything else. What's the good of it? And so, I ask you to be frank. What is the condition of our business?"

"It all depends on the undulation of credit," Pochatkin replied, after giving the matter some thought.

"What do you mean by 'undulation of credit'?"

Pochatkin began to explain, but Laptev could make nothing of what he was saying and sent for Makeichev. He appeared promptly, and after saying a prayer ate something, then, in his staid, mellow baritone, began to speak of the clerks' duty to pray day and night for their benefactors.

"Splendid, but, with your permission, I do not consider myself your benefactor," said Laptev.

"Every person ought to remember what he is and be conscious of his rank. You, by the grace of God, are our father and our benefactor, and we are your slaves."

"I am fed up with all that!" Laptev exclaimed angrily. "Please, you be my benefactor now, and explain the condition of our business to me. Kindly give up looking on me as a boy, otherwise I shall close the warehouse tomorrow. My father is blind, my brother is in a lunatic asylum, my nieces are still young; I loathe this business, and I should be glad to leave it, but, as you yourselves know, there is no one to replace me. Drop the diplomacy, for God's sake!"

They went to the warehouse to go over the accounts, and continued to work on them at home in the evening, the old man himself helping them. Initiating his son into his commercial secrets, he spoke as though he were engaged, not in trade, but in sorcery. It appeared that the yearly increase in profits was approximately ten per cent, and that the Laptev fortune, in cash and securities alone, amounted to six million rubles.

At one o'clock in the morning, after finishing the accounts, Laptev went out into the fresh air, still feeling as though he were under the spell of figures. The moonlight night was still and sultry. The white walls of the houses on the other side of the river, the heavy, barred gates, the silence, and the black shadows all combined to create the impression of a fortress; the only thing lacking was a sentry with a gun.

Laptev went into the garden and sat down on a bench near the fence that separated them from the neighbor's yard, which also had a garden. The bird cherry was in bloom. He remembered this tree as being just as large and crooked when he was a child; it had in no way changed since then. Every corner of the garden and the yard reminded him of a time long past. In his childhood, even as now, the whole moonlit yard could be seen through the sparse trees, the shadows had been just as mysterious and forbidding, the windows of the clerks' rooms had stood wide open, and then, as now, a black dog had lain in the middle of the yard. All these were melancholy memories.

Beyond the fence, in the neighboring yard, there was the sound of light footsteps. . . . "My darling, my sweetheart," whispered a masculine voice, so near the fence that Laptev could even hear the sound of breathing.

Now they were kissing. . . . Laptev was convinced that the millions and the business, for which he had an aversion, would ruin his life and end in making a slave of him; he visualized how, little by little, he would habituate himself to his position, little by little enter into the role of head of a commercial firm, grow dull, old, and finally die like any ordinary man, wretched, embittered, and plaguing everyone around him. But what was to prevent his giving up the millions and the business, and leaving this yard and garden, which since childhood had been hateful to him?

The whispering and kissing on the other side of the fence agitated him. He walked to the middle of the yard, unbuttoned his shirt over his chest, and looked at the moon; he felt like ordering the gate to be unlocked and walking out, never to return. His heart throbbed sweetly with a foretaste of freedom; he laughed for joy, imagining how wonderful, poetic, and even consecrated life might be. . . .

And still he did not move, but stood there asking himself: What is it that holds me here? He was vexed with himself and with the black dog, which, instead of running in a field, a forest, any place where it could be free and happy, lay stretched out on the stone paving. Clearly, both he and the dog were prevented from leaving the yard by one and the same thing: habituation to captivity and the servile condition. . . .

At noon the following day he went to see his wife, and, to avoid being bored, invited Yartsev to go with him. Yulia Sergeyevna was living in a *dacha* at Butovo, and he had not visited her for five days. On arriving at the station the friends took a carriage, and all the way Yartsev sang and was in ecstasy over the magnificent weather. The villa was located in a large park not far from the station. About twenty paces from where the principal avenue began, Yulia Sergeyevna sat under a broad old poplar tree waiting for her guests. She was wearing a sheer, elegant dress of a pale cream color, trimmed with lace, and in her hand she held the old familiar parasol. Yartsev greeted her and went on to the house, from whence came the sounds of Sasha's and Lida's voices. Laptev sat down beside his wife to talk of business matters.

"Why have you been so long in coming?" she asked, still keeping his hand in hers. "I sit here for whole days, watching, wondering whether you will come. I miss you so!" She stood up, passed her hand over his hair, and looked intently into his face, at his shoulders, and his hat. "You know, I love you," she said, blushing. "You are very dear to me. Now you have come, I can't tell you how happy it makes me to see you! Well, let us talk. Tell me something."

She had told him that she loved him, and he could only feel as though he had been married to her for ten years, and was longing for his lunch. She put her arm around his neck and the silk of her dress tickled his cheek; he carefully removed her hand, stood up, and, without a word, walked toward the house. The little girls came running to meet him.

"How they have grown!" he thought. "And how many changes there have been in these three years. . . . But then, one may have to live another thirteen, another thirty years. . . . Something still awaits us in the future! We shall live—and we shall see."

Sasha and Lida clung to him; he embraced them and said, "Grandfather sends his regards. . . . Uncle Fedya is not going to live much longer. . . . Uncle Kostya has sent a letter from America, with greetings to you. He's bored at the exposition and will return soon. And Uncle Alyosha is hungry."

He sat on the porch and watched his wife walking slowly along the avenue toward the house. She was deep in thought; her face wore a charming, melancholy expression and her eyes glistened with tears. She was no longer the pale, slender, fragile girl she once had been, but a mature, vigorous, beautiful woman. Laptev noticed the delight with which Yartsev gazed at her when they met, and saw a reflection of her new, lovely expression in the rapturous melancholy of his face. It was as though he were seeing her for the first time in his life. While they were at lunch on the porch, Yartsev kept looking at Yulia, at her beautiful neck, with a sort of joyous, shy smile. Laptev could not help watching them; and he was thinking that perhaps he would have to live another thirteen, another thirty years. . . . And what would he be obliged to live through in that time? . . . What does the future hold for us?

And he thought: We shall live—and we shall see.

—1895

The House with the Mansard

An Artist's Story

I

IT HAPPENED six or seven years ago, when I was living in one of the districts of the province of T——, on the estate of a landowner called Byelokurov, a young man who got up very early, went about in a long sleeveless peasant coat, drank beer in the evenings, and was always complaining to me that he never met with sympathy from anyone, anywhere. He lived in a lodge in the garden, and I in the old manor house, in an enormous salon with columns, where the only furniture was a wide divan on which I slept, and a table at which I played patience. Here, even in calm weather, there was always a humming sound in the old Amos stoves, and during a thunderstorm the whole house shook as though it were about to crack into pieces; this was somewhat frightening, especially at night, when the ten great windows were suddenly lit up by a flash of lightning.

Condemned by fate to a life of perpetual idleness, I did absolutely nothing. For hours at a time I gazed out the window at the sky, the birds, the garden walks, read everything that was brought me by the post, and slept. Occasionally I left the house and wandered about till late in the evening.

One day as I was returning home I unexpectedly came upon an estate I had never seen before. The sun was already sinking, and evening shadows lay across the flowering rye. Two rows of towering old fir trees, so densely planted that they formed almost solid walls, enclosed an avenue of somber beauty. I climbed the fence with no difficulty, and proceeded along the avenue, slipping on the fir needles which lay almost two inches deep on the ground. It was still and dark but for a shimmer of golden light high in the tree-tops, which here and there cast rainbows on the spider webs. The fragrance of fir needles was almost suffocating. I soon turned into a long avenue of lime trees. Here, too, everything was desolate and aged; last year's leaves rustled mournfully underfoot, and shadows lurked among the trees. From an ancient orchard on the right came the faint, reluctant note of an oriole—the bird, too, was probably old. And then the lime trees came to an end; I walked by a white house with a veranda and a mansard roof, and there suddenly opened before me a view of a courtyard, a wide pond with a bathhouse, a clump of willows, and on the farther bank a village with a tall, slender belfry on which a cross glowed in the last rays of the setting sun. For a moment I was under the spell of something familiar and very dear to me, as though I had seen this very same landscape at some time in my childhood.

At the white stone gateway that led from the courtyard to the open fields—a solid, old-fashioned pair of gates adorned with lions—stood two girls. One of them, the elder, slender, pale, and very beautiful, with masses of auburn hair and a stubborn little mouth, looked very severe and scarcely took any notice of me; the other, however, still very young—not more than seventeen or eighteen—also slender and pale, but with a large mouth and large eyes, gazed at me with astonishment as I walked by, said something in English, then looked confused; and it seemed to me that I had also known these two charming faces at some remote time. I returned home feeling as if I had had a dream.

Not long after this, one midday when Byelokurov and I were taking a walk near the house, there was an unexpected rustling of grass and a carriage drove into the yard; in it sat one of the girls I had seen—the elder. She had come with a subscription list to ask help for the victims of a fire. Without looking at us she very seriously and precisely told us how many houses in the village of Siyanovo had burned down, the number of men, women, and children left homeless, and what steps the relief committee, of which she was a member, proposed to take. She gave us the list to sign, then put it away and immediately said good-bye.

"You've quite forgotten us, Pyotr Petrovich," she said to Byelokurov, as she gave him her hand. "Come and see us, and if Monsieur N—— (she mentioned my name) would care to see how the admirers of his talent live, and will come with you, my mother and I would be delighted."

I bowed.

When she had gone Pyotr Petrovich began telling me about her. The girl, he said, was of a good family; her name was Lidia Volchaninova, and both the estate on which she lived with her mother and sister and the village on the other side of the pond were called Shelkovka. Her father had once held a prominent position in Moscow, and had died with the rank of privy councilor. Although they had ample means, the Volchaninovs lived in the country summer and winter, never leaving their estate; Lidia taught in the zemstvo school in Shelkovka, her own village, and received a salary of twenty-five rubles a month. She spent nothing on herself but what she earned, and was proud of being self-supporting.

"An interesting family," said Byelokurov. "Let us go and visit them one day. They will be delighted to see you."

One day after dinner—it was a holiday—we thought of the Volchaninovs and set out for Shelkovka to see them. We found the mother and both daughters at home. The mother, Yekaterina Pavlovna, who apparently had once been beautiful but now was stouter than her age warranted, suffered from asthma, and was melancholy and absent-minded. She undertook to entertain me with talk about painting. Having learned from her daughter that I might perhaps visit Shelkovka, she had hastily called to mind two or three of my landscapes that she had seen at exhibitions in Moscow, and now asked me what I had intended to express by them. Lidia, or, as she was called at home, Lida, talked more to Byelokurov than to me. Serious and unsmiling, she asked him why he did not work in the zemstvo, and why he had never attended any of its meetings.

"It's not right, Pyotr Petrovich," she said reproachfully. "It's not right. It's a shame!"

"True, Lida, true," her mother agreed. "It's not right."

"Our whole district is in the hands of Balagin," Lida continued, turning to me. "He's the chairman of the board, and he's distributed all the district offices among his nephews and sons-in-law, and he does whatever he likes. He ought to be opposed. We young people ought to form a strong party. But you see what our young men are like. It's a shame, Pyotr Petrovich!"

The younger sister, Zhenya, remained silent while they talked of the zemstvo. She took no part in serious conversation, being considered not quite grown up by her family; they still called her "Misuce," as though she were a little girl, because as a child that was her way of saying "Mrs." to her governess. She kept looking at me with curiosity, and when I examined the photograph album she explained it to me: "That's my uncle . . . that's my godfather . . ." and she drew her little finger across the portraits, childishly brushing against me with her shoulder, and I could see her delicate, undeveloped bosom, her thin shoulders, her plait, and her slender little body tightly drawn in by a sash.

We played croquet and lawn tennis, walked about in the

garden, drank tea, and then sat a long time over supper. After the huge, empty salon with columns, I felt somehow at home in this small, cozy house in which there were no oleographs on the walls and the servants were addressed politely; it all seemed very young and pure, thanks to the presence of Lida and Misuce, and everything breathed integrity. At supper Lida again spoke to Byelokurov about the zemstvo, Balagin, and school libraries. She was a spirited, sincere girl with convictions, and it was interesting to listen to her, though she talked a great deal and in a loud voice—perhaps because she was accustomed to speaking in school. My friend Pyotr Petrovich, on the other hand, who from his student days had retained the habit of reducing every conversation to an argument, was tedious, vapid, and long-winded, and spoke with the obvious desire of appearing to be a clever man with progressive views. Gesticulating, he overturned the sauceboat with his cuff, making a large pool on the tablecloth, which apparently was noticed by no one but me.

The night was dark and still as we walked home.

"Good breeding does not consist in not upsetting the sauceboat, but in not noticing it if someone else does," said Byelokurov, with a sigh. "Yes, an admirable, intellectual family. I'm terribly out of touch with nice people, terribly! And all because of work, work, work!"

He talked of how hard one had to work if one wanted to be a model farmer. And I thought: what a muddled, slothful fellow he is! When he spoke of anything serious his exertion expressed itself in a prolonged series of "er-er-er's"; and he worked exactly as he spoke—slowly, always late, never getting anything done on time. I had no faith in his capacity for business, if only because the letters I gave him to post remained in his pocket for weeks.

"And the hardest thing of all," he muttered, as he walked along beside me, "the hardest thing of all is that you work and work, and never get any sympathy from anyone. No sympathy whatsoever!"

II

I began to frequent the Volchaninovs'. Generally I sat on the lowest step of the veranda; oppressed by dissatisfaction with myself, and filled with regrets for my life, which was passing so rapidly and uninterestingly, I was forever thinking how good it would be to tear out of my breast the heart that had grown so heavy. Meanwhile, they talked on the veranda, and I could hear the rustling of their dresses and of pages being turned. I soon grew accustomed to the idea that during the day Lida received the sick, distributed books, and frequently went to the village carrying a parasol but without a hat, and in the evening talked in a loud voice about the zemstvo and schools. Whenever the conversation turned on practical matters, this slender, beautiful, invariably austere girl with the exquisitely chiseled little mouth would turn to me and in a dry tone say, "This won't interest you. . . ."

She did not find me sympathetic. She disliked me for being a landscape painter and not depicting the needs of the people in my pictures, and also for being indifferent, as she thought, to what she so strongly believed in. I remember once driving along the shore of Lake Baikal and meeting a Buryat girl on horseback, dressed in a shirt and trousers of blue Chinese cotton; I asked her if she would sell me her pipe, and as we talked she stared contemptuously at my European features and my hat; in a moment she grew bored talking to me, and with a wild shout galloped away. In exactly the same way Lida despised me as an alien. She gave no outward sign of her dislike, but I could feel it; and as I sat there on the lowest step of the veranda I experienced a feeling of irritation, and remarked that treating peasants when one was not a doctor was to deceive them, and that it was easy to be philanthropic when one had over five thousand acres of land.

Her sister, Misuce, had no such cares, and spent her life in complete idleness, as I did. As soon as she got up in the morning she would take up a book and start to read, sitting on the veranda in a deep armchair, her feet scarcely touching the floor; or she would seclude herself in the avenue of lime trees, or walk beyond the gates into a field. She spent the entire day poring over a book, but only an occasional tired, dazed look and the extreme pallor of her face revealed that this reading was a mental strain. When I arrived, as soon as she caught sight of me she would flush slightly, drop her book, and, looking into my face with her large eyes, would eagerly tell me whatever had happened—that the chimney in the servants' quarters had been on fire, or that one of the workmen had caught a big fish in the pond. On ordinary days she usually wore a light blouse and a dark blue skirt. We took walks together, picked cherries for jam, went rowing in the boat; and when she jumped up to reach a cherry or when she pulled the oars, her thin, delicate arms could be seen through the wide, transparent sleeves of her blouse. Sometimes I would sketch while she stood by my side and watched me with delight.

One Sunday at the end of July I arrived at the Volchaninovs' about nine o'clock in the morning. I walked through the park, keeping at a distance from the house, looking for white mushrooms, which were plentiful that summer, and marking the places where I found them so that later I could come and gather them with Zhenya. A warm breeze was blowing. I saw Zhenya and her mother, both in light holiday dresses, walking home from church, Zhenya holding her hat against the wind. Afterwards I could hear them having tea on the veranda.

For a carefree person like myself, ever seeking an excuse for perpetual idleness, these festive summer mornings in country houses have always held a singular charm. When the garden, all green and sparkling with dew, lies radiant and joyous in the sunshine, when there is a fragrance of mignonette and oleander near the house, when young people, all charmingly dressed and gay, having just returned from church, are drinking tea in the garden, and when one knows that all these healthy, well-fed, handsome people are going to do nothing the whole day long, then one wishes that all of life could be like this. These are the thoughts I had as I walked in the garden, and I was quite prepared to stroll about, without occupation and without aim, the whole day, the whole summer.

Zhenya came with a basket; her expression revealed that she had known, or at any rate felt, that she would find me in the garden. We gathered mushrooms and talked, and when she asked me a question she walked a little ahead in order to see my face.

"Yesterday a miracle took place in the village," she said. "Lame Pelageya has been ill a whole year, and no doctors or medicines did her any good, but yesterday an old woman whispered something over her, and she isn't ill any more!"

"That's of no importance," I said. "You don't have to seek miracles only among the sick and the old. Isn't health a miracle? And life itself? Anything that is beyond understanding is a miracle."

"But aren't you afraid of what you don't understand?"

"No, I approach phenomena that I do not understand boldly, and do not defer to them. I am above them. Man must recognize his superiority to lions, tigers, the stars, to everything in nature, even to what is beyond understanding and appears to be miraculous, otherwise he is not a man but a mouse, afraid of everything."

Zhenya thought that, being an artist, I knew a great deal and could accurately divine what I did not know. She longed for me to lead her into the domain of the eternal and the beautiful, to that higher realm where, in her opinion, I was quite at home, and she talked to me of God, eternal life, and the miraculous. And I, unwilling to admit that my self and my imagination would perish forever after death, replied, "Yes, man is immortal." And she listened, believed, and never demanded proof.

As we walked toward the house she suddenly stopped and said, "Our Lida is a remarkable person. Don't you think so? I love her with all my heart; I would readily sacrifice my life for her. But tell me"—Zhenya touched my sleeve with her finger—"tell me why you always argue with her. Why do you become so irritated?"

"Because she is wrong."

Zhenya shook her head in protest, and tears came into her eyes. "That is inconceivable!" she exclaimed.

At that moment Lida, having just returned from somewhere, was standing near the veranda with a riding whip in her hand, a graceful, beautiful figure in the bright sunlight, giving orders to one of the workmen. Bustling about and talking loudly, she took care of two or three sick people, then, with a preoccupied, businesslike expression, walked from room to room, opening one cupboard after another, finally going to the attic. It was a long time before they could find her to call her to dinner, and by the time she came we had already finished the soup.

For some reason I remember and love all these petty details and, although nothing special happened, I still have a vivid memory of that whole day. After dinner Zhenya read, lying in the deep armchair, and I sat on the lowest step of the veranda. We did not talk. The sky was overcast, and a thin, fine rain began to fall. It was hot; the wind had gone down, and it seemed as though the day would never end. Yekaterina Pavlovna, still heavy with sleep, came out onto the veranda carrying a fan.

"Oh, Mama," said Zhenya, kissing her hand, "it's not good for you to sleep during the day!"

They adored each other. When one of them went into the garden, the other stood on the veranda looking toward the trees and called, "Oo-hoo, Zhenya!" or "Mamochka, where are you?" They always said their prayers together, sharing an identical faith, and understood each other perfectly, even without words. And their attitude toward people was the same. Yekaterina Pavlovna also became accustomed to my presence, and soon grew attached to me; when I did not come for two or three days she sent to ask if I was well. She, too, gazed admiringly at my sketches, and with the same candor and talkativeness as Misuce, told me everything that happened, often confiding to me her domestic secrets.

She stood in awe of her elder daughter. Lida was never affectionate, and spoke only of serous matters; she lived a life apart, and to her mother and sister was the sacred, somewhat enigmatic figure that an admiral, sequestered in his cabin, is to his sailors. "Our Lida is a remarkable person," her mother would often say, "isn't she?"

And now, as the soft rain fell, we talked of Lida.

"She is a remarkable person," said her mother; then, with a cautious glance over her shoulder, she added in a conspiratorial undertone, "You'd have to search with a lantern by daylight to find another like her! But, you know, I'm beginning to be somewhat alarmed. The school, the dispensary, books—that's all very well, but why go to extremes? She's almost twenty-four, you know; it's time she thought seriously about herself. If you go on like that with books and dispensaries, you don't see that life is passing. . . . She ought to marry."

Zhenya, pale from reading, her hair in disorder, raised her head and spoke as if to herself, while looking at her mother. "Mamochka, it all rests with God's will." And again she was immersed in her book.

Byelokurov arrived wearing his peasant coat and an embroidered shirt. We played croquet and lawn tennis, when it grew dark sat a long time over supper, and Lida again talked about schools and Balagin, who had the whole district under his thumb.

As I left the Volchaninovs' that evening, I carried away the impression of a long, long, idle day, and a melancholy awareness that everything in this world, however long it may last, comes to an end. Zhenya accompanied us to the gateway, and perhaps because I had spent the entire day from beginning to end with her, I began to feel that I should be lonely without her, that this whole charming family was very close to me; and for the first time all summer I had a desire to paint.

"Tell me, why do you lead such a dull, colorless life?" I asked Byelokurov as we walked home together. "My life is dull, difficult, monotonous, because I am a painter, an odd person; from my youth I have been torn by envy, dissatisfaction with myself, and misgivings about my work, and I have always been poor, a vagabond. But you—you're a healthy, normal man, a landowner and a gentleman—why do you live so uninterestingly? Why do you take so little from life? Why, for instance, haven't you fallen in love with Lida or Zhenya?"

"You forget that I love another woman," replied Byelokurov.

He was referring to his friend, Lyubov Ivanovna, who was living in the lodge with him. Every day I used to see this lady, plump, podgy, and pompous as a fattened goose, walking about the garden, always with a parasol, dressed in the Russian national costume and strings of beads. The servant was continually calling her either to a meal or to drink tea. Three years before, she had rented one of the lodges for the summer, and had stayed on, apparently forever. She was ten years older than he, and kept him well in hand, so much so that he even had to ask her permission to leave the house. She was given to sobbing in loud, masculine tones, and I used to send word to say that if she did not stop I would give up my room. She stopped.

When we reached home Byelokurov seated himself on the divan and, with a scowl, fell to pondering; I walked up and down the room, stirred by a sweet emotion, as if I were in love. I wanted to talk about the Volchaninovs.

"Lida could fall in love only with a member of the zemstvo, someone who is just as fascinated by hospitals and schools as she is," I said. "Oh, for the sake of such a girl, not only could one become a member of the zemstvo, but even, as in the fairy tale, wear out a pair of iron boots. And Misuce? How adorable that Misuce is!"

Byelokurov, with his drawling "er-er-er," held forth at length on the malady of the age—pessimism. He spoke emphatically, in a tone that suggested I was debating with him. Hundreds of versts of desolate, monotonous, sun-parched steppe cannot bring on the depression that is induced by one man who sits and talks, and gives no sign of ever going.

"It's not a question of either pessimism or optimism," I said irritably. "It's simply that ninety-nine out of a hundred people have no brains."

Byelokurov took this as a reflection on himself, was offended, and went away.

III

"The prince is visiting in Maloziomovo, and sends you his greetings," said Lida, removing her gloves as she came in. "He had a great deal of interesting news. . . . And he promised to raise the question of a medical station at Maloziomovo again at the next meeting of the provincial assembly, but he says there's not much hope." Then, turning to me, she added, "Excuse me, I keep forgetting that this sort of thing can be of no interest to you."

I felt exasperated. "Why of no interest to me?" I asked, shrugging my shoulders. "You don't care to hear my opinions, but I assure you, the question is of the greatest interest to me."

"It is?"

. "Yes, it is. In my opinion there is absolutely no need for a medical station at Malòziomovo."

My irritation communicated itself to her. "And what is there a need for—landscape paintings?"

"No, not for landscape paintings either. There is no need for anything there."

She finished taking off her gloves and opened a newspaper which had just come by post; a moment later, in a quiet voice, evidently trying to control herself, she said, "Last week Anna died in childbirth; if there had been a medical station in the neighborhood she would be alive now. It seems to me that even landscape painters ought to have some sort of convictions about this matter."

"I have very definite convictions about it, I assure you," I replied. But she hid behind the newspaper as if unwilling to hear me. "In my opinion, medical stations, schools, libraries, dispensaries, under existing conditions, serve only to enslave the people. They are fettered by a great chain, and you do not sever the chain, you simply add new links to it—those are my convictions."

She raised her eyes to my face and smiled derisively, but I went on, trying to catch hold of my main idea.

"What matters is not that Anna died in childbirth, but that all these Annas, Mavras, Pelageyas are oppressed by work from morning till night, and are all ill from overwork; their entire lives they're trembling for their sick and hungry children and doctoring themselves in fear of sickness and death; they fade early, age early, and die in filth and stench. Their children grow up and it's the same story, and so it goes on for hundreds of years, millions of people living worse than animals—in constant dread, and all for a mere crust of bread. The whole horror of their situation lies in the fact that they never have time to think of their souls, never have time to recollect their own image and likeness; hunger, cold, animal fear, massive work, like an avalanche, block all roads to spiritual activity—to the very thing that distinguishes a human being from an animal, to the only thing that makes life worth living. You come to their aid with hospitals and schools, but this does not free them from their shackles; on the contrary, it further enslaves them, since, by introducing new prejudices, you increase the number of their wants; not to mention the fact that they have to pay the zemstvo for their drugs and books, which only increases their burden."

"I am not going to argue with you," said Lida, putting down her newspaper. "I've heard all that before. I will say only one thing: it is impossible just to sit with your hands in your lap. True, we are not saving mankind, and perhaps we do make mistakes; but we do what we can—and in that we are right. The highest and most sacred task of a civilized man is to serve his neighbor, and we are endeavoring to serve as best we can. You may not like it, but then, one can't please everyone."

"True, Lida, true," said her mother.

She was always timid in Lida's presence, anxiously glancing at her whenever she wanted to speak, fearful of saying something superfluous or inappropriate, and she never contradicted her, but always concurred: true, Lida, true.

"Teaching the peasants to read and write, giving them books of wretched little precepts and adages, and medical stations, can no more lessen their ignorance or lower their death rate than the light from your windows can illuminate this huge garden," I said. "You're not giving them anything; by meddling in the lives of these people you do nothing but create new needs, new obligations to work."

"Oh, my God! But we must do something!" exclaimed Lida irately. Her tone made it evident that she considered my arguments trifling and contemptible.

"The people must be freed from heavy physical labor," I said. "They must be relieved of their yoke, given a respite, so that they do not spend their whole lives at the stove, at the washtub, in the fields, but may also have time to think of their souls, of God, and to develop their spiritual faculties. This spiritual activity—the continual search for truth and the meaning of life—is the vocation of every human being. Make it unnecessary for them to work like beasts of burden, let them feel that they are free, and you will see what a mockery these books and dispensaries are. Once a man becomes conscious of his true vocation, he can be satisfied only by religion, science, art—not by these trifles."

"Free them from work!" Lida smiled. "Do you really think that is possible?"

"Yes. Take upon yourself a share of their labor. If all of us, city and country dwellers alike, everyone without exception, would agree to divide among ourselves the work that is expended in satisfying the physical needs of mankind, each of us would be required to work perhaps two or three hours a day, no more. Imagine if we all, rich and poor alike, worked only three hours a day, and were free the rest of the time! Imagine too, if in order to depend still less upon our bodies, and to work less, we were to invent machines to replace our work, and tried to reduce the quantity of our needs to the minimum! We would harden ourselves and our children, so that they should not fear hunger and cold, and we should not continually tremble for their health like Anna, Mavra, and Pelageya. Imagine if we no longer doctored ourselves, maintained dispensaries, tobacco factories, distilleries—what a lot of free time we should have as a result! All of us together would devote this leisure to science and the arts. Just as the peasants sometimes work as a community to repair the roads, so all of us, as a community, would search for truth and the meaning of life, and—I am convinced of this—the truth would very soon be discovered, mankind would be delivered from this perpetual, agonizing, oppressive fear of death, and even from death itself."

"But you are contradicting yourself," said Lida. "You keep talking about science, but you reject literacy."

"Literacy, when a man can use it only to read tavern

signs, or an occasional book that he doesn't understand—
that kind of literacy we have had since the time of Rurik;
Gogol's Petrushka has long been able to read, and yet, as the
village was in Rurik's day, so it has remained. It is not literacy that is needed, but the freedom for a wide development
of our spiritual faculties. It is not schools that are needed,
but universities!"

"And you reject medicine, too."

"Yes, it would be required only for the study of diseases
as natural phenomena, and not for their cure. If anything is
treated, let it be the cause of the disease rather than the disease itself. Remove the principal cause, physical labor, and
there will be no disease. I do not acknowledge a science that
cures," I continued, growing excited. "Science and art, when
they are genuine, aspire not to temporary, not to partial
goals, but to the eternal and the universal—they seek the
truth and the meaning of life; they seek God, the soul, and
when they are harnessed to the necessities and the evils of
the day, to dispensaries, to libraries, they can only compli-
cate and encumber life. We have plenty of doctors, chemists,
lawyers, plenty of literate men; but we have no biologists,
mathematicians, philosophers, poets. All of our intellectual
and spiritual energies have gone into the satisfaction of temporary, passing needs. . . . Scientists, writers, and painters
work hard; thanks to them, the comforts of life increase
daily, the demands of the body are multiplied; meanwhile,
truth is a long way off, and man continues to be the most rapacious, the most unclean of animals, and everything tends
to the degeneration of the majority of mankind, and the permanent loss of all the vital capacities. In such conditions, the
life of the artist has no meaning, and the more talented he is
the more bizarre and incomprehensible is his role, as, on examination, it appears that he is working for the amusement
of a rapacious, filthy animal, and supporting the existing
order. I don't care to work for this, and I will not. . . . Nothing is of any use; let the world sink to the depths of hell!"

"Misuce, leave the room!" said Lida, evidently considering my language pernicious to so young a girl.

Zhenya looked mournfully from her sister to her mother, and went out.

"Such charming things are generally said when people wish to justify their indifference," said Lida. "It is easier to denounce schools and hospitals than it is to teach or heal."

"True, Lida, true," her mother said.

"You threaten to give up working," Lida continued. "You obviously have a high regard for your work. Let us stop arguing; we shall never agree, since I value the most imperfect of these libraries and dispensaries, of which you have just spoken so contemptuously, more highly than all the landscape paintings in the world." She abruptly turned to her mother and began speaking in a quite different tone. "The prince is very much changed, and much thinner than when he was last with us. They are sending him to Vichy."

She went on talking to her mother about the prince in order to avoid speaking to me. Her face was burning, and to conceal her agitation she bent low over the table as if she were shortsighted, and pretended to read the newspaper. My presence was disagreeable to her. I took my leave and went home.

IV

Outside all was quiet; the village on the other side of the pond was already asleep and not a light was to be seen but for the pale reflections of the stars on the water. At the gate with the lions Zhenya was standing motionless, waiting to walk a little way with me.

"Everyone is asleep in the village," I said, trying to discern her face in the darkness. I could see her sad, dark eyes fixed upon me. "The innkeeper and the horse thieves are sleeping peacefully, while we respectable people argue and irritate each other."

It was a melancholy August night—melancholy because already there was a scent of autumn in the air. The moon was rising behind a purple cloud, barely lighting the road and the dark fields of winter corn on either side of it. From time to time a star fell. Zhenya walked along the road beside me, trying not to look at the sky, to avoid seeing the shooting stars, which for some reason frightened her.

"I think that you are right," she said, shivering from the damp night air. "If people, all together, could devote themselves to spiritual activity, soon they would know everything."

"Of course! We are higher beings, and if we actually realized the full power of human genius, and lived only for higher purposes, ultimately we should become like gods. But that will never be—mankind will degenerate, and not a trace of genius will remain."

When the gates were out of sight, Zhenya stopped and hastily shook my hand.

"Good night," she said, shivering; her shoulders were covered with nothing but a thin blouse, and she was shrinking from the cold. "Come tomorrow."

The thought of being left alone in this irritated state of dissatisfaction both with myself and other people terrified me, and I, too, tried not to look at the falling stars.

"Stay with me a little longer," I said. "Please."

I was in love with Zhenya. I think I loved her because she always met me when I came, and walked with me when I went away; because her face, when she looked at me, was rapt and tender. How touchingly beautiful were her pale face, her slender neck and arms, her weakness, her idleness, her books! And her mind? I surmised that hers was a remarkable intellect; I was enchanted by the scope of her ideas, perhaps because she thought so differently from the austere and beautiful Lida, who did not like me. Zhenya loved me because I was an artist; I had conquered her heart with my talent, and I had a passionate desire to paint only for her; I dreamed of her as my little queen, who one day would hold sway with me over these trees, these fields, the mists, the dawn—all this miraculous, bewitching nature, in whose midst I had till now felt hopelessly alone and useless.

"Stay with me a moment longer," I pleaded. "I entreat you!"

I took off my coat and put it over her chilly shoulders; she laughed and flung it off, afraid of looking ugly or absurd in a man's coat, and at that instant I took her in my arms and covered her face, her shoulders, her hands, with kisses. . . .

"Till tomorrow," she whispered, and cautiously, as though fearing to violate the stillness of the night, embraced me. "We have no secrets from one another. I must tell my mother and sister at once. . . . It's frightening! Mama's all right, she likes you—but Lida!"

She ran back toward the gate.

"Good-bye!" she called.

For a moment I stood listening to the sound of her running footsteps. I had no desire to go home; there was no reason for me to go there. I stood lost in thought, then slowly made my way back, to look once more at the house in which she lived, the dear, simple old house, with the mansard windows that seemed to be peering down at me like eyes, understanding everything. I walked past the veranda and sat on a bench near the tennis court in the darkness under an ancient elm tree, from where I could look at the house. In the windows of the mansard, where Misuce had her room, there was bright light, then a soft green glow—someone had put a shade over the lamp. Shadows moved about. . . . I was filled with tenderness, serenity, and satisfaction with myself—satisfaction that I could let myself be carried away and fall in love; and at the same time I was made uneasy by the thought that at this very moment, only a few paces from me, in one of the rooms of that house, was Lida, who did not like me, perhaps even hated me. I sat there waiting to see if

Zhenya would come out, and as I listened for her it seemed to me that I could hear the sound of voices in the mansard.

An hour passed. The green light was extinguished, and the shadows were seen no more. The moon stood high above the house, shedding its light upon the sleeping garden and its paths; dahlias and the roses in the flower bed at the front of the house were clearly visible, and everything seemed to be of one color. It began to grow cold. I left the garden, picked up my coat on the road, and slowly made my way home.

When I arrived at the Volchaninovs' the following day after dinner, the glass door into the garden stood wide open. I sat down on the veranda, expecting that at any moment Zhenya would appear from behind the flower bed on the lawn, in one of the avenues, or that I should hear her voice from within the house. I went into the drawing room, then into the dining room. There was not a soul to be seen. From the dining room I walked down a long corridor to the entrance hall and back again. There were several doors in this corridor and through one of them I heard Lida's voice.

"To the crow somewhere . . . God . . ." She was speaking in a loud, distinct voice, probably dictating. "God sent a piece of cheese . . . to the crow . . . somewhere. . . . Who's there?" she suddenly called, hearing my step.

"It is I."

"Oh! Excuse me, I can't come out to you just now; I'm giving Dasha her lesson."

"Is Yekaterina Pavlovna in the garden?"

"No, she and my sister left this morning for a visit to my aunt in the province of Penza. And in the winter they will probably go abroad," she added after a pause. "God sent . . . the crow . . . a piece . . . of cheese. . . . Have you written it?"

I went back by the same way I had come that first day, but in reverse; from the courtyard to the garden, past the house, then along the avenue of lime trees. . . . At this point I was overtaken by a small boy who handed me a note: "I told my sister everything, and she insists that we part," I read. "I could not bring myself to hurt her by disobeying. God will give you happiness. Forgive me. If you only knew how bitterly Mama and I are weeping!"

Then came the dark avenue of fir trees, and the broken-down fence. . . . In the field where then the rye had been in flower and quails had called, now there were cattle grazing, and hobbled horses. Here and there the winter corn was bright green on the hills. A sober, prosaic mood took possession of me, and I felt ashamed of all I had said at the Volchaninovs', and bored with life, as I had been before. When I got home I packed my things, and that evening went to Petersburg.

I never saw the Volchaninovs again. Not long ago, on my way to the Crimea, I met Byelokurov in the train. He still wore his peasant coat and an embroidered shirt, and when I asked him how he was he replied, "Thanks to your prayers." We began to talk and he told me he had sold his estate and bought a smaller one, which he had put in Lyubov Ivanovna's name. He could tell me little about the Volchaninovs. Lida, he said, was still living in Shelkovka, and teaching in the school; gradually she had succeeded in gathering round her a circle of people who were in sympathy with her ideas, and who formed a strong party; at the last zemstvo elections they had ousted Balagin, who until then had held the whole district under his thumb. About Zhenya he could tell me only that she no longer lived at home, and that he did not know where she was.

I am beginning to forget the house with the mansard, and only now and then, when I am painting or reading, suddenly, for no apparent reason, I recall the green light in the window, the sound of my footsteps echoing through the field at night as I walked home, in love, and chafing my cold hands. And even more rarely, when I am oppressed by loneliness and feeling sad, I dimly remember, and little by little begin to feel that I too am being remembered and waited for, and that we shall meet. . . .

Misuce, where are you?

—1896

Peasants

I

NIKOLAI CHIKILDEYEV, a waiter in the Slavyansky Bazaar, a hotel in Moscow, had fallen ill. His legs went numb and his walk was affected, so that one day, as he was going along the corridor carrying a trayful of ham and peas, he stumbled and fell. He was obliged to give up his job. Whatever money he and his wife had was spent on doctors; they had nothing to live on; he grew dull without work and decided that as things stood he ought to return to his village. At home even illness is easier to bear, and it is cheaper to live there. Not without reason is it said: "There is succor in the very walls of a home."

He arrived in his village, Zhukovo, toward evening. In his memories of his childhood he had pictured his home as bright, cozy, comfortable, but now, going into the hut, he was positively scared: it was so dark, crowded, and unclean. His wife Olga and his daughter Sasha, who had come with him, stared in perplexity at the large, filthy oven, which occupied almost half the room and was black with soot and flies. What a lot of flies! The stove was lopsided, the log beams in the walls were on a slant, and the hut looked as if it were about to collapse. In the foremost corner of the room, near the ikons, bottle labels and scraps of newspaper were pasted on the walls instead of pictures. The poverty! The poverty! None of the grownups was at home; everyone was out reaping. On the oven sat a flaxen-haired girl of eight, unwashed and apathetic; she did not even look at them as they came in. Below her a white cat was rubbing itself against the oven fork.

"Pussy, pussy!" Sasha called coaxingly. "Pussy!"

"She can't hear you," said the little girl. "She's gone deaf."

"Why?"

"Oh, somebody hit her."

Nikolai and Olga realized at a glance what life was like here, but said nothing to each other; silently they put down their bundles, and silently went out into the street. Their hut was the third from the end and seemed the poorest and oldest looking; the second was not much better; but the last one had a metal roof and curtains at the windows. That hut, not enclosed, stood apart; it was a tavern. The huts stood all in one row, and the entire little village—quiet, and dreamy, with willows, elders, and mountain ash peeping out from the yards—had a pleasant look.

Behind the peasants' farmsteads there began an abrupt, steep descent to the river, with huge stones jutting out here and there through the clay. Down the slope, paths wound about these stones and the pits dug by potters; pieces of broken pottery, some red, some brown, lay in heaps, and below there stretched a broad, level, bright-green meadow, already mown, over which the peasants' cattle were now wandering. The river, a verst from the village, meandered between wonderful leafy banks; beyond it was another broad meadow, a herd of cattle, long files of white geese, then, just as on the hither side, a steep rise, and at the top, on a hill, there was a village with a church that had five domes, and, at a little distance, a manor house.

"How lovely it is here!" said Olga, crossing herself at the sight of the church. "Heavens, what space!"

Just at that moment the bells began ringing for vespers (it was Saturday evening). Down below, two little girls who were lugging a pail of water looked round at the church to listen to the tolling of the bells.

"About this time they are serving dinner at the Slavyansky Bazaar," Nikolai said dreamily.

Sitting on the edge of the ravine, Nikolai and Olga watched the sunset, and saw how the gold and crimson sky was reflected in the river, in the church windows, and in the very air around them, which was soft and still and inexpressibly pure, as it never was in Moscow. And when the sun had set and the herd went past, bleating and lowing, geese flew across from the other side of the river—then all was silent; the soft light faded from the air, and the evening darkness rapidly descended.

Meanwhile Nikolai's father and mother had returned; two emaciated, bent, toothless old people, both of the same height. The daughters-in-law, Marya and Fyokla, also came home from their work on the estate across the river. Marya, the wife of Nikolai's brother Kiryak, had six children, and Fyokla, the wife of his brother Denis, who was in the army, had two; when Nikolai entered the hut and saw the whole family—all those big and little bodies moving about on sleeping-shelves, in cradles, and in every corner, and when he saw the greed with which the old man and the women ate black bread, sopping it in water, he realized that he had made a mistake in coming here, sick, with no money, and with a family, too—a mistake!

"And where is brother Kiryak?" he asked, after they had exchanged greetings.

"He's watchman for a merchant," his father replied. "He stays there in the woods. He wouldn't be a bad peasant if he didn't drink so much."

"He's no breadwinner!" said the old woman tearfully.

"Our men are a bad lot; they bring nothing into the house, but they take plenty out. Both of them, Kiryak and the old man, drink. No use hiding a sin, he knows his way to the tavern. We must have angered the Queen of Heaven!"

In honor of the guests they set up the samovar. The tea smelled of fish; the sugar was gray and gnawed; cockroaches ran over the bread and the crockery. It was revolting to drink the tea, and the conversation too was revolting—about nothing but sickness and want. And they had not finished drinking their first cups of tea before there came a loud, prolonged, drunken shout from the yard.

"Ma-arya!"

"Looks like Kiryak's coming," said the old man. "Speak of the devil. . . . "

Everyone fell silent. After a little while, again the same shout, harsh and long-drawn-out, as though it were coming out of the earth.

"Ma-arya!"

Marya, the elder daughter-in-law, turned pale and shrank against the oven, and it was strange to see the look of terror on the face of this powerful, broad-shouldered, homely woman. Her daughter, the pathetic child who had been sitting on the oven, suddenly broke into loud wails.

"What's the matter with you, pox-head?" shouted Fyokla, a handsome woman, also strong and broad-shouldered. "Don't worry, he's not going to kill her!"

Nikolai learned from the old man that Marya was afraid to live in the forest with Kiryak, and that every time he got drunk he came for her, created an uproar, and beat her unmercifully.

"Ma-arya!" The shout sounded close to the door.

"Protect me, for Christ's sake," spluttered Marya, breathing as if she had been plunged into very cold water. "Protect me, good people. . . . "

Every child in the hut began to cry, and, seeing them, Sasha too burst into tears. A drunken cough was heard, and in came a tall, black-bearded peasant wearing a winter cap, and, because his face could not be seen in the dim light of the little lamp, he was terrifying. It was Kiryak. He walked up to his wife, swung his arm, and struck her in the face with his fist. Stunned by the blow, she did not utter a sound, but only cowered, and instantly her nose began to bleed.

"What a disgrace! What a disgrace!" muttered the old man as he clambered up onto the oven. "Before visitors, too. It's a sin!"

The old woman sat hunched over, silent, lost in thought. Fyokla rocked the cradle. Obviously aware of the terror he aroused and pleased by it, Kiryak seized Marya by the arm and dragged her to the door, snarling like an animal in order to seem more terrible, but at that moment he suddenly caught sight of the guests and stopped.

"Ah, they've come," he said, letting his wife go. "My own brother with his family. . . . "

He said a prayer before the ikon, staggering and opening wide his bloodshot, drunken eyes.

"My brother and his family have come to the parental home . . . from Moscow, that is. The ancient capital, that is the city of Moscow . . . mother of cities. . . . Excuse me. . . . "

He sank down on a bench near the samovar and began drinking tea, loudly lapping it from the saucer amid general silence. He drank about a dozen cups, then lay down on the bench and began to snore.

They started going to bed. Because he was sick, Nikolai was to sleep on the oven with the old man. Sasha lay down on the floor, and Olga went with the women into the shed.

"Ay-ay, dearie," she said, lying down on the hay beside Marya. "Tears won't help your trouble. You have to bear it, and that's all. In the Scriptures it is written: 'Whosoever shall smite thee on thy right cheek, turn to him the other also.'. . . Ay-ay, dearie."

Then in a low, singsong voice she told them about

Moscow, about her life there, how she had worked in rooming houses as a chambermaid.

"And in Moscow the houses are big, made of stone," she said, "and there are many, many churches, forty times forty, dearie, and in the houses they're all gentry, so fine and so proper!"

Marya told her that not only had she never been to Moscow, but she had never even been in their own district town; she could neither read nor write, and knew no prayers, not even "Our Father." Both she and Fyokla, the other sister-in-law who sat listening a little way off, were exceedingly backward and could understand nothing. They both disliked their husbands; Marya was afraid of Kiryak, and whenever he stayed with her she shook with terror, and always got a headache from the vodka and tobacco fumes of which he reeked. And Fyokla, when asked if she missed her husband, spitefully replied, "He can go to the devil!"

They talked a little, then fell silent.

It was chilly, and near the shed a cock, crowing with all his might, kept them from sleeping. When the bluish morning light began to show through the cracks, Fyokla quietly got up and went out, and they could hear the thud of her bare feet as she ran off somewhere.

II

Olga went to church and took Marya with her. They were both in good spirits as they walked down the path to the meadow. Olga liked the wide sweep of country, and Marya felt that in her sister-in-law she had found someone close and akin to her. The sun was rising. Low over the meadow skimmed a drowsy hawk. The river looked murky; here and there a mist hovered over it, but on the farther side a strip of

light already lay across the hill, the church sparkled, and in
the garden of the manor house the rooks cawed indignantly.

"The old man's not so bad," Marya told her, "but
Granny's strict; she's free with her hand. Our own grain
lasted till Shrovetide, but now we buy flour at the tavern—
so she's angry; she says we eat too much."

"Ay-ay, dearie! You have to bear it, and that's all. It is
written: 'Come unto me, all ye that labor and are heavy
laden.'"

Olga spoke in a prim, singsong voice, and her gait was
that of a pilgrim woman, rapid and bustling. Every day she
read the Gospel, read it aloud like a sexton; much of it she
did not understand, but the sacred words moved her to tears,
and such words as "behold" and "verily" she pronounced
with a sweet faintness of heart. She believed in God, in the
Holy Virgin, in the saints; she believed that it was wrong to
offend anyone—whether simple people, Germans, gypsies,
or Jews—and woe even to those who did not pity animals;
she believed it was so written in the Scriptures; and when
she uttered phrases from Holy Writ, even though she did not
understand them, her face grew tender, compassionate, radiant.

"Where do you come from?" Marya asked her.

"I'm from the province of Vladimir. But I was taken to
Moscow long ago, when I was eight years old."

They came to the river. On the opposite side a woman
stood at the water's edge taking off her clothes. Marya recognized her.

"That's our Fyokla," she said. "She's been across the
river to the manor yard—to the stewards. She's a hussy, and
foul-mouthed—that's what she is!"

Black-browed Fyokla, with her hair hanging loose, still
young and agile as a girl, sprang from the shore and began
flailing the water with her legs, sending out waves in all directions.

"A foul-mouthed hussy!" Marya repeated.

A rickety log footbridge spanned the river, and just below it, in the clean transparent water, swam a shoal of broad-headed chub. Dew shimmered on the green bushes reflected in the water. There was a gust of warm air; it was soothing. What a beautiful morning! And how beautiful life could be in this world if it were not for poverty—terrible, everlasting poverty, from which there is no escape! Only to look around at the village was vividly to recall all that had happened yesterday, and the enchantment of the happiness that seemed to surround them instantly vanished.

When they reached the church Marya stood in the entrance and did not dare to go farther; nor did she dare to sit down, though they only began ringing for the service after eight o'clock. She remained standing the whole time.

While the Gospel was being read the crowd suddenly parted to make way for the squire's family; two young girls wearing white dresses and broad-brimmed hats came in, and with them a plump, rosy little boy in a sailor suit. Olga was moved by their appearance; from the first glance she decided that they were well-bred, cultivated, handsome people. But Marya sullenly and despairingly looked at them from under her brows as if they were not human beings, but monsters that might trample her if she did not make way for them.

And every time the deacon intoned in his bass voice, it seemed to her that she heard the cry "Ma-arya!" and she shuddered.

III

The arrival of visitors became known in the village, and by the time the service was over a great many people had gathered in the hut. The Leonychevs, the Matveichevs, and the Ilyichovs came to make inquiries about relations who were working in Moscow. All the Zhukovo boys who could read and write were packed off to Moscow and hired out as waiters and bellboys (just as those from the village on the other side of the river were apprenticed only to bakers). Such had been the custom since the days of serfdom, when a certain Luka Ivanych—a Zhukovo peasant who was now a legendary figure—had been head butler in one of the Moscow clubs, and would take none but fellow villagers into his service; and these in turn, as they rose in position, sent for their kinsmen and found places for them in tea-houses and restaurants, and from that time on the village of Zhukovo was never called anything but "Toadyville" or "Lackeytown" by the inhabitants of the neighboring villages. Nikolai had been taken to Moscow when he was eleven, and Ivan Makarych, one of the Matveichevs, who was then a headwaiter at the Hermitage Garden, found a place for him.

And now, addressing the Matveichevs, Nikolai said sanctimoniously, "Ivan Makarych is my benefactor, and I am bound to pray for him day and night, as it was through him that I have become a good man."

"God bless you!" tearfully exclaimed a tall old woman, the sister of Ivan Makarych. "We have heard nothing of him, the dear man."

"Last winter he was in service at Omon's, but this season there was a rumor that he was somewhere out of town, in a garden restaurant. . . . He has aged! It used to be that he would bring home ten rubles a day in the summertime, but now things are quiet everywhere, and it's hard on the old man."

The women looked at Nikolai's pale face, at his feet shod in felt boots, and mournfully said, "You're no breadwinner, Nikolai Osipych; you're no breadwinner! No, indeed!"

They all made much of Sasha. She was going on eleven, but was so small and thin that she looked no more than seven. Among the other little girls, dressed in long faded smocks, sunburned, with shaggy, cropped hair, she, with her white skin, her large dark eyes, and a little red ribbon in her hair, seemed droll, like some little wild creature that had been caught in the fields and brought into the hut.

"She can read, too," Olga boasted, looking tenderly at her daughter. "Read something, child!" she said, getting the Gospels from the corner. "You read, and the good Christian folk will listen."

The testament, an old, heavy volume with soiled edges, was bound in leather and gave off an odor as of monks coming into the hut.

Sasha raised her eyebrows and in a loud singsong began, "'And when they were departed, behold, the angel of the Lord . . . appeareth to Joseph in a dream, saying, Arise, and take the young child and his mother . . .'"

"'The young child and his mother,'" Olga repeated, flushing with emotion.

"'And flee into Egypt, and be thou there until I bring thee word. . . .'"

At these words Olga could not restrain her tears and began to weep. Seeing her, Marya gave a sob, then Ivan Makarych's sister followed their example. The old man coughed and fussed about, looking for something to give his little granddaughter, but he could find nothing, and gave it up with a wave of his hand. When the reading was over the neighbors returned to their homes, deeply moved and very much pleased with Olga and Sasha.

Because it was a holiday, the family spent the whole day at home. The old woman, who was called Granny by her husband and daughters-in-law, as well as by her grandchildren, tried to do everything herself. She lit the oven, set out the samovar, even carried the midday meal to the men in the fields, and then grumbled that they were wearing her out with work. She continually worried for fear someone should eat too much or sit idle. At one time she would hear the tavernkeeper's geese going along the back of the huts to her kitchen garden and would run out with a long stick, and, standing by her cabbages, which were as withered and scraggy as herself, would spend half an hour shrilly railing at them. At another time she would imagine that a crow was stealing up on her chickens, and she would rush at it with loud words of imprecation. She scolded and grumbled from morning till night, often raising such an outcry that passers-by stopped in the street.

She treated the old man unkindly, calling him a good-for-nothing, a scourge. He was a shiftless, unreliable peasant, and perhaps if she had not nagged him continually he would not have worked at all, but would only have sat on the stove and talked. He told his son at great length about certain enemies of his, complained of the insults from neighbors that he had to put up with every day, and he was tiresome to listen to.

"Yes," he would say, standing arms akimbo, "yes . . . a week after the Exaltation of the Cross I sold my hay at thirty kopecks a pood, of my own free will. . . . Yes. . . . Well. . . . All right, so you see, I'm taking my hay in the morning, of my own free will, not bothering anyone, and in an evil hour I see the village headman, Antip Sedelnikov, coming out of the tavern. 'Where are you taking it, you so and so?' he says, and fetches me one on the ear."

Kiryak had a racking headache from drinking and was ashamed to face his brother.

"What vodka will do!" he muttered, shaking his throbbing head. "You must forgive me, brother and sister, for Christ's sake. I'm not happy about it myself."

Because it was a holiday they bought a herring at the tavern and made a broth from the head. At midday they sat down to drink tea, and drank cup after cup until they all perspired; after that they began on the broth, all helping themselves from one pot. But the herring itself Granny hid away.

In the evening a potter was firing pots on the slope. Down in the meadow the girls got up a round dance and

sang songs; someone played an accordion. On the other side
of the river too, one kiln was burning, girls were singing,
and from a distance it sounded sweet and melodious. In and
about the tavern the peasants created an uproar, singing in
drunken, discordant voices, and swearing so that Olga could
only shudder and say, "Oh, Holy Fathers!"

She was amazed that the cursing was so incessant, that
those who swore the loudest and most continually were the
old men, who were close to death. And the children and
young girls listened to this foul language without being in
the least perturbed; they had apparently grown accustomed
to it in their cradles.

It was past midnight, and the fires in the kilns on both
sides of the river had died down, but on the meadow below
and in the tavern the revelry continued. The old man and
Kiryak, walking arm in arm, both drunk and bumping
against each other, went up to the shed where Olga and
Marya were lying.

"Leave her be," the old man urged, "leave her be. . . .
She's a quiet woman. . . . It's a sin. . . . "

"Ma-arya!" shouted Kiryak.

"Leave her be. . . . It's a sin. . . . She's not a bad woman."

They stood by the shed for a moment and then went on.

"I lo-ove the flowers of the fi-ield," the old man suddenly
began singing in a high piercing tenor. "I lo-ove to gather
them in the meadows!"

Then he spat, and with a filthy oath went into the hut.

IV

Granny stationed Sasha near her kitchen garden and told
her to take care that the geese did not get in. It was a hot August day. The tavernkeeper's geese could steal into the garden from the back, but at the moment they were occupied

with other matters; they were picking up oats near the tavern, peacefully chatting, and only the gander craned his neck as though wishing to see whether the old woman with the stick was coming. There were other geese that could have come up from below, but now they were feeding far on the other side of the river, a long white garland of them stretched across the meadow. Sasha stood there for a while, grew restless, and, seeing that the geese were not coming, walked away to the slope.

There she saw Marya's eldest daughter, Motka, standing motionless on a large rock, staring at the church. Marya had borne thirteen children, but only six were living, all girls, not a single boy, and the eldest was eight. Motka, barefooted and wearing a long smock, stood with the sun blazing down on her head, but she seemed to be as unaware of it as though she had turned to stone. Sasha stood beside her and looked at the church.

"God lives in the church," she said. "People have lamps and candles, but God has little red and green and blue ikon lamps, like tiny eyes. At night God walks in the church, and the Holy Mother of God and Saint Nikolai walk with him— thump, thump, thump they go! And the watchman is dreadfully scared! . . . Ay-ay, dearie," she added, in imitation of her mother. "And when the end of the world comes, then all the churches will fly up to heaven."

"E-e-ven the be-ells?" Motka asked in her deep voice, drawling every syllable.

"Even the bells. And when the end of the world comes, the good people will go to paradise, and the mean ones will burn in an eternal and undying fire, dearie. To my mama, and to Marya, too, God will say: 'You never harmed anyone, so you go to the right, to paradise'; but to Kiryak and Granny He'll say: 'You go to the left, into the fire.' And whoever doesn't keep their fast in Lent will go into the fire, too."

She looked up at the sky, opening her eyes wide, and

said, "Look at the sky and don't blink your eyes—and you'll see the angels."

Motka, too, peered at the sky, and a minute passed in silence.

"See them?" Sasha asked.

"No, I don't," replied Motka in her deep voice.

"But I do. Wee little angels flying through the sky, and their tiny wings go flip-flop, like mosquitos."

Motka stared at the ground and thought about this, then she asked, "Is Granny going to burn?"

"She is, dearie."

From the rock down to the very bottom the even slope was covered with soft green grass that made one long to lie upon it or to touch it with one's hands. Sasha lay down and rolled to the bottom. Motka, with a solemn, stern expression, took a deep breath, lay down, and rolled after her, her smock climbing up to her shoulders.

"What fun it is!" said Sasha with delight.

They walked up to the top to roll down again, but at that moment they heard the shrill, familiar voice. Oh, how awful it was! Granny, toothless, bent and bony, her short gray hair flying in the wind, was driving the geese out of the kitchen garden with a long stick.

"They have trampled all the cabbages, the devils!" she shrieked. "You thrice-cursed, you pests, may you drop dead!"

She caught sight of the little girls, threw down her stick, picked up a switch, and, seizing Sasha by the neck with fingers that were dry and hard as spikes, began thrashing her. Sasha wept with pain and terror, while the gander, waddling and craning his neck, went up to the old woman and hissed at her; when he returned to the flock all the geese welcomed him with a "ga-ga-ga" of approbation. Then Granny proceeded to whip Motka, whose smock was again rolled up. With loud cries of despair, Sasha ran to the hut to complain. Motka followed, weeping in her deep voice, without wiping away her tears, and her face was as wet as if it had been splashed with water.

"Holy Fathers!" Olga cried in amazement when the two children came into the hut. "Queen of Heaven!"

Sasha began telling what had happened; at that moment Granny came in screaming and swearing; Fyokla flew into a rage, and the hut was in an uproar.

"Never mind, never mind!" Olga, pale and upset, comforted Sasha, stroking her head. "She's your grandmother; it's a sin to be angry with her. Never mind, child."

Nikolai, worn out by the perpetual clamor, the hunger, the suffocating fumes, the stench, by now loathing and despising the poverty, and ashamed of his parents before his wife and daughter, swung his legs off the oven, and in a tearful, fretful voice said to his mother, "You must not beat her! You have no right to beat her!"

"A-ah, you're going to die there on that oven anyway, you good-for-nothing!" Fyokla spitefully shouted at him. "The devil brought you here, you spongers!"

Sasha and Motka, and all the little girls in the hut, skulked in a corner on top of the oven behind Nikolai's back, and from there listened to everything in silent terror, and the beating of their little hearts could be heard. When there is someone in a family who has been ill, long and hopelessly ill, there come oppressive moments when all those close to him, fearfully, secretly, in the depths of their souls, long for his death; only children dread the death of someone close to them, and are always horrified at the thought. And now the little girls, scarcely breathing, stared at Nikolai with sorrowful expressions on their faces; they were thinking that he would die before long; they felt like crying, and longed to say something kind and comforting to him.

He pressed close to Olga, as though seeking her protection, and in a low, trembling voice said, "Olga, dear, I can't bear it here any longer. I haven't the strength. For God's sake, for the sake of Christ in heaven, write to your sister, Klavdia Abramovna. Let her sell and pawn everything she has, and send us the money, so we can go away from here. Oh Lord," he went on in anguish, "if only I could have a glimpse of Moscow! To see Mother Moscow, if only in my dreams!"

When evening came and the hut grew dark, it was so dismal that even to speak was difficult. Granny, still wrathful, soaked rye crusts in a cup and sucked them for a full hour. After milking the cow, Marya brought in a pail of milk and set it on a bench; then Granny very slowly poured it from the pail into jugs, taking her time, evidently well-pleased that now, during the Fast of the Assumption, no one could drink milk, and all of it would be left untouched. She poured the least little bit into a saucer for Fyokla's baby. When she and Marya carried the jugs down to the cellar, Motka suddenly roused herself, slipped down from the stove, and, going to the bench where the wooden cup full of crusts was standing, splashed some milk from the saucer into it.

When Granny returned she sat down to her crusts. Sasha and Motka watched her from the top of the oven, and they were glad that she was eating forbidden food and now would surely go to hell; it consoled them, and they lay down to sleep. As she dozed off, Sasha visualized the Last Judgment: a fire burning in an enormous stove that resembled a potter's kiln, and the Evil One, all black, with horns like a cow's, driving Granny into the fire with a long stick, just as she herself had driven the geese.

V

On the day of the Feast of the Assumption, between ten and eleven in the evening, the girls and boys making merry down in the meadow suddenly raised a cry, and ran scream-

ing in the direction of the village. People sitting on the brink
of the slope at first could not make out what was wrong.

"Fire! Fire!" Desperate cries were heard from below.
"We're burning!"

Those who were sitting above looked back, and a terrifying, extraordinary spectacle met their gaze. From the
thatched roof of one of the end huts rose a column of flame
seven feet high, swirling and scattering sparks in all directions like a spraying fountain. All at once the whole roof
burst into brilliant flame, and they heard the crackling of the
fire.

The light of the moon was obscured, and now the entire
village was bathed in a quivering red glow; black shadows
moved over the ground, there was a smell of burning, and
those who ran up from below were panting and trembling so
that they could not speak; they collided with one another,
fell down, and, unaccustomed to the bright light, could
hardly see and did not recognize one another. It was frightening. What was particularly horrifying was that above the
fire pigeons were flying in the smoke, and in the tavern,
where they were still unaware of the fire, people were
singing and playing the accordion as though nothing had
happened.

"Uncle Semyon's place is on fire!" someone shouted in a
loud, harsh voice.

Marya, her teeth chattering, was running about near her
hut, weeping and wringing her hands, though the fire was a
long way off, at the other end of the village. Nikolai came
out wearing felt boots, and the children ran about in their little smocks. Near the village policeman's hut a sheet of iron
was struck. Boom! Boom! Boom! floated through the air;
and this repeated unremitting sound wrung the heart and
made one turn cold. The old women stood about holding the
ikons. Sheep, calves, and cows were driven out of the yards
into the street; chests, sheepskins, tubs were carried out. A
black stallion that was kept apart from the herd because he

kicked and injured the horses was set free and ran through the village once or twice, neighing and pawing the ground, then stopped short near a cart and started kicking it with his hind legs.

The bells in the church on the other side of the river began to ring.

It was hot near the burning hut, and so light that every blade of grass on the ground was clearly visible. Semyon, a red-headed peasant with a large nose, wearing a jacket and a cap pulled down to his ears, sat on one of the chests they had succeeded in dragging out; his wife lay face down, unconscious and moaning. A little old man of eighty with a long beard, who resembled a gnome—not one of the villagers, but apparently in some way concerned with the fire—was walking about without a cap, carrying a white bundle in his arms; the blaze was reflected on his bald spot. The village headman, Antip Sedelnikov, black-haired and swarthy as a gypsy, went up to the hut with an ax and smashed the windows one after another—no one knew why—then began chopping the porch.

"Women, water!" he shouted. "Bring the engines here! Get a move on!"

The peasants who had just been carousing in the tavern pulled up the engine. They were drunk and kept stumbling and falling; they all looked helpless and had tears in their eyes.

"Girls, water!" shouted the headman, who was drunk, too. "Get a move on, girls!"

The women and girls ran down to where there was a spring and hauled pails and tubs of water up the hill, and after pouring it into the engine, ran down again. Olga, Marya, Sasha, and Motka all carried water. The women and boys pumped the water, the hose hissed, and the headman, directing it now at the door, now at the windows, controlled the stream with his finger, which made it hiss even more sharply.

"Brave fellow, Antip!" voices shouted approvingly. "Keep it up!"

Antip plunged into the burning hut and shouted from within, "Pump! Come on—exert yourselves, good Christians, in this unfortunate catastrophe!"

The peasants stood in a crowd staring at the fire and doing nothing. No one knew what to do, no one knew how to do anything, though there were stacks of grain and hay, piles of fagots, and sheds near by. Kiryak and old Osip, his father, both tipsy, stood there, too. And, as though to justify his idleness, the old man said to the woman lying on the ground, "Why take it so hard, friend? The hut's insured—why worry?"

Semyon, addressing himself now to one person, now to another, kept telling how the fire had started. "That same old man, the one with the bundle, a house serf of General Zhukov's—at the general's, may he rest in peace, he was a cook—he came over this evening. 'Let me stay the night,' he says. Well, we had a glass, to be sure. . . . The wife got busy with the samovar—we were going to give the old man some tea, and in an unlucky hour she set the samovar in the entry, and the sparks from the chimney, you see, must have gone straight to the roof, to the thatch. That's how it was. We were nearly burnt up ourselves. The old man's cap was burned up; it's a shame!"

The sheet iron was struck unremittingly, and the bells continued ringing in the church on the other side of the river. Olga, flushed and breathless, looking with horror at the red sheep and at the pink pigeons flying through the smoke, kept running down the slope and up again. It seemed to her that the ringing sound had penetrated her soul like a sharp thorn, that the fire would never end, that Sasha was lost. . . . And when the roof of the hut fell in with a crash, the thought that now the entire village would surely burn made her feel weak, and she could no longer go on carrying water, but sat down at the edge of the slope, setting the buckets nearby;

beside her and down below the peasant women sat wailing as though for the dead.

Stewards and workmen came in two carts from the estate across the river, bringing a fire engine with them. A very young student in an unbuttoned white tunic rode up on horseback. The pounding of axes was heard; then a ladder was placed against the burning frame of the building and five men climbed it at once, led by the young student, who was red in the face and, in the tone of one accustomed to putting out fires, shouted in a hoarse, strident voice. They pulled the house to pieces a log at a time, dismantled and dragged away the cow shed, the wattled fence, and a stack of hay that stood near by.

"Don't let them break it down!" Grim voices rang out in the crowd. "Don't let them!"

Kiryak headed for the hut with a determined air, as though intending to prevent the newcomers from breaking it up, but one of the workmen turned him back and struck him on the neck. There was a laugh, and the workman struck him again. Kiryak fell and crawled back into the crowd on all fours.

Two beautiful girls wearing hats—probably the young student's sisters—arrived from across the river. They stood a little way off, watching the fire. The logs that had been pulled away were no longer burning, but continued to give off a heavy smoke; the student, who was working the hose, turned the water first on these logs, then on the peasants, then on the women hauling the water.

"Georges!" the girls called to him reproachfully, alarmed, "Georges!"

The fire was over. And only when they began to disperse did they notice that it was already dawn, that everyone looked pale and somewhat swarthy, as people do in the early morning when the last stars are fading. As they parted, the peasants laughed and made jokes about General Zhukov's cook and the cap that had burned up; they already wanted to turn the fire into a jest, and even seemed sorry that it had ended so soon.

"You put out the fire very nicely, sir," Olga said to the student. "You should come to us in Moscow. We have fires there 'most every day."

"Oh, are you from Moscow?" one of the young ladies asked.

"I certainly am. My husband was a waiter at the Slavyansky Bazaar, miss. And this is my daughter." She pointed to Sasha, who was huddled up to her trying to keep warm. "She, too, is a Moscow girl, miss."

Both young ladies said something in French to the student and he gave Sasha a twenty-kopeck piece. Seeing this, old Osip's face lit up with hope.

"Thank God there was no wind, Your Honor," he said to the student, "or we'd all have been burned out in no time. Your Honor, good gentlefolk," he added sheepishly, lowering his voice, "the dawn is chilly. . . . Something to warm a man . . . a half-bottle to Your Honor's health. . . . "

They did not give him anything; he cleared his throat and drifted off toward home. Olga stood at the top of the slope and watched the two carts fording the river, and the gentlefolk walking across the meadow; a carriage was waiting for them on the other side. When she returned to the hut she rapturously described them to her husband.

"Such good people! And so beautiful! The young ladies—like cherubs!"

"I hope they burst!" said the sleepy Fyokla maliciously.

VI

Marya considered herself unfortunate, and used to say she longed to die. Fyokla, on the contrary, found everything in this life to her liking: the poverty, the filth, the everlasting strife. She ate whatever was given her, without discrimination; slept anywhere and on anything that came to hand; and she would empty the slops right by the porch, splashing them out from the doorway, then walk barefoot through the puddle. From the very first day she conceived a hatred for Olga and Nikolai simply because they did not like this life. "I'd like to see what you're going to eat here, you Moscow gentry, you!" she would say malevolently. "I'd just like to see!"

One morning—it was by then the beginning of September—Fyokla, vigorous, handsome, and rosy from the cold, brought up two pails of water; at the time, Marya and Olga were sitting at the table drinking tea.

"Enjoy your tea!" exclaimed Fyokla jeeringly. "What fine ladies!" she added, setting the pails down. "They've taken up the style of drinking tea every day now. Better watch out you don't blow up with your tea-drinking!" she went on, looking at Olga with hatred. "That's how she got her bloated mug in Moscow, the fat slob!"

With a swing of the yoke she struck Olga on the shoulder, and the two sisters-in-law could only clasp their hands and say, "Oh, Holy Fathers!"

Then Fyokla went to the river to wash the clothes, cursing so loudly all the way that she could be heard inside the hut.

The day passed; then began the long autumn evening. In the hut they were winding silk; all except Fyokla, who had gone across the river. They got the silk from a factory near by, and the whole family worked together to earn next to nothing—some twenty kopecks a week.

"We were better off when we had masters," the old man said as he wound the silk. "You worked, you ate, you slept, everything in its turn. For dinner they gave you *shchi* and *kasha*, for supper more *shchi* and *kasha*. And plenty of cabbage and cucumbers; you could eat to your heart's content, as much as you liked. There was more strictness, too. Everyone knew his place."

The hut was lighted by one little lamp, which smoked and burned dimly. When someone stood in front of the lamp and a large shadow fell across the window, the bright moonlight could be seen. Speaking unhurriedly, old Osip told them how people used to live before the Emancipation; how in these very places, where life was now so poor and dreary, they used to hunt with harriers, borzois, bird-dogs, and when they went out as beaters the peasants were given vodka; how whole wagonloads of slaughtered fowl were sent to Moscow for the young masters; how the bad serfs were flogged or sent away to the Tver estate, while the good serfs were rewarded. And Granny too had something to tell. She remembered everything, absolutely everything. She told about her mistress, a kind, God-fearing woman, whose husband was a lecher and a rake, and all of whose daughters made unfortunate marriages: one married a drunkard, another a commoner, the third eloped (Granny herself, a young girl at the time, had helped with the elopement), and all three had died early of grief, as did their mother. And remembering these things, Granny actually shed a tear.

Suddenly there was a knock at the door, and they all started.

"Uncle Osip, let me stay the night!"

The little old bald-headed man whose cap had burned, General Zhukov's cook, walked in. He sat down and listened, then he, too, began to reminisce. Nikolai sat on the oven with his legs hanging down, listening and asking questions about the dishes that had been prepared for the gentry in the old days. They talked of cutlets, chops, various soups and sauces, and the cook, who also remembered everything very well, mentioned dishes that were no longer served; there was one, for instance, made of bulls' eyes, which was called "Waking up in the morning."

"And cutlets *maréchal,* did you make those?"

"No."

Nikolai shook his head disapprovingly. "A-ah! Fine cooks you were!"

The little girls sitting and lying on the oven gazed down unblinkingly; there seemed to be a great many of them, like cherubs in the clouds. They liked the stories; they sighed, shivered, and turned pale, enraptured at one moment, terrified at the next, and to Granny, whose stories were the most interesting of all, they listened breathlessly, afraid to stir.

Silently they lay down to sleep, and the old people, stirred up and troubled by their reminiscences, were thinking what a fine thing youth was, that no matter what it may have been like, nothing remained in memory but what was vivid, joyous, moving; and how terribly cold was death, which now was not far off—better not to think of it! The little lamp went out. The darkness, the two little windows brightly illumined by the moon, the stillness, and the creaking of the cradle, for some reason all reminded them that life was over, that it was impossible to bring it back. You doze, you slumber, and suddenly you feel a hand on your shoulder, a breath on your cheek—and sleep is gone; your body feels numb from lying still, and thoughts of death creep into your mind. You turn onto the other side—and death is forgotten, but the same old tiresome thoughts of poverty, of fodder, of the rising cost of flour hover in the mind, and before long you again remember that life is over, that it is impossible to bring it back. . . .

"Oh, Lord!" sighed the cook.

Someone was tapping very gently at the window. Fyokla must have come back. Olga got up, yawning and whispering a prayer, unlocked the door, then pulled the bolt of the outer door. But no one came in; there was only a cold draft of air from the street, and the entry was suddenly bright with moonlight. The silent, deserted street, and the moon itself floating across the sky, could be seen through the open door.

"Who's there?" called Olga.

"Me," came the answer. "It's me."

Near the door, crouched against the wall, was Fyokla, stark naked. She was shivering with cold, her teeth were chattering, and in the bright moonlight she looked very strange, pale, and beautiful. The shadows that fell upon her and the luster of her skin in the moonlight stood out vividly, and her dark eyebrows and firm young breasts were defined with particular clarity.

"Those wretches on the other side undressed me and turned me out—like this," she said. "I had to come home without my clothes—naked as the day I was born. Bring me something to put on."

"But come inside," Olga said softly; she, too, was beginning to shiver.

"I don't want the old folks to see."

Granny was already stirring and mumbling, and the old man asked, "Who's there?" Olga brought her own shift and skirt, dressed Fyokla, and then they both went quietly into the house, trying not to make a sound with the doors.

"Is that you, you slick one?" Granny angrily muttered, guessing who it was. "Curse you, you nightwalker! I wish you'd drop dead!"

"It's all right, it's all right," whispered Olga, wrapping Fyokla up. "It's all right, dearie."

All was quiet again. They always slept badly. Each one was kept awake by something troublesome and persistent: the old man by the pain in his back, Granny by anxiety and malice, Marya by fear, the children by itch and hunger. And now, too, their sleep was troubled; they kept turning from side to side, talking in their sleep, getting up for a drink.

Suddenly Fyokla started howling in a loud, coarse voice, but she quickly controlled herself, and only an occasional sob was heard; then the sobs became softer and more muffled until she was silent. From time to time they heard the striking of the hours on the other side of the river, but it was somehow strange—first it struck five, then three.

"Oh, Lord!" sighed the cook.

Looking at the windows it was difficult to tell whether the moon was still shining or whether it was already dawn. Marya got up and went out, and she could be heard milking the cow and saying, "Stea-dy!" Granny, too, went out. It was still dark in the hut, but already possible to discern objects.

Nikolai, who had not slept the whole night, got down from the oven. He took his dress coat out of a green chest, put it on, and went to the window, where he stood stroking the sleeves, fingering the coattails, and smiling. Then he carefully took it off, put it back into the chest, and lay down again.

Marya came in and started lighting the stove. She was evidently half asleep, and was waking up as she walked about. She must have had a dream, or perhaps the stories of the preceding night came to her mind, as, stretching luxuriously before the fire she said, "No, freedom is better."

VII

The "master," as they called the district police inspector, had arrived. Both the time and the reason for his coming had been known for a week. There were only forty households in Zhukovo, but the accumulated arrears in zemstvo and state taxes amounted to more than two thousand rubles.

The police inspector stopped at the tavern, drank two glasses of tea, then set out on foot for the headman's hut, near which stood a crowd of those whose taxes were in arrears. The headman, Antip Sedelnikov, in spite of his youth—he was only a little over thirty—was strict and always sided with the authorities, although he himself was poor and remiss in paying his taxes. It was evident that he liked being headman; he enjoyed a sense of power, which he was incapable of displaying except by his harshness. At the village meetings he was feared and obeyed. It sometimes happened that he would swoop down upon a drunken man in the street or near the tavern, tie his hands behind him, and put him in the lockup. Once he even locked up Granny and kept her there for a whole day and night for cursing at a village meeting to which she had come in Osip's place. Antip had never lived in a town or read a book, but somehow he had managed to pick up various bookish expressions, and loved to make use of them in conversation; for this he was respected, though not always understood.

When Osip came into the headman's hut with his tax book, the inspector, a lean old man with long gray side whiskers, wearing a gray tunic, was sitting at a table near the entry, making a note of something. The hut was clean; the walls were decorated with pictures cut out of magazines, and in the most conspicuous place, near the ikon, there was a portrait of Battenberg, the late prince of Bulgaria. Antip Sedelnikov stood by the table with folded arms.

"He owes one hundred and nineteen rubles, Your Honor," he said, when Osip's turn came. "Before Easter he paid a ruble, but not a kopeck since."

The police inspector raised his eyes to Osip and asked, "Why is this, brother?"

"Show God's mercy, Your Honor," Osip began, growing excited. "Permit me to say, last year the gentleman from Lyutoretsk said to me, 'Osip,' he says, 'sell me your hay. . . . You sell it,' he says. Well, why not? I had a hundred poods for sale; the women mowed it on the water-meadow. Well, we struck a bargain. . . . It was all right and proper."

He complained of the headman, and kept turning around to the peasants, as though inviting them to bear witness; his face was flushed and covered with perspiration, and his eyes grew sharp and spiteful.

"I don't know why you're saying all this," said the inspector. "I'm asking you—I am asking why you don't pay your arrears. None of you pay, and am I to be responsible for you?"

"I can't do it!"

"These words are of no consequence, Your Honor," said the headman. "The Chikildeyevs are certainly of the needy class, but if you will, please, inquire of the others—the cause of it all is vodka. And they're a bad lot. Without any sort of comprehension."

The police inspector made a note of something, and then, in a mild, even tone, as though he were asking for water, said, "Get out."

He soon drove off; coughing, he climbed into his cheap buggy, and it could be seen even from the look of his long lean back that he had already forgotten about Osip, the village headman, the Zhukovo tax arrears, and was thinking of his own affairs. Before he had gone a verst, Antip was carrying off the samovar from the Chikildeyevs' hut, with Granny after him, shrilly screaming, straining her lungs.

"I won't let you! I won't let you take it, you devil!"

He walked rapidly, taking long strides, and she pursued him, panting, almost falling, a bent and frantic figure, her kerchief fallen to her shoulders, her greenish hair blowing in the wind. All at once she stopped, and, like a real rebel, began beating her breast with her fists and shouting still louder in a sobbing singsong.

"Good Christians, you who believe in God! Dear friends, they have wronged me! My darlings, they're destroying me! Oh, oh, my dears, save me!"

"Granny, Granny!" said the headman sternly. "Get some sense into your head!"

Without the samovar it became completely gloomy in the Chikildeyevs' hut. There was something humiliating in this deprivation, something insulting, as though the hut had lost its honor. It would have been better had the headman carried off the table, all the benches, all the pots—it would have seemed less empty. Granny shrieked, Marya wept, and as soon as the little girls saw her they cried, too. The old man, feeling guilty, sat in a corner, downcast and silent. Nikolai, too, was silent. Granny loved him and was sorry for him, but now, forgetting her pity, she attacked him with reproaches and abuse, shaking her fists in his face. She screamed that it was all his fault: why had he sent them so little after bragging in his letters that he was earning fifty rubles a month at the Slavyansky Bazaar? Why had he come here, and with a family, too? If he died, where would they get the money to bury him? . . . It was pitiful to look at Nikolai, Olga, and Sasha.

The old man sighed heavily, took his cap, and went off to the headman. It was growing dark. Antip Sedelnikov, his cheeks blown out, was soldering something at the stove, and the air was full of fumes. His children, emaciated and unwashed, no better than the Chikildeyevs, were romping about underfoot; his wife, an ugly, freckled, big-bellied woman, was winding silk. It was an unfortunate, wretched family; Antip alone looked alert and handsome. On a bench stood five samovars in a row. The old man said a prayer to Battenberg before he spoke.

"Antip, show heavenly mercy. Give me back the samovar! For Christ's sake!"

"Bring three rubles and you can have it."

Antip puffed out his cheeks, the fire hissed and hummed and was reflected in the samovars. The old man began to knead his cap. He thought a moment, then said, "You give it to me!"

The swarthy headman looked as though he were completely black, like a wizard; he turned round to Osip and spoke sternly and rapidly.

"It all depends on the district magistrate. On the twenty-sixth of the month you can state the grounds of your dissatisfaction before the administrative session, verbally or in writing."

Osip did not understand a word of this, but it satisfied him and he went home.

Ten days later the police inspector came again, stayed for

an hour and drove away. During those days the weather was cold and windy; the river had been frozen for some time, but still there was no snow, and the people had no end of trouble because the roads were impassable. On the eve of a holiday some neighbors dropped in at Osip's to have a talk. They sat in the dark; since it was a sin to work, they did not light the lamp. There were some items of news, all of them quite unpleasant. In two or three households the hens had been taken for the tax arrears, sent to the district government office, and there they had died because no one had fed them; sheep had been taken, and while they were being carted away, tied together and moved into different carts at each village, one of them had died. And now they were discussing the question: who was guilty?

"The zemstvo!" said Osip. "Who else?"

"Of course, the zemstvo."

The zemstvo was blamed for everything—for the arrears, the oppression, the crop failure—though not one of them knew what was meant by the zemstvo. This dated from the time when the rich peasants, owners of factories, shops, and inns, had been delegates to the zemstvo, had grown dissatisfied, and took to inveighing against it in their factories and taverns.

They talked about God not sending the snow; firewood had to be hauled, but it was impossible to drive or walk over the frozen ruts. Formerly, fifteen to twenty years ago and earlier, the talk in Zhukovo had been much more interesting. In those days every old man looked as if he were harboring some sort of secret, as if he knew something, expected something. Then they used to talk of a charter with a golden seal, of the redistribution of land, of new lands, and of buried treasure; they were always hinting at something; now, however, the people of Zhukovo had no secrets at all, their whole life was as though on the palm of the hand for all to see, and they could talk of nothing but want, food, fodder, and the absence of snow. . . .

They fell silent. And again they recalled the hens and the sheep, and began discussing whose fault it was.

"The zemstvo," said Osip dejectedly. "Who else?"

VIII

The parish church was nearly six versts away at Kosogorovo, and the peasants went there only when necessary, for a baptism, a wedding, or a funeral. For regular services they went to the church across the river. On holidays, in good weather, the girls dressed in their best and went in a crowd to the service, and it was a gay sight to watch them crossing the meadow in their red, yellow, and green dresses; in bad weather they all stayed home. They went to the parish church in preparation for the sacrament. From each of those who had not managed to take the sacrament during Lent, the priest took fifteen kopecks as he made the rounds of the huts with the cross at Easter.

The old man did not believe in God; in fact, he almost never even thought of Him. He acknowledged the supernatural, but felt that it was the women's concern, and whenever religion or miracles were discussed in his presence, or a question about such matters was put to him, he would scratch himself and reluctantly say, "Who knows?"

Granny did believe, but her faith was somewhat dim; everything was confused in her memory, and no sooner did she begin to think of sins, of death, of the salvation of the soul, than want and cares took possession of her mind, and she instantly forgot what she had been thinking about. She did not remember any prayers, and usually in the evenings, before lying down to sleep, she would stand before the ikons and whisper, "Holy Mother of Kazan, Holy Mother of Smolensk, Holy Mother of the Three Arms. . . ."

Marya and Fyokla crossed themselves, fasted, and took

communion every year, but without any understanding of what they were doing. The children were not taught to pray, nothing was told them about God, and no moral precepts were instilled into them; they were simply forbidden to eat certain foods on fast days. In other families it was much the same: there were few who believed, few who understood. At the same time they all loved the Holy Scripture, loved it tenderly, reverently; but they had no books, there was no one to read the Bible and explain it to them, and because Olga sometimes read them the Gospels, they respected her and addressed her and Sasha as their superiors.

For church holidays and special services Olga often went to neighboring villages and to the chief town of the district, in which there were two monasteries and twenty-seven churches. She was abstracted while on these pilgrimages, completely forgetting her family, and only when she got home again did she suddenly make the happy discovery that she had a husband and daughter; then, smiling and radiant, she would say, "God has sent me blessings!"

What went on in the village tormented and revolted her. On Saint Elijah's Day they drank, at the Assumption they drank, at the Exaltation of the Cross they drank. The Feast of the Intercession was the parish holiday for Zhukovo, and on that occasion the peasants drank for three days; they drank up fifty rubles belonging to the communal fund, and then collected more money for vodka from each household. On the first day the Chikildeyevs slaughtered a sheep and ate it in the morning, at dinner, and in the evening; they ate great quantities of it, and the children got up at night to eat more. Kiryak was terribly drunk all three days; he drank up everything, even his boots and cap, and beat Marya so that they had to pour water over her. Afterwards they were all ashamed and sick.

However, even in Zhukovo, in this "Toadyville," once a year there was a genuine religious festival. It took place in August, when the ikon of the Life-Giving Mother of God was carried from village to village throughout the district. The day on which it was expected in Zhukovo was still and overcast. The girls in bright holiday dresses set off in the morning to meet the ikon, and toward evening they brought it to the village in a solemn procession with the cross, banners, and singing, while the bells rang out in the church across the river. A great throng of villagers and strangers filled the street; it was noisy, dusty, and crowded. The old man and Granny and Kiryak, eagerly, with outstretched hands, gazed at the ikon, and weeping said, "Protectress! Mother! Protectress!"

It was as though they all suddenly understood that there was no void between heaven and earth, that the rich and powerful had not yet taken possession of everything, that there was still a defense against abuse, bondage, the oppressive, unendurable poverty, and the horrors of vodka.

"Protectress! Mother!" sobbed Marya. "Protectress!"

But the service came to an end, the ikon was carried away, and everything went on as before; and again there was the sound of coarse drunken voices from the tavern.

Only the rich peasants feared death; the richer they grew the less they believed in God and in the salvation of the soul, and only through fear of their earthly end, and to be on the safe side, did they burn candles and have prayers said. The poorer peasants had no fear of death. The old man and Granny were told to their faces that they had lived too long, that it was time for them to die, and they did not mind. Nor did they hesitate to say in Nikolai's presence that when he died, Fyokla's husband Denis would be sent home from the army. And Marya, far from fearing death, regretted that it was so long in coming, and was glad when her children died.

They had no fear of death, but had an exaggerated terror of all sickness. It required a mere trifle—an upset stomach, a slight chill—for Granny to wrap herself up, lie on the oven, and start moaning loudly and incessantly, "I am dying!" The old man would rush off for the priest, and Granny would receive the sacrament and extreme unction. They frequently talked about colds, worms, and tumors that moved about in the stomach and rolled up under the heart. Above all, they feared catching cold, and for this reason, even in summer, wore heavy clothing and warmed themselves on the stove. Granny loved being treated, and often drove to the hospital, where she said she was not seventy, but fifty-eight; she thought that if the doctor found out her real age he would not treat her, but would tell her it was time for her to die instead of taking medicine. She generally went to the hospital early in the morning, taking two or three of the little girls with her, and came back in the evening, hungry and bad-tempered, with drops for herself and ointments for the little girls. Once she took Nikolai with her also, and for a fortnight afterwards he took drops and said he felt better.

Granny knew all the doctors, and medical assistants, and quacks for twenty miles round, and not one of them did she like. At the Feast of the Intercession, when the priest made the round of the huts with the cross, the deacon told her that in the town near the prison there lived an old man who had been an army surgeon's assistant and who was good at working cures; he advised her to try him. Granny took his advice. After the first snowfall she drove to the town and fetched a little old bearded man in a long coat, a converted Jew, whose face was covered with blue veins. Just at that time there were people working in the hut: an old tailor in terrifying spectacles was cutting a waistcoat out of some rags, and two young men were making felt boots out of wool. Kiryak, who had been discharged because of drunkenness and now lived at home, was sitting beside the tailor mending a horse collar. It was crowded, stuffy, and fetid in the hut. The converted Jew examined Nikolai and announced that it would be necessary to cup the patient.

He applied the cups, while the old tailor, Kiryak, and the little girls stood and watched, and it seemed to them that they saw the disease coming out of Nikolai. And Nikolai, too, watched how the cups adhering to his chest gradually filled with dark blood, and he felt as though there actually were something coming out of him, and he smiled with satisfaction.

"That's fine," said the tailor. "God grant it will do you good."

The converted Jew put on twelve cups, then another twelve, drank tea, and drove away. Nikolai began to shiver; his face looked sunken, and, as the women said, shrank up into a little fist; and his fingers turned blue. He wrapped himself up in a quilt and a sheepskin coat, but he felt colder and colder. Toward evening he became restless; he asked to be laid on the floor, and begged the tailor not to smoke. Then he grew still under the sheepskin, and toward morning he died.

IX

Oh, what a cruel, what a long winter!

By Christmas their own grain was used up and they had to start buying flour. Kiryak, who now lived at home, caroused in the evenings, terrifying everyone, and mornings he always was tormented by headache and shame; he was a pitiful sight. Day and night from the cattle shed came the bellowing of the starving cow—a heart-rending sound to Granny and Marya. As if to spite them, there were severe frosts and high snowdrifts continually; and the winter dragged on. At Annunciation there was a real blizzard, and snow fell at Easter.

But after all the winter did come to an end. At the beginning of April there were warm days and frosty nights; winter would not surrender, but one warm day overpowered it at last, and the streams began to flow and the birds to sing. The whole meadow and the bushes near the river were drowned in the spring floods, and the area between Zhukovo and the farther bank was one vast sheet of water, from which, here and there, flocks of wild ducks took wing. The spring sunset, flaming, with magnificent clouds, gave to every evening something extraordinary, novel, and improbable, the sort of thing that seems unbelievable when one sees the very same colors and clouds in a picture.

Swiftly, swiftly flew the cranes, with mournful, summoning cries. Olga stood at the top of the slope and gazed for a long time at the flooded meadow, at the sunshine, at the church, which looked bright and, as it were, rejuvenated; her tears flowed, and she gasped for breath, so passionate was her desire to go away, anywhere, even to the ends of the earth. It was already decided that she should return to Moscow to go into service as a chambermaid, and that Kiryak should go with her to get a job as a porter or something of the sort. Oh, to get away quickly!

When the ground was dry and the weather grew warm they made ready for the journey. Olga and Sasha, with knapsacks on their backs and bast sandals on their feet, left at daybreak; Marya came out to see them off. Kiryak was not well and remained at home for another week. Olga said a prayer, looking at the church for the last time; she was thinking of her husband, and though she did not weep, her face puckered up and became unsightly, like an old woman's. During the winter she had grown thin and plain, her hair had turned a little gray, and instead of her former attractive appearance and pleasant smile, her face now had a resigned and sad expression from the sorrows she had lived through, and there was something dull and fixed about her gaze, as if she did not hear.

She was sorry to part from the village and the peasants. She remembered how they had carried Nikolai out, that a service for the repose of his soul had been ordered at almost every cabin, and how everyone had wept, in sympathy with her grief. In the course of the summer and the winter there

had been certain hours and days when it seemed that these
people lived worse than cattle, and it was terrible to live
with them; they were coarse, filthy, dishonest, and drunken;
they did not live together in peace, but continually quar-
reled, because they did not respect but feared and suspected
one another. Who keeps the pothouse and makes drunkards
of the people? The peasant. Who embezzles and drinks up
the community, school, and church funds? The peasant.
Who steals from his neighbor, sets fire to his property, and
bears false witness in court for a bottle of vodka? Who, in
the zemstvo and other meetings, is the first to raise his voice
against the peasants? The peasant. Yes, to live with them
was terrible. Yet they were human beings, they suffered and
wept like human beings, and there was nothing in their lives
for which one could not find justification: oppressive labor
that made the whole body ache at night, cruel winters, poor
crops, overcrowding, and no help, and no place from which
it could be expected. Those who were better off and stronger
could do no good, as they themselves were coarse, dishonest, drunken, and swore just as foully; the pettiest official or
clerk treated the peasants like tramps, addressed even the
county headman and church wardens in contemptuous
terms, and thought he had the right to do so. And, indeed,
can there be any sort of help or good example from greedy,
grasping, dissolute, and slothful men who visit the village
only in order to insult, despoil, and terrorize? Olga recalled
the pathetic, degraded look of the old people when in the
winter Kiryak had been taken off to be flogged. . . . And
now she felt sorry for all these people, painfully so, and as
she walked on she kept looking back at the huts.

After accompanying them for two miles, Marya said
good-bye, then fell to her knees, pressed her face to the
earth, and began wailing, "Again I am left alone, poor
me . . . poor, unhappy . . ."

And for a long time she went on wailing like this, and for
a long time Olga and Sasha could see her, still on her knees,

still bowing and clutching her head in her hands, while the rooks flew over her.

The sun rose high and it began to get hot. Zhukovo was left behind. Walking was pleasant. Olga and Sasha soon forgot both the village and Marya; they were cheerful and everything entertained them: an ancient burial mound; a row of telegraph poles running one after the other and disappearing on the horizon, their wires humming mysteriously; a farmhouse framed in foliage, from which there came the scent of dampness and hemp, a place that for some reason seemed to be inhabited by happy people; the skeleton of a horse, a solitary gleam of white in a field. And the larks trilled unflaggingly, the quails called to one another, and the cry of the corn crake sounded as though someone were rattling an old iron door handle.

At midday Olga and Sasha came to a large village. There on the broad street they encountered the little old man who had been General Zhukov's cook. He was hot, and his red, perspiring bald head shone in the sun. He and Olga failed to recognize each other; then, looking round at the same moment, they did recognize each other. Without a word each continued on his own way. Stopping before the open windows of a hut that seemed newer and more prosperous than the rest, Olga bowed down, and in a loud, thin, singsong voice said, "Good Christians, give alms, for Christ's sake, whatever your mercy may bestow, and in the kingdom of heaven may your parents know eternal peace."

"Good Christians," Sasha chanted, "give, for Christ's sake, whatever your mercy may bestow, and in the kingdom of heaven . . ."

—1897

The Darling

OLENKA, THE DAUGHTER of the retired collegiate assessor Plemyannikov, was sitting on the little porch that faced the courtyard, lost in thought. It was hot, the flies were annoyingly persistent, and it was pleasant to think that it would soon be evening. Dark rain clouds were gathering from the east, bringing with them an occasional breath of moisture.

Kukin, a theater manager who ran an amusement garden known as the Tivoli, and who lodged in the wing of the house, was standing in the middle of the courtyard staring up at the sky.

"Again!" he said in despair. "It's going to rain again! Every day it rains; every day, as if to spite me! I might just as well put a noose around my neck! It's ruin! Every day terrible losses!"

He clasped his hands, turned to Olenka and went on, "That's our life for you, Olga Semyonovna. It's enough to make you weep! You work, you do your very best, you worry and lose sleep, always thinking how to make it better—and what happens? On the one hand, the public is ignorant, barbarous. I give them the very best operetta, a pantomime, magnificent vaudeville artists—but do you think that's what they want? Do you think they understand it? What they want is slapstick! Give them trash! And then, look at the weather! Rain almost every evening. It started the tenth of May and it's been raining incessantly ever since—all May and June. Simply dreadful! The public doesn't come, but I still have to pay the rent, don't I—and the artists?"

The next day toward evening the clouds again appeared, and, laughing hysterically, Kukin said, "Well, go on, rain! Flood the whole park, drown me! Bad luck to me in this world and the next! Let the artists sue me! Let them send me to prison—to Siberia—to the scaffold! Ha! Ha! Ha!"

And the third day it was the same. . . .

Olenka listened to Kukin gravely, silently, and sometimes tears would come into her eyes. She was so moved by his misfortunes that she ended by falling in love with him. He was an emaciated little man with a yellow face and hair combed down over his temples; he spoke in a thin tenor voice, twisting his mouth to one side, and despair was permanently engraved on his face; nevertheless, he aroused a deep and genuine feeling in her. She was always in love with someone and could not live otherwise. First it had been her papa, who was now ill and sat in an armchair in a darkened room, breathing with difficulty; then it had been her aunt, who used to come from Bryansk every other year; and before that, when she was at school, she had been in love with her French teacher. She was a quiet, good-natured, compassionate girl with meek, gentle eyes and very good health. At the sight of her full, rosy cheeks, her soft, white neck with a dark little mole on it, and the kind, ingenuous smile that came over her face when she listened to anything pleasant, men thought, "Yes, not bad!" and smiled too, while the ladies present could not refrain from suddenly seizing her hand in the middle of a conversation and exclaiming in an outburst of delight, "You darling!"

The house she had lived in since birth, and which, according to her father's will, was to be hers, was located on the outskirts of the city on Gypsy Road, not far from the Tivoli. In the evenings and at night when she heard the band playing and skyrockets exploding, it seemed to her that it was Kukin at war with his fate, assaulting his chief enemy, the apathetic public; then her heart melted, she had no desire to sleep, and when he returned home at daybreak she would tap softly at her bedroom window and, letting him see only her face and one shoulder through the curtain, would smile tenderly at him. . . .

He proposed to her and they were married. And when he had a good look at her neck and her plump, fine shoulders, he clapped his hands together and exclaimed, "Darling!"

He was happy, but as it rained both the day and the night of the wedding, his expression of despair remained unchanged.

They got on well together. She presided over the box office, looked after things in the garden, kept the accounts and paid the salaries; and her rosy cheeks, her sweet, artless smile, shone now in the box-office window, now in the wings of the theater, now at the buffet. She began telling her friends that the most remarkable, the most important and essential thing in the whole world was the theater—that only through the theater could one derive true pleasure and become a cultivated and humane person.

"But do you suppose the public understands that?" she would ask. "What it wants is slapstick! Yesterday we gave *Faust Inside Out,* and almost every box was empty, but if Vanichka and I had put on some kind of trash, then, believe me, the theater would have been packed. Tomorrow Vanichka and I are putting on *Orpheus in Hell.* Do come."

Whatever Kukin said about the theater and the actors she repeated. Like him she despised the public for its ignorance and indifference to art; she took a hand in the rehearsals, correcting the actors, kept an eye on the conduct of the musicians, and when there was an unfavorable notice in the local newspaper, shed tears, and then went to the editor for an explanation.

The actors loved her and called her "Vanichka and I" and "the darling." She was sorry for them and used to lend them small sums of money, and if they deceived her she wept in secret but did not complain to her husband.

They got on well in the winter too. They leased the municipal theater for the season and sublet it for short periods to a Ukrainian troupe, a magician, or a local dramatic club. Olenka grew plumper and was always beaming with satisfaction, while Kukin grew thinner and yellower and complained of terrible losses, although business was not bad during the winter. He coughed at night and she would give him an infusion of raspberries and linden blossoms, rub him with eau de Cologne, and wrap him in her soft shawls.

"What a sweet precious you are!" she would say with perfect sincerity, as she stroked his hair. "My handsome pet!"

At Lent he went to Moscow to gather a new troupe, and without him she would not sleep, but sat all night at the window looking at the stars. She likened herself to the hens, which also stay awake all night and are uneasy when the cock is not in the henhouse. Kukin was detained in Moscow, wrote that he would return by Easter, and in his letters sent instructions regarding the Tivoli. But on the Monday of Passion Week, late in the evening, there was a sudden, ominous knocking at the gate; someone was hammering at the wicket as if it were a barrel—boom! boom! boom! The sleepy cook, splashing through the puddles in her bare feet, ran to open the gate.

"Open, please!" said someone on the other side of the gate in a deep bass voice. "There is a telegram for you!"

Olenka had received telegrams from her husband before, but this time for some reason she felt numb with fright. She opened the telegram with trembling hands and read:

IVAN PETROVICH DIED SUDDENLY TODAY AWAITING
THISD INSTRUCTIONS FUFUNERAL TUESDAY.

That was exactly the way the telegram had it: "fufuneral"
and the incomprehensible word "thisd"; it was signed by the
director of the operetta company.

"My precious!" Olenka sobbed. "Vanichka, my precious,
my dearest! Why did we ever meet? Why did I know you
and love you? Whom can your poor forsaken Olenka turn to
now?"

Kukin was buried on Tuesday in the Vagankovo cemetery
in Moscow. Olenka returned home on Wednesday, and as
soon as she reached her room sank onto the bed and sobbed
so loudly that she could be heard in the street and in the
neighboring courtyards.

"The darling!" said the neighbors, crossing themselves.
"Darling Olga Semyonovna! Poor soul, how she grieves!"

Three months later Olenka was returning from mass one
day, in deep mourning and very sad. It happened that one of
her neighbors, Vasily Andreich Pustovalov, the manager of
Babakayev's lumberyard, was also returning from church
and walked with her. He wore a straw hat, a white waistcoat
with a gold watch chain, and looked more like a landowner
than a merchant.

"Everything happens as it is ordained, Olga Semyonovna,"
he said gravely, with a note of sympathy in his voice, "and
if one of our dear ones passes on, we must take ourselves in
hand and bear it submissively."

Having seen Olenka to her gate, he said good-bye and
went on. All day long she seemed to hear his grave voice,
and as soon as she closed her eyes she dreamed of his dark
beard. She liked him very much. And apparently she had
made an impression on him too, because not long afterwards
an elderly lady whom she scarcely knew came to have coffee with her, and as soon as she was seated at the table began
to talk of Pustovalov, saying that he was a fine steady man

and that any marriageable woman would be happy to marry him. Three days later Pustovalov himself paid her a visit. He did not stay long, not more than ten minutes, and said little, but Olenka fell in love with him—she was so much in love that she lay awake all night, inflamed as with a fever, and in the morning she sent for the elderly lady. The betrothal was arranged, and the wedding followed soon afterwards.

After they were married Pustovalov and Olenka got on very well together. As a rule he was in the lumberyard till dinnertime, then he went out on business and Olenka took his place and sat in the office till evening, making out bills and dispatching orders.

"Every year the price of lumber rises twenty per cent," she would say to customers and acquaintances. "Why, we used to deal in local timber, but now Vasichka has to travel to the province of Mogilev every year for wood. And the freight!" she would add, covering her cheeks with her hands in horror. "The freight!"

It seemed to her that she had been in the lumber business for ages and ages, that lumber was the most important and essential thing in life, and she found something touching, dear to her, in such words as girder, beam, plank, batten, boxboard, lath, scantling, slab.... At night she would dream of whole mountains of boards and planks, long endless caravans of wagons carrying lumber to some distant place; she dreamed of a whole regiment of 8-inch beams 28 feet long standing on end, marching on the lumberyard, beams, girders, slabs, striking against one another with the hollow sound of dry wood, all falling, then rising, piling themselves one upon another.... When she cried out in her sleep, Pustovalov would speak to her tenderly, saying, "Olenka, what's the matter, darling? Cross yourself!"

Whatever ideas her husband had became her own. If he thought the room was hot or business was slow, she thought so too. Her husband did not care for entertainment of any kind, and on holidays stayed at home, and so did she.

"You are always at home or in the office," her friends said to her. "You ought to go to the theater, darling, or to the circus."

"Vasichka and I have no time for the theater," she would reply sedately. "We are working people, we're not interested in such foolishness. What's the good of those theaters?"

On Saturday evenings they would go to vespers, on holidays to early mass, and as they walked home side by side their faces reflected the emotion of the service. There was an agreeable aroma about them both, and her silk dress rustled pleasantly. At home they had tea and buns with various kinds of jam, and afterwards a pie. Every day at noon, in the yard and beyond the gate in the street, there was a delicious smell of borsch and roast lamb or duck and, on fast days, fish; no one could pass their gate without feeling hungry. In the office the samovar was always boiling and the customers were treated to tea and cracknels. Once a week they went to the baths and returned side by side, both very red.

"Yes, everything goes well with us, thank God," Olenka would say to her friends. "I wish everyone were as happy as Vasichka and I."

When Pustovalov went to the province of Mogilev to buy timber, she missed him dreadfully, and lay awake nights crying. Sometimes in the evening Smirnin, a young army veterinarian to whom they rented the wing of the house, came to see her. They chatted or played cards, and this diverted her. She was especially interested in what he told her of his domestic life. He was married and had a son, but was separated from his wife because she had been unfaithful to him, and now he hated her; he sent forty rubles a month for the support of the child. Listening to all this, Olenka sighed, shook her head, and was sorry for him.

"Well, God keep you," she would say, accompanying him to the stairs with a candle. "Thank you for passing the time with me, and may the Queen of Heaven give you health."

She always expressed herself in this grave, circumspect

manner in imitation of her husband. Just as the veterinarian was about to disappear behind the door below, she would call to him and say, "You know, Vladimir Platonych, you ought to make it up with your wife. For your son's sake, you should forgive her! The little fellow probably understands everything."

When Pustovalov returned she would tell him in a low voice all about the veterinarian and his unhappy life, and they both would sigh, shake their heads, and talk about the little boy, who very likely missed his father. Then, by some strange association of ideas, they both stood before the ikons, bowed to the ground, and prayed that God would send them children.

Thus the Pustovalovs lived quietly and peaceably, in love and complete harmony for six years. Then one winter day, after drinking hot tea in the office, Vasily Andreich went out without his cap to dispatch some lumber, caught cold, and was taken ill. He was treated by the best doctors, but the illness had its way with him, and after four months he died. And again Olenka was a widow.

"Whom can I turn to, my darling?" she sobbed, after burying her husband. "How can I live without you, miserable and unhappy as I am? Good people, pity me!"

She went about in a black dress with weepers, gave up wearing a hat and gloves for good, seldom went out of the house except to go to church or to visit her husband's grave, and at home she lived like a nun. Only after six months did she take off her widow's weeds and open the shutters of her windows. Occasionally she was seen in the mornings, going with her cook to the market, but how she lived and what went on in her house could only be surmised. People based their conjectures on the fact that she was seen drinking tea in her garden with the veterinarian, that he read the newspaper aloud to her, and that, on meeting an acquaintance in the post office, she said, "There is no proper veterinary inspection in our city, and that's why there is so much sickness around. You often hear of people getting ill from milk or catching infections from horses and cows. The health of domestic animals ought to be just as well looked after as the health of human beings."

She repeated the ideas of the veterinarian, and now was of the same opinion as he about everything. It was clear that she could not live even a year without some attachment, and had found new happiness in the wing of her own house. Another woman would have been censured for this, but no one could think ill of Olenka; everything about her was so natural. Neither she nor the veterinarian spoke to anyone of the change in their relations, and tried, indeed, to conceal it, but they did not succeed because Olenka could not keep a secret. When his regimental colleagues visited him, while she poured tea for them or served supper she would talk of the cattle plague, the pearl disease, the municipal slaughterhouses. He would be dreadfully embarrassed, and when the guests had gone, would seize her by the arm and hiss angrily, "I've asked you before not to talk about things you don't understand! When we veterinarians are talking among ourselves, please don't interfere! It's really annoying!"

She would look at him in amazement and anxiously inquire, "But, Volodochka, what am I to talk about?" Then, with tears in her eyes, she would embrace him, begging him not to be angry, and they were both happy.

This happiness did not last long. The veterinarian went away with his regiment, went away forever, as the regiment was transferred to some distant place—it may even have been Siberia. And Olenka was left alone.

Now she was quite alone. Her father had died long ago; his armchair lay in the attic, covered with dust and with one leg missing. She grew thin and plain, and when people met her in the street they did not glance at her and smile as they used to; clearly, her best years were over and behind her, and now a new, uncertain life was beginning, one that did not bear thinking of. In the evening, as she sat on her porch,

Olenka could hear the band playing and skyrockets going off at the Tivoli, but this no longer called up anything to her mind. She gazed indifferently into her empty courtyard, thought of nothing, wished for nothing, and later, when darkness fell, she went to bed and dreamed of the empty courtyard. She ate and drank as though involuntarily.

Above all—and worst of all—she no longer had any opinions whatever. She saw objects about her, understood what was going on, but could not form an opinion about anything and did not know what to talk about. And how awful it is to have no opinions! You see a bottle, for instance, or rain, or a peasant driving a cart, but what the bottle, the rain, or the peasant may be for, what the significance of them is, you cannot say, and could not even for a thousand rubles. When Kukin was with her, or Pustovalov, or later, the veterinarian, Olenka could explain everything, could express an opinion on anything you like, but now there was the same emptiness in her mind and heart as in her courtyard. It was painful, and bitter as wormwood in the mouth.

Little by little the town was spreading in all directions; Gypsy Road was now a street, and where the gardens of the Tivoli and the lumberyards had been, houses sprang up and lanes formed. How swiftly time passes! Olenka's house grew shabby, the roof was rusty, the shed sloped, and the whole yard was overgrown with tall grass and prickly nettles. Olenka herself had aged and grown plain; in the summer she sat on the porch, and her soul was empty, bleak, and bitter; in the winter she sat at the window and stared at the snow. There were times when a breath of spring or the sound of church bells brought to her on the wind would suddenly provoke a rush of memories; then her heart melted, her eyes brimmed with tears, but this lasted only a moment, and there was again emptiness and uncertainty as to the purpose of life. Bryska, the black kitten, rubbed against her, purring softly, but Olenka was not affected by these feline caresses.

Was that what she needed? She wanted a love that would take possession of her whole soul, her mind, that would give her ideas, a direction in life, that would warm her old blood. She shook the black kitten off her lap and said irritably, "Get away! Go on! There's nothing for you here!"

And so it was, day after day, year after year, no joy whatsoever, no opinions of any sort. Whatever Mavra the cook said, she accepted.

One hot July day, toward evening, when the cattle were being driven home and the whole yard was filled with clouds of dust, someone unexpectedly knocked at the gate. Olenka went to open it herself and was astounded at what she saw: there stood Smirnin, the veterinarian, his hair gray, and in civilian dress. All at once she remembered everything and, unable to control herself, burst into tears, dropping her head onto his breast without a word. She was so moved that she scarcely was aware of going into the house and sitting down to tea with him.

"My dear!" she murmured, trembling with joy. "Vladimir Platonych! What brings you here?"

"I have come here for good," he said. "I've retired from the army and I want to settle down and try my luck on my own. And besides, it's time for my son to go to high school. He's growing up. I am reconciled with my wife, you know."

"Where is she?" asked Olenka.

"She's at the hotel with the boy, and I'm out looking for lodgings."

"Good heavens, my dear, take my house! Lodgings! Goodness, I wouldn't take any rent for it," cried Olenka, growing excited and weeping again. "You live here, and the wing will do for me. Heavens, how glad I am!"

The next day they began painting the roof and whitewashing the walls, and Olenka, with her arms akimbo, walked about the yard giving orders. Her face beamed with her old smile, and she was animated and fresh, as though she had waked from a long sleep. The veterinarian's wife arrived, thin and homely, with short hair and a capricious expression. With her came the little boy, Sasha, small for his age (he was going on ten), chubby, with bright blue eyes and dimples in his cheeks. No sooner had he entered the courtyard than he began chasing the cat, and immediately his gay and joyous laughter could be heard.

"Auntie, is that your cat?" he asked Olenka. "When she has little ones, please give us one of her kittens. Mama is terribly afraid of mice."

Olenka talked to him, gave him tea, and her heart grew suddenly warm and there was a sweet ache in her bosom, as if this little boy were her own son. In the evening when he sat in the dining room doing his homework, she gazed at him with tenderness and pity as she whispered, "My darling, my pretty one. . . . How clever you are, my little one, and so fair!"

"An island," he read aloud from the book, "is a body of land entirely surrounded by water."

"An island is a body of land . . ." she repeated, and this was the first opinion she had uttered with conviction after years of silence and emptiness of mind.

She now had opinions of her own, and at supper she talked to Sasha's parents about how difficult the lessons were for children in the high school, but that, nevertheless, a classical education was better than a technical course, because it opened all avenues—you could be a doctor . . . an engineer. . . .

Sasha started going to high school. His mother went to Kharkov to visit her sister and did not come back; his father used to go away every day to inspect herds, and he sometimes was away for three days together. It seemed to Olenka that Sasha was quite forsaken, that he was unwanted, that he was being starved to death, and she moved him into the wing with her and settled him in a little room there.

For six months now Sasha has been living in her wing. Every morning Olenka goes into his room where he lies fast asleep, his hand under his cheek, breathing quietly. She is always sorry to wake him.

"Sashenka," she says sadly, "get up, darling. It's time for school."

He gets up, dresses, says his prayers, and sits down to breakfast; he drinks three glasses of tea, eats two large cracknels and half a buttered roll. He is still not quite awake and consequently ill-humored.

"Now, Sashenka, you have not learned your fable very well," Olenka says, gazing at him as if she were seeing him off on a long journey. "You are such a worry to me! You must do your best, darling; you must study. . . . Pay attention to your teachers."

"Oh, leave me alone, please!" he says.

Then he walks down the street to school, a little figure in a big cap, with a knapsack on his back. Olenka silently follows him.

"Sashenka-a!" she calls. And when he looks round she thrusts a date or a caramel into his hand. When they turn in to the school lane he feels ashamed of being followed by a tall, stout lady; he looks back and says, "You'd better go home, Auntie. I can go alone now."

She stops, but does not take her eyes off him until he has disappeared into the school entrance. Ah, how she loves him! Not one of her former attachments had been so deep; never before had her soul surrendered itself so devotedly and with such joy as now, when her maternal feelings have been quickened. For this little boy who is not her own, for the dimples in his cheeks, for his cap, she would give her whole life, would give it with joy and tears of tenderness. Why? But who knows why?

Having seen Sasha off to school she goes quietly home, contented, serene, full of love; her face, grown younger in the last six months, beams with joy; people meeting her look at her with pleasure and say, "Good morning, Olga Semyonovna, darling. How are you, darling?"

"The lessons in school are so difficult nowadays," she says, as she goes about her marketing. "It's no joke. Yesterday in the first class they gave him a fable to learn by heart, a Latin translation, and a problem. . . . You know, it's too much for the little fellow."

And she begins talking about the teachers, the lessons, the textbooks—saying just what Sasha says about them.

At three o'clock they have dinner together; in the evening they do the homework together, and cry. When she puts him to bed she takes a long time making the sign of the cross over him and whispering a prayer. Then she goes to bed and dreams of that faraway, misty future when Sasha, having finished his studies, will become a doctor or an engineer, will have a large house of his own, horses, a carriage, when he will marry and have children of his own. . . . She falls asleep, still thinking of the same thing, and the tears run down her cheeks from under closed eyelids, while the black cat lies beside her purring: mrr . . . mrr . . . mrr. . . .

Suddenly there is a loud knock at the gate and Olenka wakes up, breathless with fear, her heart pounding. Half a minute later there is another knock.

"It's a telegram from Kharkov," she thinks, her whole body trembling. "Sasha's mother is sending for him. . . . Oh, Lord!"

She is in despair, her head, hands, and feet are cold, and it seems to her that she is the most unfortunate woman in the whole world. But another moment passes, she hears voices: it is the veterinarian coming home from the club.

"Well, thank God!" she thinks. Gradually the weight on her heart lifts, and she feels relieved; she goes back to bed and thinks of Sasha, who is fast asleep in the next room, sometimes crying out in his sleep, "I'll give it to you! Go on! No fighting!"

—1898

Selected Bibliography

Avilova, Lydia. *Chekhov in My Life: A Love Story.* Trans. David Margarshack. London: Methuen, 1989.

Callow, Philip. *Chekhov: The Hidden Ground.* Chicago: Ivan R. Dee, 1998.

Chudakov, Alexander P. *Chekhov's Poetics.* Trans. E. Cruise and D. Dragt. Ann Arbor, MI: Ardis, 1983.

Clyman, Toby, ed. *A Chekhov Companion.* Westport, CT: Greenwood Press, 1985.

Debreczeny, Paul, and Thomas Eekman, eds. *Chekhov's Art of Writing: A Collection of Critical Essays.* Columbus, OH: Slavica, 1977.

de Sherbinin, Julie W. *Chekhov and Russian Religious Culture: The Poetics of the Marian Paradigm.* Evanston, IL: Northwestern University Press, 1997.

Eekman, Thomas A., ed. *Critical Essays on Anton Chekhov.* Boston: G. K. Hall, 1989.

Hingley, Ronald. *A New Life of Chekhov*. New York: Alfred A. Knopf, 1976.

Jackson, Robert L., ed. *Chekhov: A Collection of Critical Essays*. Englewood Cliffs, NJ: Prentice-Hall, 1967.

——,ed. *Reading Chekhov's Text*. Evanston, IL: Northwestern University Press, 1993.

Karlinsky, Simon, ed. *Anton Chekhov's Life and Thought: Selected Letters and Commentary*. Evanston, IL: Northwestern University Press, 1997.

Kataev, Vladimir. *If Only We Could Know! An Interpretation of Chekhov*. Trans. and ed. Harvey Pitcher. Chicago: Ivan R. Dee, 2002.

Kirk, Irina. *Anton Chekhov*. Boston: Twayne, 1981.

Llewellyn-Smith, Virginia. *Anton Chekhov and the Lady with the Dog*. Oxford: Oxford University Press, 1973.

Nabokov, Vladimir. "Anton Chekhov." In *Lectures on Russian Literature*. New York: Harcourt Brace, 1981.

Pritchett, V. S. *Chekhov: A Spirit Set Free*. New York: Random House, 1988.

Rayfield, Donald. *Anton Chekhov: A Life*. New York: Henry Holt, 1988.

——.*Understanding Chekhov: A Critical Study of Chekhov's Prose and Drama*. Madison: University of Wisconsin Press, 1999.

Simmons, Ernest J. *Chekhov: A Biography*. Boston: Little, Brown, 1962.

Troyat, Henri. *Chekhov*. Trans. Michael Henry Heim. New York: Dutton, 1986.

Turkov, Andrei, ed. *Anton Chekhov and His Times*. Trans. Cynthia Carlile and Sharon McKee. Fayetteville: University of Arkansas Press, 1995.

Wellek, René and Nonna D., eds. *Chekhov: New Perspectives*. Englewood Cliffs, NJ: Prentice-Hall, 1984.

READ THE TOP 20
SIGNET CLASSICS

ANIMAL FARM BY GEORGE ORWELL

1984 BY GEORGE ORWELL

NARRATIVE OF THE LIFE OF FREDERICK DOUGLASS
  BY FREDERICK DOUGLASS

BEOWULF (BURTON RAFFEL, TRANSLATOR)

FRANKENSTEIN BY MARY SHELLEY

ALICE'S ADVENTURES IN WONDERLAND &
    THROUGH THE LOOKING GLASS BY LEWIS CARROLL

THE INFERNO BY DANTE

COMMON SENSE, RIGHTS OF MAN, AND OTHER
    ESSENTIAL WRITINGS BY THOMAS PAINE

HAMLET BY WILLIAM SHAKESPEARE

A TALE OF TWO CITIES BY CHARLES DICKENS

THE HUNCHBACK OF NOTRE DAME BY VICTOR HUGO

THE FEDERALIST PAPERS BY ALEXANDER HAMILTON

THE SCARLET LETTER BY NATHANIEL HAWTHORNE

DRACULA BY BRAM STOKER

THE HOUND OF THE BASKERVILLES
  BY SIR ARTHUR CONAN DOYLE

WUTHERING HEIGHTS BY EMILY BRONTË

THE ODYSSEY BY HOMER

A MIDSUMMER NIGHT'S DREAM BY WILLIAM SHAKESPEARE

FRANKENSTEIN; DRACULA; DR. JEKYLL AND MR. HYDE
  BY MARY SHELLEY, BRAM STOKER, AND ROBERT LOUIS STEVENSON

THE CLASSIC SLAVE NARRATIVES
  EDITED BY HENRY LOUIS GATES, JR.

Classics of Russian Literature

THE BROTHERS KARAMAZOV
Fyodor Dostoyevsky
Four brothers, driven by intense passion,
become involved in the brutal murder of their
own father.

CRIME AND PUNISHMENT
Fyodor Dostoyevsky
The struggles between traditional Orthodox
morality and the Eurocentric philosophy of the
intellectual class are the potent ideas behind this
powerful story of a man trying to break free
from the boundaries imposed upon him by
Russia's rigid class structure.

WAR AND PEACE
Leo Tolstoy
In this broad, sweeping drama, Tolstoy gives us
a view of history and personal destiny that
remains perpetually modern.

ANNA KARENINA
Leo Tolstoy
Sensual, rebellious Anna renounces respectable
marriage and position for a passionate
affair which offers a taste of freedom and a
trap of destruction.

**Available wherever books are sold or at
signetclassics.com**